ANGELS DINING AT THE RITZ

OTHER BOOKS BY JOHN GARDNER

James Bond Novels
Licence Renewed
For Special Services
Icebreaker
Role of Honour
Nobody Lives For Ever
No Deals, Mr Bond
Scorpius
Win, Lose or Die
Brokenclaw
The Man from Barbarossa
Death is For Ever
Never Send Flowers
SeaFire
Cold
Licence to Kill (from the screen-
    play)
Goldeneye (from the screenplay)

Suzie Mountford Books
Bottled Spider
The Streets of Town

The Boysie Oakes Books
The Liquidator
Understrike
Amber Nine
Madrigal
Founder Member
Traitor's Exit
Air Apparent
A Killer for a Song

Derek Torry Novels
A Complete State of Death
The Cornermen

The Moriarty Journals
The Return of Moriarty
The Revenge of Moriarty

The Kruger Novels
The Nostradamus Traitor
The Garden of Weapons
The Quiet Dogs
Maestro
Confessor

Novels
Golgotha
Flamingo
The Dancing Dodo
The Werewolf Trace
To Run a Little Faster
Every Night's a Bullfight
The Censor
Day of Absolution
Blood of the Fathers (writing as
    Edmund McCoy)

The Generations Trilogy
The Secret Generations
The Secret Houses
The Secret Families

Autobiography
Spin the Bottle

Collections of Short Stories
The Assassination File
Hideaway

For further details, please visit the author's website:
www.john-gardner.com

ANGELS DINING AT THE RITZ

John Gardner

This first world edition published in Great Britain 2004 by
SEVERN HOUSE PUBLISHERS LTD of
9–15 High Street, Sutton, Surrey SM1 1DF.
This first world edition published in the USA 2004 by
SEVERN HOUSE PUBLISHERS INC of
595 Madison Avenue, New York, N.Y. 10022.

British Library Cataloguing in Publication Data

Gardner, John, 1926-
    Angels dining at the Ritz. - (Detective Suzie Mountford series)
    1.   Mountford, Suzie (Fictitious character) - Fiction
    2.   Women detectives - England - London - Fiction
    3.   Detective and mystery stories
    I.   Title
    823.9'14 [F]

    ISBN 0-7278-6045-3

Typeset by Palimpsest Book Production Ltd.,
Polmont, Stirlingshire, Scotland.
Printed and bound in Great Britain by
MPG Books Ltd., Bodmin, Cornwall.

*This book is for
Lisa Moylett*

*With undying thanks
for taking over when the
going got tough*

Author's Note

This is the third book in the series following a young woman detective sergeant, Suzie Mountford, through World War II, and we have now reached 1942. The first all-American air attack on occupied Europe took place on 17th August of that year. Twelve B17 Flying Fortresses bombed the railway marshalling yards at Rouen, escorted by a gaggle of RAF Spitfire IXs. No aircraft from 302nd Bomber Squadron, 33rd Bombardment Group, 8th USAAF took part in that attack because none existed: there was no 302nd Squadron and no 33rd Group in the 8th USAAF at that time.

No aircraft flew from a base at Long Taddmarten fifteen miles or so from King's Lynn, because Long Taddmarten does not exist.

The brave men who were the crew of *Wild Angel* did not exist either. If I have accidentally used names of people who were members of the 8th USAAF I apologize: all mine are fictitious, as are the police officers working in Norfolk, and those depicted as coming from Scotland Yard.

However, events on board *Wild Angel* are drawn from the published reminiscences of officers and men of the 8th USAAF.

Also, while I know the first raid took place on the date above, other raids have been scheduled at random – the targets were targets but maybe not on the days I assign them.

The thing that is real is the spirit of the times.

John Gardner

There were angels dining at the Ritz,
And a nightingale sang in Berkeley Square.

Eric Maschwitz:
'A Nightingale Sang in Berkeley Square'

One

This is the BBC Home and Forces Programme. The time is eight o'clock on Monday 17th August. Before the Morning Service, here is the news and this is Alvar Lidell reading it. Downing Street and the War Office have announced that General Bernard Montgomery has taken command of the Eighth Army in Cairo. General Montgomery has replaced General Gott, who was killed ten days ago when the aircraft in which he was travelling was shot down, and . . .

. . . It is reported from Moscow that the German Sixth Army has now reached the outskirts of Stalingrad. There is heavy fighting in the area . . .

. . . The Home Office has issued a communiqué saying that during last week's night raid by the German Luftwaffe on East Anglia there was a direct hit on a mental hospital in Colchester resulting in many casualties. The Home Secretary, Mr Herbert Morrison, referring to this incident, said that it was another indication of the Nazi lack of respect for innocent lives . . .

. . . In Norfolk, three members of the same family have been found shot dead in their home near King's Lynn. The Norfolk Constabulary are treating the deaths as murder and Scotland Yard has been called in. The victims have not yet been named . . .

Tommy Livermore was with the Deputy Assistant Commissioner (Crime) in his office on the fifth floor of New Scotland Yard, the big turret room looking down on the ornate

1

gates; the Reserve Squad called in early because of the killings in Norfolk.

'Ascoli?' For a moment he sounded as though he'd never heard the name. Then he repeated it. 'Ascoli? Right, Arthur?'

'Max Ascoli,' the DAC (Crime) prompted, frowning because Livermore's mind seemed to be elsewhere.

'Max Ascoli KC. You don't forget a name like Ascoli, do you?' Tommy smiled to himself. 'Max Ascoli who defended ...?'

'Goldfinch, yes. *That* Max Ascoli, Tommy.' The Deputy Assistant Commissioner (Crime) was a big man, tall and broad with iron-grey hair, the manners of a courtier and that sleek just-shaved look to his jowls whatever the time of day. He was particularly nice when it came to people like Detective Chief Superintendent Livermore because of his title – the Honourable Thomas Livermore – though nobody at the Yard ever called him that, and the Press referred to him as Dandy Tom because of the detail and eccentric cut of his Savile Row suits.

The DAC (Crime) was a bit of an arse-licker who held the Royal Family and members of the so-called aristocracy in respect; as, of course, did most people.

'Sands-Ascoli, Lincoln's Inn, Arthur.' Tommy sounded speculative, then added the address. 'Did one hell of a job for Goldfinch. I'd never met him before the Goldfinch trial, but I've known Willoughby since I was a kid. Ned Sands was a friend of my pa's.'

Willoughby was Sir Willoughby Sands KC, whose father, Ned, had formed the Sands–Ascoli partnership with Max Ascoli's father, old Sam Ascoli, died 1937, Coronation year when George VI and Queen Elizabeth were crowned in Westminster Abbey, a huge event surrounded by much pomp and ceremony: special mugs handed out to the kids with pictures of the new king and queen on them; public ox roasts up and down the country; great rejoicing and a lot of legless drinking everywhere.

'My pa used to say if I ever murdered someone I should send for Ned or Will Sands.' He gave a mirthless little laugh. 'Never did, but by heaven, Max Ascoli did the trick for Golly Goldfinch.'

'He had good expert witnesses, Tommy. Did him proud, and we all knew that Golly Goldfinch was – to use the technical term – a raving loony. Max Ascoli simply put the seal on it, demonstrated it to the world.'

'And now he's dead?'

The Deputy Assistant Commissioner nodded and even made the nod appear to be the action of a mourner: solemn and grief-touched. 'Max Ascoli, his wife, Jenny, and the boy, Paul, seven – eight – years old, poor little sod.'

'Strewth! You think it's connected with Goldfinch?'

'Highly unlikely.' Count of three. 'How could it be? Golly's banged up at His Majesty's pleasure.'

A picture of the girl, Lavender, came into Livermore's head, but he didn't mention her out loud. Lavender was still around, somewhere or other. They'd never caught her and that rankled; Lavender was Golly Goldfinch's cousin and suspected of all kinds of nefarious doings connected with some of the murders they'd felt Golly's collar for. Then he nodded, saying good thing Golly was banged up, and the DAC knew what he was thinking – we'd have been certain about it if Goldfinch had been topped. Tommy Livermore often said they should have topped Golly Goldfinch and had done with him. 'Doesn't matter a snowball in hell that he was unhinged. We had him bang to rights over sixteen or more murders; maybe a *lot* more if we hadn't stopped counting. Should've hung the little bugger, my view, heart.'

And Suzie Mountford would nod vigorously because when Tommy had one of his hanging moods on him the only thing you could do was agree. After all, he should know. He had attended the execution of the one person they'd got for aiding and abetting Goldfinch. 'Swift as an arrow from the Tartar's bow, as the Bard says,' his terrible smile. 'There one minute, gone the next. Pierrepoint knows the job. Sticks him on the trap, talking to him all the time, reassuring him, "You'll be all right with me, son," steps back, trips the lever and he's gone. *Kur-lunk.* Doesn't cost the taxpayer a penny once the execution's paid for. Should've happened to Goldfinch. Just over a minute from entering the condemned cell to stretching his neck. Dead humane.'

And if anyone dared oppose him and suggest capital punishment was barbarous, Detective Chief Superintendent Livermore would make an angry sound and say, 'Yes, and the earth's flat, I suppose. Eye for an eye and a tooth for a tooth. That's the sensible way.'

In fact he had been holding forth on the death penalty to three of his sergeants – Billy Mulligan, Molly Abelard and Suzie Mountford – when the DAC had called him up to the fifth floor about the killings of the Ascoli family in East Anglia, Long Taddmarten, fifteen miles south of King's Lynn, which was why they'd all got the early phone calls.

Now he went back to his fourth floor office, dramatic front pages of the *Police Gazette* gilt-framed on the walls and the little model guillotine on his desk. He called in Billy and told him the score, left him in charge, then sent for Molly Abelard, Suzie Mountford, Ron Worral and Laura Cotter, who did photographs and crime scenes, a DC called Peter Prime, very good with fingerprints, and another DC by the name of Free, ballistics and firearms, also good with local organization out in the sticks.

He got them into his office together with Brian, his driver, and another driver name of David Rooke, predictably called 'Doc' or 'the Doctor' because of his initials, D.R.

Tommy was about to give them the story so far when his telephone rang, the red one direct from the switchboard.

It was the Clerk of Chambers, Adrian Russell, who broke the news to Willoughby Sands when he arrived a little after nine on the Monday morning. Russell stood waiting as Sir

Willoughby shuffled, wheezing, up the stairs. In chambers they tried to keep clients well away from the front hall when Willoughby Sands KC arrived, just in case they formed the opinion that the famous barrister was on his last legs. Those stairs took their toll and invariably the great man got into the hall red-faced, breathless and in a condition of near collapse.

Lugging a briefcase and a cloth bag of books, Willoughby fastened his bright watery eyes on Russell, grey and with a new pallor somehow tinged with fear; the secretaries, gathered outside Russell's domain at the end of the hall, looking like the chorus of a Greek tragedy, one of them weeping.

'What's this?' he snapped, preparing to receive terrible news. Perhaps it was his son with the 8th Army in the Libyan Desert, or his wife, whom he'd left less than an hour previously. She'd been a little peaky of late. Heavens, she rarely complained. 'Come on,' he said, modulating his voice. 'Something's up. What is it?'

Russell fidgeted, moving from one foot to the other, and not meeting his eye. 'I think, in your office, sir.'

Willoughby sighed and moved towards his door. Old Russell was past it really, looked scruffy, he thought, not for the first time, but what could you do? Russell had stayed on because he knew the chambers, knew the partners, had known them for thirty-four years. Couldn't get or train a younger man in wartime, damn it. But the problem remained: Russell was becoming unkempt, shabby, a greasy Dickensian figure in chambers.

Willoughby flopped into the old captain's chair behind his desk, dropping the book bag and the briefcase, still out of breath, his heart thumping in his ears, thinking that he must lose some weight – he was always conscious of his permanent obesity, his greed. Lord, make me slim but not just yet.

The door closed behind Russell.

'I'm sorry, sir,' his clerk's voice matching his age, something Willoughby Sands had not noticed before. 'It's Mr Max, sir . . .'

'Max? What about Mr Max?' Max Ascoli, the other partner in Sands–Ascoli, Lincoln's Inn. Four or five years Willoughby's junior, Max Ascoli, but following well in his father's footsteps – old Sam Ascoli, who had formed the partnership with Willoughby's father, Ned Sands, a legend down the Bailey.

'He's dead, Sir Willoughby.'

'Dead? Can't be bloody dead. Spoke to him on the telephone last night.'

'Nevertheless, sir, he's dead.'

Oh my God, Willoughby thought. Max takes Jenny and the boy to Norfolk and that oversized cottage to avoid the bombs, then catches it from some stray Heinkel unloading from six thousand feet over King's Lynn.

'How?' he asked. 'Another Baedeker raid?' The so-called Baedeker Raids were the bombings supposedly picked personally by Hitler from the Baedeker guidebooks, reprisals for the RAF bombing of Cologne. The *Luftwaffe* now targeted the great cathedral cities of England – Exeter, Bath, Norwich, York and Canterbury.

'No, Sir Willoughby. Mr Max was murdered. Shot to death in his home, sir. Shot in the face, the Chief Constable said.'

'Christ in an MG! His face?'

'His face, sir.'

'Jesus on a tandem! I'll have to ring Jenny,' his hand moved towards the telephone.

'No, sir. No good, sir. All three of them – faces shot away with a twelve-bore, they said.'

'All three?' voice rising to a squeak. 'When?'

'Sometime during the night, Sir Willoughby. Early hours. The Chief Constable of Norfolk thought you should know. Said they were getting the best possible people on to it. The Yard.'

'Damned right I should know. All three? Jumping Jesus!'

Adrian Russell didn't hold with Willoughby Sands' blasphemous language. He winced every time a colourful description of Our Lord came out of his boss's mouth. In fact he had on one occasion remonstrated with him, to which Willoughby had replied, 'I apologize if it offends you, Russell. But I'm certain My Maker is big enough and powerful enough to understand what help His name is in banishing tension and frustration in me. Personally, I think He approves, and I'm sure He doesn't mind.'

His hand again went out to the telephone and he asked the chambers' switchboard operator to get him Whitehall 1212, the number for Scotland Yard's Private Branch Exchange (PBX). Until relatively recently every man, woman and child was aware of that number for it was the one the BBC urged you to call with information or in an emergency. Since the mid-1930s that had changed and the 999 number had replaced it.

'Whitehall 1212,' a female answered from the Yard, and Sir Willoughby Sands asked for Detective Chief Superintendent Livermore. '. . . Reserve Squad,' he added, and when the Honourable Tommy Livermore answered, he identified himself: 'Tommy? Willoughby Sands.'

'Yes. Willoughby, I'm terribly sorry.'

'You on to it, Tommy?'

'Yes, Will, we're just leaving.'

'Get him, Tommy.'

'Of course, Willoughby.'

'And keep me informed. This is *very* personal.'

'Yes, Willoughby.'

Tommy cradled the instrument and Suzie raised an eyebrow and made a comical face. 'That was Willoughby,' she said softly out of the corner of her mouth.

'Have care, Susannah.' Tommy looked straight into her eyes. 'You're not too old for me to—' He stopped, pulling himself together, coughing, realizing where he was. Suzie blushed to the tips of her toes, remembering some of the games they played over weekends, the servant and the strict master. She liked those games. So did Tommy. The squire and the young serf: highly stimulating.

Tommy gave them the bare facts. Max Ascoli KC, the silk who had defended Golly Goldfinch last year, murdered – though the body had yet to be identified. The whole family, wife and child, all found in Ascoli's country house – 'It's called a cottage, Knights Cottage, but I think we'll find it's something more substantial.' Tommy also told them he understood the three victims' faces had been almost blown away, all of them as though their killer wanted them obliterated. They were on the case, going in two cars: Brian would drive the Wolseley and the Doctor, David Rooke, the Railton they'd borrowed off the Sweeney. The claret one.

Last year down the Old Bailey, Max Ascoli hadn't done much defending in the Goldfinch case because Golly had pleaded guilty, diminished responsibility. Ascoli simply had to keep his client from taking that nine o'clock walk and going down the drop with a noose round his neck, and he did that admirably with the aid of trick cyclists and other specialists. Now he was dead and his client still alive in a place for the criminally insane.

Brian drove Tommy Livermore, Suzie and Molly Abelard (who else?); Doc, in the Railton, had Ron Worral, Laura Cotter (snaps and crime scenes), Peter Prime (dabs), and Dennis Free (guns and locals). They drove in convoy, not stopping anywhere except five minutes at a pub for a pee, stretch the legs. The two cars left just before nine, four hours later –

'Very flat, Norfolk,' Tommy said, stretching and doing his Noël Coward voice to match the line from Coward's play *Private Lives*, the imitation not really very good. 'Very flat, Norfolk, that's why they're building all these aerodromes so the RAF and the USAAF can get out there and bomb the buggery out of the Nazis. See what I mean?'

They were passing the perimeter track of an aerodrome where big planes were taxiing, landing and taking off all the time: mostly RAF, Halifaxes and Lancasters and a couple of twin-engined jobs nobody could recognize – everyone learned aircraft recognition, fact of life. The girls craned their necks, peering at the strange shapes: you didn't get to see many real aeroplanes close up if you spent most of the time in London.

A few miles further on – a gorgeous afternoon, deep-blue sky, burning sun – Suzie asked, 'Can we talk about the case, Chief?'

'Yes, please,' added Molly.

Tommy shook his head. 'I've already told you. You know exactly what I know: a house called Knights Cottage in Long Taddmarten—'

'I think they just call it Taddmarten round here,' Brian said from behind the wheel.

'Three bodies, two male, one a child, and one female. All three shot in the face with a twelve-bore; that's all I know, three people called Ascoli. Okay?'

A couple of minutes later, Tommy Livermore said, 'About an hour.' No explanation.

It was just after two o'clock.

They understood just after three o'clock on that summer afternoon when Tommy gestured – 'That must be Long Taddmarten over there, Church of St Mary Magdalene.' The gesture was simple, a flick of the hand towards the wide clear horizon and the sharp grey spire and huddle of buildings, silhouettes against the deep blue.

They had long left the Fenlands behind and were in the flat rolling country, surrounded by farmland: fields of corn as far as the eye could see. Right up to the edge of the world, Suzie thought. She'd never been in East Anglia before, never seen the sweep of land as though God had levelled it out, put in the odd roll or hump of grass, the occasional tree, sometimes a little stand of them unexpected against the skyline. You looked and knew that it went on for ever and a day.

'The field of the cloth of gold,' Tommy murmured as though he was also awed by the sight – the ribbon of straight road cutting through the rustling, slightly bending, rippling corn – then, far away, a mite to their left, came a sudden flash, like the sun glinting off a piece of glass, a heliograph set just above the ears of corn.

Fair waved the golden corn, Suzie heard the hymn in her head, and for a second was with her mum and dad in church at harvest festival, back in the happy time before Daddy died and Mum got remarried to the Galloping Major: back when life had seemed fair and happy, all safely gathered in.

Sitting directly behind Tommy, she craned sideways to try and see what the little light flash was, narrowing her eyes against the sun's glare on this hot afternoon. And she saw, five miles away, the sun reflecting off the wing of a big aircraft lumbering into the sky, silver and straining upwards. Then, drowning the car's engine, there came a sheet of sound, a funnel of noise from the four great radial Wright Cyclone engines propelling the flashing silver aircraft, still low, crawling into the air from the aerodrome they called Long Taddmarten, home of, among others, the 302nd Bomber Squadron from the 33rd Bombardment Group of the United States 8th Army Air Force.

Brian slowed down and they all looked to the left at this magnificent beast, silver except for a letter on the tail, bristling with turrets and guns, men in place, flaps extended to give the wings more lift to take the weight of the fuselage and all it held growling upwards, wheels tucked away. Forward of the cockpit canopy, painted on the nose was a tough-looking woman, a brunette with a cigarette hanging out of the side of her mouth, a halo tipping away above her head, wings sprouting from her back, a glass of booze in one hand and a broken lyre in the other, the long robe she wore hoicked up to show her black lacy underwear and the aeroplane's name stencilled beneath – *Wild Angel*.

It was eleven minutes past three and already another aircraft was lifting off from the airfield – there were six in all.

'The famous B-17,' said Brian. 'The Flying Fortress.' Fortresses were still taking off from the field when the Wolseley, closely followed by the Railton, pulled into the small square – really an oblong – the centre of Long Taddmarten.

Captain Ricky LeClare USAAF sat in the left hand seat at the controls of *Wild Angel* as they bumped and banged their way up to their operational height, towards Southwold on the coast, orbiting, gently sliding in and out of formation until they were all set. Next to Ricky, Bob Crawfoot lounged in his seat, trying to look relaxed – they all *were* relaxed, excited but with little fear, because they would soon be in the defensive formation that made the Flying Fortresses formidable and invulnerable, could pour a wall of fire down on any aircraft that tried to attack, from any quarter. The guns of all the aircraft linked together: wall of death.

Six B-17s out of Long Taddmarten, plus another six from Bassingbourn.

LeClare scanned the instruments and tried to get his mind round it all, seeing his training over the last couple of years coming to fruition. They were going out to bomb the railroad marshalling yards at the French city of Rouen and this would be pretty special because it was the first all-American attack on occupied Europe – 17th August 1942. He could hardly believe it. Ricky LeClare, at thirty-one, was an old man in the squadron – almost ten years since he had taken his Masters at U.Va., Charlottesville, his mind slid to the words of the Saturday-night, after-the-game song that made it all seem like yesterday –

> *'From Vinegar Hill to Ivy Road,*
> *We're gonna get drunk tonight.'*

In his mind's eye, all he could see was the blood.

Two

There were four of them waiting in the Residents' Lounge of the Falcon Inn: big men, precise with no wasted movements, solemn as priests, grave as mourners, little humour and less give than an iron bar – that's what Suzie Mountford thought. They were the cream of Norfolk CID and three of them had come all the way from Norwich.

Tommy and his team had come all the way from London.

As they'd driven into Long Taddmarten Tommy Livermore told Brian to pull over to the left, 'About twenty yards up,' he said, where the road narrowed, the buildings cramming in on either side, then widening into the basic oblong in the centre of the village, though they still called it a square – 'Taddmarten Square' on the black and white picture postcards, a little market there once a week, Wednesdays. Rows of cottages, peppered with a few three-storey buildings, some Tudor beams and the occasional shop, ran higgledy-piggledy the length of both sides of the oblong, and where the road narrowed again, going north, with lanes for two-way traffic, there was a short row of cottages blocking off the top of the square. Behind them the equivalent area to the south where the road widened was blocked off by a garage, a cave of a place: corrugated-iron roof, one petrol pump out front, scruffy, 'Ralph Taylor Repairs' in dirty white over the garage doors and another notice propped against the pump saying, 'Speciality Bicycles • Bought & Sold • Repairs'. Made sense, what with the petrol rationing and everything: most cars up on blocks for the duration. The entire garage was painted a flat, sickly green: nauseating.

As they got out of the cars Tommy said they had to find the Falcon Inn because he'd been told that was where they were staying. He looked around, sniffed the warm air and said, 'Obviously the centre of the universe, this part of the village.' To the left he saw a Christmas-card Tudor pub, the Bell, big wooden bell painted brass on the hanging sign, then four shops, the signs above them weathered with age, faded by the sun, washed out by rain, the first of them: 'Family • Daryl Wood • Butcher'; a butcher, plump and bald, standing in the doorway – probably Daryl himself. Then 'MFH Fox, Baker and Confectioner'. To the right of his shop window a legend was affixed to the grey wall in gold letters, each two feet high. 'TUROG' it said, name of a bread like Hovis, the capital T a dropped cap. At the far end they had 'Cogger, Ironmonger' – sold everything from nails to numbers for your door. Last, at the very end, there was 'Chamberlain' and he obviously had tinned food and groceries, cigarettes, when there were any, matches, tinned food and dry goods, sweets, firelighters, all imaginable things, Kilner Jars, candles and caps for toy pistols, kids shooting each other down all over the place.

Across the road from the shops, there it was, the Falcon Inn – big hanging sign with a large bird, talons curled, wings cupping the air as it swooped towards its prey. The Falcon Inn stood in the centre of the village, quite a large building, square, grey and Georgian – grey only where you could see the stone, the front covered with Virginia Creeper, thick vines of it, trimmed around the big multi-paned windows. Be a picture in the autumn, Suzie thought and she saw, some forty yards behind it, the church spire, sticking out like a grey deformed finger.

Two young women with prams stared at them from a bus stop as though they'd never seen men and women from London before; an elderly man in a grey suit with a cap jaunty on his head led a reluctant dog on a lead, and two boys up to no good cycled past, tall in the saddle, watching without looking at them.

Timeless, Tommy thought. This kind of place would have
the same names in its records over centuries, repeated again
and again in baptisms, weddings and funerals, in the magis-
trates' court, on the war memorials, in the church: same
names at Agincourt and Arras, Crécy and Cambrais.

'You must be the gentlemen from London.' The landlord's
wife – Mrs Staleways – looked uncertainly at Suzie, Molly
Abelard and Laura Cotter, as if trying to work out their sex.
'We've only got four doubles and six singles.' Unsure who
would require what, how and when. 'They're waiting for you
in the Residents' Bar,' she added, almost accusingly, indicating the half-glass door across the hall, a bit to the right.

'Then we'll leave our cases here and sort out the rooms
later,' Tommy said with a dazzling smile, melting her heart.

Mrs Staleways was a rotund little woman with a sticking-
out large backside they couldn't see because she was behind
the desk. Hetty Staleways, wife to Len, mother of Beryl and
Christopher. 'It's a terrible business,' she volunteered.

'It is indeed,' Tommy agreed, looked around at his assembled team and said quietly, 'Suzie, Molly, with me. The rest
of you mingle with the locals. Glean. Tell Brian and Doc to
park the cars. Behave yourselves.' He cocked his head in the
direction of the opaque glass of the door on which was
inscribed 'Residents Bar & Lounge', in gold, very smart.
'Beauty baffles brains,' he winked at Suzie, then turned back
to Dennis Free, still near the reception desk. 'Dennis, nip
over to Chamberlain's, get a *Daily Mail* and the local paper.'

'What's Chamberlain's?' Free shook his head.

'Use initiative. It's the general store across the road. Bound
to stock newspapers. He'll also have a lot of gossip. Take
Laura with you. Be a cosy couple out for the day. Return
with rumours and idle chat.'

'Right, Guv.'

'Any more for the *Skylark*?' Tommy said with another all-
purpose grin, and for a second Suzie thought they could be
off on a day trip, maybe to the seaside: pink sticks of pepper-

mint rock, candyfloss and cheeky kiss-me-quick hats, going down to the sea, tucking their skirts up in the legs of their pants, the men putting handkerchiefs on their heads knotted at each corner, warding off sunstroke; the girls and women rucking up their skirts without embarrassment, frequent sight on English beaches.

He knows what he's doing, Suzie considered. He's surrounding himself with women, keeping the local force on their toes. Won't know what they're dealing with.

Meekly they followed Tommy through the door and there met the solemn men from Norwich, and the one from King's Lynn.

To Suzie they all looked well past closing time, while Tommy thought that collectively they had the personality of a brick wall.

The heavyset, tall one with beetle brows and arrogance in his sneer unwound himself, slowly put down his coffee cup and rose. 'Tommy,' he said with a smile, holding out both hands in greeting.

Hello? Tommy thought. This one's taking liberties, we've never been introduced yet he's treating me like an old flame. Head gnome, I'll be bound. Head gnome buttering me up because I'm supposed to be a gent, an Hon. He took the man's hand.

'Brew,' the man said introducing himself. 'Harold Brew. Detective Chief Superintendent Brew. Officer in charge Norfolk CID.' He grasped Tommy's hand and tried to give him the Masonic handshake, at the same time stepping in close and grasping Tommy's right forearm with his left hand.

It felt like a judo move or one of the new skills they were teaching the Home Guard: unarmed combat, they called it. Serious-eyed and straight-faced, they believed a quick course in basics would make the old men and young boys into serious killers.

Tommy nodded. 'Harold,' he said with feeling and quickly snapped out introductions: 'DS Mountford, Suzie Mountford.

DS Abelard, Molly Abelard. Highlights of the Reserve Squad. My right-hand men.' He spoke gravely, as though he always told the truth and Brew hurriedly introduced the other three: a DI called Glynn Roberts, another DI name of Allee, plus the DCI in charge of King's Lynn CID, Eric Tait, big, stern and serious – hardly a smile, beaky nose, eyes slightly hooded and extravagantly tall.

Tait said, 'It's an honour to have you down here, sir.' Must have been six foot six in his stocking feet. 'Rangy' was a good word.

Spoiled the mood for Tommy, who hated all the class snobbery that went with his pedigree – The Honourable Thomas Livermore, heir to his father's title – Earl of Kingscote.

'Privilege to be here,' Roberts muttered with little sincerity, while DI Allee nodded, not meeting his eye. All out of their depth, Tommy reflected, possibly believed in fairies and good luck charms, wanted to touch him to ward off evil, share in the supposed legend: the gentleman detective, dying breed. Never lived, he thought, simply a conceit for authors of detective fiction: Lord Peter Wimsey, or Albert Campion and Detective Inspector Roderick Alleyn. Figments, fragments set to solve paper puzzles, nothing to do with the real life that came up to their necks, over their heads in this fifth decade of the twentieth century. Gentlemen detectives: the stuff of fiction that people liked to think crossed the line into real life.

Now he said, 'Just here to get on with the job,' then asked what information they could give him and the story began to come out, dribs and drabs, shreds of evidence.

What had happened was that Piglet, the Ascolis' dog, had barked and whined most of the night outside the cottage. Knights Cottage: six bedrooms, three bathrooms, library, dining room with original sixteenth-century fireplace, drawing room, sun room, usual offices. Mature garden, two acres. More your high-class villa than a cottage, just as Tommy had suspected.

Knights Cottage stood some fifty yards from the nearest house at the north end of the village, almost on the boundary itself on the King's Lynn road. The nearest neighbours – a long-retired military man, Colonel Matthews, and his lady – at Roundhill House had complained to the village bobby, PC 478 Walter Titcombe, telephoned him first thing, early. Titcombe proceeded warm footed to Knights Cottage, where the stupid, floppy oddity, Piglet, upper-class mongrel, a lot of Spaniel crossed with a sexually obsessed Yorkie called George, leaped at him, but not happily.

Piglet – so named by the boy Paul Ascoli during his Winnie the Pooh period – was a bit of a joke. He liked to play with the pigs that inhabited a field just behind the garden of Knights Cottage, big muddy sty of a place he only had access to if someone left the door open in the red-brick wall that hemmed in the garden. Odd thing was the pigs weren't frightened of the dog: all got on like fleas in a palliasse. Piglet could growl or bark at them and they took no notice, just romped together. Bob Raines, the farmer who owned the pigs, claimed to have caught the wretched pup trying to mount one of his young sows and said of him, 'That'n be a nasty-minded pooch, but clever an' well-named, Piglet. Keeps quiet up in the top field with my pigs, then goes back to Knights Cottage and barks like a traction engine.' People were divided about Raines's idea of congress between the dog and the pigs because the same farmer had once claimed to have owned a cat with an owl's head. Unlikely.

But there were many who disliked Piglet: butcher Darryl Wood's delivery boy, Ernest, for one. Piglet would lay into him, barking, snarling and snapping like a hound from hell when he came over to deliver Jenny Ascoli's meat – not much of it now the rationing was settling in. The postie, Bernie Carpenter, approached Knights Cottage with daily dread even though Piglet usually only savaged his postbag.

But that morning, 17th August, Piglet had wakened Colonel and Mrs Matthews, barking away at 6 a.m. Later, the colonel said he had some idea that he'd heard Piglet barking in the night. Barking and whining, sure of it, pulled out of sleep for a few seconds and heard him, loud and close, then sank back into sweet oblivion.

PC Titcombe was a big man, broad, red-face and a waxed moustache, Sherwood Foresters in the '14–'18 show, a sergeant, promoted in the field, came out to become a policeman in 1918 and was bloody good at it. Had the knack of policing a village. Knew about village hierarchy: knew who to butter up and whose ear he could clip; who to warn off and who to encourage; polite to the ladies, friendly and flirtatious with the housemaids, helpful to the landlords and tradesmen, and the scourge of potential villains. They said of him that Walter Titcombe knew when to pounce and when to be blind, especially where the licensing laws were concerned. Had an uncanny knack with the girls, knew instinctively which ones he could pluck, out there behind the graveyard wall; also had a strange way with animals, who seemed to sense his legal power in the village.

Piglet was running around in circles outside the back door of Knights Cottage and began barking and whining as soon as he saw Wally Titcombe; ran to him and then back to the door, pausing to look at the policeman. Intelligent dog, Titcombe thought, telling me something: knew there were horrors, maybe more, unpleasant on the other side of the door.

The door was slightly ajar and Piglet waited for him to push it fully open, making sure he was following through the dark utility room with its smell of boot polish and sets of shoes on newspapers near the copper with its fireplace below, in the brick surround. Titcombe's nan had had a copper just like it. As a child he'd sit in there for hours of a Monday morning as she got the fire going, then began to steep the clothes in the tub, pushing them round, stirring them with the wooden tongs and the dolly, pulling them up and rubbing them on the washboard. Steam and sweat everywhere. His nan had been consumed by the work, every Monday, all day dollying the wash, rubbing, scrubbing, putting it through the mangle, then out to dry.

The utility room led into the wide kitchen with an arched ceiling, some free-standing cupboards on the far wall and a large old Welsh dresser near the door which led on through what had once been the servants' hall – only Walter knew the Ascolis only had a daily woman who sometimes came in to help with the cooking if they had a dinner party, or people there for the weekend. The Ascolis were held in high regard in the village in spite of their odd name.

An oval table took up most of the room, the overhead lights, two of them, were on and the blackout frames in place over the two windows. The table was set for three people and there were two silver toast racks, a cruet and large cups. They obviously used the servants' hall as a breakfast room.

There was one door to the left, open, leading to three steps and a short passage to a door, functional and lined in green baize, before which Piglet lay shivering, whimpering, flat on the ground, distressed, plainly frightened, head turning back towards Titcombe, eyes wide, brown and filled with apprehension. Whining.

'Good boy,' Titcombe patted the animal's head and its body wriggled again. As Titcombe said later, 'Like he was tryin' to squirm hisself through the flagstones, dig hisself down to hell and back.'

PC 478 Titcombe drew his truncheon from its long pocket in his trousers, put his shoulder to the green baize door and pushed.

He couldn't recognize Mr Ascoli, who lay on his back in the centre of the hall, dressed in pyjamas and a dressing gown, blue with pinkish piping on the sleeves and lapels, fancy and with decorative frogging. Long marks of slime and what looked like blood came out from under the corpse's arms, dark silvery rails, as though he had been pushed across the stone floor of the hall, leaving the trail behind him.

19

'I knew it were him by his hair, that's all, 'cos his face was obliterated,' Wally Titcombe said when he was struggling over his report. 'His face . . . well it were as if hundreds of hornets had swarmed on him, stung him to death, leaving holes in his flesh as well as their stings, holes the diameter of cigarette butts some of them.'

In the middle of the face there was a larger ragged hole where his mouth had been, not a mouth any more, just a dark hole. No lips.

PC 478 Titcombe, in spite of experiences on the Somme and elsewhere in France, was physically shaking as he began to search the rest of the house. It took almost half an hour to discover Max Ascoli's wife, Jenny, in the master bedroom, a horrible sight, and the boy, Paul, in his room, still tucked up in bed but with his face blasted by a shotgun, obviously fired while he slept.

When he had searched the entire house, Wally Titcombe telephoned his superiors in King's Lynn. He used the family phone in Knights Cottage, wrapping his handkerchief round the handset, telling the operator that he was speaking from Taddmarten 37 and this was official police business.

Detective Chief Inspector Tait from King's Lynn told Tommy that when he looked at the crime scene his impression was that the Ascolis were the victims of some murderous vagrant – or vagrants – who had come upon the house, asked for food or money and were rebuffed. 'I think they returned later for old-fashioned vengeance,' he told Tommy, who, though he had yet to visit the scene of the crime, felt the theory could be a little simplistic.

But who knew?

They could see the target area, the city of Rouen, from ten miles away, the sky so clear that afternoon, bright and peaceful flying at 23,000 feet over northern France, with Ricky LeClare keeping the stabilizers of the lead aircraft just in the right position above *Wild Angel*'s nose. The lead aircraft was *Butcher Boy* and their Group Commander sat in the co-pilot's seat, just as the Commanding General of VIII Bomber Command – Ira Eaker – rode in the lead aircraft of the second flight, *Yankee Doodle*.

Over the Channel, four RAF squadrons of Spitfire IXs joined the formation to give cover as far as the target, and Bob Crawfoot, who claimed to be half Sioux Indian, grinned happily from the co-pilot's position, watching the French countryside slide past below. 'Lookit those RAF boys and their dinky little planes.' He sucked in through his teeth, shouting loudly, hearing the words in his ears, his mouth inside the oxygen mask there at 23,000 feet. 'Lookit them move. Boy-o-boy. Betcher they dangerous little boogers.'

The Bombardier, Wilton Truebond, lay in the nose, looking down at France, thinking he had never imagined a country could be that pretty from the air. England had astounded him. Now France was showing that it was a different country: different kinds of farming, different road systems – no hedgerows for one thing. Different! Different! Different! For Lieutenant Will Truebond it was all new because he came from Minnesota, where they said there were only two seasons – winter and road repairs.

Until he joined the Army in 1939 Truebond had never ridden a train or an airplane. His longest journey was the monthly ride in his father's car to the Twin Cities – Minneapolis–St Paul. When he did his bombardier's training he flew out of Randolph Field, Texas, and the first bombs he dropped were on the sand and rock ranges, not a hint of green. Until they began the long flight to Europe Will Truebond had viewed only the arid geography of Texas from the air. England was a revelation. And now France.

Even though the weather had been mostly grey and dismal in the month since he'd arrived at Long Taddmarten, the lush-ness of the countryside never failed to amaze him: the long age and beauty of the trees, the organization of farmland, the sweep of a soft horizon, like the curve of a woman's breast.

It was all so different to the settings of his youth and life back home in the little town of Frozen Bend, Minnesota, pop. 11,235. At school they'd called it Frozen Butt and that was about it.

When this was over, he thought, I'll spend my life travelling the world and seeing everything.

Ricky LeClare came on over the interphone, as they then called it, 'Okay, Bombardier, you okay? We'll be over the target in eight minutes, positioning for the bombing run.'

'Roger that, Skipper,' and Will put his face into the scope of the Norden bombsight, with its two gyroscopes and the four knobs he used to position the aircraft and the bombs. Once the bombing run began it would be Will Truebond who would be flying the plane: the Norden bombsight linked to the autopilot so Truebond would virtually fly the ship, with LeClare monitoring the course on the PDI – the Pilot Direction Indicator – while the bombsight did all the complicated math, working out height, wind, direction, speed of *Wild Angel* and all the other complicated stuff until the bombsight knew they were in the right place, throbbed an electrical pulse that released the ordnance and sent it screaming down to the target – or near enough whichever came first.

'This baby'll do all the work for you long as you feed it the correct information,' his first bombsight instructor said. 'So good, the Norden, that it'll drop a bomb in a pickle barrel from ten thousand feet.'

Will Truebond didn't subscribe to that boast any more, but he still repeated it, and the rest of the stuff his instructor said. 'The Norden'll even make you coffee if you treat it right. Who knows, it might even be better'n your girlfriend. You got a girlfriend, Truebond?'

'Back home, Sergeant.'

'Keep her there then, son. You gonna get horny, get horny about your Norden bombsight.'

When he received his commission and the General pinned

on the silver wings, one of the first people to salute him had been that tech-sergeant instructor. Proud moment.

Will Truebond concentrated on the cross hairs, manipulated the four knobs, selected the British-made 600-pound General Purpose bombs; his head full of noise, the constant blast of the engines; the scent of oil and rubber in his nostrils inside the oxygen mask, and that singular smell of the B-17's interior; the cold air breathed in that was oxygen; his body rising and juddering, then falling with the ship, as the target, the Rouen-Sotteville marshalling yards – the permanent way, the rolling stock, repair shops and the big locomotive workshop – slid into view far below them and the Norden worked its magic, releasing the bomb load.

The ship leaped upwards when the weight was detached, the autopilot uncoupled from the Norden and Ricky LeClare again took control, holding her steady in the turn as Jimmy Cobalt, up at his navigator's station in the nose with Truebond, gave him the course for home.

LeClare gave the instruction to little Willie Wilders, their radio op, to send the code word, saying that the bombs had been dropped. Willie sent it straight off in Morse, then climbed back up to the dorsal gun position.

Will Truebond still had his eyes on the target way below. Through the sight he seemed detached from what was really going on, waiting for the bombs to straddle the target: he never saw them. He glanced up to starboard and saw two small dark clouds appear, suddenly forming out there beyond the right wing; then realized what they were and saw another and another with a bloom of scarlet deep within, heard the pistol-crack like lightning striking nearby, and felt the ship wallow and buck. They were trying to kill them – this was flack from around the target – and he felt real fear, the darkness in his gut and the twitch of his sphincter muscles.

Within a few minutes they were back with the fighter escort, the Spitfires, heading for home at the far end of their range, everybody cock-a-hoop and shouting over the interphone, saying they had done it, what a great job, they'd whupped the Krauts' asses for them; told them the Yanks had arrived.

The only people dissatisfied were the air gunners, swinging their turrets or mountings with no targets to shoot at, desperately needing to prove themselves. They had been turned out of gunnery school at Fort Myers, Florida, where they'd trained in AT-6s and O-47s, having no communication with the bored pilots, who had to drop a wing as your signal to start shooting at the drogue towed by another pilot who didn't care. When you got back they always discovered the camera guns were not working and the whole business had been a waste. The only time they managed to fire the .30 or .50 calibre guns was on the ground in a mocked-up turret. They'd spent hours learning to strip the weapons and clear stoppages, more time being lectured on defensive formations and even longer hours on aircraft recognition, knowing who not to shoot at in a moment of trigger-happy fear. They knew they could do it, but deep down wanted to face an attack by fighters, at the same time as fearing such an experience: needing the blooding.

Tim Ruby in the upper turret swung the guns round, a complete circle, then held them a shade to port as he watched the Spitfires bucking around in their formation heading for home – little Timmy Ruby, the baby of the crew, looked fifteen, had the heart of a lion.

Tech-Sergeant Henry Corkendale was the port waist gunner, with Sergeant Piakesky in the starboard position, standing back to back in the freezing cold, wrapped up with electrical suits, helmets, scarves and heavy gloves, cold and scared behind the goggles, the open holes uncomfortable, bare to the elements.

Corky yelled when he saw the two dots growing bigger until he could see the outlines, recognized the head-on view and heaved the heavy .50 calibre gun in their general direction, then watched as some of the Spits dropped towards them, chased them, and in that moment he loosed off some ammunition as though he was helping. Bob Pentecost, squashed upside down in the ball turret, swung his guns around, looking to see what Corky was shooting at, and found nothing.

Peliandros, the tail gunner, family originally from Athens, Greece, was jumpy all the way back and Tim Ruby in the mid-upper turret immediately behind the pilot's position, developed a twitch, everyone getting on with their jobs, tired and cold now, the euphoria dissipated.

As they came back up to the French coast, there was more flack, looking pretty as it puffed out its black and grey clouds, below and above them, no danger, not coming really near, though Peliandros swore that more 109s began to prod at the Spits but got chased off.

They crossed the British coast where they had crossed on the way out, Southwold, nice English watering hole, and began the let down towards Taddmarten. It was just before seven that evening – 19.00hrs – when *Wild Angel* started to make its approach to Taddmarten. Truebond looked out of the nose, seeing the houses and the church and feeling they had come home. For the first time he felt this *was* home. Really home, reaching out and putting its arms around the whole crew: Long Taddmarten, home of the 302nd Bomber Squadron from the 33rd Bombardment Group, sharing the base with two RAF Spit squadrons and one squadron of Beaufighters.

Ricky LeClare felt it as well. Glad to be home in one piece: elated, boisterous, noisy, cocksure. They had taken the war to the enemy and come home safe. They were kings, they were gods.

At seven o'clock Tommy Livermore was just talking about leaving and Suzie thought: Leaving? We've only just arrived.

Three

She had been the first person to reach the accident in which her father was killed, fifty yards or so from their front gate – years ago now. Since that time Suzie had been proud that she could look at bodies and mutilations without turning a hair. Like most good middle-class girls she had been brought up not to show emotions or grief in public, not to visibly cling to others for support. This had translated into the police ethic of not showing shock or fear before 'civilians': being undemonstrative and in control at all times. She believed it showed strength of character, which in some measure it did.

She thought she'd seen it all, including the decapitated body of a nasty little man in Soho when she was working out of West End Central; but these faceless bodies in Knights Cottage were something else: a whole family brutally and quickly done to death in their home.

In the drawing room, the baby grand was covered with framed photographs: mostly of Max with the good, rich and beautiful. There were others though, demonstrating what a happy family they were: Paul at various landmarks in his young life; Paul with Mummy and Daddy; Mummy and Daddy on their wedding day. Willoughby Sands, Tommy pointed out, was best man – the male smile said 'chums'.

Looking at the body, Tommy said, 'Photographs are worse, heart. Frozen for all time.' But she doubted it as she looked at Ron Worral stepping carefully around Max Ascoli's body, using first his eyes, then the camera. She had to drag her eyes away from the holes in the man's face and the congealed blood and then upstairs to the even more horrible sight of Jenny Ascoli hurled backwards, face shredded, in the doorway of the main bedroom.

'Jenny is woken by the shot, heart – tell me if this makes sense.' Tommy led her up the stairs slowly, one slow tread at a time. 'She wakens, eyes pop open and, for a moment, she doesn't know what has woken her. *Bang!* Or *bang-bang!* She sits bolt upright. It takes a few seconds but she knows something's wrong so out she gets in her modish pink silk nightie. Stands by the bed, frightened, listening, hears someone on the stairs and goes to the door. Our killer has loaded again – if he needs to – and bang . . .'

Her face was ripped away, just a big smudge of blood where her features had been minced off, the muzzles less than a foot from the face.

Looking past the body, through into the main bedroom, there was a large and striking watercolour on the wall: a stretch of battered coastline, fishing boats pulled up on a harsh stone beach, three of them on ramps with chocks holding them upright, the sea grey and cold, almost indistinguishable from the pewter sky, storm clouds hanging to the east.

Tommy turned and walked across the landing to the passage that led to the child's room. Suzie followed, glanced down and saw DCI Tait and another pair of plainclothes officers come in through the front door. Tait stopped, puzzled, looking at Ron taking the photographs with Laura Cotter in attendance, Peter Prime and Molly Abelard dusting for dabs. He called up, 'Tommy, my boys've taken all the pictures.'

'Yes, old bean, but I like my lads to get plenty of practice.'

'Ah.' Tait shook his head. 'The ambulance is waiting. Can they remove the bodies?'

Tommy came to the head of the stairs and looked down

at Tait. 'Don't think so, heart. I've got Professor Camps driving up from London. Think he'd prefer to look at the corpses in situ.'

Camps, one of the great experts in medical jurisprudence, forensics and pathology: Francis Camps, up there with Keith Simpson, Bernard Spilsbury and Donald Teare, big medical wheels.

Jesus, Suzie thought, what a bastard Tommy's being. With reason. The whole phalanx of big guns who'd greeted them at the Falcon had behaved in an odd way: they'd toadied to him, showing a sort of mock deference that, she saw, had made him angry. Dandy Tom getting his own back, 'Pissing into the wind,' he would say, laughing. But he had got to them. She saw it in the livid tinge to Tait's cheeks and the anger in his eyes.

As he turned away, Tommy muttered, 'Serve 'em right. Shouldn't have joined,' and dragged Suzie back to the matter in hand, talking as they walked. Her job was to listen, comment, look and watch, point out inconsistencies, pick him up on anything that didn't mesh. Her eyes and ears were the tools of her trade now.

'You really got Camps coming down for the bodies?' she asked, and Tommy stopped walking.

'Course not. The quack from King's Lynn's perfectly capable,' grin. Then, 'You'd better tell them they can take the bodies as soon as Ron's done the snaps of the ones up here. Then come back to the boy's room, eh?'

She nodded, 'Right, Chief,' and went off to the stair head, calling down to Ron, who was taking a final close-up of Ascoli's mashed and punctured face. She thought of some picture she had seen of a face covered in growing greenery, as though the flesh had been seeded, the blades of grass cutting through the skin, bizarre and somehow frightening. 'If you've finished down there, they can remove Mr Ascoli, Ron,' she called down.

'I thought—'

'They can take him off to King's Lynn; and the others when you've finished.'

Ron Worral smiled and nodded: knowing the Chief as well as anybody.

Tommy Livermore stood blocking the doorway of the boy's, Paul's, room. 'Don't know whether you should come in here, heart.'

Too late, for she was already past his left shoulder. 'Shit,' she said under her breath, opened her mouth to speak, but Tommy finessed her, treading on whatever she was about to say.

'Paul didn't even wake.' He put a hand on her arm and she tried to look everywhere but the bed. Frog aeroplane kits made up neatly, painted correctly – a Handley Page Hampden, a Hurricane and a Fleet Air Arm Skua with wings folded – all standing in line along a shelf. The books, *The Boy's Book of Aeroplanes*, *The Boy's Book of Knowledge*, D. H. Parry's *Sabre and Spurs!*, a tattered and elderly set of *Arthur Mee's Children's Encyclopedia*, inherited from his grandfather probably, she thought, then allowed her eyes to drift back to the horror.

The bedclothes drenched in blood and a stain slashing up the headboard and then the wall, reaching about six feet high.

'The lad's either still asleep, or pretending, so chummy slides up to the bed, sticks the muzzle under the chin, couple of inches away and looses off – I think both barrels . . . Yes?'

Suzie doesn't reply, just stands in the doorway, shivering slightly trying to take her eyes away from the bed with the dark-stained, dry, stiff sheets and blankets.

There is a cough from behind them. Dennis Free is on the landing.

'Dennis?' Tommy says, not raising his voice.

'Chief, there's a Purdey twelve-bore, double-barrelled shotgun in Max Ascoli's study. Hasn't been fired in a long time.'

'Other half of a pair?'

'Most likely, Chief. Thought you should know.'

'Thank you, Dennis. Now, Suzie . . .'

Suzie didn't stay to hear the question. She gave a little sob, couldn't stop shaking, and did a kind of quick dance step, twisting her body to the left, hopping behind Tommy and Dennis Free, then running down the stairs, out of the front door: out to the sunshine and Brian and Doc, standing by the cars.

'Suzie . . .' Tommy called again from the landing.

Outside, Brian followed her, two steps, and called out, 'You want to sit in the car, Skip?'

She doesn't reply, just shakes her head rather wildly, like a wet dog, surprised to find she's crying. In her head pictures of the dead revolve, full of blood: her father mangled in sliced metal, a dozen other horrors, the little man decapitated in Soho to the three bodies behind her now in Knights Cottage, their faces scrubbed away with the 12-bore shot, and the child taken in his sleep.

'Heart, what is it?' Tommy comes up quietly behind her, his hand first on her shoulder, then the fingers straying to her cheek, touching the tears. 'What is it?' understanding what was going on and wanting her to put it into words, clean out her mind, scour the final emotional release, the bottled-up terrors from all the dead she had encountered over the years. She feels wrung out, desolated, reaches up, placing a hand on his shoulder, eyes brimming. 'Tommy. Sorry. How do you deal with it?' Meaning the final full stop of sudden death. 'How do *you* feel about death, Tom?'

His face slid into a sad half smile. 'Oh, I'm agin' it, heart. Definitely agin' it.' His face reforming into a grin.

She blinked – bravely through the tears, she thought – starting to come down from the feeling of shock. Typical of Tommy, making light of the most terrible aspect of life and the horror of it all ending so suddenly.

'Get in the car, heart.' Patting her shoulder. 'We'll go back to the Falcon and you can get yourself together.' He called

Brian, then made his excuses: 'Got to have a word with Molly.'

'Want to sit in the back, Skip?' Brian asked and she didn't even acknowledge him, still drowned in a mixture of emotions, just climbed in and slumped into the back seat where, presently, Tommy joined her and they purred back to the inn.

'Molly's following. I've organized some food with our soignée landlady, the fair Madame Staleways.'

The description was so inappropriate that, in spite of herself, Suzie smiled weakly. Then she asked if she'd have time to unpack.

'Don't unpack, heart. We're not staying tonight. Back to the Smoke, then up here again sometime tomorrow or Wednesday.'

'But we've only just got here.'

'I know. Comes with the job, old love. Got to sneak around Lincoln's Inn and talk to old Willoughby Sands, him of the paunch, big arse, full of smart legal chatter.'

'Tommy.' Chiding him, more out of habit than anything else.

'Either go to his chambers or see him at home: Hampstead. You'd like it there, heart. Very swish, dontcherknow.'

'Really?'

'We haven't got enough on the Ascolis and I don't want to leave it to Billy Mulligan. I've not done me job: bad planning, old love. Me, the one who usually has everything tied up. This time I didn't. Ropey do, heart. Thought we'd have a file on the Ascolis, because they settled here, in Britain, at the turn of the century: ice cream makers, did cakes and other titbits. Made their fortunes by 1910.' He gave a little laugh, reached over and squeezed her hand. 'All well and good but we've got no real detail. You see what happened in Knights Cottage as a bit of revenge, sudden, like Tait suggested? Vagrants? Tramps? Travelling people?'

As they pulled into the Falcon so the Flying Fortresses

were returning to the base up the road, landing on the main runway and taxiing round to the hardstandings, the frying pans. The engines roared, then dropped down as they stalled out for their three-point landings, then grumbled again as they taxied, spluttering to a halt. They could be heard all over the village, the sounds funnelling through the old streets.

'Ascolis killed by vagrants, my impression,' Tait had said.

Suzie put her brain back in gear, then said she really didn't see some vagrant creeping back to do for the people who had, possibly, refused them some kind of assistance, a tip or food. Tommy nodded. 'Me neither, and I don't see Max being high-handed to beggars. No marks on the wall either.'

'Marks?'

'Vagrants, beggars, gypos, didicoi, milestone inspectors: they all do it, signal soft touches and hard cases with a chalk mark. Special signs. Should learn them, heart.'

Aloud, Suzie said, 'Oh?' then wondered why DCI Tait had suggested vagrants in the first place. 'No evidence to support it: not as yet,' she said, then went to her room – a single next to Tommy's huge double at the front of the building, over-looking the square. She washed, changed and went down with her small case stuffed with overnight things and her schoolgirl toilet bag.

Molly had arrived and sat waiting near the dining-room door. Tommy came down a couple of minutes later.

'Well, GPO were fast enough, good,' he announced. 'Set up a telephone in my room, new number, account to the Yard, no SNAFUs. Not yet.'

The dining room was almost empty.

They sat at a window table and were waited on by Beryl Staleways – a thin soup, dry lamb cutlets, over-cooked pota-toes and carrots – an unappetizing Sunday dinner on a warm August Monday evening which ended with rhubarb and a lumpy custard. 'I thought the London British restaurants were bad,' Tommy said, raising his eyebrows and glancing across the room at Beryl, lumpy as the custard and with BO redolent of rodent – *en masse*.

During the meal Tommy had talked almost non-stop, giving his instructions to Molly. 'Curry-comb the place,' he said. 'Then Hoover it, and after that you collect every scrap of paper and begin to sort through it. Go to the back of drawers, riffle through books, don't be shy about diaries and personal letters.' He continued in that vein until the rhubarb arrived.

Molly said the lamb was spectacularly bad.

'Old ewe,' Tommy agreed.

'My grandma,' Molly told them, 'was a bit of a Mrs Malaprop. She thought E-W-E was pronounced eewee. Used to call me her eewee lamb.'

Suzie laughed, but Tommy smiled weakly and said he'd had an aunt who once said they'd backed a winner at Newmarket that had made them 'Rich beyond the dreams of ambergris', capping Molly's story to the extent that Suzie didn't really believe him. Sometimes Tommy liked to be king of the castle as far as wit was concerned. It was one of his least pleasant sides.

The balance of the team arrived, chattering and looking satisfied with themselves. 'You going to warn them?' Tommy asked of Molly.

'Let them find out the hard way.' Molly laughed. 'Chief, the Press 're around, outside.

They came out, Tommy and Molly walking ahead, Suzie just behind, a little to the left, 'The bodyguard position,' Molly had once told her, and the Press came out from under the flagstones: two reporters and a blocky looking man with a camera.

'Chief Super, what's the latest?' they were asking, clamouring.

Tommy waved them away, and the guy with the camera began taking pictures: *click, click, click*.

'I want them working nine, ten hours tomorrow; want this part tied up. If you've any spare time get 'em all chatting up the locals – gossip, rumours, the usual . . .'

'Don't worry, Chief.' Molly, grave and unsmiling. *Click . . . click . . . click.*

'. . . start harassing their doctor in King's Lynn, name of Locust. Peter Locust. Locals call him Plague for obvious reasons.'

Tommy was still talking to her as they folded themselves into the back of the car. 'I'll leave a message for you in the morning, or trace you and give you a list of where we expect to be – over at Sir Willoughby Sands's to start with, either in his chambers or his house, depending on the arrangements WDS Cox has made for us. Don't know where after that, but we'll keep in touch. Be good, Molly, and keep the team under the lash.' Grin, raised hand, 'Right, Brian, let's go.'

As the Wolseley turned on to the main road that ran along the perimeter of the air base, so they were met by what looked like a factory turning out at closing time, bicycles by the dozen and a couple or three jeeps sweeping out of the main gate: GIs on bikes, sergeants, T-sergeants, M-sergeants, WOs, officers in various states of dress – No 1 uniforms, olive-green shirtsleeve order, even officers in their pink and greens – and on all sorts and conditions of bikes, men's bikes with the crossbar, women's bikes without a crossbar, some of the shorter men riding kid's bikes; there were bikes with baskets across the handlebars and bikes with saddlebags: Ralph Taylor in the Square must be doing a roaring trade. Everyone smiled and some shouted to one another. Many smoked cigarettes; some had cigars in their mouths. They were the Yanks, the guys who had come to show little old England how a war should be fought: arrogant with a mix of wanting to please and a need to have a good time.

The bicycles were heading towards the village and its pubs, while Tommy noted the jeeps went fast along the road towards the relative sophistication of King's Lynn. These were young men, some of them risking their lives in the skies of northern Europe. These were men far away from home and the social disciplines of family. Many would drink more than was good for them; some would pick up local girls and try to do what they'd never think of trying on with their serious girls back home. All too soon they would discover that the British country girls tended to say yes – footloose no doubt in the absence of their boyfriends, now wedded to HM Forces. Looking at the massed squadrons of cyclists in uniform, Tommy felt the stirring of an idea. 'Heart?' he said in the Eton drawl. Suzie found the Eton drawl to be the facet of Tommy that she liked least. His 'language' she could put up with, and the occasional farting in bed – 'The old Scotch warming pan,' as he'd say – but the Eton drawl always indicated something sneaky was about to surface: it was his twitch, his tic, his almost deliberate signal of a new idea, good or bad.

'Heart?'

'Yes, Tommy.'

'Don't you think we should cast an eye on Max, Jenny and the Yanks? See if they had dealings. Never can tell with the Yanks, heart, eh?'

'Absolutely, Tommy.'

She put it on the back burner of her mind. Left it simmering on a low light so that it would be well done after they returned from quizzing Sir Willoughby Sands and anyone else who might add to their knowledge of the Ascoli family.

Some forty miles inland from Long Taddmarten, off the road between Haddenham and Huntingdon, up a tree-lined drive and surrounded by a high brick wall topped with broken glass set into cement, lay Saxon Hall. That afternoon it had been visiting hours at Saxon Hall Hospital, known locally as the lunatic asylum or, incorrectly, the Spike, which was usually slang for workhouse.

Among police officers and members of the legal profession Saxon Hall was spoken of with some reverence as 'The Hall' because within its stern walls were two large wings set aside for the Criminally Insane: very tight and secure with several separate wards for males and females and never the twain shall meet. This was where Golly Goldfinch – Two-Faced Golly – was being kept at His Majesty's pleasure. And that afternoon, Golly Goldfinch, of Ward C1, had a visitor: a tall, plump lady with hair long and brushing her shoulders, black as nightshade, thick pebble spectacles and a limp.

'Who you then?' Golly asked quietly. There were four 'patients', as they were euphemistically called, in Ward C1, which had only one way in and out: a triple-locked steel inner door and an outer door that was made of solid oak with reinforced panels and a speaking tube to contact anyone inside. The windows set high along one side were big, arched, covered in wire mesh and protected on both sides by bars. Facing this wall were the four cubicles – solid, thick metal walls and a steel door with standard Judas squint. The doors were locked each night from eight until seven the next morning except in an emergency.

Golly was the only one with a visitor this afternoon. Since he had been at The Hall his only visitors had been police officers who came to talk him into admitting to more killings than they knew about, hoping to be able to cross out some that were still on the books. He also saw the psychiatrist once a week, taken to his office by the large Mr Bolt – Christopher Bolt the Chief Nurse/Warder, big with a small, rather silly moustache – and his oppo, Mr Sidney Snow, tall, thin and dogmatic. Golly had the same line for them, never tired of it – 'You going to bolt me in then, Mr Bolt?' and 'Going to snow today, is it, Mr Snow?' – this last becoming tedious in the middle of August. Golly didn't imagine that they'd get fed up with these questions, thought they were the soul of wit, but the two men could've thumped him if they got the chance.

'You've forgotten what I look like, Golly?' The woman brushed hair back from her face and smiled, giving him a slow wink behind the thick specs. They sat facing each other at a small table in the main association area of the ward, near

Golly's cubicle, or his cell as he thought of it: bed, metal cupboard, bolted to the wall, and the writing desk that folded flat.

'I never seen you before.' In a bit of a sulk.

'Oh, come on now, Golly. Course you seen me before, your Auntie Harriet. Your mum's younger sister . . .' She had a broad country accent, Berkshire, Hampshire maybe.

'Mum never had a younger sister.'

The psychiatrist had said he might not recognize her and she had agreed it had been a while since he'd seen her – 'Only I thought that, as how Golly has no other family – 'cept that no-good sister of his – it's my duty to come and see him.' All potential visitors had to be interviewed by one of the doctors before they were allowed to see the prisoner, as well as being vetted by the institution's executive staff, who were fairly slapdash.

'Golly, of course she did. You remember me really, Golly. Course you do,' this last almost whispered. Then she dropped her voice even more, barely a breath in what seemed to be a different voice entirely: 'Kill with the wire, Golly. You remember *that.*'

Mr Bolt and Mr Snow were playing some card game, quietly, over by the door. Mr Chris Williams and Mr Billy Green were talking to the other patients, sitting and chatting away quietly, down the far end, by the door to the Ablutions: more steel, unlocked only when a patient needed to be in Ablutions, accompanied by a warder . . . nurse.

Golly looked up sharply now and peered at his aunt, leaned forward a little in his chair and saw her eyes and the smile.

'Shit,' he said, awestruck. 'Oh,' he said. 'Ah! Yes. I know who—'

'Course you do, Goll,' said Lavender, who had got the long black wig from a mate who worked for a theatrical costumier and could get things like wigs and padding, which she was using now to put on weight; she'd also borrowed the terrible old suit she wore and the dykey shoes, mannish brogues, polished like a conker. 'I'm your Auntie Harriet, though I'm not surprised you didn't recognize me because I haven't seen you since before the war: 1938, was it?'

Lavender was a whore, and being a relative of Golly's had used him as a minder in the two rooms she worked out of off Rupert Street in London's West End, spit and a stride from Piccadilly where the whores, now in 1942, were coming into their own: the Piccadilly Commandos.

'Yeah, about then,' Golly grinned and gave his familiar 'huh' of a laugh. '1938 or '39, I forget.'

'Thirty-eight,' said Lavender firmly. Golly would move out on his own if she wasn't careful – liked making up his own stories – and the laugh, she knew, often got out of hand: drew attention to himself. The last thing either of them needed was attention.

Quietly she asked Golly what the screws behind her were doing.

'Minding their own business,' he told her, 'and they're nurses, not screws.'

'I know what they are. Officially those men are called Nurse/Warders,' Lavender said with feeling. The ones she could see, at the other end of the ward, were not interested in what she and Golly were talking about. Why should they be? Nobody could possibly escape from Saxon Hall, could they? 'I know exactly what they are,' she continued. 'And the real problem is . . .' long pause, then speaking without moving her mouth, like a ventriloquist, '. . . getting you out of here.'

'Can't be done,' Golly trying to do the same trick – *Ant ge un.*

'Oh, yes it can.' She smiled and he could sense the old Lavender under the smile. 'I've a foolproof plan. Piece of cake.'

'Piece of cake,' he repeated not moving his lips – *Eas o' ake.* Then, 'The judge said I was at His Majesty's pleasure and the brief said that meant for ever and ever. Amen. Told me that. And Mr Bolt he said it was for always. He said it was for ever *and a day*. Those were Mr Bolt's words.' Golly looked up and his eyes opened wide just at the moment Lavender sensed someone behind her.

'Mr Bolt said what was for ever and a day?' Christopher Bolt, standing just behind her, large as life and twice as natural. 'Talking about me, Golly?'

Golly swallowed and looked away, couldn't look Mr Bolt the Chief Nurse in the eye, six foot one with bulging muscles because he spent time with the dumb-bells and weights. 'Nothing, Mr Bolt.'

'Wocher mean, *nothing*, Golly?'

Lavender, as nice Auntie Harriet, adjusted her glasses, looked straight at Bolt and told him the poor boy was bewailing his fate. 'He knows they're never going to let him out of here, Mr Bolt. Never in a hundred years.'

'No, miss. No, they're not going to let him out, not even if the Angel Gabriel blows his trumpet tomorrow forenoon. They'll not even let him out then.' Bolt nodded and walked down the ward to the other men at the far end while Mr Snow let himself out of the main door and went for his break, cup of tea, a wad and a Wills Woodbine fag. The only brand available that week.

Nobody near them now.

Low, under her breath, Lavender in her deep disguise and right in the character she had created for herself whispered, 'Listen, Golly, listen really well. This is what we have to do, and your side is easy . . .'

Later, when the visiting time was over, Mr Bolt himself escorted her back to the lodge that was really a kind of guard room at the main gates, the protected entrance and exit to Saxon Hall. As they walked, Lavender limping along slowly as Harriet Goldfinch, younger sister to Ailsa, Christopher Bolt spoke, 'When we was talking in there, miss – I am right, it is miss, isn't it?' Looked down at her, smiled a knowing smile. Twinkle.

'Yes, Mr Bolt. Yes it's miss, always has been and I suppose always will be now.'

'When we was talking in there. You spoke of your nephew as "a poor boy". "A poor boy bewailing his fate," you said.'

'I did, yes.'

'You think of him as a poor boy, miss?'

'I do, Mr Bolt. Yes, of course I do. The boy's had his liberty taken away from him, and, unless I'm mistaken, you keep him subdued with drugs. You keep him quiet and pliable, yes?'

A curt nod from Mr Bolt.

'He is lost to the world. Lost to me, his living relative, and he's classified insane, my nephew,' Miss Harriet Goldfinch said, almost tearfully.

'Perhaps, miss, you should think of all those folks that your nephew, Golly, killed. The people he strangled with the piano wire; the people he crushed the life from; think about them and their relatives, who'll never see *them* again because of Golly.'

'They only proved he killed one. Charlotte Fox she was.'

'Yes, Miss Goldfinch. They only *had* to prove one, but what about the others? Patricia Cooke from near Stratford-upon-Avon, Marie Davidson from Trumpington, Mary Tobin found on Ealing Common, Geraldine Williams, Newcastle, Gillian Hunt in her Birmingham flat, Pamela Harwood—'

'You seem to have made quite a study of my nephew, Mr Bolt,' she snapped.

'Don't need to make a study, miss. Your Golly never stops talking about them, croons hisself to sleep reciting their names. . . . Obsessed by them.'

'Even when he's subdued by your drugs?'

'Especially when he's had the drugs. Gets what they call a heightened perception of things. I hear he goes into a lot of detail when he talks to Dr Cornish. A. Lot. Of. Detail.'

'Then I trust Dr Cornish knows how to help him.'

'Indeed he does, miss. Helps him a great deal, I gather.'

Something not quite as it should be, Christopher Bolt thought to himself as he watched the elderly, rather common lady, waddle her way out of the gates and along the barbed wire-flanked drive heading towards the second checkpoint, the one in the brick wall topped with broken glass.

Couldn't quite put his finger on it, but Christopher Bolt had a nasty little sense of irritation about Harriet Goldfinch: something that didn't quite fit. Have to keep an eye out for her on the next visiting day.

Take a closer look.

Four

A fter making a couple of telephone calls they went to Willoughby Sands's house near Hampstead Heath. A quiet road, large old Victorian mansions, lots of gable ends with painted white boards, big sash windows, and outside the trees in full dying summer leaf, August dust on them. Not much bomb damage around here, but the council had taken away the gates and railings from the front of the houses, to help make tanks and aeroplanes. They never did of course – make tanks and aeroplanes – because the metal from railings couldn't be turned into tanks, 'planes, guns or bombs. Probably made people feel good though, letting all the railings go. The dogs loved it, had a field day.

Inside it was cool and neat and Lady Sands, who greeted Tommy with a kiss and Suzie with a limp handshake, said you couldn't get the staff these days, murder running a big house without staff, unfortunate choice of words in the circumstances. She went on to say she was trying to train a new general-purpose servant. 'On the dim side,' she told them. 'Dim as a Toc H lamp.'

Then Sir Willoughby came in, roly-poly like a caricature on legs. The pair together reminded Suzie of Laurel and Hardy, Lady Sands small and thin, Willoughby downright fat, but full of energy, fiddling with his tie.

Stanley, pick up those tools.

But Ollie, I only wanted to . . .

Tommy started it. 'Will, I want to talk about Max Ascoli.

42

Run down the family history. Inside story from the wise, y'know, get it from the horse's mouth.'

Will Sands gave a high whinnying sound and Suzie was surprised that such an experienced barrister could stoop to that kind of music-hall humour. In the back of her head she heard Tommy Trinder, the comedian, doing his 'You lucky people' catchphrase.

'Come to the fount of all wisdom,' Tommy said with his Eton drawl. 'I know you must be feeling it badly. Last thing you'll want to do . . .'

'Do what I can,' from Willoughby. 'You know that. I want you to get the bastard. Best I should keep going anyway but couldn't stay in chambers: two families intertwined you see. Sands–Ascoli.'

Lady Sands interrupted, said, 'If you'll excuse me I'll go and attempt to train this fifteen-year-old cretin they've sent me from the Labour Exchange: teach her how to work a carpet sweeper,' left a dazzling smile behind her. It seemed to linger in the drawing room after she had closed the door. But Suzie caught Tommy rolling his eyes to heaven.

'Imogen really didn't care for Jenny Ascoli,' Willoughby grinned, speaking quietly, embarrassed. 'Felt knowing her socially was a shade infra dig.'

'Why?' Suzie asked and Willoughby Sands gave a huge shrug, shaking his head and raising his arms. 'Who can tell? I do not understand the female mind. Particularly I do not understand my wife's mind.' He laughed, deep and heartfelt. 'She gets on with everyone else, know what I mean?' His face showed that it was all a mystery to him. 'Virgil got it right. *Varium et mutabile semper Femina.* Eh?'

'Wasn't any good at geometry, old thing.' Tommy did his side-on smile – one corner of his mouth turned up showing his teeth – the one he called his terrible smile.

'"Fickle and changeable always is woman."'

'Thank you.'

43

Suzie thought that maybe she should give up now while she was a step ahead.

They waited and finally Willoughby said, 'Anthony – Antonio – Tony Ascoli came to England from Rome around 1889–1890, sometime about then. Came with his wife, Clara, and the three bambini: Salvatore – whom friends called Sammy – Benito and the toddler Fredo. They settled first in Manchester, but Sammy came south: Oxford to read Law. Came up to Magdalene in the Michaelmas term 1891. They had money, big success in Rome with ice cream and confectionery. Never understood why they left Italy. Lot of rumours of course . . .'

Not for the first time Suzie wondered why Oxford University had a college dedicated to St Mary Magdalene whose name they pronounced 'Maudlin'. Never could work out the vagaries of university traditions.

'What kind of rumours?' Tommy sprawled in an easy chair and Willoughby in the middle of an old-fashioned Chesterfield, taking up most of it, the Chesterfield covered in white with little rosebuds dotted around. Suzie sat on a Victorian nursing chair in the far corner by a long curved bay window looking out on to the garden, big floral decoration on a table set in the bow: colourful. On the opposite wall there was a large oil: Venice, the waterfront adjacent to the Piazzetta di San Marco: a corner of the Doge's Palace with the pillar topped by a statue of St Theodore and the other pillar, in the foreground, surmounted by the Lion of St Mark. Dramatic scene with a storm brewing, lightning in the wings. She had an idea that this was a copy of some more famous painting, but couldn't place it. They used to carry out executions between those two columns. Suzie knew because she'd spent a week there with her family back in the peace of childhood, sometime in the thirties. Got her bottom pinched in Venice boarding a vaporetto: nice. Had it fondled in London, on a crowded tube train only last week: not so nice. One of the things she vividly remembered about that

trip to Venice was the guide telling them about the executions, all gruesome and loving it. That and the bottom
pinching. Sexual arousal in Venice: what could have been
better?

'Rumours?' Willoughby sighed. 'Rumours that the Ascolis
had crossed someone. That was the favourite. Huge row,
threats, vengeance-is-mine sort of business . . .' Waving a
hand, indicating it was a load of rubbish.

'*Someone*?' Tommy queried.

'Yes . . . Someone. Never had details. Dame Rumour you
know, Tommy.'

'No. You *knew* Sammy; knew him well, I guess. After all
he was your father's partner in chambers. He must have said
something. The real story, the reason why the family came
to England.'

'Oddly, Tom, he didn't. None of the Ascolis ever referred
to it, steered clear of it, changed the subject if asked, but
there were other tales – that old Antonio had run away from
Rome with some ice-cream recipe, or a secret piece of equipment for the confectionery trade. Another one was that
Antonio'd had an affair with some girl in royal circles and
it was a big scandal, something went wrong. Either the girl
had killed herself – you know, hot Italian blood – or she was
up the loop and he'd run away with his wife.'

Tommy gave his screwed-up face 'looking at the ceiling
look', the quizzical one, right eyebrow raised. But Willoughby
Sands continued:

'Old Antonio liked the ladies. Come to that, all the Ascolis
were fond of the horizontal waltz, and chose women who
were enthusiastic, enjoyed the zig-zig as well, all of them.'

Tommy gave a long series of nods, understanding the
Ascolis.

'Beginning of the century they didn't all lie back and think
of England y'know. All the Ascoli men picked girls who
knew what it was for and liked it with some fervour. Vines
have tender grapes; let him kiss me with the kisses of his

45

mouth: for thy love is better than wine: Song of Solomon stuff.'

Of course, Suzie thought, he means the beautiful romantic side of love, romantic and physical sides. I bet poetic old Willoughby's full of it. Suzie wondered if this was the reason Imogen hadn't liked Jenny Ascoli, the sex thing. Perhaps. Maybe didn't like Willoughby either, could be.

Willoughby smiled thinly, raising his head, looking Tommy in the eyes. 'Not getting too technical for you, am I, Tommy?'

'Not at all. If it gets difficult I'll ask my translator.' He grinned at Suzie. 'Any truth in that last one, Anthony and the royal lady?' Tommy, clipped now, the drawl gone.

Suzie noticed that Willoughby had taken over the drawl. 'Couldn't say, old boy.' Long pause as though waiting for Tommy to step in again. 'Fact is the family came over from Rome, Antonio trawled the country for some kind of an in. I mean they were a cut above your normal tradespeople. Yes, they were in the ice cream and confectionery business but they didn't actually sweat in kitchens or wait on tables in cafés.' Broad smile and a nod. 'Sammy though – well, Salvatore'd set his heart on the Law, and they had to have pulled some strings because Sammy got into Magdalene no problem. No problem about reading Law either. Come to think of it they must have had one hell of a pull because Sammy had to have become an English citizen by the time he was called to the Bar. And there was his wife – now I *do* know the truth about *that* . . .'

'That's a blessing,' Dandy Tom muttered. 'Blessing and a boon.'

Sammy met Cynthia Hope-Jones at a ball in December 1894. The waltz was *the* dance and they danced the waltz that night till the early hours. 'Marked her card. Every dance, as I heard the story. Soon as he saw her, Sammy decided he'd lay siege to her: bring in his big guns, trundle on the ballistas and howitzers.'

Cynthia was a striking redhead – and you know how Italians can become obsessed by redheads – tall and slim of figure with grey eyes and a slinky smile.' He gave a slinky smile of his own. 'I remember my father, the guv'nor, tellin' me.' Willoughby leaned back, closed his eyes then opened them, wide and innocent. 'Back then, "slinky" had two meanings. It meant sneaky or underhand, and Cynthia certainly still had a sneaky smile when I first met her twenty years on.'

'Two meanings?' Tommy snapped.

'You don't want to bother with the second one, I assure you.' Willoughby leaning forward, sincere, nodding just as he would when trying to avoid going down some dangerous line of questioning in court, wrinkling his nose.

'So, Sammy and Cynthia . . . ?' Tommy prodded him.

'Yes.' Willoughby seemed short of breath for a moment as though he'd been running or suddenly aroused by a memory. 'Clicked,' he said. 'More than clicked really from what my guv'nor said. Met at that Christmas Ball 1894 and *had* to marry in April '95. Desperately in love of course, but no end of a stink, the guv'nor told me. The Hope-Joneses were military: Colonel Sir Wilson Hope-Jones, Household Cavalry. Sir Wilson threatened to horsewhip old Sammy – nearly did, I gather. Lived in a state of armed truce. Sammy called him "Colonel" to his dying day. Cynthia said to him, "Daddy, what shall Sammy call you, now he's part of the family?" "Oh, hup, ah, hup yes. He can call me Colonel." Old boy was killed 1916. On Haig's staff and his car caught a stray shell – one of ours, I believe. Blew him to buggery.'

'So, Cynthia was, to use your own colourful expression, up the loop?'

'If you'll pardon my coarseness, young woman,' to Suzie. 'Yes, bun in the oven, caught out, up the spout, in the Pudding Club, whatever takes your fancy, Tommy.'

'And the result was?'

'Bit of a tragedy actually. A boy, Phillip – Fillipo.'

Exaggerating the Italian accent. 'He wasn't quite right,' tapping his forehead with the fingers of his right hand. 'Had to hide him away in some clinic. Switzerland, somewhere near Thun, round that way. Then Cynthia just couldn't get pregnant again. Ironic really and it wasn't for want of trying. I know. The guv'nor used to say they were at it like stoats. Caught them once in chambers late at night. Laugh? Lord he used to laugh like a drain. Talked about it. Said Sammy would complain to him about Cyn wearing him out. Couldn't get enough. Sammy and my guv'nor formed Sands–Ascoli in 1910. Max was born eight years earlier, 1902, apple of Sam's eye, and both of Cynthia's. He was adored and spoiled rotten.'

'And they all lived happily ever after.' Tommy stretched, head going back, perfectly at ease. At his most dangerous, Suzie thought.

'Happy as Larry.'

'You got on with Max?'

'Just about his best friend, seven years older than him, but he joined chambers a year after the guv'nor brought me in.'

'So when was that?'

'1924. Never looked back.'

'And he had no problems? He was good?'

'Good, he's outstanding. *Was* outstanding. Well, you saw him in action, Tommy, the fellow he defended . . . the one you'd put away. What was his name, Goldmark, Goldfish . . . ?'

'Goldfinch. Adam Arthur Goldfinch. Golly Goldfinch. Strangler extraordinary. Loopy as a bat and dangerous as a scorpion.' Tommy took a deep breath and was about to launch himself into his 'hanging's-really-too-good-for-them' speech.

'Golly Goldfinch, yes. I came along to watch Max on that one. No defence of course but he did the job, kept him alive, had him put away at HM's pleasure. Good result. Knew the right people to bring in, that trick cyclist from Harrow. Brilliant. Perfect match. And the other fellow, the sociologist. Unusual line of questioning. You still looking for whoever primed the bloke? Directed him?'

'We know exactly who did that, who became the voice in his head. We know who she is and why she did it. Trouble is she didn't leave a forwarding address.' A slim smile, flicking on and off. 'Defence Max's main thing, was it?'

'He liked defence, though his great successes were when he prosecuted. All a challenge. Bit of an actor with a lot of law in his head. Very quick on his feet as well, great co-ordination between brain and limbs. You must recall some of his cases . . .' and it looked as though they were off on a journey through Max Ascoli's professional life. But not quite yet.

Tommy asked, 'Anyone in particular still living who might feel less than happy with Max?'

'A few. Your boy Golly Goldfinch may think it's Max's fault that he's locked up in some Government institution for the rest of his natural. There are a few like that. Take Lucan MacRoberts . . .'

'The schoolgirl killer?'

'That's what the papers called him.'

MacRoberts, an itinerant builder's labourer, had been charged with murdering two schoolgirls, one fourteen years old, the other almost fifteen, on Putney Heath in 1932. But he appeared to have an unbreakable alibi involving four other labourers he claimed to have been with over the two days during which the killings had taken place – 6th and 7th June '32.

'The girls were strangled and raped, caught while they were taking a short cut, separately, across the heath.'

Tommy nodded back at Willoughby, signifying that he had read about it, one of the famous cases of the '30s.

Willoughby said there was a lot of circumstantial evidence to link MacRoberts with the murders, but the man was said to have been working with four friends doing repairs for an iffy builder, putting some dodgy plumbing right in some equally dodgy houses near West Hill, spit and a stride from Putney Heath. The police couldn't break the four men alibiing MacRoberts. Stalemate.

'At the time we had an inquiry agent permanently working for Sands–Ascoli, name of Phillip Poole. Good un. In fact his son Dick works for us now. Phillip got himself close to these itinerant labourers, got the inside story.'

Max Ascoli, it seemed, suspected MacRoberts was passing a bit of dropsy to the other lads giving him an alibi, doing some thieving to save his neck and pay for the story. Poole went through the records of the four alibis, eventually got details of jobs they'd been sacked from – petty theft and the like, no police action taken: theft, fiddling, bad time-keeping, drunkenness. 'They all had stuff in the past they'd have rather kept hidden, and the people they'd worked for weren't bashful about talking to Phil Poole. In the end they sang like the proverbial canary: veritable canary glee club.'

When it came down to it, MacRoberts's defence were calling all four of the men as witnesses to establish the alibi. 'Whole case revolved round them,' Willoughby said.

But Max demolished the lot: starting in a friendly way, implying he had only a couple of routine questions, leading them down a path strewn with deadly obstacles, and finally teasing, then bludgeoning the truth out of them, laying them bare, knocking them into a corner where they finally condemned themselves through their own muddled stories.

'As it turned out, the defence only called two of them, and after hearing the first one go to pieces it was too late. MacRoberts was found guilty of rape and murder, but the psychiatrist's report led the judge to reluctantly sentence him to be held at His Majesty's pleasure. Screamed at Max, MacRoberts did, just as he was being taken down, "I'll get you, you slimy bastard. I'll do for you." Or words to that effect.'

'A lot of them say things like that.' Tommy smiled. 'I've even been at the receiving end of similar curses.'

'Yes, and MacRoberts meant it. Wouldn't put it past him to try masterminding a murder from his cell at Rampton.'

'Others?'

'A handful, yes. We all collect them along the way. All barristers do, but few take it seriously.'

'Max?'

'I doubt it. Max is – *was* – a fairly relaxed person. Christ, I can't yet believe he's gone.'

'He has, I've seen him.' This time Tommy wasn't smiling.

Suzie often thought that Tommy Livermore should have been a barrister, told him so more than once. 'Don't look good in one of those stupid wigs, heart. Not my style,' usual flippant self. Now he was batting questions off Willoughby Sands like a fast game of table tennis: probing into Max Ascoli's professional career.

He went through some of Max's big cases, using the melo-dramatic names Fleet Street assigned to them at the time, making them sound like detective stories by Agatha Christie or Dorothy L. Sayers. The Edmund Diamond Mystery, for starters, the mystery being that Mr William J. Edmund didn't have the diamond he sold to a syndicate for almost a million pounds sterling – lot of money back then, middle thirties. On that occasion Max Ascoli put Edmund away for fifteen years. Then there was the Vicarage Murder: the vicar, the Revd Arthur Hilton, returning after evensong one Sunday to find his wife of two months – Ruth, ten years his senior – battered to death in the bedroom. Eventually Arthur Hilton was arrested on very slim evidence, but Max untangled the threads in court and laid out a thoughtful and damning case which led to the vicar taking his last walk with the public hangman. Revd Hilton was, beneath the cloth, a man just like any other and craved money and a life in which to spend it. The week he was married was the week that he took out a £500,000 insurance policy on his new bride.

The Affair of the Gold Tooth followed soon after, then the Greased Lightning Killings and the Laddie Green Kid-napping, possibly Max's most notable trial, the result of which sent four men directly to jail for thirty years each.

Tommy thought maybe he should look more carefully into

those whom Max had sent to prison for significantly long terms.

For almost an hour and a half, Sir Willoughby Sands discussed the cases of his partner, Max Ascoli, skilfully and with elan: Willoughby talking quietly, absorbed by what he was saying almost as though he was celebrating Max's life and gaining some form of comfort by doing so.

Finally, Tommy led him towards what had occurred in the past twenty-four hours. 'Who gave you the news, Will?'

'Of Max's death? Adrian Russell, my Clerk of Chambers. Told you, didn't I?'

'And who told *him*?'

'Somebody from the Yard. Fredo and Helena had people call on them. And Freda, Benito's widow's staying with Fredo and Helena at the moment. Copper turned up at the house, Montpelier Square. Said they'd been trying to get Freda for hours, in Scotland where she lives for most of the year.'

'The local lads went round to Montpelier Square, eh? Handy really: they probably picked up their rations at Harrods first. You know where they came from? I mean was it the local nick, or did the Yard really send them?'

'I've no idea.'

'What number Montpelier Square?'

Willoughby told him and Tommy got to his feet. 'Good of you, Will. Good of you to put up with us for so long. Invaluable.' He gathered up his notebook and Suzie saw him glance towards her, out of the corner of his eye really, just a tiny movement of his head at almost the same time as Imogen Sands came back into the room with a tray of coffee: well, a silver coffee service with the usual appurtenances, six different kinds of sugar including the coloured crystals, and what Tommy always called 'those horrible dinky little cups'.

Dandy Tom had drunk a large cup of black coffee the previous night when they got back to Suzie's flat in Upper

St Martin's Lane – said it always helped him rise to the occasion – and it did with spectacular results.

'Oh, you going?' Lady Sands asked, sounding happy about it.

''Fraid so, old dear,' Tommy, all light-hearted with matching smiles.

'Have some coffee, Tom, please.'

'Couldn't, heart, got things to do, people to see. Got to sharpen the old handcuffs and clean off the magnifying glass, rub down the truncheon with linseed oil.'

'If you must, then. Should've brought it in sooner, but been a bit occupied with the cretin.'

'Of course.'

'Oh, I did take a cup of tea to your man, to your chauffeur.'

'Brian,' Tommy said, his smile turning into a smirk. Most unattractive, Suzie decided. 'Good show. He'd appreciate that.'

'Yes, I thought he looked like a tea person.'

'You have the most wonderful instinct, Imo.'

'Yes,' she said, the drawl catching up with her now. *Yerse.*

Suzie followed Tommy to the door, where he stopped, half turning, hand on the brass doorknob. 'Where were you on Sunday night, Will? Sunday night and the early hours?'

'He was here all evening. Back from chambers around five, didn't go out again. Stayed in all night. Slept with me.' Imogen quick. Like a blur.

'See ourselves out,' Tommy said and hustled Suzie towards the front door. 'Can't stand Imogen,' he whispered when they got outside.

At the car he leaned into the front passenger window. 'Brian, we'd like to go to Montpelier Square when you've finished your tea: don't rush on our account.'

Five

Some of the photographs sitting in silver frames on the baby grand were duplicates of the ones they'd seen in the late Max Ascoli's house at Long Taddmarten. Now Tommy Livermore and Suzie Mountford were in Fredo's home, Montpelier Square: high ceilings and wonderful old furniture, expensive wallpaper and nice pictures, including an obscure Turner and a Canaletto, both here in the drawing room. Venice in Knightsbridge.

Pride of place on the baby grand was a large photograph of Max and his bride Jenny in their going-away clothes. She looked small and vulnerable with luscious blonde hair high on her head. Max looked tall and proud, smiling down on her with a possessive expression.

The photographs all contained Ascolis, living and dead, with famous people and with each other, showing what a close family they all were. If you knew the Ascolis and they regarded you as friends, they would help in time of trouble. If you were in any danger the Ascolis would close around you and protect you, fight off all comers. They were all loyal and true to friends. Brave and steadfast: made you part of their society, part of their gang.

Tommy caught a whiff of gangsterism about the Ascolis, power hanging around on the fringes of the British upper classes. It was that odd cross between fragrance and the reek of corruption. He wondered again about their place in the United Kingdom, why they had come here, how they had settled seamlessly into an almost aristocratic stratum.

Suzie thought of the British army she'd learned about in school, the kind of army that formed a square to hold off the enemy, mainly your Zulus or your Indian mutineers: the square that didn't break unless the Gatling was jammed and the colonel dead, regiment blinded with dust and smoke with some kid shouting, 'Play up! Play up! And play the game!'

Old Tony Ascoli was there in a lot of the photos, him and his wife, Clara, in front of the country house they'd owned near Bicester in Oxfordshire, or the other one up near Balmoral; also plenty of them with the three boys growing up: Sammy, Benito and Fredo, Sammy dead now but snaps of him and Cynthia with Max growing up, happy families. Benito with Freda before he was killed in 1937 – motor accident near Monte Carlo, on one of those dangerous mountain roads that snake along towards Italy. Freda had been with him at the time and walked away from the wrecked car – a Bentley, naturally, fit for the captain of industry that Benno had outwardly become. Willoughby Sands said that in private Freda claimed she was asleep when the crash occurred, but reckoned that Benito had become confused, forgot he was driving in France (it was always happening, she'd said) and crossed over to the left side of the road – bang, head-on into a van. It made Suzie reflective, sad because the van that killed her father had drifted over to the wrong side of the road outside her family home near Newbury, on the Kingsclere Road.

The widow Freda sat, straight-backed, quite close to the baby grand not really looking her fifty-eight years. More a well-preserved forty, Suzie thought. A slim, lithe forty with an unextinguished sensuality in her movements. 'Panther, I thought, heart,' Tommy said later.

Fredo and Helena, his English wife, sat together on a long divan and they didn't look much older than their wedding photo with Benno the best man and bridesmaids neither Tommy nor Suzie could identify, Fredo maybe greying a little now, clear blue eyes that always seemed to have a hint of amusement in them, dancing and twinkling.

'I'm sorry to intrude,' Tommy began, sounding genuinely concerned, and Suzie looking soberly grave, backing him up. Grief was a nationwide experience now in time of war. People dreaded the knock at the door, a policeman or a telegram. Too many remembered the telegrams from the Great War and the deluge of misery they brought.

Fredo raised a hand, 'Our nephew, Max?' He started, the voice flat, no particular accent and no trace of his Italian lineage. 'We know he's dead, with Jenny and young Paul. But we have no details.'

'One of my colleagues came to see you, I understand.'

'An inspector, uniformed, from Scotland Yard. With a young woman police sergeant. They were very kind, but said they hadn't got the full story.' Fredo was an exact man, a man careful in speech and a neat man in dress and habits, from his carefully combed hair to the clean manicured fingernails.

'No.' Tommy didn't look any of them in the eye, looked down at the carpet and across the room instead. 'Do you mind if we sit down?' Not waiting for a reply, he settled himself on to the arm of the long sofa facing the divan, casual and relaxed. Suzie found a padded stand-chair and sat, awkwardly to attention, doing a little rumba movement with her buttocks to settle.

Tommy said, 'I'm afraid the details aren't very appetizing. The ladies may—'

'The ladies'll be fine.' Helena Ascoli was a tall, striking woman, with a steel-tipped glint in her eye, svelte, not a pound of extra fat on her hips, wearing a summer cotton dress, pink and blue pattern, beautifully tailored, long legs, her make-up perfect and her hair, dark with a hint of grey, impeccable: Harrods beauty salon perhaps. The tough quarter of a bridge four, Suzie thought: the kind who never forgave a partner's error, played to win.

'They were shot.' Tommy spoke quietly as though he didn't want them to hear him.

'Yes, we knew they were shot.' One of the women – Suzie wasn't quick enough to see which one.

'Shot. Yes, we knew that much. Just.' Fredo simply repeating the word.

'With a twelve-bore shotgun.' Tommy still kept it low, and added, even lower, 'In the face. All three of them.' He paused and this time looked at each of them in turn, saw them absorbing it, wincing as they tried to picture the circumstances. 'I wanted to get the rest of you together, the remainder of the Ascoli family, see if you had any ideas. Anyone's name who maybe had reason to hate Max.' Pause of around three seconds. 'Just to be certain: you are Freda Ascoli. Benito's widow –' turning to the other woman – 'and you're Helena, Fredo's wife . . . ?'

'I prefer to be called Freddy,' said Fredo. Freddy.

'The three of you are basically all that's left of the Ascoli family, yes?' He'd bet that Benno called himself Ben. Benny.

'Not *quite* the whole family.' Freda's voice was gruff, throaty: a sexy voice, Tommy thought, attractive. If Freda spoke in a crowd and you heard that voice you would immediately turn towards her: match the face to the voice, instantly interested.

'No. There are your children of course.'

'I've two sons fighting for king and country in North Africa. Ben's and my sons. Emelio and Vittorio.'

Ben (told you so): good old English names, Tommy thought and with the thought heard Freda again, 'Emil and Victor.'

Freddy gave the grin of a simpleton. 'And I have three girls. Wouldn't you know it? Three girls to bring up, pay for, marry off. All intelligent, pretty and naughty as elves. Maria, Francesca and Margherita.' He gave a roguish grin, shrugged and said, 'Mary, Frances and Margaret. All Ascolis and each one a special joy of my heart.'

'My heart as well,' Helena not wanting to be left out.

Tommy let it all pause for a couple of seconds, two beats of a conductor's baton. 'So, that's the entire Ascoli family: The three of you here, Mary, Frances and Margaret, plus Emil and Victor. The entire clan extended from those who came and settled in the UK from Rome in 1889?'

Freddy nodded. 'Now Max and his family are gone, yes. Yes, settled here in 1889 or '90, nobody seemed certain of the date and I was still a babe, learning to walk, toddling.' He toddled up his left forearm with the first two fingers of his right hand. 'But we have relations who remain in Italy. Antonio had two brothers: Luigi in Perugia, and Guido in Milan. Both dead now of course, but we have cousins, male and female.'

'They in the same line of business as you: ice cream, confectionery, cafés?'

'On a smaller scale, but yes.'

Since the end of the previous century the Ascolis' name had become synonymous in Britain with cream cakes, ice creams, tea, coffee, neat little sandwiches, and even neater little waitresses.

'Often wondered why your family left Rome in the first place?' Said as though he couldn't care less about the answer, just interested. For the record.

'That is family business. Not for the wider world.' For the first time Freddy sounded serious, as though the lightness had drained out of him.

'The reason is for the Ascoli family alone,' Freda very straight and solemn.

Tommy wondered if there was some special ceremony once someone married an Ascoli, or when an Ascoli child reached the age of twenty-one: a ritual to pass on the family secrets.

Suzie thought of the Masonic Order.

'So, the Ascoli family in the United Kingdom consists of the three of you plus your five children?'

Freddy spread the fingers of his right hand, holding it out, palm down, and tilting it: *comme ci comme ça*. Then he looked first at his wife, then at Freda. They both nodded. 'There is one other,' he said, and Tommy looked at him blankly. He had once instructed Suzie, 'When somebody begins to offer information you should appear disinterested. That way you get more, heart.'

'Two if you count Fillipo, Max's brother. You know about Max's brother?'

Tommy nodded, didn't speak even though he really wanted to know where the man, Fillipo, was, where he was being looked after. If he was still alive of course.

'Okay. You ever hear of a woman, Paula Palmer?'

Tommy shook his head.

'Paula Palmer is a painter: watercolourist. Well-known for her Norfolk scenes.' Freddy smiling as though he was looking at a pleasing picture now. 'Does wonderful studies of the coastline, also some quite famous paintings of Norwich. There is a series of Norwich Cathedral, four pictures of the cathedral in the four seasons. Also a similar set of Ely Cathedral. She is much in demand as a book illustrator.'

Both Tommy and Suzie recalled the painting they'd glimpsed in the master bedroom of Knights Cottage, the grey sea and sky with small boats propped upright on the dark beach.

'So, she's a painter. Paula Palmer? What else?' Tommy, flat, dull but profitable.

'She has a daughter.' Freddy made a gesture with both hands this time. 'Very pretty girl, the daughter. Sixteen, maybe seventeen years of age, name of Thetis, blue eyes and hair the colour of champagne.'

'But really an Ascoli?'

Freddy nodded. 'When Max was Ned Sands's pupil in chambers, he was, naturally, Ned's junior for a number of serious cases, capital cases. One was at the Norwich Assizes. Rex v Betteridge. A murder. Ned prosecuted. Often did in Norwich. Had connections there.'

A young woman cleaner had been stabbed to death while

at work, doing Paula Palmer's kitchen. Girl called Betteridge, Christine Betteridge: seven stab wounds, the body found by Paula Palmer, who claimed to have been working in her studio in the garden of her house in King's Lynn. Christine Betteridge was her daily.

'Made her an important witness, put her into close contact with Max.' Freddy now in the jugular vein.

'This was when?'

'Twenty-four. February 1924. Basically Max was there to see that Paula was innocent and free: the local law, at one stage, had designs on Paula for the murder.'

'And you're saying . . . ?'

'Max had an affair. A most passionate affair. There was a kind of doomed obsession about it, and the girl, Thetis Palmer, is the result.'

Doomed obsession, Suzie thought. Crikey!

'Who knows, or knew about this?' Illegitimacy could still be a serious disgrace: in the Church of England an illegitimate male could not become a priest, and a girl often carried the stigma of being a bastard, or the mother of one, to the grave.

'The whole family,' Freda unsmiling, thought it should remain a secret. 'Max did everything he could: complete gentleman.'

'Practically everyone,' Freddy explained. 'Sammy certainly knew because Max was a straightforward young man. Didn't hide anything. Went to his father for advice. There were other serious issues.'

'Ah.' Tommy waited for Freddy to give him the full SP – as they said in the Job.

'The victim, the cleaner, Christine Betteridge, was in a violent, disastrous marriage. The husband was abusive, a difficult drunk, unstable. Murdered her of course, after a terrible fight the night before. Just came to where she was working and stabbed her to death.'

Tommy remembered now, or partly recalled reading about the case. 'Didn't he try to blame someone else?'

'His defence was crazy, a pile of melodramatic rubbish with just enough piquancy to make it a front-page story.' Freddy glanced away, as though he had lost the story's thread. 'He accused Mrs Palmer of killing the girl. And she had no alibi. Had been on the premises all morning, alone with Christine Betteridge.' For a second he appeared to be tongue-tied. 'On the face of it, Paula Palmer had the opportunity, the means and the motive. In the cold light of the courtroom it looked very dodgy, enough to lure the unwary. I think Ned described it as a wrecker's lantern.'

'Motive?' Tommy asked and got no reply.

'Together Ned and young Max turned it around, called Miss Palmer as a prosecution witness, and Betteridge was found guilty, sentenced to death. A month later the sentence was commuted to life imprisonment.'

'Motive?' Tommy asked again.

Freddy contorted his face into a wry expression and gave another shrug. 'There was motive if you believed the fantastic story told by Betteridge. It is a tedious and wild tale. Doesn't help much.'

'Try me,' Tommy drawled.

'Palmer was her maiden name, used it professionally, but she was married, still in her teens, to a wealthy man. Barnard, Eric Barnard of Barnard's Electric Malt, a vitamin substitute which, he claimed, helped just about anyone from pregnant mothers to adolescent girls: rejuvenated the lot. Magic elixir in the twenties and thirties.'

'I recall the advertisements,' and Tommy saw in his head the big red letters Barnard's had used, sparks coming out of a jar – *She Can't Do Without It* the ad said, a little tag at the top to say who couldn't do without it: *Nursing Mother, Adolescent Schoolgirl, Convalescent Woman, Growing Boy – he can't do without it.* According to Mr Barnard few people could live without Barnard's Electric Malt. Made a fortune from it.

'Made millions,' Helena said. 'The girl did very well for

herself.' *Gel*. 'They hadn't lived together for some time, but they were still married then.'

'And?' Tommy asked, waiting, sitting on the arm of the sofa, so relaxed he could have gone to sleep by the look of it.

'It was the old, old story,' Freddy didn't look him in the eye. 'Thirty-five years difference in age. That was the real problem, she was a neglected wife, and very young. Looking back on it I think Eric had probably lost his get-up-and-go, if you follow me . . .'

'Hard on your heels.'

'The story was outrageous, pure melodrama. Betteridge claimed that he and his wife . . .'

'. . . little Christine?'

'. . . the victim. Christine had rock solid evidence that Paula Palmer was planning to skedaddle. But not until she had cut herself a large slice of her husband's fortune. She was, Cyril said – that was his name, Cyril Betteridge, poor fellow – going off with her lover of three years, Edgar Turnivall, after she'd grabbed a ludicrous amount of cash. Part of the plan was to elope to Cap d'Antibes. I ask you.' Huge shrug.

Tommy gave Freddy his understanding nod: the one with a lot of comprehension in the eyes. 'I suppose she put the bite on Paula, please excuse the terrible Americanism, I heard it in a film, "put the bite on".' Silly grin, what was he playing at? 'And when she did, I presume he argued that Paula stabbed her to death in a fury.'

In her head Suzie heard Tommy lecturing her in investigative techniques. 'Never assume, never presume,' he taught.

'That's how he told it in his defence. Paula must've flown into a rage and stabbed her. Big kitchen knife, used it for carving the Sunday joint.'

'One could get a decent Sunday joint back then, 1924.' Tommy sounded wistful and Suzie thought of the joints they still had from the Home Farm at Kingscote Grange, the family seat. 'What was the solid evidence?'

Freddy gave another of his shrugs. He was good at shrugs, Freddy, got them down to a fine art, angle of the shoulder just right. 'There was a letter, supposedly written by Paula to her lover, to Edgar Turnivall Esq. The salutation was simply, "Darling", no date, then a lot of stuff about how wonderful it would be when they went off together, mass of purple prose, bodies mingling, joined for eternity, waited for each other since the dawn of time and some sexual heavy stuff, that kind of thing. Know what I mean?'

'Of course. Parlourmaid's fiction kind of thing.' Tommy appeared to wince, and Suzie thought 'you old cheat', knowing he wrote the most wonderful lovey-dovey purple prose.

Just before the final showdown with Golly Goldfinch she recalled the note he had left under her pillow:

> For the Chinese this year may be
> the Year of the Snake,
> But for me it will always be the
> Year of the Small of Your Back.

Then only last week she had found a fragment, again under her pillow:

> I bury myself in the long-limbed looseness
> of your body,
> And dream of time past and a glorious
> time future with you.

Then Tommy asked, 'What was the real clincher, Freddy? The fact that convinced the jury?'

'No fellow called Edgar Turnivall. Nobody knew him, nobody'd heard of him, least of all Paula Palmer. Denied all knowledge. No such bloke. Couldn't be found, figment of Cyril's imagination.'

'Paula Palmer the painter, eh. The beautiful girl Max fell
for? Max had the affair and Miss Palmer – professional name
– had the child. Max didn't marry her?'

'She told Max about the child the day he drove up to break
it to her that they were finished.'

'But he fell for her?' Tommy asked, a shade heavily, Suzie
thought.

'Load of bricks. Hook, line and sinker, yes.'

'You're sure of this?'

'Absolutely. Young Max was totally smitten. Went around
in a daze. Talked to me about it. Talked to Sammy as well.
I remembered it clearly yesterday, when we got news of his
death. I thought of him, how he was at that time. It was so
refreshing, he looked like a cartoon character KOed by love,
or sex or whatever it was. I mean he was forever smiling and
I thought I could detect a ring, like the one around Saturn,
round his head with blue birds flying in it.'

The two Ascoli women nodded, thinking their memories
of the time when Max was dashing up to Norfolk at every
possible chance. 'Talk of marriage,' Helena said.

'Bought the ring,' Freda added.

'And she told him she was pregnant when he went up to
tell her it was all off? Why was that, Freddy? Why did Max
call it off if he cared for her so much? Hook, line and sinker,
you said.'

Freddy sighed, shook his head, looked at his shoes and
said, 'Like two peas in a pod they were: thought we could
hear wedding bells. Then Max called it off. Called it off when
he found there actually was an Edgar Turnivall. That would
be around March, April, 1925.'

A lot more to it than that – Tommy could feel it – a longer
tale, more twists and turns. 'Exciting,' he said under his
breath. 'Exciting and dead dangerous, lawyer and client, bloody
hell, almost like doctor and patient.'

'Where did Jenny fit into all this?' Tommy realized he had
not yet brought Jenny under the microscope.

'My dear man, Jenny was about half a decade into the future: well, three, four years or so.'

'Ah.' Tommy began to do the sums in his head. A picture of all those Americans on their bicycles crossed his mind, then the aircraft lifting off from Long Taddmarten. 'How did Max and his family take to the sudden influx of our American Allies?'

'Well, Jenny of course loved it.' Freda sounding surprised as she spoke.

'Why was that?' Suzie chipped in.

'Jenny's American of course.' Helena in high dudgeon, as if to say these people're from Scotland Yard. How dare they not know the basics.

'One of you will be down before the inquest, I hope?' spoken as a question.

'When will *that* be?' Helena still up there.

'I should imagine sometime next week. We'll need one of you to identify the bodies. Need an independent identification, even though there's—'

'I'll do it,' Freddy trying to smooth things over. 'We'll be down, but I'll do it.'

'It'll be in King's Lynn.'

Freddy nodded, the others were not looking at him.

'Ask a silly question . . .' Tommy remarked as they were walking back to the car. Now why did they suddenly get all antsy?

'The isle is full of noises,' Captain Ricky LeClare said, looking up at the ceiling of the Officers' Club, on his seventh bourbon, salting his beer first, then drinking the bourbon chaser.

'The what is full of what, Skipper?' First Lieutenant Will Truebond had knocked back his sixth bourbon and he looked at Captain LeClare as though his pilot had set him a difficult puzzle.

'The isle is full of noises,' Ricky repeated, a little louder this time.

'Sure is,' Bob Crawfoot agreed.

'You know what I'm saying, Bob?' Ricky was having a tiny difficulty with focusing, one eyelid drooping. 'Good old Bob Crawfoot, Half man, half tepee. The isle is full of noises.'

'What isle?' Truebond finding it exceptionally difficult.

'We had a teacher at school,' LeClare spoke with care, as though his speech was negotiating a line of stepping-stones over a fast river. 'Name of Cohen. We called him "Chunks", don' ask me why. Chunks Cohen, real smart guy. Shakespeare. Very good on Shakespeare. Said that Shakespeare wrote for all men and for all ages and he was right. "The isle is full of noises", that's Shakespeare. *The Tempest.*'

'Shakespeare's damned boring,' from Bob Crawfoot. 'Had to study a Shakespeare play in high school. Did a thing about a guy killed a king. Wife helped him. Witches, battles, killing, blood, lot of blood, all that stuff but all those words. *Mac . . . MacFuck* it was called, something.'

'You don't say.' Will Truebond grinned.

'He didn't say.' Bob Crawfoot began to giggle.

'No, s'right. Listen, this isle is full of noises with us and the RAF taking to the skies all the time, and the fucking *Luftwaffe* coming over dropping bombs when they feel like it. Now the isle is jumpin': thousands of soldiers ridin' around in their tanks, cluttering up the roads in their Brenda gun carriers, whatever they're called – weren't meant for it these roads – and they're practising shooting all over the place, rehearsing bombing, throwing hand grenades, shootin' all kinds of shit. The isle is full of fuckin' noises and Shakespeare wrote that.'

Lieutenant Will Truebond took a long drag on his Camel cigarette, blew out the smoke, 'You're talking outa your ass,' being philosophical.

There hadn't been an operation today but they'd had to fly, up there training, flying in the right formation for attack, the one where you could cover every possible approach by cones of fire from the guns. That was damned dangerous as well because if you flew into cloud you couldn't see the other guys. People had been killed practising the formation flying: left the pilot's arms aching and his eyes red and sore searching the skies and the gunners got twitchy thinking they'd seen other airplanes when it was only a darker area of cloud, or a reflection. When people were killed on these training flights, which they often were in those days, the USAAF did not always issue a bulletin – not good for morale – kept quiet; only people on the base knew. Next of kin were told they had died serving their country. Died bravely.

'If they stand us down at the weekend,' Ricky LeClare said dreamily, 'I think we should all go up to London, see the sights. Go as a team.'

'Good idea,' Truebond nodded, sipped his drink again. 'Family outing. Everyone?'

'The toot ensemble.' Ricky grinned. 'May have to live with the others soon, the word is we're gonna have to live together, each crew and the ground crew in a Quonset. Get to know one another. Become a family.'

'You mean live with enlisted men, NCOs?' Crawfoot sounding shocked. 'Never heard the like.'

'Talking outa his ass,' Truebond repeated, once more with feeling. 'Anyway, we got a hop here this weekend. With the RAF guys, lot of their WAAFs.'

'Well, next weekend, then.'

As they came out of Freddy Ascoli's Knightsbridge house, walking to the car, Tommy said it all gave them something to think about.

'I'd like to read the case file, Cyril Betteridge,' Suzie said, sounding a shade cheeky.

'Not yet,' Tommy told her.

'Why not?'

'Because *I'm* going straight back to the Yard to ferret it out and read it. You, Susannah, are en route to Somerset House.'

Somerset House: the Public Records Office where they kept all England's register of those who were hatched, matched, dispatched and more besides.

'To look into the Ascolis' background?'

'You've got it, heart. Every bit of paper they have in there with the Ascoli name on it, I want it all copied and put in a new file. And you look very carefully to see on the birth, marriage and death certificates what nationality they officially owned to, all the subsidiary forms. Then we can look elsewhere to find the legality of their cause. I want to know when they got travel documents, passports and the like, I want to know everything.'

'You've got it,' Suzie agreed.

Brian would bring the car back at five. Tommy said, 'We want no slacking, heart.'

Suzie went in and set about the work with half her mind on what Freddy, Helena and Freda had said about Max.

He didn't follow anything up regarding Turnivall. As far as they were concerned this was the first time a policeman had been told that an Edgar Turnivall existed, Freddy had said: scared them rigid.

As for Thetis, Max behaved in an exemplary fashion: owned to the child, negotiated through a solicitor for visiting rights, and provided for her. The child regularly spent time with him. When he married Jenny, she was told that there was one non-negotiable factor – Thetis Palmer. He paid for her schooling, her clothes, pocket money, took her on holiday: was a father to her.

Jesus, Suzie thought, somewhere in these terrible, faceless killings the fact of Thetis Palmer's existence had to fit in.

Six

Suzie came out of Somerset House just before five o'clock feeling well pleased with herself: a good two hours' work done including a couple of telephone conversations above and beyond the call of duty.

Brian was waiting for her in the Wolseley: looked unhappy and bad tempered, kept fidgeting with things, asked if she minded him smoking – as if she ever had – offered her a cigarette and lit up for both of them, Suzie sitting next to him as he pulled out into the moderate traffic.

'What's the matter, Brian?'

'Nothing,' bristling. 'Nothing. It's okay, Skip.'

Which it wasn't. You could see irritation under the surface, and she knew already. At least she could guess.

'Come on, Brian. It's *me* you're talking to.'

'Bloody Dandy Tom,' grunted in an angry voice. 'Sorry, Skip. Shouldn't go on.'

'What's up then?' Knew it. Brian was in the midst of a fling-a-ding, run round the park, with Molly. Nobody supposed to know, but of course they all did. Back at the Falcon, Suzie had noticed that they'd chosen rooms next to one another: they'd be creeping in and out all night; felt guilty because she'd be doing the same thing herself with Tommy. Not for the first time she asked herself why she was so much in Tommy's thrall: bound to him with iron; steel padlocks on the iron. Well, when she thought about it in any depth, he *had* made a woman of her, and she supposed that she loved him: wasn't quite certain.

begin
John Gardner

'Tommy dealing from the bottom again?'

'Not getting on with it,' Brian still disgruntled.

'Getting on with what?'

'This bloody case. Now he says he'll have to talk to bloody Willoughby Sands again. Tomorrow.'

'So we're not going back to Norfolk tonight then?'

'No.'

'And you're missing Molly?'

'What d'you think?'

When she had first spotted what was going on, Suzie had told Tommy, who already knew. Nothing slipped past Tommy: he was a walking, talking repository of facts, true, false and too difficult. She had also said that she didn't think Molly was that kind of girl, to which Tommy, in his infuriatingly laconic manner, said, 'You're all that kind of girl, heart. Give or take the dykey few.'

Which was saying a lot for Tommy's perception because Suzie had, since first meeting, thought of Molly Abelard as belonging to the Dykey Few (Scotland Yard Branch) and it came as a surprise to discover that she was sexually as hetero as apple blossom, if that's what it was.

I'll be with you in apple blossom time, she sang in her head.

Molly, who had suffered in her life, was the Reserve's expert in unarmed combat and small arms, permanently cleared to carry a pistol. Recently she'd done a refresher course up in Scotland at the Commando Training Unit, where they didn't really hold with women, except in bed or in the kitchen, no shoes on. The rumour was that the big hairy commandos had been shaken stupid by Molly, while Tommy had spread the story that she hadn't gone to do a course at all, she had gone as an instructor.

Brian was still disconsolate when they got back to the Yard, said he'd stay with the car. Wouldn't come up to the fourth floor. 'If the Chief needs me he can send someone down for me.'

70

When Suzie got to his office Tommy was telling a filthy story to Billy Mulligan and one of the lads called Dave.

'"I told my husband that we had to do something special for your retirement and he said, 'Fuck him, give him a fiver.' The bacon and eggs was my idea."'

They roared with laughter, but Tommy was po-faced and just said, 'Well, there you are, Sergeant Mountford. What news on the Rialto?'

She told him the news she had gleaned from Somerset House: all the Ascolis claimed to be British citizens. But she had rung the Home Office, talked to a friend she'd been at school with: no mention of Ascoli in their files, the ones on granting citizenship. Liz Parsons, the friend, beautiful, radiant with a brain the size of Middlesex and striking gold hair. The chaplain used to smile at her and quote Eliot: 'Weave, weave the sunlight in your hair.'

'You're absolutely certain?' Tommy had his gimlet eye out, boring into her head.

'I can give you the dates,' and she started to reel them off: Antonio Ascoli died in February 1920, aged 87, and his wife, Clara, two years later, aged 80: both listed as British citizens. Sammy married Cynthia Hope-Jones, April 1895. Sammy was just 26 years old and put himself down as a British citizen as, later, were his offspring, Fillipo and Maximus. Benito married Freda Harkness in 1904: he was almost 30 – bit of a late developer that one, but definitely down as a true British citizen, as was his wife and two sons.

She took a deep breath. 'Sadly old Benno died in that car accident, June 1937, and is buried in Menton: British as a bulldog, and only sixty-three on his last birthday.

'And Fredo, barely six months old when he was brought into the United Kingdom in 1889. Married Helena in 1917 just before he left for the Western Front, to join his squadron, flying his SE5a.' She pursed her lips. 'Old Freddy's a dark horse, three times mentioned in dispatches and a DSC; nearly went west, shot down twice and walked away from the wreckage both times, something that didn't happen often in those days. Ended up an ace, toast of the town, sent back to Blighty to tour the training squadrons and show off to the civvies in the closing months of the war.'

'Brave fellow.' Tommy frowned. 'Brave or lucky. I wonder which?'

Bit of both, probably. She didn't say it aloud.

'Where the hell did you get all the lingo, heart? Going west and coming back to Blighty, eh?'

'The Galloping Major, who d'you think?'

'Yers,' with his funny look, nose tucked to one side, like Will Hay, schoolmaster comic, sniffing, 'Good morning, boys.'

The Galloping Major was Suzie's stepfather, though she could never recognize him as such, Major Ross Gordon-Lowe DSO, big hero of the Great War, he liked to think. Her mother had married him out of desperation, Suzie's father leaving them without the money to complete her brother James's education. Suzie couldn't bear the idea, yet her mum, Helen, seemed to manage all right. There had been some years of uneasy truce and it still wasn't totally worked out between them – the Galloping Major and Suzie.

'So how'd you reckon the Ascolis became British?'

'There's nothing on paper.' Suzie gave him what her mum would've called an old-fashioned look, with the right eyebrow taking on a life of its own.

'Suzie?' Billy Mulligan popped his head round the door. 'Someone wants you on the blower: female, says she's from the Home Office, name of Liz Parsons.'

She indicated Tommy's phone, getting both his permission to use it and giving Billy the nod to have the call transferred. After a few seconds the phone tinkled weakly and she picked it up. 'Mountford,' she answered.

'Suzie, it's Weavie,' being the name they called her at school after the T. S. Eliot the chaplain used to spout at her. In retrospect they all thought the chaplain probably lusted after Weavie – in the nicest possible way of course.

72

'Yes, Weavie. What's going on?'

'Had rather a find, Mounty.' Mounty – what they had called her at school, Mounty Mountford. 'One of your Ascoli chaps had himself down as British in 1895, yes?' *Ya*, she pronounced it.

Suzie told her yes, Sammy was married that year. British subject. Mounty Mountford the moss-brained minge someone had written in one of Suzie's exercise books from the fifth form, Va, though she doubted that the person concerned knew what 'minge' really meant. The nuns wouldn't have had a clue. Everyone was convinced that the nuns didn't go to the lavatory and they certainly didn't know about sex. Bridget Herring, the scamp of the Upper 5th, tried to explain it to Sister Mary Anna one day and was given double detention for having a filthy mind.

'Well, he wasn't British.' You could almost see Weavie's grin of triumph, talking about Sammy Ascoli. 'Though he was British by 1902. They all were.'

'How come?'

'I had another run through the files, I mean it's a proper glory hole down in our Registry, bags and bags of filing cabinets, you can walk miles around them and I'm not exaggerating. I quickly ran through the As again – thousands of them – and there's a letter from HM the King. 1902, King Edward VII – Bertie as we call him down here.'

'And?'

'And I can't give you sight of it until my boss has cleared it with the Minister, but he will tomorrow. Can you drop in?'

'What's it say?'

'Basically, HM wrote asking for the entire Ascoli family to be made British citizens without bothering with formalities.'

'Crikey!'

Suzie put her hand over the mouthpiece, asked Tommy when they were going back to East Anglia and he told her tomorrow afternoon.

'About lunch time, Weavie, so for heaven's sake stay in and wait for us. I'll be bringing my boss. Detective Chief Superintendent the *Honourable* Tommy Livermore.'

'Not Dandy Tom?' Weavie was a dreadful snob, read all the crime stories in the *Express* and *Mail*.

'Himself, Weavie. Stay in and you'll get to touch the hem of his raiment.'

'Don't think I'll wear a raiment tomorrow,' Tommy said, then asked what was going on.

'King Edward VII asked for the Ascolis to be made British. No formalities. It's in a letter.'

'As you would say, Suzie, crikey!'

Of course it wasn't as straightforward as that, but they didn't find out the details until the following afternoon. Had a lot to get through before then.

'The King himself, eh? Wonder what the Ascolis did for him?'

'Perhaps he liked ice cream.'

'Probably did, but he liked the ladies better than anything.'

'Maybe an Ascoli lady tickled his fancy.'

'In 1902 there were a limited number of ladies in the Ascoli family.'

Brian drove them back to Upper St Martin's Lane and Suzie felt uncomfortable because he was morose and mono-syllabic, all the way. She was concerned that he'd start talking about Tommy and herself, then dismissed the idea: whatever his moans, however chocker he became, Brian would always remain loyal to Tommy, if not to her.

Tommy told Brian to pick them up around eight forty-five in the morning, well, didn't tell him but sort of asked him if he minded – Tommy always terribly nice when giving an order.

'Here, 'bout eight forty-five, quarter to nine, please, Brian, if that's okay.'

'Not much of an option, sir.' He drove off without even saying goodnight. Not like Brian.

'What's up with him?' Tommy asked as they climbed the

stairs, hand in hand like a pair of sixteen-year-olds obsessed with each other.

'He's a man, Tommy. Having a sulk.'

'What's he got to sulk about?'

'Path of true love and all that.'

'Had a spat with Molly?'

'No, you fool. He's not *with* Molly. Stuck down here.'

'Not my fault, heart.'

'He doesn't know that.'

'You mean he blames me.'

'Course he blames you.'

'Thinking like a bloody woman.'

'No, Molly's probably thinking like a woman. He's probably rung her and she's blamed him.'

'I can't help that can I? Shouldn't have bloody joined.'

'Tommy, I wouldn't know. We've got precious little food in by the way.' Afterthought.

'Going out to dinner, heart. My treat.'

So Suzie put on some glad rags: the swish dress she had bought at Swan and Edgar's, the blue one that cost £2.18s in their sale just after Christmas, when they came back from spending that amazing time at Kingscote Grange, when his parents had actually approved of her. The blue one with the bow on the shoulder, the plunging neckline and the pencil-slim skirt: Tommy liked it, said she looked dead classy in it.

So they went down to Bertorelli's with its oak panelling and Italian ambience, still there even though they were at war with Italy; had minestrone, then veal on a pile of spaghetti in a rich tomato-based sauce, onions in there as well and loads of garlic – didn't matter because they both had it.

Tommy didn't settle, worrying about the case.

'What're we actually doing tomorrow?' she finally asked, bringing it to him because he wouldn't talk about work unless she led him into it: Tommy was a gent about things like that. She just wished he would stop the coarseness, the old Scottish warming pan, and the language.

75

'Nine fifteen at Lincoln's Inn, Willoughby's chambers. Rang him tonight.'

'You're going to ask him more questions?'

'Wouldn't be going if I wasn't.'

'Couldn't you ask him on the phone?'

'Absolutely not. Have to see the whites of his eyes.'

'Oh, Tom, Willoughby's not in the frame.'

'Why not? Close to the family, probably guardian of some of their secrets. Course he's in the frame. Got to talk to him about Jenny Ascoli, and the girl Thetis. Funny name for a girl, Thetis.'

'Why not? Greek myth. Thetis was a sea nymph, mother of Achilles, I think.'

In her mind she heard a phrase from some poem she'd once learned or heard – *Thetis wrote a treatise . . .* What was it? She heard music: *Oh I do like to be beside the seaside.* Didn't have a clue why.

'Probably why Max felt a bit of a heel.' Tommy chuckled. 'Achilles heel.'

She had to tell him he shouldn't laugh at his own jokes.

'I think we've also got to find out about the invisible Edgar Turnivall.'

Max called it off when he found there actually was an Edgar Turnivall.

The waiter bent over their table and asked what they'd have for pudding. 'There's not really much of a choice, I'm afraid,' shaking his head in a gesture of regret.

'I'll have the baked apple and ice cream.' Tommy looked up at him. 'As long as the ice cream's Ascoli's.'

'Of course it is, sir. And for madame?'

She'd have the same.

'Won't be able to have it after the 31st August.' Tommy sounded like a soothsayer telling her to beware the ides of August, but they'd already gone, Suzie thought. Ides of August was the 13th, she remembered, though could never have said what the ides were. 'Why?'

'Because of our mingy government. No more ice cream's going to be allowed after the end of the month.'

'Spoilsports.' She was shocked at this news.

'DCI Tait,' Tommy said and it took a moment for Suzie to realize that his naming the head of King's Lynn CID had nothing to do with the forthcoming ban on ice cream.

'What about him?'

'We decided his theory didn't wash. That it didn't feel like killings done by vagrants on a sort of whim: unplanned.'

'Right. Strikes me that it was very well planned. No spontaneity about it.'

'Absolutely, so what do you think it was, Suzie? What did it feel like to you, heart?'

She didn't think about it, just came out with it. 'An execution.'

'Mmmm.' Agreeing. 'Exactly. As though old Pierrepoint had come in and taken each of them, stood 'em over the trap, then worked the lever – in this case a pair of triggers.' Tommy nodded. 'Wiped the smiles off their faces, eh?'

She thought that Tommy could be freezingly cold-blooded at times, thinking of Max Ascoli lying on his back on the grey stone slabs, the floor of the hall at Knights Cottage, his face wiped clean of everything, pitted with 12-bore shot.

'So why,' he went on, 'would an experienced police officer hazard a guess at it being a sudden passing fancy: murder on the spur of the moment, when it so obviously isn't?'

When they finally left, going out into the street – the waiter pleased with the tip Tommy had given him – darkness was just starting to creep across London, nights beginning to draw in even with double British Summertime. Ten o'clock. A couple of weeks ago it wasn't even dusk until around 10.45 p.m.

Tonight the bombs started to fall around eleven thirty. A shock because there hadn't been any raids for a while.

'Damn.' Tommy put down his book: they were like an old married couple now, sitting up reading their books until one or the other wanted the lights out: he was reading Graham Greene's *Brighton Rock*, while Suzie had just started chapter one of Daphne du Maurier's *Rebecca*: Last night I dreamt I went to Manderley again.

'Shit!' whispered Suzie, the girl who wanted Tommy to tone down his language.

As the siren wailed so they heard the first two *whumps*, bombs falling, not far away, somewhere the other side of Charing Cross, down towards the river, she thought, not far away at all. Windows rattled and they felt the bed tremble, sound of fire engines and in the sudden comparative silence the odd drone of aircraft: German aircraft with the engines unsynchronized, a strange throbbing, double-throbbing sound, once heard never forgotten.

'You want to go down?' Tommy asked, meaning to the shelter in the building's basement, or further afield to the Underground, the Tube.

'Not really. I'm comfy here. Don't want to get out. You?'

'Not fussed.'

Suzie couldn't recall the last time they went down to the shelter. If he had asked, she wouldn't have minded going up on the roof, see the bombs as they burst, wonderful splodges of crimson, lighting up the place for miles, for a minute perhaps, then the glow as buildings started to burn. Suzie liked the bombs: found them exciting.

'Know what your father told me, Tommy? The belted earl?'

'What?'

'Said he'd been down to the village shop. Bought a big packet of oatmeal, for the porridge. When cook opened it up there was a special competition thing inside.'

'They're always having competitions: the oatmeal people.'

'Yes, but this one had a finishing date of July 1937.'

'He tells that to all the girls.'

'Do the windows, Tom.'

He grumbled but got out of bed as three more bombs came down, again off by the river, then another two. He slipped behind the curtains and raised the sash windows, three of them, lifting them about ten inches. You always opened the windows slightly, guard against the glass shattering if they had a near miss.

Back in bed he switched off the bedside lights. 'Let's have a bit of a cuddle, heart.'

'Thought you'd never ask.'

So they had a bit of a cuddle while bombs came down over the next hour, fire engines and ambulances drove through the night, the ack-ack thudding away hardly hitting anything, and above them the Heinkels', Junkers' and Dorniers' engines throbbed, two beats to the bar. Unsynchronized.

Well, eventually one thing led to another.

'I love that little thing you do when we both know we're on the right wavelength.'

'What? This?'

'Oh, yes, Sukey. Yes. Oh, that's so nice. Oh.'

'Oh! Oh!'

'Herrrooooooooooh!'

'Ouf!'

Golly Goldfinch was called Two-Faced Golly Goldfinch because, looking at him head on, he seemed to have two faces. Birth defect: a cleft running at a slight angle from his receding hairline to the bridge of his nose, then down his nose so that it kinked; put one nostril higher than the other, right higher than the left in a sort of lightning mark, like a rune. Then the cleft ran down through his lips and his chin, splitting the face in half. It was fairly hideous and made it very difficult not to be recognized. Instantly identifiable. He wondered how Lavender would keep him hidden if she got him out of Saxon Hall. He used to manage it in the old days, before they arrested him. It was down to that lady policeman, the bitch. Spoiled everything now the world had seen his picture.

Tonight he lay in bed in the Ward: had only taken half his medicine. These screws – not screws, nurses – were lazy, didn't stand over you and watch you take your pills, two yellow and two blue. Tonight he'd only taken one of each. Aunt Harriet – Lavender really good at dressing up – had told him to begin tonight so he'd have some in reserve; he could expect the postcard any day, she'd said. When he got the postcard it was a signal.

The only good thing about the medicine was that the creatures didn't come any more, the huge spider-like things that would creep across the floor towards his bed. The woman didn't come either, the one who told him where to go and who to kill, whispered it in his ear. Dr Cornish had told him he wouldn't hear the voice in his ear any more once he began taking the medicine. Wait, he started to think, something wrong: very wrong. He had known who it was, who told him where to go and who to kill. Just out of reach in his head. Maybe taking less of the medicine would bring it back to him. The name, who the lady was.

The important thing was to get away – got to get that right. Golly had it all straight in his mind, knew exactly what to do. Bit of soap and a bit of baccy, make himself sick. Get them all worked up about his health. That's the way to do it, what Mr Punch said, Judy going Oh-dear-dear-dear, using the swizzle.

Really he was wide awake still. Usually he felt tired by this time, ready to drop off into the land of dreams: and what dreams. He started to giggle and had to clamp his mouth shut, put his hand over it, otherwise Mr Jim Bolitho the head night screw – nurse – would come down and there would be trouble.

Golly thought he would have to do it all when Mr Bolt was on. Golly reckoned he had the measure of Mr Bolt.

Seven

'Weavie, this is Detective Chief Superintendent the Honourable Tommy Livermore. Sir, this is my friend Weavie, from school.' He didn't like her saying *Honourable*, but she had warned him.

'Heard a lot about you, Weavie. Charmed.' Tipped his hat with a big goofy grin, like Felix the Cat. Suzie wanted to kick him.

Later he said, 'You're right, old dear. She is the most amazingly lovely girl. Adore the hair, glisters like the real thing.'

'"Men, when they lust, can many fancies feign."' She quoted, thinking Sir Willoughby isn't the only one who can do great poets. Mounty Mountford the moss-brained minge. Little girls are terrible: grinning in her mind, they remembered all the sexual bits like 'making the beast with two backs', and the part in *Hamlet* about lying between a maid's legs, and country matters.

But this was on the way to Long Taddmarten, in the afternoon, about half past two, quarter to three. Before that, in the morning, they had gone to the Sands–Ascoli chambers in Lincoln's Inn, where Willoughby Sands sat behind a desk the size of a tennis court, covered with papers and legal briefs tied up with pink ribbon. The stooped and ageing Clerk of Chambers, Adrian Russell, showed them in, a thin husk of a man, very deferential but seedy – unkempt white hair and slight tremor in his hands. If it had been a film, toothless Moore Marriott might have played him in a grubby suit.

Willoughby opened his arms in a gesture that said,

'Welcome, what can I do for you?' Aloud he said, 'You have more questions? I came down here early—'

'Good,' from Tommy, serious.

'. . . came down here early. I can give you half an hour.'

'Sorry, old love,' Tommy even more serious. 'You have to give us as long as it takes. We're the coppers, Will. You have some of the answers.'

'We'll see.'

'First off,' Tommy began nice and relaxed, 'First off why did you never think to tell me that Jenny Ascoli was an American?'

'Why not? Didn't play a part in matters. She's a British citizen . . . *was* a British citizen when she died. Spent twenty-one years in Virginia being an American, met Max, became British, gave birth, died British.'

'Yes and living cheek by jowl with a damned great American Air Force base the past few months. Who knows what baggage she could have brought from the States? Just give me the story.'

Willoughby Sands puffed out his cheeks in a strange blowing motion, filled his cheeks with air and blew it all out, rolling his lips. Twice. 'Really I don't see . . .' he began, then saw the way Tommy was looking at him and changed his mind. 'All right . . . June, nineteen hundred and twenty-eight. Max was invited to speak at a conference in New York. New York Bar Association. Gave two talks on the British Legal System. Crowd of lawyers there, tongues hanging out. Max had a whale of a time, went over and came back on the *Mauritania*, sister ship to *Lusitania*, the one the Germans sank – U-boat, 1915. First class of course, all the trimmings, all paid for. Max thought it was his birthday.' A pause, as though he was about to deliver some great secret, then a frown, 'I think it was *Mauritania*, but I could be wrong.' Shook his head, frowned again.

'On the first night of the return journey he was introduced to Miss Virginia Anstead and her lately widowed mother,

Mrs Mabel Anstead. The recently departed husband and father was Senator James Anstead of the Democratic Party, lashings of cash, big spread in Virginia, tobacco; had become a senator almost by default.

'Virginia Anstead was just twenty-one, ma and daughter making their first visit to Europe. Five-and-a-half-day trip to Southampton: Jenny and Max, bingo, hit the jackpot, three cherries in a row – which didn't endear him to Mabel, who was a somewhat foolish woman, not a social asset. Want more?'

'If there is more. I thought her name was Jenny?'

'Virginia Jennifer Angela Anstead. Preferred Jennifer, Jenny. Told me once that all eligible girls in Virginia were called Virginia. There were jokes about it. Virgin for short but not for long, sort of thing.'

'And that was it? American heiress meets eligible bachelor on board liner?'

'Sailed off into the sunset, yes. Marriage made in heaven, I thought. Jenny was the right thing for him – once she got Ma out of the way.'

'Which she did?'

'In no time flat, don't ask me how but Ma left straight after the wedding, St Margaret's Westminster of course. Came back once, '34 I think, to see her newly born grandson, young Paul. That was it. Hasn't returned since.'

'And Jenny was happy?'

'As a sandgirl. Loved it, couldn't get enough – of being a legal wife that is. Brilliant, great organizer, splendid hostess, the whole magic thing. Looked like a permanent honeymoon from where I was sitting. To make their happiness complete the boy came along, Paul, he would be what? Now? When he died? Eight? Around there. Lively, intelligent. Max said he'd teach him to enjoy the good things in life. Jenny clucked around, mothered him.'

'Jenny ever go back?'

'The States? No. Happy being a wife, mother, homemaker

all that kind of thing. House in London and the so-called cottage in Norfolk. Max took on a new lease of life. This business is a real tragedy. Dreadful. Disaster.'

'How did she take to the daughter, Thetis?'

Willoughby's eyebrows shot upwards, surprised. 'Not supposed to show amazement. Obviously the family's told you. You're honoured.'

'No, Will, I'm a policeman. They felt I should know.'

'And I'm used to keeping family skeletons in the cupboard,' which Suzie thought strange, barrister thinking the family would keep quiet. Obviously Max had never made a secret of being the child's father.

As if voicing her thoughts, Tommy said, 'But it wasn't a family skeleton, was it? I get the impression that Max was proud to be her father. Didn't mind who knew.'

Willoughby burbled, 'Well, I don't . . . I don't think . . . What really . . . ?'

'Has she been told?'

'About her father's death? Yes. A close friend of the family told her mother, who broke it to the girl.'

'And I'm going to have to see her, Will.'

'You are? Yes, of course you are.'

'Where do I find her?'

'With her mother in King's Lynn. With Paula Palmer.' He recited an address and Suzie wrote it down in her pocket book.

'Which gets us to Paula Palmer and the accusation against her: the story Betteridge told during his trial.' Thought for a moment, then seemed to change tack, swerved to the chase. 'Max had an intense and passionate affair with Paula? They were even on the brink of marriage?' Raised questioning eyebrows.

'True. I know where you're taking this, Tommy. Why don't you sit down.' Since they had arrived in Willoughby Sands's office, Tommy had remained standing in front of the desk as though taking the high moral ground to conduct his interrogation. Now he slowly folded himself into one of the easy chairs. There were three of them and a small settee, the room was so big.

'Max had this potent affair, marriage in the wings, almost had the banns read, bought the ring.' Tommy sat back, contented, hands lying lightly across his stomach, like a man waiting to listen to the King on the wireless after a good Christmas lunch.

'Yes,' Willoughby brisk, no nonsense.

'And suddenly, when everyone's expecting to go to St Margaret's Westminster for the society wedding of the year, they have to put a notice in *The Times*: marriage between Max Ascoli and pretty Paula Palmer of King's Lynn will not take place. People go into hiding. Oh, the shame of it all. As an Ascoli said to me, "She told Max about the child the day he drove up to break it to her that they were finished." Will, old love, I need the whole story because the Ascoli in question went on to say, "Max called it off when he found there actually *was* an Edgar Turnivall."' Again, Tommy presented the picture of a satisfied, contented and superior man. Suzie knew this to be part of the Livermore effect, his personal interrogation technique. *Get the subject to dislike you, heart. Difficult in your case but with me it's easy, I can turn on a sixpence, become a know-all, clever bugger in a second.* Grin, touches his cheek, eyes never leaving Willoughby Sands, Tommy Livermore on the Job, digging away. 'Edgar Turnivall, Paula's supposed lover, the one the Betteridges were going to peach to her husband, the mogul Barnard.'

'And if that *was* true, our Paula would have a great motive because she hadn't yet drained off enough money from hubby. Makes Paula sound a real cow.' Tommy straight-faced and unpleasant, spitting it out.

'Doesn't it? Yes. A dark lady. Absolutely true. All of it. She got a fair old whack of cash from hubby by the by. Worked out very well. Came out of the blue because Barnard had another lady, came in one day and asked Paula for a divorce

– just before Betteridge went to trial. Did the decent thing and allowed her to sue, got himself caught with the lady, a Miss Wright – ironic moniker, eh?' Willoughby grinned at Tommy. 'Interesting though, she's a most undemanding lady in some areas.' Cheshire Cat, Suzie thought. Then, almost a whisper, 'I told you about Phil Poole, didn't I?'

'Enquiry Agent extraordinary, yes.'

'As a precaution Max sent Phil off on a search. Told him to turn over every stone and find Edgar Turnivall – this was before the case had even come to trial, when he caught the first whiff of Betteridge's defence.'

Willoughby Sands gave a weak smile.

'Give me the full SP, Will.'

'Phil Poole starts scratching around. Really thorough, goes through hotel records, does the voters list locally and, later, in other cities, ever widening circles. Comes up with his hands empty. There is nobody called Edgar Turnivall. Nobody. What's more he can't get anybody to say they've seen Paula with a man they don't recognize, not her husband. He comes away with seven Davids, five Alexanders, three Alans, sixteen Dorises, three Ethels and a Patrick – that's only the young ones. Goes through the parents and the grand-parents who're still alive and takes a look at them. Many are at the other end of the country. Not one, on that first pass, had any connection with Paula and there were no Edgars. Plenty of Turnivalls, no Edgars, nary a one. Phil was a great professional sleuth, did it in his sleep.'

Willoughby said there wasn't a stain on Paula Palmer's character when she left the court. 'In the clear. And you know however hard people try to hide in an adulterous affair, a private dick always catches them out. Nobody came up with anything: not a whisper, not a hint, not even a, "Well, that woman's no better than she ought to be. I know because three years ago I saw her crossing the street with another man." He currycombed the country, looked at an incredible number of people. Scoured the land, looking for a non-existent man.'

Tommy shifted in his seat, 'And in the end, months later, he found somebody.'

'That's another story, Tommy.'

'It's an awful lot of work for one man to take on.'

Willoughby looked up under his eyelids, as if sneaking a peep at some cheat-sheet in an exam. 'Phil Poole wasn't just one man, Tommy. Had a regiment of contacts, people out in the world, beavering away, digging down the mines where a million diamonds shine and all that. There they were in council offices up and down the land, in the streets, in shops, newspaper offices, even in police stations.'

'Really?' Tommy said without enthusiasm. He liked to think that police officers were not there to help passing enquiry agents, private dicks, people whom he regarded as civilians. 'On the beaches and landing grounds as well, were they?' Parodying Churchill's famous speech.

'Phil was a bit like Sherlock Holmes, with his Baker Street Irregulars, Tommy. We paid him well and he paid for assistance. If he hadn't got friends in police stations – even at the Yard – Phil wouldn't have got to the truth. If it was the truth.'

'Tell me about it, Will.' Tommy smiling now.

Naturally, Max had spent a great deal of his time in East Anglia, doing this that and the other. 'Mainly the other, and particularly after the trial when the love affair was too hot not to cool down, if I may borrow the song. It was just one of those things, Tom, and on one of those days a police sergeant gave him a tinkle on the blower. Said, "Phil, we've got something in the CID storeroom here at King's Lynn that'll put hair on your chest. Give you a bit of a start. Put starch in your pencil, so to speak."'

Willoughby said that after the murder, and Betteridge's first statement, the local CID had taken a lot of stuff from Paula's house – 'River Walk', 'though it was a fair way from the river – River Great Ouse. Overlooked it, panoramic view.'

Most of the stuff was returned after the trial. Most of it,

but not quite all. Willoughby said, 'You know how it happens, Tommy.' They hadn't got round to dealing with some of the things. One in particular: a little box of letters taken from the studio. Letters to Paula from all kinds and conditions of men and women. And to be fair, Paula probably didn't even remember that one note was there.

'It was quite short but it made old Phil's heart turn over. "Darling," it said, dated 28th September 1924 – the Betteridge trial just finishing up in Norwich and Paula Palmer's name dragged through the mud, then pulled out and dried off by the prosecution – by Max – and the affair was getting stronger every day.'

The letter said (good, strong hand, no extra flourishes):

> I think we should leave things just as they are for the time being. No telephones and only the occasional letter or card. Destroy this as with the others then keep to the agreed dates, Tuesdays and Thursdays, when this has all blown over. It's been a long time, but now it's coming to an end. Keep up the fiction of E.T. I love you for ever and long for the waiting to end.
> Ever yours, Frank.

'Obvious who E.T. was: Edgar Turnivall.'

'A *nom de lit*,' Tommy chuckled.

'And you know what was stupid? They all make silly mistakes. It was on printed notepaper, a smart address in Bury Street, spit and a stride from St James's Palace. Oh, what a tangled web we weave, eh?'

Tommy had perked up. 'And?' he asked.

'And Phil went along and set up shop, initially on Tuesdays and Thursdays but he saw the fellow within a couple of weeks. Smart but a shade dodgy, that's how he described him. Tall, slim, well dressed, didn't seem to have a place of work; carried himself well. Phil said he thought chummy was a professional drone. Turned out he was a professional soldier.

Guards officer. Francis St John Elph – the Wiltshire Elphs, who were all feeling the pinch, descended from Jean Francis d'Elphé, came over with Duke William, 1066 and all that. Give her her due, Paula didn't go near . . . Not till later.'

'Well, she had Max sewn up by then . . .'

'True, but I couldn't work out if she'd given Captain St John Elph the heave-ho. I mean it was pretty clear they'd been carrying on a while . . . or . . . Anyway, I told Phil Poole to stay schtum for the time being. Till we saw which side the loaf was buttered, eh?'

'Let me guess,' Tommy smiling now, cheerful as a bug in a rug. 'You all waited for three or four months?'

'Seemed to be the prudent way.'

'And did she come?'

'March 1925. Met in public and it seemed they were giving their letters and keepsakes back. Met at the Charing Cross Hotel. He was exceptionally emotional. Phil thought this could be au revoir and not goodbye. Happily wrong.'

'He'd told her to destroy the one letter you had?' *Destroy this as with the others.*

'Ever known a woman who destroys the stuff? Not likely, they all hang on to the epistles against a rainy day, Tommy.'

'And you eventually told Max?'

'Knocked him stupid. He was like a crazy man, thought he might do himself a mischief to be honest. Then he calmed down, went cool as the proverbial cucumber. Then he went ice cold. You know that wonderful biblical expression, "And the iron entered into his soul." That was Max. I think he had loved her beyond belief. I also think he went a little mad.'

'Dashed up there and she told him about the child. He responded by saying it was all over. What did you think, Will?'

'It was odd. Reversal of fortune.'

'When was the last time you saw them together?'

'About two weeks before – maybe three weeks, have to look at my diary for '25.'

'And how were they? How were they together?'

'It's a long time ago, but my memory of it was that they were immersed in each other. Laughed, joked, locked eyes, total happiness.'

'Must've been difficult for you, knowing what you did – or at least suspecting it.'

'It was *all* difficult.'

'Then, couple of weeks on you know for certain that there'd been someone else, St John Elph; and you tell Max.'

'Phil told him, showed him the evidence.'

'And he was stunned?'

'Poleaxed.'

'Then he calmly goes to King's Lynn and tells her it's all off. What did he say to you? How did he explain it?'

'He said there was no other way. There was a possibility that Betteridge's story was true. However slight that possibility, he couldn't risk marrying her. Talked about cutting out infection. Hard, but necessary. Brave devil, Max. Changed man as well. Until he met Jenny. One of the difficult things to remember is how young Max was. In his early twenties yet moving his career uphill fast.'

There was a long silence, over a minute, and Suzie found she was almost holding her breath.

'What happened about, what's his name, Francis St John Elph?'

Willoughby Sands looked away, turning, glancing out of the window. 'We checked on him now and again. Like you fellows we keep things open. Phil retired and his son, Richard – Dick – took over. Phil must've taken him through everything. So Dick carried on where his father left off. Same network in place, I should think.'

'She see him again, Paula?'

'No. No, she didn't. Not to our knowledge. Dick topped it up every few months: checked where he was, with his regiment or at home. Gave up his commission, went up to Wiltshire. Father had the house and estate, run down going to buggery. Worked there, ran it. Have to admit he got the place on its feet again. Came back into his regiment in '39, they took him back, in his forties by then. Killed in France during the retreat to the Channel. Well, he was missing presumed killed. Didn't turn up in the German lists of prisoners.'

'Case closed then?' Tommy stood again, raised eyebrows, his questioning look.

'Absolutely.'

'And Paula?'

'Changed. Kept her head below the parapet; dedicated herself to Thetis. Max got on with his career. Worked like a dervish: twenty-eight hours a day, that sort of thing.' Sir Willoughby looked at his shoes, then up at Tommy again. 'As I said, got to remember how young Max was. Still sewing his oats probably. Paula was maybe his first real love. Can you recall the Sturm und Drang of that, Tom? First true love? Ropey kind of time, eh?'

Tommy half nodded and swiftly changed the subject. A shade too swiftly for Suzie's liking. 'Will, tell me, what happened to Phillip, Fillipo, Max's elder brother? He still alive?'

'Oh yes, he's still alive, and he's still living in the place where he gets looked after, treated like a king. Secure and loving. Most of the nuns're saints.'

'And it's where?'

'Nursing home run by a most understanding order of nuns, just outside Thun. Damned great Gothic building. Creepy actually.' The nuns were a nursing order – Sisters of the Order of Compassion, 'Schwestern des Ordens des Mitleides,' Willoughby Sands told them in faultless Hoch Deutsch. 'Mother houses were in Basle and Paris. Just outside Thun, called Alpenruhe, Peace of the Mountains, which shows that the Swiss do have a sense of humour.'

'You would know this, would you? Personally?'

'For a few years it was my job to visit and check up on Phillip. Make sure of his state of mind.'

'And he's been there all his life?'

'Apart from the first three, four years, yes. It was clear early on that he was never going to be a social animal. Great shame, he's a nice fellow to look at, but . . .'

Tommy glared, then asked what was actually wrong with Phillip.

'Better let the family explain. Not for me to go into.'

Tommy looked pensive, Suzie watching him, then he sighed. 'Ah, Thun. Once said a final goodbye to a girl on Thun railway station,' Tommy mused and Suzie thought, Oh, really? Never told me about that.

You could never tell with girls, held the past against their men. Always wanted to know what the competition had been, way back before they'd even met. Was she better than me? And he'd say, 'No, heart. Different.' And it would be maddening

Tommy nodded and looked solemn and said that was all for now.

Brian drove them to the Home Office where they met Weavie, who introduced them to her boss. In turn her boss showed them the now famous letter that hadn't come from King Edward VII himself of course, but had been written by an equerry – dated 20th April 1902.

Sir,

His Majesty has instructed me to ask you if you would kindly receive the Ascoli family, from Italy, and enrol them as British citizens without any formal let or hindrance. Issue them with passports etc. Be good enough to inform me when this has been done. The details of the said Ascoli family are on a separate sheet enclosed.

His Majesty also commends to you the wonderful ice cream made by the Ascoli family.

I am, sir, your obedient servant –

'I told you he must have liked the ice cream,' Suzie said with a straight face.

They lunched at the Ritz. Brian found himself a nearby pub that did good sandwiches. After that they set off on the return journey to Long Taddmarten.

'There are puzzles, motives and more puzzles,' Tommy said, stretching himself out in the back of the Wolseley, where he promptly went to sleep.

Tommy could do that, go to sleep on a clothesline: anywhere, anytime. 'Coppers can do it,' he would say. 'Comes from being regular and hoarding sleep. You hoard up the sleep while you're working, stockpile it, then draw on it as soon as you stop.' Load of rubbish of course, absolute load of old bunny, but he did have the knack, go to sleep anywhere.

When he woke he repeated his last sentence. 'Puzzles, motives and more puzzles.'

'What're you on about now, sweetheart?' She could talk like that in front of Brian, but had to watch herself when anyone else was around. It was like what her old granny used to call 'language'. When she first joined the Met, Suzie got used to using 'shit' and 'bugger' all the time. Went home to stay with Mummy and the Galloping Major after the course was over, at Hendon. First morning, goes down and there is a superlative breakfast waiting for her, her mum sitting there with the Galloping Major stuck behind his *Daily Telegraph*. Suzie rubs her hands, takes in the bacon, eggs, tomato, sausage, feels the wonderful scent in her nostrils and can almost taste the crisp toast and coffee. Rubs her hands together and says, 'Whoa. Shit hot!' And realizes she's just made a terrible gaffe. Good little middle-class girls didn't use gutter language. Shocked Mummy beyond measure. She told the story to Tommy who said, 'When I was eight or nine, I heard one of the farm hands using the word that rhymes with "luck" so I used it. My ma asked my pa what it meant. Unusual.'

Now, in the car, 'I'm on about puzzles, motives and more

puzzles, heart. Puzzle number one – why were the Ascolis given the waiver to become British citizens? Number two – why would the Ascolis *want* to become British citizens? Then, what's the truth about Paula and the Christine Betteridge murder?'

He turned, smiled what he called his terrible smile. 'D'you think Paula still holds a grudge? D'you think she's wild enough and mad enough to drive through the night, take a twelve-bore shotgun, smoke out Max, his wife and his child? And what of Francis St John Elph missing presumed dead. Is he? Or is he alive, sneaked back to England, home and beauty, shrouded with the night, crept up on Knights Cottage, slipped inside, taking a twelve-bore to the family?'

'And what about the Yanks—?' Suzie began.

'More options than an Agatha Christie.' The terrible smile again.

'. . . on that aerodrome, anyone who remembers Virginia Jennifer from the days in the State of Virginia—'

'Commonwealth,' Tommy corrected.

'What?'

'They call it the Commonwealth of Virginia. The Old Dominion.'

'Oh. Well is there anybody at Long Taddmarten aerodrome who holds some kind of bitterness going back to the first twenty-one years of her life?'

Tommy was silent for a few seconds. Then – 'Come to that, heart, is there anyone on that aerodrome who remembers the Ascoli family from Italy? Think of the Italians who've become American citizens, perhaps one of them could hold a murderous malevolence towards the family! Wants revenge on Max's house and all who live in it. Think about that?'

'Yes, Tommy, and think about some villain who comes romping into Long Taddmarten, asks around, finds out who the wealthy folk are; then goes to burgle the Ascolis, gets caught, grabs Max's shotgun, sends them all sailing into eternity.'

'Good point,' Tommy closing his eyes and going back to sleep.

Later they'd call the St-Nazaire docks a 'milk run', but today, in the afternoon, going on four o'clock, little Tim Ruby died over St-Nazaire: the first of *Wild Angel*'s crew to be killed.

They had dropped their bombs and Ricky LeClare was turning the ship back into formation, giving her some power to catch up and slide behind the lead airplanes, when the flack batteries got it just right, explosions all round them, mainly away to the right but one alongside – the crimson bloom, the dirty smoke and the crack – more of an explosion this time that pushed them off towards the port side.

Ricky knew they'd been hit, felt it like a big slap behind him, behind and almost above him with the ripping patter of shrapnel going in. *Wild Angel* bucked, swung just like it did on take-off, but he felt the response when he corrected, knew that none of the control surfaces had been hit. A minute later he knew that Tim Ruby had bought it. Willie Wilders in his radio op's little bay was alerted by something, got up, staggered forward and saw Timmy's legs hanging there in his harness and the blood everywhere, dripping. Most of the plexiglas in the upper turret covered in Ruby's blood.

Five pieces of shrapnel had ripped, hot, through the turret, little pieces catching Tim Ruby in the cheeks, lacerating his head, then the big lump, size of a man's hand, slashed in, razor sharp, went through the fleece-lined collar of his B-3 jacket, caught him in the neck, like a scythe, opened up his carotid artery, the hot life blood pumping out to the rhythm of his decreasing heartbeat, spraying everywhere.

Timmy Ruby felt the jab of pain, then began to black out, fighting for breath. Then he was floating, happy on that visit to DC with his ma and pa when he was six, seven maybe: warm day walking beside the Reflecting Pool and seeing Abe Lincoln sitting up there in stone. 'Look at Honest Abe Lincoln, son,' his father said, saying it close by him again now. Far away he heard music and there he was, dancing with Billie-Anne Davis at the High School Prom, only a couple of years ago. Billie-Anne hard against him as they swung around together, wonderful feeling her body close to his, hot, sweaty and lovely. Gonna stay with her for ever. 'Billie-Anne, I love you, gonna stay with you for ever.' Then, out on College Hill, in the long damp grass, 'Billie-Anne, move your bottom a little and bend your knees. That's it. Oh baby.' Happy as he started to lose the picture, dropping into whatever else was there.

When they got back to Long Taddmarten, firing flares, bright red to let them know they had a serious casualty on board, they took the rest of the crew away from the ship. Bob Pentecost, cramped and easing himself out of the ball turret, saw the upper turret and threw up, retching on the grass while the medical orderlies shepherded the others away, getting them in a couple of command cars that had been sent out.

The squadron's first casualty. Tim Ruby, not yet twenty years of age. Killed in action.

Eight

Brian got them back to the Falcon Inn, Long Taddmarten, at chucking-out time: Yanks happy with their lot being shepherded from the bars, several of them supported by other Yanks; some with local girls who looked ready for action; some throwing up against the wall, not used to the tepid English beer; some singing loudly. Inevitably there was a scrum around the bikes, neatly stacked against the side walls of the building, and there were those who had arrived on bicycles and now made the sensible decision to weave their way back to the aerodrome on foot.

Captain Ricky LeClare had left half-an-hour earlier with Juliet Axton, tall, dark and rounded. He'd met her when she was serving dinner for Max and Jenny Ascoli, taken a long look at her while she was putting the plate of veal cutlets, cauliflower and pommes duchesse in front of him, knowing in the look that it could happen any time.

Ricky and Juliet were now heading steadily to the woods known locally as the spinney and to Ricky as a woods, well-known courting place. Ricky's intention, to shag Juliet's brains out, not difficult.

Inside the Falcon Tommy had worked some magic, said nothing to Suzie but greeted the landlord's wife, 'Got here all right then, Mrs Staleways?'

'Oh, yes sir, indeed they did, all ready for you just like the gentleman told me.'

Tommy said they'd have them in his room, collecting Molly

Abelard on the way. 'Need you to give me your report, Molly.
The boys and girls happy?'

'What have you done?' Suzie having the sense not to call
him Tom or darling in front of Molly.

'The food is so dreadful.' Molly getting it even before
Suzie had made the connection with what Dandy Tom had
been up to.

'The boys and girls happy, Molly?' Tommy repeating the
question.

'Not particularly. Been cementing Anglo-American relations tonight though; some of them're a bit whistled.'

Up in Tommy's room Mrs Staleways and her plump
daughter, Beryl, still smelling of rodent, arrived together
bearing plates. Piles of beautifully prepared sandwiches –
little triangles – and soup plates brimming.

'Got Dover, my pa's man, to drive over with some
comestibles,' Tommy announced. 'Nothing special, the
family leek and potato soup recipe, and some chicken breast
sandwiches, touch of French mustard. The soup's rather
special.'

'This one's yours, sir,' Ma Staleways placing a plate in
front of Tommy, a pile of sandwiches bearing a small blue
flag on a cocktail stick stuck in the topmost sandwich.

'What's different about yours?' Suzie asked, suspicious.

Tommy smiled, Mrs S. and daughter were leaving, almost
backing out of the room, bowing now they had been informed,
by Dover, that he was an aristocrat, son of an earl. 'Mine
have a little drop of salad cream on them.' Tommy's terrible
smile again, more a grin this time.

'Salad cream?' Suzie's face all wrinkled in disgust. 'Salad
cream? That's what my mum used to call imitation mayon-
naise.'

'Yes, and I bet she pronounced it My-on-aize.'

'It's dreadful stuff, Tommy.'

'I prefer it.' And that was that. When Tommy preferred
something to the real thing you couldn't do anything about

it; liked gravy only made with Oxo, a dash of Bovril perhaps, nothing else would do for him.

They silently sampled the soup.

'Gosh this is good, Chief,' from Molly.

'We had some of this at Christmas, didn't we, sir?' Suzie showing off.

'Yes, the day Billy Mulligan came down.' Nya nya-nya nya nya. 'Family secret this: made by angels for heroes.' Pushing his plate away and reaching for the neat crustless sandwiches.

At this point Molly produced the folders. She was an incredibly tidy and neat person, would make a good wife for Brian one day, but not just yet. Tommy said if they married they'd be immediately separated and moved out of the Reserve Squad: sent to different corners of the area ruled over by the Met (said the same about himself and Suzie. Who knew? she thought). Now, Molly showed her neatness by producing the folders: stout, thick card filing folders, different colours; she was noted for them, sign of her organizational skills.

The blue one contained the autopsy reports from the mortuary in King's Lynn. Tommy flicked through them and asked, 'No surprises?'

'No surprises, Chief. Tiny pinch of chloral in Max Ascoli's bloodstream but he has a small prescription for sleeping tablets in the medicine cabinet in his bathroom.'

He slid the folder over to Suzie, who glanced through the reports, seeing one had died because the 12-bore shot had smashed the jaw and ripped out the soft tissue around the throat, lacerating the windpipe. She reckoned that was little Paul but she did not dig too deeply. Her eyes straying down the other pages took in the shattered cheekbones, the shot giving ocular trauma, cracking the skull in one case and doing Lord knew how much damage to the mouth and teeth.

The second folder was Molly's general report. Tommy glanced down this, then asked Molly to tell him the highlights, 'In your own words, not in the jargon.'

Molly said they had been through the house from top to bottom sending some samples – mainly odd spots of blood found in strange places – off for forensic testing. Pete Prime had done the fingerprints and there were a lot that couldn't be matched to the Ascolis.

Dennis Free had gone along with Laura to Roundhill House, down the road, and interviewed Colonel and Mrs Matthews.

'Anything new there?'

'No, Chief. The colonel ran over the dog barking again, settled in his mind now that he had been woken by it much earlier, around four he thought.' Which would be accurate because the doctor gave the time of death somewhere between four and five, around there: three at the earliest, five the latest. Apart from that the colonel and his lady had been visitors twice, invited for dinner at Knights Cottage with other local worthies: vicar and his wife, Mr Dorn who travelled to King's Lynn every day, big solicitor and councillor; wife was a bit of a drip, Mrs Matthews remarked. Molly said that Colonel Matthews's main contribution was that he considered PC 478 Titcombe a good man, 'Good ex-serviceman, make a capital detective.' Molly doing the voice. Tommy snorted. Mrs Matthews appeared to be obsessed by Jenny Ascoli's clothes: 'Had some very expensive things, Worth and Schiaparelli; also extraordinary jewels, diamond brooches and the like.'

'It was from her that Dennis got the name of the Ascolis' daily, Mrs Axton and her daughter Juliet. Mrs Matthews had tried to poach them and failed. So I went and had a word with the Axtons, Chief. Got some useful gen.'

Tommy looked at her sideways, didn't really know what to make of Molly using Raff slang, 'gen'. She would come into the Reserve Squad office, fourth floor of the Yard, saying all hearty, 'What's the gen, chaps?' Infuriated people.

Tommy reached for another sandwich and took a healthy bite, closing his eyes as the flavours mingled, lighting up his taste buds, looked happy as if he had taken nectar into his mouth. Three long chews, 'What kind of gen, Molly?' as though the word gen was something he had to explore.

'As well as doing the daily work, Mrs Axton would take Juliet to help in the evenings when they had a dinner party: do the veg, take things in and out of the oven, Juliet would serve at table, nice slender girl, all the usual, at Jenny Ascoli's beck and call.'

Tommy nodded and took another mouthful of his sandwich: all perfectly natural.

'Mrs Axton was talkative. Remembered the names of the grand ladies and gents who were guests of Mr and Mrs Ascoli.'

'Yes,' Tommy drawing it out in his drawl.

'Well, his old chum Sir Willoughby Sands was a regular visitor; his daughter, Thetis Palmer from King's Lynn, also a regular, pretty young thing, still at school but drank wine with the best of them, I'm paraphrasing of course . . .'

'Of course.'

'And more recently, and most regularly, the whole crew of one of those American bombers, "the Flying Fortification things", as Mrs Axton put it.'

'Ah.'

'Bomber they called *Wild Angel*. Very jolly these men were. Fair made our Juliet blush with their flirting. Flirted with Mrs Ascoli an' all. Not all of them officers either, officers and NCOs all mixed in together, didn't seem right.' So Mrs Axton again.

'Did they now?' Tommy took another bite of sandwich and Suzie, nibbling hers, thought how good they were, wouldn't mind a bit of salad cream herself though, liked it in spite of what Mummy always said.

By this time, Molly had pushed a new folder across the table, lovely crimson colour, the new folder, bulging, wouldn't lie flat. 'I've started going through the desks, drawers, papers. Came across these, locked in a small private safe in Max Ascoli's study.'

101

'Left unlocked?' Tommy looking a shade stern, suspicious.

'No. Locked. Dennis Free did the honours. He's excellent with locks. Locks and firearms, very much his thing.'

The letters, in both pockets of the folders, were still in their envelopes, two packages of them tied with ribbon, same kind of pink ribbon they used on legal briefs. Tommy pulled out one of the piles, started picking at the ribbon, began undoing it.

Suzie watched him, saw the extraordinary concentration and wondered why. She shifted to look on the first envelope, addressed to Max Ascoli, Sands–Ascoli, Lincoln's Inn, London. Above it the date stamp. 4th June 1941, King's Lynn, and marked 'Private & Personal. For Mr Ascoli's eyes only.'

Tommy slid the first envelope out, fingers going inside to pull out the folded four pages; saw the salutation, 'My Dearest Darling Max', looked at the date below the scrawled address 3rd June 1941, then flicked the pages over to glance at the signature. Tommy went still as a rock. Suzie saw it as well and felt herself go cold. June 1941, signed, 'I love you ever, P xxxxx'. She saw Tommy's right eyebrow levitate, and he started to push the letter back using his fingertips, turning the whole pile over: removing his hand and glancing sideways at Suzie.

'Right. Molly, anything else, anything at all?'

'Not really, Chief. Crime scene's well secured. Oh, one thing,' looking pained. 'That local bobby, Titcombe.'

'Make a good detective according to Colonel Matthews,' superior smile.

'All very well for you, Chief, but I think he believes the colonel. He's been bothering seven kinds of hell out of me, "Anything I can do to help, Sarge? . . . I think that looks a bit dodgy, Sarge . . . On the Somme, Sarge, we always . . ." Know what I mean, Chief?'

'Tell him to bugger off.'

'Takes no notice, Chief. Thinks he's fireproof. Well, you'll see for yourself tomorrow when you're there.'

'Won't be there, Molly, not tomorrow.'

'Oh?'

'No, you're in charge of the crime scene. We'll be over in King's Lynn most of tomorrow. Sleep well.' Dismissed. As they reached the door, 'Oh, Suzie, yes, can you hang on a minute. Need a quick word.'

Molly smiled a know-it-all smirk as she closed the door behind her.

'You see who that letter was from?' Tommy asked without looking at her. He was undoing the ribbon on the second bundle and spreading them all out, fingertips only, across the little light oak card table at the foot of his bed. Said, 'This is going to take a long time.'

'All night. What're we in for tomorrow: King's Lynn?'

'Seeing the daughter, Thetis, and her mother who may well be the "P" as in "I love you ever, P".'

'Or somebody who wants us to think she's the "P" in "I love you ever, P".'

'Good girl,' he smiled, the terrible smile again. 'You're really getting the hang of things, heart.'

Condescending bugger, Suzie thought but didn't say anything.

'That's it tomorrow, P and Thetis?'

'If our friend Wills comes up smiling we could have another visit to make . . .'

'Oh, who . . . ?'

'No, not the famous Chinaman, O Who, someone else, Jack Bennett. Any the wiser?'

'No.'

'Good. So we really can't take all night. Want to be fresh for it. Anyway, what would people say?'

'Selected highlights, then?'

'Gems from the letters of P. Yes. Let's see what the sequence is . . .' He started to sort the envelopes, fingertips only on the pointed edges, arranging from the date stamps. They ran from October 1939 until last week, 6th August 1942 – between fifty and sixty letters in all. 'I'll look at the beginning and the end.' Drawing two of the envelopes towards him. 'The Alpha and Omega. You pull out a couple at random.'

Suzie reached out, found one envelope dated August 1940 and another in December 1941, manipulating them with the tips of her fingers.

'Woa!' Tommy unleashed a minor roar. 'I've got the whole thing. Love is in the air. Romance hits home. Listen to this. He carried on reading: "Darling, darling, darling" – all the darlings, eh.'

> So angels were dining at the Ritz tonight. Tonight it happened, as I knew it would. Max, I have kept the faith as you told me. I have waited, calmly, didn't even believe everything when I saw you had married. You said, wait and I'll come, and there you were, dining alone at the Ritz with the other angels, and I saw you and knew the moment had arrived when you looked up and smiled. Did you know I'd be there with my agent, Johnny? Oh, Max, the waiting's been long and hard . . .

Tommy paused, looked up at her. 'Well, heart, if these're the real thing old Max Ascoli was a bit of a dog. October 3rd 1939.' He bowed over the pages on the table and moved his lips, muttering the rest of the text.

'"You haven't changed one jot. Dear God it's so good to have you close again. Is next week going to be okay? Age certainly hasn't wearied you, Maxie."'

'Maxie, eh, hot bloody Maxie . . .'

What was it Willoughby had said? *They were immersed in each other, Max and Paula.*

Suzie said it didn't seem to have changed by the summer of 1940 either, 'Just when we were moving towards our own little moment of truth, Tom.'

'Yes, and wonderful that was. Been meaning to ask you, heart, will you marry me?'

'I thought you said we couldn't because of being moved apart by the powers that be.'

'I've had a word with the powers that be, my darling. They've promised *that* won't happen.'

'When was this?'

'End of last week, heart. Been waiting for a suitably romantic moment.'

'Tommy.'

Later, lying on the bed, Suzie thinking about creeping back to her room, Tommy said, 'This thing's getting more like an Agatha Christie every hour.' He was back to using the Eton drawl. 'Like the Poirot things, fellow wearing out all his little grey cells. You wrote this in a book, they wouldn't believe you. It's so Agatha Christie it's almost confusing – a young reach-for-the-stars barrister has an incredible reputation in his early twenties, falls in love with a suspect he helps clear, guaranteed true love for ever. Then thinks twice about it when he finds out she could just be guilty after all, and is also carrying his child. Meets and marries fabulous American girl and ends up shot to death with his wife and son, their faces blown away. What a story, especially as he's come from a dodgy old Italian ice-cream family. It's got all the elements of a great saga, but how do we untangle the facts? Now it seems he may have been having a ring-a-ding-a-doozy with the first girl. How do we sort this one out, heart?'

She said she didn't know but she'd sleep on it and could they, perhaps, start piecing together the letters because they appeared interesting in more ways than one. She didn't mention the fact that she had started to wonder about actually marrying him.

Tommy said, 'Maybe, heart.' Then he said, 'Good night,' turned over and went to sleep. She drifted off as well, woke at four in the morning, tiptoed out and went back to her room. Slept like a large log.

* * *

There was a window high up in the wall opposite his bed, first thing he saw whenever he opened his eyes as soon as the door was unlocked and opened. As ever, he saw it this morning, the daylight slamming in between the bars and the safety netting on both sides of the window. There was no escaping from Saxon Hall.

Mr Edgehill was on duty, supervising the medication and the ablutions. Nobody was ever left alone during morning ablutions, but Mr Martin Edgehill was decent, a nice bloke, treated you right. He saw Golly take his two pills (well, he only really took one of them but nobody could tell, the spare went into the seam he'd picked open in the khaki battledress trousers they wore during the day). As soon as Golly was out of bed, Mr Edgehill issued him with his safety razor. Patients were not allowed to clean their razors after shaving; the screws just took them back and cleaned them for you after you finished, washed and dried them while you had your breakfast.

Breakfast was served at the big round table in the association area away from the cubicles. Golly saw it as he walked to his place, other patients having a laugh with Mr Edgehill and Mr Colls, who served them. 'I'll have the kedgeree, please, my man.' 'Just toast and coffee for me my good fellow.' They all did it, using their version of smart upper-crust accents.

This morning, Golly didn't say anything, his mind focused on the postcard lying next to his place on the table: picture of somewhere called Bath Abbey. 'I've visited this lovely church today. Hope you are okay. With love Auntie Harriet.' And three XXXs and an O. Three kisses and a hug. He'd take the hug, please, and all the kisses, lots of tongue, licking around his teeth. Lavender could do all that and he'd get it soon. The card meant it would be tomorrow night. Later he'd go through what he had to do. Get the sliver of soap and the ball of tobacco out of their hiding places, and then . . .

'What's the matter, you not hungry then, Golly?' Mr Martin

Edgehill barking at him, pulling him from his secret thoughts. 'Come on, Golly. It's your favourite. Kippers today. Think of all them fishermen risking their lives to get kippers for your breakfast.'

'Yes, Mr Edgehill. Sorry, Mr Edgehill. Pass the vinegar, please, Parks.'

Parks was in for killing two kiddies. None of them really liked Parks. Maybe, Golly thought, maybe he should . . . Then he saw Mr Edgehill's paper and stopped, frightened.

'Can I have a look at your paper, Mr Edgehill?' he asked after they'd cleared away. They were allowed to read and do things on their own for half-an-hour after breakfast.

'Don't throw it away, Golly. I want to take that home when I go off duty.'

He had been right. There they were, damned great picture of them. Headline on the page said, TOP DETECTIVE INVESTI-GATES FAMILY KILLING IN TADDMARTEN. The picture showed all three of them, three people he hated. The lady policeman he'd tried to kill with the wire, the big bastard of a copper who'd wrestled him to the ground – bloody Livermore, gave evidence at the trial. And the other lady policeman, the one who had a gun pointed at him. Great nasty hairy woman.

Taddmarten wasn't that far away from where he'd be going. Had Lavender arranged it? Did Lavender want him to get the bastards this time? He'd soon know. He'd know tomorrow night.

Nine

'Mummy will be down in a minute. Thetis Palmer, slim as a lath, brown as a berry, eyes with a sparkle, hair like spun gold – all the clichés – smiled at them, asked them to sit down, said she knew what it was about: Daddy was dead; didn't seem shaken or sad about it; didn't have the level of grief they'd expect; but seemed exceptionally nervous; nerves shattered like broken bone.

Blue eyes and hair the colour of champagne, Freddy Ascoli had said, and he was right. Pity about the nerves, fingernails bitten ragged, hands unsteady, fiddling.

She wore a blue Airtex shirt and a pleated skirt, sky-blue colour, skirt ending just above the knee, swung as she walked, pre-war skirt.

Later, on their way back to Taddmarten, Tommy was to remark on the sixteen-year-old. 'Advanced for her age. Eminently rompworthy.' And Suzie nearly slapped him. But it was true, very adult for her sixteen years, as they were to discover. 'Well,' Tommy had added, 'give it another black-berry season, eh?'

But now, Suzie thought, here she was, Thetis, nervous as a newt out of water, eyes roaming, not looking them in the face, hands restless, her heart, her sixteen-year-old heart, turning over and over and over, like to bet on it, Suzie would.

The rooms in these smart middle-class houses were all very similar, high ceilings. Beautifully furnished, decorated with flair. No photos of the Ascolis here though, except some of Thetis Palmer, an Ascoli really, growing up with a tall, kind of statuesque woman, long hair falling down one side of her face like Veronica Lake. And there *was* one with Max, her father, standing with a hand on her shoulder.

On the walls there were paintings, almost certainly Paula Palmer's work, spare, bleak, wind-swept beaches and cliffs with a lot of sea in there, pewter crawling up to the gunboat sky.

The door opened, nice solid oak door, big brass door knob, and in came the statuesque woman from the photos; the one with the red hair down to her shoulders, her body straight and slender moving inside the tailored clothes – clothes chosen to set off the body: navy-blue dress with white polka dots, neat neckline with a white collar. Over the dress she wore a matching coat, kind of matinee jacket, short, made of the same light silky material, dead smart, close-fitting dress and a loose jacket, pearls around her throat, matching earrings, and on her feet lovely navy court shoes, looked Italian, bought before the war like Thetis's skirt, couldn't get stuff with all that material in these utility days.

Red hair.

You know how Italians can become obsessed by redheads, Willoughby Sands talking about Cynthia, Max's mother.

Hadn't thought of Paula Palmer as a redhead somehow. Now Suzie could see why Max's and Paula's affair had been so passionate, all-embracing, obsessive.

It was not what you expected of an artist, a painter. An artist you expected to find in an old skirt and shirt, dabbed around with paint, maybe brushes pushed into her hair and a spot of paint on the nose, possibly gym shoes. Artists didn't usually come smart county, but this one did.

'You all right, darling?' putting an arm round Thetis, whose eyes had just started to brim a little as Paula Palmer held out the other hand to Tommy, more to be kissed than to shake, and introduced herself, 'I'm Paula Palmer, Thetis's mother, how do you do?' voice husky to match the sexy long legs, waiting for Tommy to introduce himself and then Suzie.

'I'm sorry to have kept you waiting. Look, does Thetis
have to stay for this? She's upset enough as it is.'

Really?

'I would like a word with her,' Tommy said, 'an official
word,' being gentle, making it sound like a bit of routine, so
Suzie moved over behind the girl, indicating that she'd look
after her, Tommy introducing them both.

'Official?' Paula's hair was drawn back in a bun that on
some people would look severe, not on Paula with the full
body of hair.

'Has to be official,' Tommy said with a smile. 'It's a murder,
triple murder . . . rather serious.'

Paula said she realized that but did they have to subject
Thetis to an interrogation?

'Not an interrogation,' Tommy told her. 'More a quick
question and answer session, quick chat. Quiet and easy,
couple of questions and they'd be done.'

'She's so young, I just thought . . .'

'Sixteen,' Tommy said. 'Sweet sixteen. Sixteen-year-
olds're serving in the Home Guard, being taken on training
flights in the ATC, trying to join up in the WAAF, ATS and
WRNS, being devious about it, fiddling their ages.'

Come to think of it, how old was Paula Palmer? Looked
late thirties if that; more likely to be forties with a sixteen-
year-old daughter. Incredible, she looked fresh and young,
fit, almost a gym teacher type.

'Thetis,' Tommy began. 'Thetis, when did you see your
father last, when?'

'Two weeks ago. Weekend, Daddy had a dinner party, some
of the American boys came over.' No hesitation but shaky.

Tommy nodded. 'From the aerodrome, Taddmarten?'

'Yes, a crew that Daddy and Jenny'd got to know, they
called their Flying Fortress *Wild Angel*. They were nice.
Treated me like an adult. Going to give me a tour round *Wild
Angel*. We laughed a lot. Their captain had known Jenny
Ascoli years ago . . .'

110

'In Virginia, at the University, Charlottesville,' Paula supplied and Tommy behaved as though he hadn't heard her.

'You speak to any of the boys later, after the party? On the phone? Get notes from them?'

'No, but Daddy was going to have another party . . . This coming weekend . . . They were all going to be there . . . Then . . . then going to the dance on the base – the aerodrome . . . A hop the Yanks called it . . . Celebration Hop . . .'

And she began to cry.

'Come,' Tommy said, soft voice. And again, 'Come . . .' an arm went out and Suzie realized that he hadn't a clue, didn't know how to comfort the girl, so she moved in and was somewhat roughly pushed out of the way by Paula, 'I'll see to her . . .', arms round her, hugging her tightly, so Suzie stepped back.

'You're all right Thetis? Okay? It's all right, darling, I'm here.' Paula close, cheek to cheek.

'For the record,' Tommy said, voice up, slightly louder. 'Just for the record, where were you, Thetis, Sunday night, Monday morning?' Trying to get away from the swell of emotion, pressing on with things.

Thetis said, 'Here,' the word launched on the aspirate, shot out, then, 'Oh,' realizing what he meant, and another 'Oh! Here of course.' A strangled sob.

But it had worked, he thought, slapped her back from the tears. 'And you, Mrs . . . Miss Palmer.'

Tiny pause, just long enough to be registered.

'I was here as well. I can vouch for Thetis, we can vouch for each other. I was away on the Monday. An appointment in London. My agent, I'm a painter, not unsuccessful. My agent, Johnny Goodman, old friend. There's been an offer for a series of paintings I've done. Johnny rang, wanted me to go up, he runs a gallery, the Goodman Gallery, Bruton Street, off New Bond Street. A considerable sum of money's involved. I was with Johnny later that day when the news broke about Maxie.'

111

Suzie thought, the news broke, no names, at around nine that morning. BBC. *Home and Forces Programme.*

Maxie, she thought.

'You left Thetis alone here?' Tommy asked, the mildest hint of aggression.

'No, I have an exceptionally good housekeeper, Mrs Goode, Emily Goode – with an *e*, we joke about it. And a daily, comes in early, Mrs Crane. I'm careful about domestics. I have to be, you see . . .'

'We know,' Tommy said quickly, stressing that she was an open book to them, knew everything.

Paula stepped back, made a little moue, lifting her chin, tilting her head.

'You went unusually early.' Thetis, eyes still red, tears trickling straight down, as if designed especially, making deltas on her cheeks. But she'd said it now, as if accusing her mother.

'There was a phone call, early, six in the morning, from Johnny.' Paula back in the conversation.

Thetis said she thought it was much earlier. 'I went back to sleep. I had some silly idea it was sometime around three or four. Can't really remember.'

'Even Johnny wouldn't ring at four in the morning. No, I saw Mrs Crane. She'll tell you. I got the milk train. Left the car at the station.'

Suzie nipped in, 'You have petrol?' suspicious. Only a few weeks before, in July, even the basic ration had been done away with and other restrictions were tightened.

Paula Palmer didn't even look in Suzie's direction, answering directly to Tommy. 'Just enough. I'm a nurse with the ARP and have to use a car to get to the first-aid post on the other side of town if there's a raid.'

Tommy nodded, turned back to Thetis. 'That was the last time you saw your father, then, the dinner party at Knights Cottage?'

The girl nodded, mouthing, 'Yes,' they could hardly hear her.

'I'm so sorry,' Tommy meaning it, turning to Paula. 'And what time did you get back from London?'

'Sixish, I think,' she looked over at Thetis, querying, seeing if she remembered.

'She got in about six fifteen,' the girl said. 'I had got myself some supper because I was going to the pictures to see *Citizen Kane*. Mummy came in and told me about Daddy. Awful shock.'

'So you didn't get to go to the pictures. Pity, *Citizen Kane*'s good.'

Callous bugger, Suzie thought, still knowing there would be a reason for his behaviour. She also remembered what Willoughby had said – *A close friend of the family told her mother, who broke it to the girl.*

'And you, Miss Palmer. How did you feel?' Rounding on her, hostile, wanting to know even though he'd warned Suzie that, at this stage, they shouldn't let her know how much they knew – or thought they knew – Tommy's right fore-finger was stabbing towards Paula Palmer, accentuating his hostility. Suzie wondered if this was calculated, reminding her of Christine Betteridge's murder here, in this house.

'How do you think I felt?' she snapped. 'My daughter's the one person in this life who means anything to me. There was a time when I'd link that with my daughter's father, he's been damned good, kept his word about everything. Even after all these years I sometimes wonder if I'm over him yet.' The whole short speech delivered in a way that you could almost taste the lightning in the air, and feel the sharp steel out of its scabbard.

Tommy was a gent when the chips were down, apologized with style. 'Miss Palmer, I am so sorry. Unforgivable of me, course you have the same feelings as—'

'And what would make you think I didn't?' Quite clearly regarding his last remark as patronizing, which made him express more humility.

'What else can I say? I . . .'

'Nothing, I think you've said enough, Chief Super-intendent.'

'Got my rank right,' he said later. 'Means she was listening. A sharp lady and you couldn't take her for anything else but a lady.'

In the present, in her house, 'River Walk' in sight of the River Great Ouse, Tommy took a further chance. 'You've never married, Miss Palmer?'

'I haven't, have I? Not since Eric Barnard that is, and when I divorced him I reverted to my maiden name,' she threw back at him, waiting for three or four beats before adding, 'That doesn't mean I'm inexperienced in life. Quite the opposite. One might as well be hung for a sheep as a lamb.' Little brittle laugh. 'That was clear to me, after Thetis was born – and happily I can say this in front of my daughter – quite clear that I was going to be treated as one of the town's scarlet women, so I didn't allow it to hold me back.'

Tommy smiled at her and quoted the Bible, 'Let him who is without sin—'

'Quite.'

'. . . cast the first stone.'

That seemed to be a breach of the barriers: a moment of mutual respect after which they appeared to treat each other as equals, and Tommy indicated that Thetis could leave them for the time being. 'I'll come back next week,' he told Miss Palmer. 'When I have more facts. We're really only in the early stages of the investigation.' Then, as they got to the door, 'Mrs Palmer, how did you actually hear about the killing of the Ascolis?'

'Our doctor, Fran Collins, was asked to break the news. She actually came here, saw Mrs Crane, who said I was in London, even mentioned I could be contacted at the Gallery. Fran rang me there.' She switched the conversation, 'Do you think you're going to . . .'

'Find the culprit?'

'Yes.'

'Believe me, we usually do. There are leads now . . . We'll have to see.' He paused, the usual pause in the hope that she would need to speak, fill in the blank space. Then – 'Miss Palmer, this offer you've had, is it for one of the cathedral sets? Norwich or Ely?' Let her know they were aware of her work.

She shook her head, 'No. How well do you know King's Lynn?'

'I don't. I know it's an old port, built around the river mouth and that's about all. I don't think I've ever been here before, maybe once as a child, but not in recent years.'

'There are some wonderful mediaeval streets that lead down to the quays on the river. I did a set of four paintings of one of those streets at different times of the year. It's the light that's so good. Juxtaposition of the buildings to sea and the sky. The light.'

'Like Venice?'

'Venice is more dramatic, yes, but like Venice, the light. I did four paintings, each from a slightly different perspective: in a thunderstorm, in summer sunlight, in snow and with a grey autumnal sky.'

'And the offer is good? I mean financially good?'

'Oh, yes.' And that was all she said on the matter.

'Tried to prise the price out of her, but she wasn't having any,' Tommy said in the car going to their next appointment on the edge of the town. 'What d'you make of them?'

'Which one, Paula or young Thetis?'

'I can't see the girl being implicated in the murder of her father, don't think fratricide's her thing. Unless she really heard the telephone ring in the night, summoning Paula out to pick up the killer on the fringe of Long Taddmarten, and was being influenced to keep quiet. After all she had a car and petrol. Very handy.'

'Silent Thetis, eh?'

'Maybe. As for Paula I think she'd kill, heart. Tough as old boots. Maybe has killed once, could do it again.'

They had been driving east, to the outskirts of the town, the dwellings dribbling out. Eventually Brian tipped his head back, and slowed the car. 'This it, Chief? Row straight ahead, on the left?'

There were four cottages, detached but all looking like those cottages you get in jigsaws, thatched, roses fading around the door on a wire frame, the last of the summer, lupins, foxgloves and hollyhocks in the front garden, peas, beans, carrots and spuds round the side with a couple of rows of lettuces: flowers and veg nearly all done now in the dog days of summer.

'Number twenty-nine, right, Chief?'

'Right.'

'It's this one here, on the end.' Brian could pick out a number on a door at fifty yards, even further. Among the vegetables round the side there was a home-made bird scarer on a tall piece of four by two, a yellow aeroplane with a big tail and a propeller that buzzed round in even a light breeze. The movement frightened small birds away from the lettuce but didn't do anything for the slugs.

'Who lives here, then?' Suzie asked.

'Jack Bennett.'

She sighed, 'And who's Jack Bennett?'

'Retired police sergeant. Detective sergeant actually. Used to work in the nick here in King's Lynn. He's the one who picked up the telephone one day and spoke to Phil Poole the Sands-Ascoli gumshoe, said, "Phil, we've got something in the CID storeroom here at King's Lynn that'll put hair on your chest."'

'Oh, *that* Jack Bennett,' Suzie grinned.

He turned out to be a tall, grey man not really likeable: unhappy, unfulfilled, Suzie thought. The cottage lacked a woman's touch: the flowers left in the garden, none in the house; everything was on the outside, inside there was clutter.

'John Eustace Bennett?' Tommy held his warrant card at eye height, his hand stock still, fist bunched.

'Yes,' swallow, like Thetis, nervous.

'Detective Chief Superintendent Livermore. One of my sergeants telephoned you?'

Another 'yes'.

'Reserve Squad, Scotland Yard. What the papers sometimes call the Murder Squad.'

A slow smile spread across Bennett's face as he relaxed.

Tommy introduced Suzie. 'Thought we were the rubber heels, did you, Jack?'

'Possibly,' he said, giving nothing away. 'What's this about? The girl who rang me didn't say.'

'It's germane to the triple murder we're investigating out at Taddmarten.'

'Poor Max Ascoli, yes. Terrible. Is it going to take long, what you want with me?' He had motioned them inside, indicating chairs, pausing even to offer a drink. There was a large and vulgar globe in one corner of the small living room, the kind of thing you saw in American films set during the fifteenth or sixteenth century, but the globe slid open to reveal an interior bottlescaped with whisky, gin, rum and brandy. Suzie wondered if the former detective sergeant was a bit of a toper.

'It going to take long?' he asked again now, as if time was, as they say, of the essence.

'Just as long as it takes.' Tommy gave a wicked little smile and seated himself across from the globe, leaning back in the armchair, all the time in the world.

'I normally wouldn't worry, but I've got a popsy coming to see me.'

Tommy frowned at this use of Raff slang. Jack was a former policeman, he would have argued, no right to misappropriate Raff slang. He said, 'A popsy, eh? At your age?'

'Guv, you don't know what it is to be retired. You spend forty years in the Job, racing around from arsehole to breakfast time, never knowing if you're on your arse or Easter Day, then suddenly, nothing. Not a bloody thing. No office, no nick, no cases. Set adrift. There's nothing worse than retiring. I promise you.' He looked up and saw Suzie grinning. 'I beg your pardon, Sarge.'

'No hobbies?' asked Tommy.

'Just the usual. Oh, I *am* in the Home Guard, but that's like Fred Karno's Army most of the time. Serious, but playing soldiers when it comes down to it. Didn't even find time to get married, Guv. The Job consumed me.' Coppers always spoke of their vocation as The Job.

'Home Guard could hold Jerry up for half-an-hour, it'd be worth it.' Tommy was straight faced, meant it. More to himself he said, aloud, 'I suppose I'm lucky. When I'm put out to grass I've got a farm to run.'

'Right, Guv.' Bennett sat himself down opposite Tommy and waited, head thrust forward, expectantly, almost taking charge.

Why isn't he a reserve copper? Suzie wondered. Must ask Tommy, look into it.

'Want you to cast your mind back,' Tommy being leisurely, as though starting to tell a story. 'Nineteen twenty-five. Betteridge had been found guilty, sentenced to death, then commuted . . .'

'Yes, that was odd for a start,' Bennett's head moved up and down. 'Nasty bugger that Betteridge, deserved to be topped, I reckoned.'

'You'd investigated Paula Palmer.' A statement.

'Sort of.'

'What's that mean?'

'Nobody's heart was in it, but there was pressure. Somebody wanted her looked at, wanted her drum turned over.'

'You had some items brought in from her drum . . . er . . . her house – from "River Walk".'

'Yes, we did.'

'And you rang Phil Poole and told him.'

Bennett gave a little smile, moved his head from right to

118

left, dipping towards his shoulders. 'Well . . .' drawing it out, 'Well, it wasn't as simple as that.' Then his face went grave again. 'Oh, Lord, Guv, I'm not going to get into any trouble for that am I, after all this time?'

With brutal frankness Tommy told him, 'You did tamper with potential evidence. Gave something away that was not yours to give. Just tell me what happened. What occurred?' Being pedantic.

Jack Bennett sighed in a kind of embarrassment, then gave a gesture signifying defeat. 'Started with Phil Poole,' his face now closed off where before it had been frank and welcoming. 'Phil arrived with the great Ned Sands and his junior, Max Ascoli, fresh-faced lad, eager. Phil didn't even have the decency to come by a different train. Word came back to us and by the next morning he was here, in King's Lynn. Within thirty-six hours he had his team assembled and working for him: two girls in the Council Offices, a young bank clerk, a quite senior member of the executive staff at the hospital, me and another copper.'

'How . . . ?' Tommy began.

Bennett raised a hand. 'Lunchtime, in the snug bar of the Bull. Don't ask me how he got his info but he was there, where I usually went, well at least three, sometimes four, times a week. He was sitting waiting for me and had me sewn up in less than half-an-hour.'

'Money?' Tommy asked, his face showing slight disgust.

'It was implied, then denied. But that wasn't what worked.'

'So, what did work?'

'Phil was extraordinary, had a presence, a personality. Just won you over. He said something like, "I work for the briefs who've come up for the trial. If you ever feel like answering the odd question, or telling me something you think I should know . . . Well, I'll be eternally grateful."'

'That sounds like money.' Tommy was sitting bolt upright, his tone flat.

'I asked him what he meant and he said, "I've told you. I'll be eternally grateful. Could do you a favour sometime. Don't get the wrong idea, I'm not talking dropsy."'

'So you passed things on.'

'No, Guv. No, I didn't. Not until a year later. Never give him anything 'til then.'

''Til the letter?'

'Right, but it was only one of sixty or seventy.'

'Sixty or seventy letters from the same person? You're sure?'

Well, Suzie thought, seventy-odd letters passing between Paula and her lover E.T., and fifty-odd letters hidden away by Max Ascoli, the beloved Maxie, purporting to be the record of a resumed love affair between Max and Paula when Max was supposedly obsessed by his wife, Jenny.

Looked like a permanent honeymoon from where I was sitting, Willoughby Sands said. Well, we now wonder? Suzie thought.

'Course I'm sure, Guv. I was the only one to sift through those letters. I read them. Christ they were sexy. I wondered, seriously wondered if they were real.'

'Were you meant to read them?'

'Don't know really. My guv'nor, DI Crook – great name for a copper – told me to get anything we had back to Miss Palmer. There was this one box, shoe box, Clark's Shoes, stuffed full of letters. I took a look, all from the same bloke, all full of love talk and then sex talk. Obscene a lot of it, like I said.'

'If she wasn't going to publish she hasn't broken the law then.' Tommy being painfully witty.

Bennett nodded, didn't smile, obviously thought he was being serious.

'You showed any of the letters to your DI?'

Bennett shook his head. 'He was dealing with a nasty little assault case. Didn't want to bother him. Anyway, it's a long while ago now. Nineteen twenty-five, Christ, a lifetime ago.'

'Quite,' said Tommy, looking hard at him, eyes like sparklers. 'So why did you send it to Phil Poole?'

'Knew it would interest him. I spoke to him and we all knew what was going on between his boss's junior and the Palmer woman. So I give it him.'

'And there were no kickbacks?'

'No one said a word. We didn't see that much of Maxie afterwards though.'

They drove back to the Falcon, Taddmarten, in a golden, buttery dying sunshine and Tommy asked Suzie what she thought of Jack Bennett. 'Didn't like him,' she said. 'Don't know why but wouldn't trust him as far as I could throw him.'

'Not far then,' Tommy grinned and put his hand around the top of her arm, feeling the muscles.

Tonight there were no treats from Kingscote Grange, so they were reduced to eating from the Staleways menu, which wasn't bad, home-cured ham and chips with some slightly soggy cabbage.

Tommy talked shop throughout. 'Discovered I was at school with the Raff station commander at the "drome",' he said. 'Chap called Raleigh Ridsdale, Group Captain. Talked to him tonight, got us invitations to the hop on Saturday night. Having dinner with him first – you're invited, Molly, and Suzie – dinner, then the dance, it'll be fun, all ranks dance, including the Yanks, the Waafs'll be queuing up no doubt.'

'And the locals,' said Molly who had just joined them. 'I had a drink in the public bar tonight and the men're scandalized at the way – I quote – the women're hurling themselves at the bloody Yanks. One of them said the girls round here are all wearing these new American knickers – one yank and they're off.'

Tommy sniggered obligingly and then Molly asked if he knew anything about a bomb disposal team coming in the morning.

'Didn't I tell you, Moll? I've asked them to put these newfangled metal detectors over the ground, find the shotgun maybe.'

After dinner Suzie went up to his room and they discussed going through the batch of Paula's letters to Max.

'Notice you didn't mention them to la Palmer,' Suzie a shade spiteful.

Tommy grinned, baring his teeth, 'Not a complete fool, heart.'

Outside it started to rain. Heavily with some thunder in the distance.

Suzie stood up while Tommy still leafed through papers. She wandered over to the window and moved aside an inch of the heavy blackout material – cost a fortune to keep the light in these days. Peering out she said, 'This has set in, it's going to be horrible out there tomorrow.'

'Good job we're staying in doing the letters then, heart.'

'I'm going to bed then,' and she was out of the door before he could object, didn't feel like being pumped by Tommy tonight, ignored the strangled cry from behind the door and headed for her room, then felt guilty about it.

It was still raining in the morning.

Ten

Golly woke in the dark and heard the rain and thought today is my day, and shivered with excitement under the bedclothes, hugging himself. He was always aware of his broken face, too aware of it, but only occasionally was he aware of his broken mind. Today he knew he was not as other men, his brain on fire, and was happy because it would be his difference that would help him get out of this place: his predatory instincts and his cunning. And Lavender's cunning.

Then he wondered if he had dreamed the visitations and knew he hadn't. For two nights someone really had unlocked his cubicle door, come in and squatted beside the bed, whispering instructions. It was not like the old days when a woman had told him who to kill with the wire. This was a man and he whispered very close to Golly's ear, sometimes snarling, told him he must time things right.

He didn't reason that this had to be one of the night staff, but somehow thought it could be Mr Edgehill, possibly Mr Colls, but Golly could never have explained how that thought came into his head. He remembered the advice though. It's a matter of timing: got to be dark by the time they decide to get you out and into hospital, take you to Addenbrook's in Cambridge, take you in an ambulance. 'Don't worry, Golly, your auntie's going to have help from inside Saxon Hall, never do it otherwise.'

Start it gently, start it early and work up to the real thing in the evening, just getting dark. That was the advice and he had the little cake of soap, bit bigger than a sixpenny piece, and the Player's Navy Cut cigarette stowed away.

Mr Christopher Bolt offered him Post Toasties at breakfast.

'Not hungry, Mr Bolt.'

'Come on, Golly, you've got to eat breakfast.'

'I'm off colour, Mr Bolt. Be all right later.'

'What colour would that be then, Golly? Sky-blue-pink or black as a badger's whatsit?'

They made him try some Post Toasties with milk and sugar. At the thought, Golly found he really felt sick. The thought of it all did it, and he ran and threw up on the polished floor. They made him clean it up himself and he was put on floor polishing for the rest of the morning up until the stand easy – coffee and biscuits – at eleven.

Then he wondered if it was taking only half of his medicine that had brought back the voices. When he had first come to Saxon Hall Dr Cornish said the tablets they gave him would stop any voices coming into his head. Wondered if it was that doing it now. He liked Dr Cornish: he'd miss him.

Molly had appointed herself chief knocker-up. She banged on all the team's doors at half seven unless you put a do not disturb sign out. This morning she dragged Suzie up from a vivid dream.

Suzie dreamed regularly of her dead father, always different but somehow refreshingly she consistently met him in the same place, a celestial golden summer corn or wheat field.

Whenever she met him in dreams, since his death, her father had grumbles – eternal rest was actually eternally being busy, wearing him out, always being chivvied by beings Suzie presumed were angels. This time he missed her mum. 'I do wish your mum'd get a move on and join me, Suzie. I miss her so and we get no timetable here to tell us when to expect a loved one. Not till the last minute anyway.'

As she washed and dressed, so the dream shook Suzie into

turmoil. You expected to be together with your beloved after death, but Mum had married the Galloping Major after Daddy had been killed, so what would happen? Would she be reunited with Daddy, or would she wait in some limbo until the Galloping Major arrived and would *they* be reunited and where would that leave Daddy? Also worrying was that he never mentioned her sister in these walks through the golden summer cornfields that were nearly recognizable as the corn-fields of her youth, ones that she would stroll through in the summers of her adolescence.

It was all confusing and worrying.

Tommy was already in the dining room when she got down. 'Want a few minutes over at the charnel house before we start on the letters,' he said. 'You game?'

'I'm always game.'

'Weren't game last night, heart.' Eyebrow cocked, quizzical look.

That made her feel guilty and she mumbled some rubbish about not feeling up to much last night.

Tommy grunted and they ate the watery kippers in silence until Molly, trim, shining and ready to take on all comers, arrived at the table. She talked of the minutiae of the inves-tigation, results of the blood samples that had been sent to forensics in Hendon, the number of fingerprints that had been lifted from Knights Cottage that didn't match those of the three family members or the staff.

Prints had been taken from the trio of corpses, and they had tracked down Mrs Axton and daughter Juliet and taken their prints. Peter Prime, their fingerprints man, had con-cluded there were other odd traces in the house and also a persistent number of one other, unidentified, set of prints. These had been made recently and were, Prime would bet his pension, the killer's prints. 'Been all over the house,' he said, 'wandering around, peering in cupboards, peeping in drawers. Probably had plenty of time after he'd killed them. Had the run of the place.'

'You think we're going to get the metal detectors today, Chief? Find the weapon?' Molly asked.

'Not if it goes on hissing down like this,' bite on his toast and marmalade. 'Don't suppose they'll use the things in the pouring rain.' Grin, 'Should imagine sparks fly out of their bums if they use them in a drizzle, let alone a deluge. Funny stuff electricity.'

Then he told Molly to stand by because Max's uncle Freddy was coming over tomorrow to formally identify the bodies.

'That'll be nice,' Molly said and Tommy gave her a swift grin and said that on Saturday they'd all be going to the dance at the aerodrome, 'Best bib and tucker.'

'Haven't brought me bib, or me tucker,' Molly crowed and even Suzie had to smile.

Brian drove them to Knights Cottage, and when he switched off the car's engine the background music became the sibilance of the rain as it drenched the leaves of nearby trees. They ran, almost hand in hand to the banded oak door while Molly followed up with the keys, there to stand guard over the house while Tommy did whatever he was determined to do.

Suzie asked what they were looking for, standing in the hall, where the flagstones still held traces of Max Ascoli's body, the smears of blood and some small traces of mud, the front door half open and Molly just inside in her grey trench coat, hands jammed in the pockets.

'Don't really know, heart. Read this article about an American murder cop who prowls around a crime scene, just mentally sniffing the air, sees what comes into his head. I'm probably too straightforward a bloke to do it: mumbo-jumbo stuff, but thought I'd try.'

'No harm, Tommy.'

'What I thought . . .' and he began pacing the hall, then climbed the stairs, muttering to himself, much as he had done when they were last there – *'Jenny is woken by the shot, heart – tell me if this makes sense.'*

For a good half-hour Tommy roamed. He stood for a long time just looking at the open master-bedroom door, then went inside and stared at the painting, the battered coastline, the fishingboats on the harsh stone beach, upright and tipped, the sea behind them grey and cold, the pewter sky and the storm clouds.

Suzie could still catch the iron scent of blood in this place, and felt the oppressive tingle of the horrors that had happened here, also she sensed that Tommy was getting something from just gazing around, standing in this place that had seen the last violent end to an entire happy family.

But she was wrong. 'Only thing I feel here is that whoever did this was fucking mad,' Tommy finally said. 'Who'd put a gun to the head of a sleeping eight-year-old?'

From a couple of hundred yards away came the hullabaloo of four Wright Cyclone engines.

The new upper turret gunner was called Sol Schwartz and he had thrown up in the head off the crew room. Nobody could blame him because he had inevitably heard what had happened to little Tim Ruby.

Today they were going to bomb the big submarine base at St-Nazaire, attacking high, around four hours from start to finish. *Wild Angel* came off the concrete uncomfortably close to the wood at the end of the runway, lifted into the air with everything straining and Ricky LeClare crossing himself as the big airplane scrabbled for height, dropped a wing, corrected, then disappeared into the low cloud.

It was a difficult and dangerous climb out. They had thought the whole thing would be scrubbed because of the heavy rain, but the Met Officer said they would be above the weather by 6,000 feet and the front would end by the time they reached the Channel. They tried to believe this as the airplane juddered, wallowed and scratched at the insubstantial sky, a thick blur of cloud and rain lashing against the plexiglas of the windshields and turrets, the rain making runnels, pouring down in little rivers and roads, lakes and ponds, whipped by the wind. Willie Wilders, in the area they called the radio room, was hanging on to the handle of the escape hatch like grim death and praying to God to let them come through this without the terrible sudden lurch revealing another Fort, climbing beside them, followed by the rip and splinter of the collision they all feared: the bang and the huge ball of flame consuming them.

At just over 6,000 feet they burst from the solid dark-grey wall of mist and rain into the glare of sunlight and the bowl of blue that reached above to infinity. In front of them the first three Forts that had taken off just before them. From his position in the tail, Peter Peliandros watched and smiled, as *Fertile Myrtle* breasted through the murk below, followed by *Lana May*, about a minute later and too close.

Ricky opened the taps and the Wright Cyclones roared as he caught up and slid into position behind *Jamaica?*, *Purty Baby* and *Iza Comin'*. Within fifteen minutes they were in their defensive formation and nosing across the Channel, clear far below in the distance the submarine pens at St-Nazaire they would attack from 25,000 feet.

'Those other ships ahead, Rick?' Crawfoot asked, squinting, peering into the peppered air over the target.

'No, brother, that's their ack-ack.' It was like a solid wall in front of them.

'Jesus,' cursed Bob Crawfoot. 'You mean we gotta fly through that?'

'If we want to bomb the target that's what we have to do.'

'Jesus,' said Crawfoot, once more with feeling.

For the best part of three hours they sat in Tommy Livermore's room, Tommy and Suzie, facing each other across the table, the letters spread out in front of them, sorted into chrono-logical order, letters from P, certain now that they were from Paula Palmer to Max Ascoli – Maxie – from October 1939 until last week, the final one just before death had brought a full stop to a romance started in the twenties, dropped brutally then picked up again in the first falter of war.

They read pieces to each other, passed the letters to and fro, making notes as they went.

'Don't really believe it, heart.'

'Difficult,' Suzie shrugged.

'They read like letters written with the express purpose of building a story.' Tommy screwed up his face as if in some agony, and went on to say that from the outset they were asked to believe that Max had dropped P for Paula like proverbial bricks when the invisible lover became exceptionally visible. 'She's supposed to have slunk off but remained true to old Maxie. Lived in the shadows, had his baby, went on through life just living for the day when he relented. A day he had foretold. A likely story. What, fourteen-odd years of it? Can't see the Paula Palmer we saw yesterday sitting meekly bringing up baby, watching Max marry, seeing that Thetis had days out with Daddy?' He shook his head slowly.

'We're going to need some handwriting analysis.'

'I've asked Molly to send someone over to King's Lynn. Ask Paula nicely.' Pause, sigh, 'Mind you, heart, I've no doubt that our Paula wrote these letters, and if by any chance it's true I'd like to know where the others went.'

There were huge gaps in the correspondence: things referred to in some letters never went to their inevitable conclusion, and in many cases P referred back to things she was supposed to have written in earlier letters now missing from the collection.

'So, she put these together by design, for some reason?'

'Why not? If she spent all that time waiting for him she could've built up an explosive head of steam. What if that telephone call *was* at three or four in the morning like Thetis thought? What if P had set the whole thing in motion: seen to it that someone was in Taddmarten already? Set it all up, sent whoever over with her letters to leave in Knights Cottage after he'd finished them off?'

'Why?'

'Why what?'

'Why leave the letters there?'

'To give us the bare bones of her tale. How she'd waited year after year while he became the great barrister he was destined to become, standing aside while he married the American girl . . .'

Suzie didn't see it, shook her head, remarked on the various purple passages, like the long, highly adolescent poem in which she put herself and Max together from the beginning of time:

> We were together in the cave,
> Wrapped in skins;
> And again at Hastings
> For our sins;
> When William came, and
> Down the ages,
> Century by century,
> Clasped in each other's
> Minds and bodies until now.

'I mean, how sentimental can you get,' Tommy rolled his eyes. 'It's pure girls' school Lower Fifth. I don't see the woman we spoke to yesterday writing that kind of drivel – certainly not the woman who paints those pictures.'

'The burning bush's quite good.'

'Ah, you mean . . .' He sifted through the letters, finding the right one and reading: '"And when I was naked you hadn't forgotten what you said all those years ago, my red hair, you smiled and, 'the burning bush,' you said."' He pulled a face. 'Yes, heart, it rings true but why would she tell him what he'd said? He knew what he'd said. It's scene writing. She'd never repeat it to him. Why?'

'And what if we find these are genuine?' Suzie smirked at him.

Softly, almost under his breath, he sang, 'a woman is two-faced: a worrisome thing that leaves you to sing . . . On the whole, heart, we should regard these letters as a red herring.'

Blues in the Night, Suzie thought.

'Until it's proved otherwise.'

Tommy nodded his assent.

They flew through the wall of flack, shells exploding all around them, not one ship touched, Ricky hanging on to the control yoke, Crawfoot ready to take over if something happened to him, *Wild Angel* bucking and groaning all through as they turned west to fly directly over the submarine pens, Will Truebond in control now as he hunched over the Norden sight and the bombs screeched down to the thick concrete and steel below.

The bomb doors didn't close when Ricky flicked the lever, so Bob Crawfoot went back and cranked them manually as they turned north again, going out over the sea and back to England and the base. When the bomb doors were open they produced extra drag you didn't need when you wanted to get the ship out of there in a hurry. They had just crossed the French coast, heading out to sea, almost free of the flack, when they were hit.

The 88 mm shell exploded a few feet from the starboard wing root, showering the starboard inner engine with shrapnel, ripping at the fuselage and starting a fire in the radio room. Mercifully Willie Wilders was unharmed, grabbed a fire extinguisher and started to tackle the fire beginning to burn holes in the fuselage.

At the same moment another shell exploded somewhere near the far end of the catwalk running back towards the tail, pieces of hot metal punctured the fuselage and exploded one of the oxygen bottles close to the waist gunners' positions.

LeClare and Crawfoot now wrestled with the controls, fighting to keep the aircraft level as it fell out of formation, losing height, spluttering and stuttering, showing signs of mortality.

Wilders was now throwing burning debris out, through the hole burned in the fuselage within the radio room. He stamped out the remaining fire and came out on to the catwalk to find that the explosion of the oxygen bottle had resulted in a wall of flame just behind the waist gunner positions.

Getting to the catwalk, Wilders saw Corky Corkendale, terrified of the blazing fire, climb up and throw himself out through the port gun hatch, while Piakesky began to climb on to the starboard hatch and got himself stuck over his machine gun, the lead on his electrically heated suit tangled with the barrel.

Wilders grabbed at the struggling Piakesky and dragged him back into the aircraft, shouting at him to help put out the fire, thrusting an extinguisher into his hands. Then he went forward, over the bulkhead, pulling another extinguisher from its position close to the flight deck. When he got back the flames were just as bad, catching hold, and Piakesky gone, so he started to douse the flames with foam, the heat already starting to melt the metal of the fuselage around the waist gun positions. He sprayed until the fire was well damped down, smoke filling the airplane, gushing out of the waist gun hatches. Dropping the extinguisher, he turned to go forward again, get another extinguisher, make sure the fire was definitely out. Then, glancing back, he thought he saw movement in the smoke looking towards the tail, his eyes and throat full of smoke. He moved back and there was the tail gunner Pete Peliandros, crawling on all fours on the catwalk.

Peliandros had been hit, coughing blood out on to the floor, moaning as he moved slowly. Wilders couldn't hear him, but knew instinctively that he was making a noise.

Wilders gently helped him towards where the radio room had been, saw that the Greek guy, Pete Peliandros, had been wounded in the back, probably punctured his left lung. He laid him out, rested his head on his own parachute, which he hadn't yet put on, and gave him a morphine injection, like they'd been taught, ripping the gunner's electrically heated suit leg, using his knife, then cutting his pants leg and the long underwear to the thigh and injecting him.

When Peliandros seemed to be comfortable, floating off, happy on the drug, feeling no pain, Wilders went forward to tell Captain LeClare, reporting on the considerable damage – using the interphone – and the fact that the waist gunners had used their 'chutes, terrified of the flames.

'Take them a while to get home then,' LeClare said, concentrating on keeping the ship level and trying not to lose any more height, down to around 7,000 feet now with one engine out and the prop feathered.

Like the Met people had predicted, the wet front had passed through quickly, and when they crossed the British coast it was bright and sunny, visibility for miles, but they were down to 2,000 feet and still dropping, everyone willing *Wild Angel* to keep flying. The airframe creaked a lot, juddered occasionally and groaned like a badly hung door. Eventually, down to a little over 1,000 feet, LeClare called everyone on the interphone and told them to hang on to their hats, he was going in to the first airfield he saw. They found one, ten minutes later, Earls Colne west of Colchester, home of the 94th Bombardment Group. Willie Wilders stayed on the catwalk with Peliandros, cradling him, keeping him comfortable, not able to give him more morphine. They fired four or five flares to attract attention and bring them running to old *Wild Angel* once she was down. If she got down.

LeClare extended the flaps as far as they'd go, but *Wild Angel* flew like a brick, both the captain and Crawfoot hauling on the control yokes as she dropped, dumping herself solidly on to the grass, rolling and slowing for around seventy yards with the motors cut back to idle. Then with a harsh grunt the starboard wing, weakened at the wing root by the 88 mm ack-ack, folded like a piece of silver paper and they slewed around and came to a smoking, steaming rest, everyone scrambling out as fast as they could, except Wilders, who stayed with Peliandros until the medics climbed in and took him off, Wilders fussing around them.

Sol Schwartz also had to be helped out: he'd hardly moved in the upper gun turret, just sat there paralysed with fear and unable to operate normally. A month later he was sent home, invalided out, flew no more missions.

For his heroism that day, little Lieutenant Wilders from Wallace, Idaho, son of a silver miner, received the Congressional Medal of Honor. *Wild Angel* was marked for salvage and nothing was ever heard of the gunners, Piakesky and Corky Corkendale: presumed drowned, got out in panic too soon.

That afternoon the guys at East Colne filled them with booze, then sent them back to Taddmarten in a command car, where they went through the post-operation interrogation and sat down to a meal around four thirty in the afternoon, steaks and fried potatoes with ice cream and apple pie to follow, all of them shaken, relieved to be home.

Fifty-odd miles away, in Saxon Hall, Golly Goldfinch was sweating on the top line, on the edge of setting the ball rolling to get out, escape. Do the impossible.

Eleven

Lavender's real name was Rosemary Lattimer. Lattimer after the dodgy geezer she'd married in a moment of insanity, Reg Lattimer. Later, Reg was killed in a pub brawl, left Lavender a widow, which didn't matter much because she was already on the game, a little room off Rupert Street in Soho with Golly Goldfinch as her minder and the nice house she'd bought out in Camford – 14 Dyers Road. She had other names, Daphne Strange, Poppy Turner, Jenny Partridge, Eunice Williams, Miss Whippy – generic name for when she did a spot of the old discipline. Now, on the outskirts of Newmarket, in the four-roomed flat she shared with her friend Nora MacSweeney, people knew her as Midge Morrison. They knew MacSweeney as Queenie – Lavender's bit of fun, Queenie MacSweeney.

They also knew them both as enthusiastic amateurs, aimed to please blokes and did for a price. The bogies in three counties knew Lavender as Trudy East and she was wanted throughout the British Isles as Rosemary Lattimer, also known as Lavender, just the one name. The rozzers even had a photograph of her, didn't look like her anymore, used wigs, dyed her hair, wore specs, sometimes limped and dressed differently: 'Mistress of disguise, me,' she'd say to Queenie, who cackled with mirth. Queenie had a cackle, couldn't have tinkled bell-like if you paid her. Exuberant and evil were Queenie's other names.

Few people in the Newmarket/Cambridge area had any idea that the hearty sporting girl, good fun-loving and pleasurable, who was Midge Morrison really was a devious female villain. In truth she was about as funny as a black widow spider and as sporty as a boa constrictor. She had lived in the flat on the outskirts of Newmarket since late in 1940, established herself there when she had to do a moonlight from London following a tip-off from a bent copper.

Her friend Queenie was also known to the police and, if it was possible, had an even worse reputation and quite a long criminal history including theft, assault and battery, robbery with violence and, though it was never proved, attempted murder. She was no better news than Lavender, mainly because she was an intuitive criminal, the problem being that she had no intuition. Queenie would react without thinking ahead, something that could well be her eventual downfall.

However, it was Queenie who'd discovered the vital element they required to extract Golly from Saxon Hall. Queenie, with her cheeky little face, long legs and tidy dishwater blonde hair, was in the saloon bar of the Fox Inn – often went there with Lavender – early evening, ten past six, listening to an elderly bloke chatting away to the innkeeper, saying just when he and his wife had got settled into their little cottage the wife insisted they go to see her sister in Edinburgh, leaving tomorrow morning and would the innkeeper take a look at the cottage if ever he was passing? Away for at least a week, maybe ten days, and he couldn't abide the sister. 'Always making cow's eyes,' he said, and had a mouth on her like a fishwife. Personally he saw no reason for that, the use of foul and unpleasant language, this distinguished-looking man, grey hair smooth as silk, called the landlord Bert, knew him.

'He seems a nice old geezer,' Queenie said when he'd gone and she was alone with the landlord, Bert.

'Yeah, nice enough but I haven't got the time or the petrol to go up and look at his place while he's away.'

'Right,' Queenie said, not showing any interest.

136

'He's only just retired, nice little pension, look after you those colleges.'

'What, Cambridge?'

'Was head porter in one of them colleges. Cambridge.'

'They tell me that's a good job.'

'Excellent.' The landlord was polishing the head porter's glass, dimpled pint glass, with a handle. 'Your friend not coming in tonight, then?'

'She'll be in later, I 'spect.'

'Started in the college at fifteen, that fellow told me, been there ever since. Like the Army.'

'So where exactly does he live that's so difficult?' Queenie asked in just the right tone, neither sounding inquisitive nor wanting to take advantage.

'He's my neighbour, and this pub's fairly remote.' The land-lord was right there: four, five miles out of Newmarket on the Cambridge road. Lavender and Queenie would travel some distance on the Newmarket–Cambridge bus to have a few drinks out at the Fox Inn. Police didn't often visit there and most of the clients were farmers, landed gents, hunting folks, farm labourers. In the summer, like now, Lavender and Queenie would take a walk out near the haycocks and have a go in the cool of the evening. Nobody talked because that was a good secret to keep close – pound a go and no ques-tions asked. Good money.

In a couple of weeks or so it would be harvest time and that would be a different story 'cos, as Lavender said, you'd scratch your bum to buggery lying in the stubble with your little drawers off. Cover it with a price rise of fifty per cent. They all knew the price went up to £1.10s when they were ploughing the field and scattering.

'Your neighbour, then.' Queenie sounded surprised.

'You go a mile on towards Cambridge and the road forks left, well, a track really, room for one and a half cars only. Snake Rise they call it because it used to lead to Snake Farm that burned down in Coronation Year. Go 'bout five mile up

Snake Rise and there's a pair of cottages on the left, use to be tied cottages for Snake Farm. They been knocked into one and done up, lick of paint, a couple of walls knocked out, chimneys repointed. Called them Snake Cottage, pretty bloody obvious. That'ud be in nineteen and thirty-nine and they were auctioned. Nice but remote. I wouldn't like to live that far out, but he seems happy enough. Haven't met the wife though.' *Event met the wife though?* In the East Anglian dialect every sentence from the landlord, Bert, sounded like a question.

She wanted to ask if Snake Cottage was on the telephone, but didn't like to draw attention to her interest. Lavender came in later, around eight, and they sat in the corner, heads together, drinking the sweet sherry they liked.

Lavender had spent the early part of the evening with a Yank officer from 322nd Bombardment Group at Bury St Edmunds, where they were just getting the aerodrome ready. 'Very generous,' Lavender said. 'Brought us a whole ham, I'll cook it tomorrow. Whole ham and a fiver, coming again next Wednesday. We'd better look at this Snake Cottage.'

This was a few nights ago and they'd caught the late bus back, then gone down to the lock-up garage near Newmarket Station, and got their little Austin Seven they hid down there, dark blue, only took it out when it was imperative. Last year Lavender had run the gauntlet and gone up the Smoke to see some of her contacts, got petrol coupons and some dodgy paper said they worked for a firm supplied waitresses for the Yank aerodromes in their special clubs, helping the American Red Cross and serving at the PX, so they could flash it if a copper stopped them late at night.

Nobody stopped them that night and they drove right past the cottage in the gloaming, saw there was a line going from the telegraph pole to the cottage, so it would do them very nicely, had a telephone. Drove past the next night – when the ex head porter and his missus were gone – and took a look at the doors and windows, made sure they had locks that would give up when they saw you coming.

Ideal. Got a friend in Bath to post the card to Golly the next day. So now, late in the afternoon of today, Golly was preparing to leave, while Lavender and Queenie were lying low, having broken into Snake Cottage a few hours before they needed and now it was eight forty-five, still light when they made the telephone call, 999, getting the ambulance. 'It's my husband,' Lavender sobbed, 'I think he's stopped breathing. Complained of pains in his chest.' The right story, gave the address and put the phone down quick. She wore a jet-black wig, good one from her friend in theatrical circles, hair brushing her shoulders and a bit of a fringe to almost hide her eyes framed in small round spectacles set in wire.

As they waited, Lavender remarked that she didn't think the pinky-red carpet quite went with the turquoise curtains or the exposed beams. 'Too sophisticated,' she told Queenie. 'Cottage like this needs more of the chintz country look with plain furniture, not the upholstered chairs and settee.' Lavender said she'd have decorated in a more simple style.

The ambulance took almost twenty-five minutes to arrive from Newmarket, great square boxy thing, crap brown with a Red Cross on the side and two men in dark-blue battle-dress in the front. Lavender ran out, weeping and wailing so that the men were immediately intent on quietening her, being gentle and solicitous. Queenie was stationed behind the solid door to the main living room, an old police truncheon in her right hand. The girls wore dark navy-blue slacks and lighter coloured shirts and both were big, not fat you understand, but big boned, with muscular strength in their arms. There was another old truncheon on the table in the little hall, next to the telephone. These two girls were ruthless, had been since they were fifteen.

The taller man, Ted the driver, went on ahead, hurrying with a satchel over his shoulder, anxious to get to the patient. 'He's on the floor in the living room,' Lavender called between sobs, doing her Sarah Bernhardt – could've won awards – distracting the other ambulance man, name of Len, short, stubby and smelled of fish, clinging on to his arm and doing real tears, a trick she'd learned early in life.

Ted barrelled into the house, took the right turn through the little archway and the door, half ajar, looking for a body, cannoned into the room and Queenie stepped from behind the door and landed a hearty crack on the back of his noggin. He grunted half way down, like the proverbial poleaxed animal, rolled over and lay still. Queenie thought she had done for him, then saw his chest rising and falling, heard another groan.

In the hall, Lavender, still weeping, getting into the role, allowed Len to precede her through the front door, grabbed the truncheon off the table and cracked him on the bonce, behind the right ear, knew the spot, sending him down and out on the carpet.

They had brought handcuffs, the ones they used for the strange clients who asked to be tied up. 'Restrain me and I'll be your slave,' one had said to Queenie. Turned out he wanted to crawl around on all fours and be pelted with windfall apples.

Lavender rolled Len into the living room and they handcuffed the two men together, then again, looping their arms around the heavy, polished mahogany table legs, wiping down the handcuffs.

'Sleep well,' Lavender said quietly and one of them moaned, still out and unhappy.

They had broken into the house by Queenie going through an unlocked kitchen window out the back, unlocking the front door – the key on a hook in the hall. Now they let themselves out of the back door in the kitchen, the Austin Seven outside where they'd left it, out of sight. They'd both put on dark navy-blue battledress blouses, Lavender's with an oval, red ARP badge on the breast, both with military gas masks over their shoulders and the truncheons slid down inside their slacks.

Lavender drove the ambulance and Queenie had the Austin Seven following, now doing the first dangerous part, getting to within five miles of Saxon Hall to a little lay-by where they could leave the Austin Seven behind a screen of laburnum bushes. Queenie stashed the car and joined Lavender in the cab of the ambulance. From there they drove to a piece of rising ground, away from any A or B main roads, to the high ground looking down on the tree-lined drive, the broken-glass topped wall and the bulk of the wards set aside for the criminally insane at Saxon Hall. At the top of the rise they parked in a thicket shielding them from view, switching off the engine and lights. There they sat waiting for the signal they prayed would eventually come from the squat little building, attached to the wards by a covered walkway, and used as a chapel by the inmates.

By lunchtime Golly was really pulling the not-feeling-well stroke, saying, 'Don't worry, I'll be okay.' Playing the martyr, so they finally thought they'd call his bluff, make him see a doctor, but the only doctors on duty were the trick cyclists, the ones some people called head shrinkers. So they gave him some aspirin and told him to have a lie down. As he went to his cubicle he complained of feeling sore down the right-hand side of his tummy, near the groin.

Eventually he came out again and ate a reasonably hearty meal. Needed the food for later: needed it to throw up.

Early in the evening Dr Cornish came down to check his patients were okay, took Golly's temperature and pressed his tummy on the right side. Said to Mr Bolt that it could be a grumbling appendix, keep an eye on him: slight temperature but if it went up, or there were other symptoms, he was to telephone Addenbrooks Hospital in Cambridge.

Golly had got his temperature up simply by thinking about it – a good trick. Now he didn't want any supper and either Mr Bolt or Mr Snow came in to see him every half-hour, kept a bit of bread and cheese for him in case he got peckish. Then, at nine o'clock, Mr Edgehill and Mr Colls came on, night staff. Mr Bolt told them to keep an eye on Golly.

At half past nine, Golly went to the bathrooms, secretly swallowed half the tobacco and the piece of soap. Went back to his cubicle and threw up, started groaning and moaning, saying his side hurt, being unwell, threw up all over Mr Colls, who had to go and get changed while Mr Edgehill rang for the duty officer.

At twelve minutes to ten they telephoned Addenbrooks and spoke to the senior doctor in Emergency. The ambulance left Addenbrooks at five past ten and Mr Edgehill – a deeply religious man? – went off down the walkway to the chapel, said a prayer and drew back the blackout, flashed the signal with his torch to Lavender and Queenie up on the rise. He then went back to the ward and said he'd travel with Golly to the hospital, got the restraints and fitted them round Golly's wrists and ankles, Golly moaning like the wind in the deep mid-winter, gagging and throwing up, feeling really ill now that the soap and tobacco were doing their worst.

In the ambulance tucked away in the thicket above Saxon Hall, Lavender and Queenie sat, tense and twitchy. The signal confirmed that Addenbrooks Hospital had been rung and an ambulance was on the way. Quietly they had slid into the high risk period, allowing fifteen minutes or so to pass before they drove fast to Saxon Hall, the Devil's Island of hospitals for the criminally insane.

An ambulance direct from Cambridge would take a while. Danger was that the hospital could well have one nearby, on its way back from a call: no way of telling. Had to take the chance. Coming across a genuine ambulance would alert everybody, even Bruce Edgehill, whom they had recruited and won over as their inside man weeks ago, would deny everything and turn on them quick as kiss your arse, as Lavender said during the planning. The two girls had seduced him in pubs and on the lush grass of summer meadows. Liked his greens, our Bruce.

They waited for around seven minutes before Lavender said, 'Let's go. Now.' Her throat dry, muscles taut, in the driving seat. She turned on the engine, slipped into first gear and let out the clutch, heading over the rough ground until they met the road around three miles from Saxon Hall.

They reached the outer gates and someone had phoned ahead from C Block, C1 Ward and they were let through, down the avenue of trees to the entrance doors, a checkpoint where they had to wait with the engine idling and the rear doors open, ready for the patient, whom Mr Edgehill brought out with a couple of junior nurses. They had Golly on a trolley – what the Americans called a gurney – wrists and ankles trussed up in leather restraints with chains and locks. Together they manhandled him into the back of the ambulance, Mr Edgehill, red-faced with his little bristling tash, saying he would ride with them, make sure of security, so Queenie stayed in the back with him, Golly lying there looking white-faced and giving a fair imitation of final agony, repeating like a child, 'I hurt . . . I hurt . . . Tummy hurt . . . Feel sick . . . O Lord . . .'

Basically Golly was a child, the kind of child that tears wings off butterflies, thinking nothing of it, except he killed people then laughed, thought it was a joke.

At last they got the doors closed and took off with a roar, Lavender hammering the engine, heading off to the lay-by and the Austin Seven behind the laburnum screen.

Around three miles out, they passed an ambulance going in the opposite direction, showing more light than it should, racing along in the dark, painted by moonlight, its little bell ringing as it went through a tiny hamlet, ten dwellings, a church and a pub, not big enough to show on anything but an Ordnance Survey map, one inch to the mile.

That'll be for Saxon Hall, Lavender thought. Another ten minutes or so and the cat'll be out of the bag, all hell breaking loose, coppers on the lookout, setting up barricades. Quite like old times. She remembered the Christmas of 1940 when Golly had told her about staying at his mum's in rural Hampshire and sneaking past roadblocks made up of police

and Home Guard. Tonight he'd be doing it in style. Gently
her foot pressed down on the accelerator and the vehicle
gained speed.

Ten minutes later they were at the lay-by with the screen
of laburnums hiding the Austin Seven where the ambulance
neatly pulled in.

Bruce Edgehill, jumping down with Queenie behind him,
said they'd better use Golly's restraints on *him*, leave him
there like a trussed turkey, handed Queenie the keys as he
left the ambulance.

'Good idea,' Queenie said, hitting him hard on the back
of the head with her truncheon. 'Make it realistic,' she panted,
hitting him again, on the ground, and again and again,
crushing his cranium. Bruce Edgehill didn't even cry out,
just lay down and died. They had determined that Edgehill
couldn't be left alive, too much of a risk, knew too much,
could name them both. Also he'd done it for greed and sex,
so he couldn't be allowed to survive.

Lavender had taken the keys from Queenie, began to
unshackle Golly, who still felt rough – 'That really you,
Lavender? Oh my goodness. Here we go then, I don't half
feel sick. Really buggered.'

'You'll be all right now, Golly, soon get over the sickness.
I got a nice piece of fish back home for you.'

'Oh, ah. With boiled potatoes, yes? And a little bit of
vinegar? Don't want chips.'

'It'll be fine, Golly love. You'll be safe with us.'

'History, that's what it is,' as he tried to sit up. 'We made
history, didn't us, Lavender? Made history getting out of the
Hall.'

And the moonlight fell across his face, revealing him in
all his hideous glory, the deep ravine cut up the forehead
into the hairline, then down, dividing the nose into what
appeared to be two separate parts, and again through the lips,
lifting half and dropping the other side, sending the teeth
into two levels, up and down, cleaving the chin. Golly was

tired, but panted out his strange laugh – *uhu-uhu-uhu* – then gave a strangled little cry, 'Free, Lavender! Free! Free!'

Behind the bushes, Queenie turned the key in the Austin Seven.

And the engine wouldn't fire.

'Shit!' she cursed, then again, 'Shit 'n'abortion!' That still didn't do the trick and by this time Lavender and Golly had arrived at the car, Golly still complaining and Lavender breathless. She pushed Golly into the back, told him to lie down, then settled in next to Queenie who was still trying to start the engine, panicking as she did so.

Lavender peered down. 'You've flooded the carburettor, Queenie: you idiot, close the choke!'

'What's the choke?'

'There.' Lavender slammed the choke closed. 'Now wait. She won't start for a minute.'

Queenie lowered her head to see the choke. 'Oh, that's where I usually hang my bleedin' handbag.'

'Well, it's the choke. Controls the air in the fuel mixture when you're starting.'

'What's gone wrong then?'

'You pulled the bloody thing out and left it out. The mixture's all wrong, flooded the carb. Try it again . . . Just a quick turn.'

Still the engine didn't fire. 'Christ, Queenie, who taught you to drive?'

'You have to be taught?'

The engine turned over.

'Again.'

This time it fired.

'Touch on the accelerator. Gently. Right, off we go . . . Bloody hell, Queenie, what we got a bloody kangaroo in the tank?'

'I can't see,' Queenie complained.

'Well, take it gently.'

They turned out of the lay-by and began moving up the

road, heading back towards Newmarket, gingerly, going across country, taking side roads, dodging, weaving and navigating by moonlight, Queenie driving with the kind of care with which you fail your driving test. Lavender giving directions.

'Where we goin' then, Lavender? Where we goin'?' Golly, whooping, excited.

'You feeling better then, Goll?'

'Just a bit. Where we goin'?'

'Babylon, Goll.'

'How many miles to Babylon then, Lavender?'

'Three score and ten, Goll.'

'We get there by candlelight, Lavla?' It was his unfortunate pet name for her when they first met in their twenties.

'You just lie down and keep still, Golly. Don't want anyone seeing you. They'll know by now. Know you're out. Just pray we don't get any nosy coppers sniffing round.'

They got back to the flat just before midnight, knowing that the news had been out since about half-past ten, saw the police nipping around the main roads which they'd avoided, active all over the place.

Queenie volunteered to drive the car back to their lock-up and hitch a ride back. 'Never know, might get lucky.' She cackled.

'Well, this is cosy,' Golly said when Lavender let him into the flat. 'I have my piece of fish now, Lavla?'

'Course you can, Goll, and now I've got you out, there's a lot of work for you to do. Lot of people to take care of.' Lavender had her own schedule, including the demise of some villainous people not all that far away in the University City of Oxford, where she planned to gather rich pickings from criminal schemes. Undergraduates were fair game, she thought, and some of them had money. Had it all planned.

Golly gave a throaty chuckle. 'I know the first one.' The hideous grin, with the slanted mouth and cock-eyed teeth. 'Special, and all mine. That lady policeman that caused all the trouble before.'

'You think that's wise, Golly?' Lavender hadn't bargained for this.

'Yeah. Yeah, I do. And she's near here ain't she, the lady policeman. Saw it in the paper. Yeah, that'd be good,' and he started to giggle, his voice rising, the giggle becoming wild, so that Lavender had to shut him up sharply, knew Golly of old and was aware that the giggle was a sign of him getting out of control.

'Golly, exactly why would you really bother with the lady policeman?'

'Because she's responsible,' he snapped back. 'Her and that Honourable bloke, that Honourable Livermore dick.'

'For what?'

'For putting me away. For everything, for locking me up, for tying me down with them pills that Dr Cornish give me.'

'I suppose.' Lavender found it easier to go along with Golly's flights of fancy when she could follow his reasoning. He had killed to her orders, and finally been caught. His anger at that turn in circumstances was manifest. The people who had caught him and put him away had become those who were responsible for him and the bad things that happened to him.

Golly would insist on these folk paying the price.

Molly joined Tommy and Suzie in the dining room of the Falcon Inn. She was distracted and tired following an afternoon tying up ends and seeing to the housekeeping of the murder inquiry. The food was execrable: warm water with a dash of Oxo masquerading as Brown Windsor soup and a tired piece of scrag-end with over-boiled potatoes and the ubiquitous waterlogged cabbage as vegetables of the day.

Tommy pushed his plate away and asked if they had a morsel of cheese, 'just to stave off the agony of hunger'.

Mrs Staleways, our Hetty, came bustling up, smiled, almost bowing to their aristocratic guest and mumbled something about having a little extra and she shouldn't really give it to residents but seeing as how it was him, and Beryl came along with a nice hunk of bread and a piece of mousetrap the size of a half-brick. Beryl still niffing of rodent.

Tommy took a sliver of cheese and a fistful of bread and began feeding himself with apparent distaste. Later he told Suzie this was the worst cheese he'd tasted in a month of Sundays.

'You get that handwriting sample from Paula Palmer?' he asked Molly, who shook her head, sadly.

'No, Chief. I had Dennis out there this afternoon. Came back about an hour ago. Waited, Paula and Thetis were out for the day, Mrs Goode told him, so he said he'd wait. He did. About half six there was a telephone call, Paula saying they wouldn't be home until very late. Dennis comes back, reckoned they'd been out so long that they wouldn't be receptive to giving handwriting samples when they got back. I told him, yes, he did right.'

Tommy nodded, chewed and nodded again. 'We can drop in tomorrow. Suzie can anyway.'

'Over there tomorrow, Chief?' Suzie asked.

'Reckon so. We've got Freddy Ascoli coming up, with the ladies I'd imagine but I'm only letting Freddy do the formal ID. Don't fancy Freda and Helena getting the vapours over the corpses. Freddy's different. Must've seen corpses in France, RFC boys usually saw some bodies.'

'You going over first thing, Chief?' Molly playing with the food on her plate, pushing it around, didn't fancy it.

'Possibly. I'll talk to Freddy later this evening and arrange matters. We could be over for a while because I want to see DCI Tait, Führer of King's Lynn CID, talk to him about this bloody silly business of the killer possibly being a vagrant. Try to set him right.'

They had cups of tasteless coffee in the Residents' Lounge, then Molly went off to make sure the other boys and girls – as she called them – were okay. 'Thought they'd try to get a meal somewhere else,' she said, not telling anyone where the somewhere else was: being like Dad, as the posters said, keeping Mum. Molly left and, eventually, Suzie said she wanted to go to bed, went up the stairs with Tommy on her heels.

'Come in for a little while or stay the night, heart.' Tommy laid a hand on her arm.

'You mind, Tom, not tonight, I'm really tired, just want to get my head down.'

'Fine. Fine. Maybe tomorrow, eh?'

'Of course, Tommy.' She was confused. Six months ago she wouldn't have needed asking twice, she'd have been in there like the proverbial rat up a drainpipe, couldn't get enough. Going through a phase, wondered how Fordy O'Dell was getting on, still flying his Spits, Wing Commander O'Dell with whom she'd been unfaithful to Tommy. Once only. One-night stand. Never told Tommy and still felt guilty.

Will you won't you, will you won't you, will you join the dance.

She went on tiptoes, made sure there was nobody else on the landing and kissed Tommy lightly. 'See you tomorrow, Tommy darling.'

'Bright and early, heart.' Taking it like a man.

Suzie undressed, put on her dressing gown, went along to the big bathroom marked *Ladies*, washed out a pair of stockings – wondered if she could get any nylons from the aerodrome when they went to the dance on Saturday – and had a strip-down wash, the water not being hot enough for a bath, only allowed five inches these days and here they actually had a five-inch mark on the bath, painted red line.

She went back to her room, pulled on her pyjamas and got into bed, reading her book, *Rebecca*, couple of pages, and she dropped off then wakened suddenly, light still on. Must switch the light off, laid her head back on the pillow, closed her eyes then heard what had wakened her before.

A quiet scratching at the door.

Twelve

The scratching turned into a soft knocking, deliberate and persistent on her door.

Suzie slid from the bed, unsteady for a moment, then, finding her balance, ran softly on tiptoe to the door: put her ear to it, then her lips.

'Who's there?' Just loud enough.

And the answer bounced back like a distorted echo, 'It's me. Tommy. Let me in.'

Oh, Tommy, not tonight . . . the words formed in her head and she was about to let them come out.

'And Molly,' she heard.

'Open the door,' Tommy commanded.

'It's not locked.' Not a gremlin in sight, so she hadn't locked it. She hadn't locked it because of getting out of there in the dark: if there was a raid or a fire, wanted to be able to sail straight through. People locked their outer doors in cities, but not always. Out in the country, she reasoned, there was no need, which was strange seeing as how only a little way up the road someone had walked into Knights Cottage and blown the faces off the residents.

She stepped back.

Dandy Tom Livermore and Molly Abelard came in looking grave and slab-faced; though Molly was distinctly tousled, her neat trench coat belted over blue pyjamas, very sexy. With Brian, Suzie thought, and it went through her head that she must be really furious to have been disturbed by Tommy.

'Never, never leave your door unlocked again, Suzie. Never

150

go out of this room alone. You wait for one of us to be with you; you never stray off by yourself, got it?'

'I'll even sleep across your door,' said Molly, meaning it, the one hundred per cent serious glint in her eyes.

They both meant it and their intensity rocked her.

'What's happened?'

Tommy closed the door behind him. 'Golly Goldfinch's done a runner from Saxon Hall.'

'But . . . Saxon Hall's . . .'

'Yes, it's impossible, nobody escapes from Saxon Hall, Suzie, but Golly just did; and he had some help.'

Her stomach turned over, rolled and looped, felt like going down in a lift, fast. She even swayed to and fro on her feet, as if about to faint.

They walked her back towards the bed; Tommy putting a hand under her left armpit to steady her.

'I've talked to Golly's head doctor, fellow called Cornish. Tells me he's forever going on about the women he killed. Remembers and recites all the details. But he also talks about you, heart, calls you "the lady policeman" and how he wants to get even. Cornish reckons he could be coming after you. And me, possibly, come to think of it.'

There, in an instant, in the twinkling of an eye, the memories flooded back, not in the form of pictures; instead she conjured Golly Goldfinch into a smell, plugged into her nostrils – a horrible stench of dog's breath, blended with the sour rotting vegetation smell she vividly recalled from that one close call when Golly tried to kill her. And almost did. In her head she heard the frightening creature's great, low sigh of pleasure as he exhaled.

'How?' she asked, meaning how the blazes did Goldfinch manage to escape from Saxon Hall?

'Told you, heart, he had help.' Tommy made himself comfortable, sat down next to her on the side of the bed. 'Could well have been that bitch Lavender, for all I know. There were two women. Stole an ambulance. Golly obviously feigned illness. They thought he had the beginnings of appendicitis. Everything done by the book, but these girls were in dead earnest. One of the so-called male nurses, who are the screws at Saxon Hall you understand, went along with Golly in the back of the ambulance. They killed him. Found him with the ambulance in a lay-by, skull bashed in.'

There was silence for around fifteen seconds. 'What do we do?' Suzie asked, foundering, feeling as though she would drown.

'What can we do? We get the local law to follow up leads, if they have any, and we get on with our investigation. The trick is making sure you're covered at all times. Someone stays with you wherever you go. If we're really careful there's no reason for you to come to any harm.'

He looked around as though checking that Golly hadn't by some cunning got himself into the room already.

'Molly is armed, you know that. Always is. Only person in the Met with permanent clearance to carry a firearm. Tomorrow I'm going to get the okay to carry one myself.'

Suzie noticed that he didn't offer to get permission for her to carry a pistol. Not surprising because she wasn't the best pupil ever with a gun. There had been a nasty incident on the firing range at Hendon, and another in an underground range where Tommy had taken her for instruction. He had ruled that she was firearms dyslexic, and she had to go home and look up 'dyslexic' in the dictionary to realize that he meant she was totally inept with weapons.

'Do more damage to yourself than the villains, heart.'

Now Tommy turned to Molly. 'Better go back to bed, Moll. Need you sharp as a razor tomorrow. Get your beauty sleep,' and he gave a little twitch when he spoke, a half smirk and a lift of one eyebrow, knew well enough that Molly was doing the horizontal conga with Brian.

With an unexpected flurry of embarrassment Molly left, saying she'd make certain that Suzie had company down to breakfast, giving Tommy her version of the evil eye to speed him on his way.

When Molly had closed the door, Tommy moved infinitesimally closer and said that now he was here why didn't he . . . ? To which Suzie told him to leave her be, but not quite in those words.

'Tommy, darling, please no, not tonight. I'm tired and this news has done nothing to help my nerves. Look, I'll lock the door and won't let anyone in but you or Molly. Please, Tommy.' She opened her eyes wide and gave him the longing look she knew did the trick with him, so he nodded, got up, kissed her head lightly and departed.

'Thanks love,' following him to the door, squeezing his arm, locking up when he'd left and shooting the bolts at top and bottom.

In truth, Tommy understood, because he also was unnerved by the news: this was the worst thing that could happen to them. Tommy, in spite of his lapses of taste – a besetting sin since childhood – his offhandedness, his crude jokes, his occasional superiority, loved Suzie, heart, soul and body. She had captivated him like no other person on their first meeting. Beneath his suave and dapper exterior, Tommy would have grave difficulties existing without her for she had become an extension of himself. He was also conscious that there was a significant age difference.

When he thought of Golly Goldfinch, Tommy saw the man with a gargoyle face, scaled like some slimy reptile. He thought of him trying to kill Suzie, choking her with the piano wire, like he had done to so many others. Deep down, Tommy feared Golly as much as Suzie feared him: the man was a walking killing machine with about as much emotion in him as a standing stone, quite capable of killing anyone who got in his way. Even murdered Suzie's sister, Charlotte, by mistake, so single-minded was he when the need to take life was on him.

As for Suzie, in the afterburn of the news that Golly was

out and about, she couldn't sleep, tossed and turned and didn't get a wink, she told herself when she woke in the morning to the Wagnerian crash of Molly's morning knock-up. In fact if she was entirely honest she would admit to being in a light doze, certainly nothing like a deep and dreamless sleep.

Molly accompanied her to the bathroom along the corridor, waited for her and shepherded her back to her room, then Tommy came and took over: out of bed, dressed, shaved and smelling of Trumper's Bay Rum.

'All set, heart?'

'Just doing my stockings, Tom.'

'Good,' the lascivious smile that was really quite nice because it showed that he was truly interested.

'Better this morning, heart?' Watching her clip the suspender to her stocking top, showing a generous slice of thigh. Tommy Livermore never tired of that view.

'I wasn't unwell.' Now the other one.

'Didn't want my company. Got a sense that all wasn't right between us. Haven't put my foot in it or anything, Suzie?'

'Course not. I was just a bit tired, then the news and all that . . . You got the okay for a weapon?'

'Up at sparrow fart, heart. Yes. Couple of phone calls and that nice Mr Tait from King's Lynn sent one over in a car.'

'We're meeting him later?'

'Yes, and I need you there to see fair play. Not altogether happy with him, Tait.'

'No?'

'No. Got a horrible feeling he was trying to lead the gentlemen from the Yard up the garden path, all glory, laud and honour to the local man. Understand, heart?'

'He would do that?'

'You'd be surprised, sweetheart. These country coppers can be sly as foxes.'

The army had arrived. Two 15-cwt trucks and a jeep. Half-a-dozen men in battledress and camouflaged smocks, a sergeant with a fierce handlebar moustache, and a smart young officer, talking in the hall to Molly, who was treating him with great deference.

'Good, the brown jobs've made it at last.' Tommy guiding Suzie into the dining room to face the morning agony of breakfast: solid egg yolks, tomato and mushrooms over-cooked, sausage and bacon undercooked, toast leathery and burned, as Tommy would say, 'Black as a badger's whatsit.'

Molly came in. 'I'm getting a ride in a jeep,' she said all of a twitter. 'I'm going up with Captain Skeggs, show him the ropes. I'm going to get them to cover the Knights Cottage grounds first, then go on to wherever you recommend, Chief.'

'I'd say take a run along the grass verges, the main road, beside the aerodrome boundary, eh? Should think it'll be closer to home though. Bet whoever did it disposed of the weapon in the garden. If not there then it'll be a very long way off.'

'Sounds fine to me, Chief. I'll be back before you leave.'

'Good.' Tommy sniffed the air as Beryl served his break-fast. 'Oh, good, Grape Nuts again.' He loathed Grape Nuts.

'What time *are* we leaving?' Suzie feeling better now, here among people, the day's chores starting, a sense of normality. She wouldn't need reminding not to go off on little private jaunts.

'We're meeting Freddy Ascoli at the hospital around eleven thirty.'

'So we go around ten thirty?'

'Only if I think it's safe to leave Molly with the pongos. Don't fancy Brian's chances now, eh?' he chuckled. 'Old Molly: real black gee-gee.' Another chuckle, deeper, almost a belly laugh.

They picked through the food, eating what was edible, and drinking the grey, weak coffee. Molly returned just as they were in the last stages of the meal.

She was a trifle breathless. 'Captain Skeggs has invited

me to his mess,' rosy, flushed and smiling. She told Beryl she only wanted some coffee and toast.

'Coffee and charcoal, eh?' Then Tommy winked at Suzie, 'Told you so. These Royal Engineers have good messes, plenty to drink, reasonable food. All the fun of the fair.'

'You're going?' Suzie asks Molly.

'I'm thinking about it,' she doesn't look Suzie in the eye.

Tommy grins, 'That Captain Skeggs, persuasive fellow.'

Molly nods, and Tommy spots the headlines of a paper being read at the next table. Sets him off talking about the latest war news – the British and Canadian Commandos landing at Dieppe and the fighting going on around Stalingrad.

'I was there the day before we declared war,' Tommy told them.

'What, Stalingrad?' Suzie and Molly both, like a Greek chorus.

'No, Dieppe. Had a couple of weeks off in Nice, dashing back to dear old Blighty before the balloon went up.'

'Couldn't the Duke of Westminster have given you a lift home in his yacht?' Suzie having a go at sarcasm.

'Already left.' Tommy didn't miss a beat. 'And we couldn't get on a boat, had to go to Boulogne. Ended up in Folkestone.'

'Who's the "we"?' Suzie asked.

'My father and mother. We were big on family holidays before the current bit of unpleasantness. Remember my mother called it Folke-stone, as if it was two words.'

Suzie gave a sickly smile as he took a deep breath, as though ridding himself of memories, and said, 'Come on then, Susannah. Time we were on our way. Drop you off, Molly, I expect Captain Skeggs is waiting.'

''Spect he is,' big smile and looking predatory in the trench coat: ready for anything. 'Any more instructions, Chief?'

'Tell you when we get there, see the pongos at work.'

Brian drove them to Knights Cottage, a nicer day, sun shining and the sky unmarked. Tommy said they'd better go and see the boys doing their job in the garden; so Molly led them through the house and on to the terrace at the back. Three of the soldiers were painstakingly sweeping the lawn and borders to and fro in wide arcs with metal plates attached to poles, each man with a backpack from which thick wires traced to the equipment, each with headphones.

'This is Captain Skeggs, Chief.' Molly introduced the tall and slender officer who had a definite eye for one person only – a grin forty feet wide all over his stupid pink face. 'This is my chief, Trevor,' she said. 'Detective Chief Superintendent Livermore.'

Chinless wonder, Suzie thought, only bum fluff on his jowls. Old Brian would be more reliable: she'd tell Molly to stick with Brian.

'Trevor Skeggs, sir.' The captain stuck out his hand. 'We've met before. Last New Year's Eve, I came to Kingscote Grange, to the ball. We spoke.'

'Oh, yes. Trevor Skeggs. You're Snuffy Skeggs's boy.' And that was that, it was patently obvious that Tommy had no real recollection of meeting young Skeggs, who explained that the men were sweeping the ground with what he called glorified metal detectors. 'Crude, but they do the job.' The other men slowly followed behind the sweepers, investigating any possible 'find'.

'Better do the meadow behind.' Tommy pointed to the field in which Bob Raines kept his pigs, where Piglet, the sexually ambivalent dog, sniffed around to get his oats. 'Take no notice of that farmer, Molly. Just get it done. Nice to have seen you again, Skeggs. Good huntin'.' Turn, swing the arm, march off. Dead military.

As they walked back through the house, Suzie remarked that the ground was still damp. 'But they didn't seem to have sparks coming out of their bums.'

'What you bloody talking about, Suzie?' he grumped.

They noticed that Brian was out of sorts during the drive over to King's Lynn.

* * *

157

Golly didn't know where he was at first, waking up in the strange room, hearing the wireless playing next door. Then he remembered the escape and drummed his heels on the mattress under the sheets.

He had a full memory, all the details, by the time Lavender came in with his breakfast: bacon and eggs, fried bread, some fried potatoes, a tomato and a sausage, toast on the side. She got extra rations from a local butcher, and some of the Yanks: services rendered.

'That looks good, like my old mum used to do it. You're a real sport, Lavla.' He stretched out and gave a happy groan. 'Goin' to have a good rest today, nobody around to chivvy me about.' Propping himself up on the pillows and tucking in.

Lavender said she'd be going out with Queenie a bit later on. 'Thought we'd take a ride over to Long Taddmarten, have a look round.'

'What's at Long Taddmarten then?'

'That's where your favourite person is, Goll. Where that lady copper is, poking her nose into a murder there. Three murders.'

'Yeah. Yeah I read about that. Someone shot that bastard responsible for getting me into Saxon bloody Hall. Saxon bloody Hole more like. Bastard!'

'Well, you said you wanted to get even with her and that other copper, so we reckoned, Queenie and me reckoned, as how we should go over and take a peep. Come back and report to you what the chances are.'

'Queenie?' Golly grinned. 'Nice name. Didn't get to meet her last night, did I? Not proply anyway.'

'Not proply, Goll, no. But you will.'

'That was good, Lavla. Getting me out, and it's good you going to check up on that bitch of a lady policeman.' He looked up and grinned his lopsided grin with the teeth showing on the right side. In Saxon Hall they'd talked about the dentist having a go at straightening those teeth. Golly didn't like the sound of that.

'All right, Goll. I've had a ham cooking and I'll leave you a few slices for your dinner, but you mustn't set foot outside this flat. Don't even go out the front door and look down the stairs. Understand?'

'Course I unnerstand, my sweet-smelling Lavender,' chuckle. 'Course I do. I wouldn't go out. Not use to it, am I?'

What had really happened was that Lavender told Queenie Golly was all set to knock off the female pig who was over with that Dandy Tom Livermore, famous copper, in Taddmarten investigating the murder of the Ascoli family, barrister that defended Golly.

'Not that he did much to defend him 'cos he was behind bloody bars in the end. Hospital they call it, that Saxon Hall. Bloody loony bin, that's what it is, and Golly don't deserve that, stuck in a loony bin. Trouble with Golly is that once he gets an idea in his head he won't settle till it's done.'

So they decided to take a butchers, see what chances could come up while the bloody woman was on the case: take a look at where they were staying, the coppers, how careful they were being.

Having told Golly about fifty times that he mustn't go out, they got him some books, *Wizard*, *Hotspur* and *The Champion* – comics really – with a spare copy of *Film Fun* that the newsagent had hanging around – 'Be careful,' the newsagent said. 'That's last week's *Film Fun*, if your kiddie's already had it you'll be in trouble.' Lavender told him her kiddie hadn't seen it 'cos he'd just come out of hospital in Cambridge, and what with one thing and another the newsagent said what a terrible thing that was, the ambulance from Cambridge, and the fellow killed and that loony on the loose. 'You keep your door locked at night, my duck,' he said to Lavender, fancying her a bit and letting her know it.

'Bugger,' she said to Queenie. 'Won't be able to go in there again, he'll be wanting to know how my kiddie is.'

'He will, an' he'll be wanting to study the hidden secrets

of your body, Lavender an' all.' Queenie was a forthright young woman.

So they got their Austin Seven out, took the comics back to Golly – parked round the corner and walked back to the flat, two storeys up from the ground floor of Lime Tree House – told him again he wasn't to go out no matter how late they got back, and Golly said, 'Don't you worry about me. I'm going to have a nice kip,' and off they went.

Golly had a giggle because he knew what else he was going to do, have a bit of a wank and stretch out in the luxury of it all. He even had a poke around the flat, looked in all the drawers and held up pieces of Lavender's and Queenie's undies, chuckling at the little pants they wore and the bits of lace they'd sewn on them, getting a hard-on like a stag's antler. He'd be okay for the rest of the day. Time enough for that Suzie girl. Time enough. She wouldn't be going anywhere, would she?

Freddy Ascoli was waiting for Tommy and Suzie, alone, loitering and neatly dressed in dark clothes outside the hospital. Even said it was nice to see them again in his precise way.

'You're on your own then?' Tommy asked.

'Not going to put the ladies through this. They're coming down as soon as we know about the release of the bodies: organize the funeral.'

'You can probably arrange that today. Go to the coroner's office. We've just about finished with them.'

Then, getting no response, he said, 'This isn't going to be easy for you,' ushering him through the doors into the hospital's reception and emergency area where the coroner's representative was waiting for them, a lugubrious pale-faced man who introduced himself as Eland Alder. The name appeared to throw Freddy who asked him to spell it. He did and Freddy was none the wiser: Eland with a long 'E' seemed to be unfamiliar to him. Perhaps it was something to do with his Italian heritage, Suzie thought.

'We have the bodies in a room like a chapel of rest, Mr Ascoli, but there is one big problem.' They waited for an explanation. Finally Alder continued. 'As you probably know . . .' They were walking down corridors all the time and Eland would stop to acknowledge other members of staff as they went. 'As you probably know, the faces of the deceased are damaged beyond possible repair, so we have bandaged the heads. If you cannot identify any, or all, of the bodies we can remove the bandaging. It'll take a little longer but we should allow you all possible assistance.'

Freddy acknowledged this helpful suggestion, though Suzie noticed that he was a shade paler than when they'd met him outside. Eland Alder led them through a door marked 'Mortuary', into a small waiting area with chairs and a vase of flowers on a table below a crucifix and an attendant standing ready to assist.

'D'you mind, Chief?' Suzie asked, having no desire to view the bodies again. Tommy nodded, asked Freddy if he was ready and gave the nod to Alder, who led the way through the next door, then again through another to the right, into the cold room where the bodies were on view: on hospital trolleys in a row, covered nicely with white sheets, each with a large red cross on them – always a big cross for C of Es or RCs.

Alder gently removed the sheets, folding them on to the back of chairs standing beside the trolleys. The three bodies were dressed in loose white robes, a long frock for Jenny and white satiny pyjamas for Max and Paul, soft white socks and slippers on their feet so they wouldn't go forward into eternity barefoot.

'Dear God,' Freddy said, crossing himself. Indeed, the heads were not visible: each covered in a fastidious, if bulky, bandage, the whole in a seamless cotton wrapper – great white egg-shape rising from between the shoulders – making it look as if all three of them had been topped off with candyfloss.

'You going to be able to identify them?' Tommy asked, and

Freddy gave a long nod. 'Oh, yes. That's Paul, I'd know him
without his cheeky face; and yes, that's Jenny, those're her
hands; so, by process of elimination, that must be Max, and
it is, the bulk of his body tells me, his height and his hands.
Those two rings are his, one was very special, Grandfather
Antonio left it to be passed on to Sammy's first son.'
　'But he wasn't Sammy's first son.'
　'No, but Max was the one who got it. You really couldn't
count Fillipo.'
　And Tommy jumped in, 'Freddy, what was really the matter
with Fillipo? Phillip?'
　Staring to the front, not turning his head to look at him,
Max Ascoli's uncle Fredo.
　'You all right?' Alder said, and Tommy turned, saw Freddy,
clinging to the trolley on which his nephew's body lay in the
satin pyjamas and with the white bulge where his head had
been.
　They got to him before he crumpled, held him up, helped
him to the door where Suzie was waiting – rushed over to
assist, eyes averted from the bizarre interior of the cold room.
　'I'll get you a cup of something. Coffee. Drop of brandy.'
Alder shuffled off and Tommy stood back, his shoulder
touching Suzie's shoulder, giving Freddy air.
　'I'm sorry. Bit of a shock that's all.' Freddy gulped. 'I
think not seeing the faces was worse than seeing them.'
　'Know what you mean.' Tommy gave Suzie a sideways
look and nodded.
　Then Alder returned with a thick china cup and saucer,
the cup steaming with black coffee, the scent filling the air
around them. 'I've put a little brandy in the cup.'
　'By God, that smells like the real thing. Can almost taste
it.' Tommy animated for a second.
　'It *is* the real thing,' but Alder made no move to give
anyone else a cup. 'We've a little stock. Helps when
someone's had to look at their loved ones, shattered and
mangled like Christmas Pudding mixture. Helps a lot.'

'Thanks for that,' Suzie muttered to herself.

'Anywhere I can take Mr Ascoli? Be alone for a while?' Tommy wasn't asking, he was ordering.

Eland Alder said there was a little office they used behind the waiting area, and when Freddy's colour came back he showed them the way.

'You asked me about Phillip. In there, you asked.' Freddy sitting in a chair now, still taking deep breaths, but pulling himself out of the nervous shock he had felt.

Tommy nodded, said, yes, all the Ascolis had mentioned him, but everything was hinted at. 'Haven't had the full hand, if you know what I mean.'

'Lovely little chap.' Freddy, in his neat dark suit with the pressed lapels, didn't look at them, let his eyes stay on his hands, as though he was examining them, concerned lest his fingers were not clean. 'Lively little fellow, full of fun. Intelligent, enquiring mind. Then one day, out of nowhere, he strangled two pet cats, did it with his bare hands. Strangled the two pussies then beat the dog, Dodger, to death with a poker. Laughed like a little drain, thought it no end of a lark. "Look what I done. Put the cats and the dog to sleep." Dodger's blood all over the place.' Pause, then, as though for effect, 'And that was only the start of it, not quite four years of age.'

Suzie felt a bit sick and Tommy asked, 'What did the doctors have to say?'

'Couldn't give any cause. Psychotic of course. Psychotic and dangerous. Dark and bloody dangerous. There were a couple of other incidents . . .'

'What?'

'He attacked a nurse. Nursery nurse. Name of Clotilde, French girl. I mean really attacked, at four years, went for her with a mallet, shattered her knee, would've stoved her head in if other servants hadn't been near. Can you imagine it? A toddler.'

'And the other thing?'

163

'Ah, that was more difficult. He tried to harm Sammy. He hid behind a door. Stood on a chair and hid behind his father's door, battered him with a walking stick, an alpenstock actually. Knocked him down, but there were other people around. Knocked him down and shouted what passed for obscenities at him.'

'Such as?'

'Would you believe Reckitt's Blue, Sunlight Soap, Coleman's Mustard and Bile Beans? The names of items he'd seen in the kitchen and memorized. He would call people things like, "You . . . you . . . Peak Frean," the biscuit people you know. "You damned Bovril." These words became his curses, his swearing.' Freddy shook his head, full of mournful memories and pain. 'They laughed at it to start with. Not after he attacked Sammy, though.'

God in heaven, Tommy thought. God save us, my whole world is filled with these aberrations, these dark people. The loathsome Golly was hard enough. Now this, a family who had spawned someone like Phillip. Fillipo.

As though picking up on his thoughts, Freddy said, 'And they called him Pip. I remember when Sammy told me. "Pip tried to brain me with an alpenstock," he said as though it was an everyday occurrence.' Another shake of the head, 'And it would've been if they hadn't put him away.'

'Which they did?'

'Almost straight off. Poor old Sammy had ten stitches in his scalp. They saw a doctor in Harley Street, who advised he should be put away. I mean, over forty years ago, Mr Livermore. Things a lot different then.'

'They're not all that advanced now,' Suzie said, thinking of some of the hospitals around for the demented and mentally bereft.

'It was the dying days of the nineteenth century, then. Funny how that hop into a new century renders so much obsolete. But Sammy was good at heart. He dug around, wanted the best for Pip. Found these good sisters –

Schwestern des Ordens des Mitleides. Sisters of the Order of Compassion. We all saw him, several times at Alpenruhe.'

'Near Thun.'

'Near Thun, and damned creepy.'

'Willoughby Sands used the same expression – creepy.'

'And he had more opportunities to savour it. Went over regularly. I think he even went over a couple of years ago, early 1940 before the balloon really went up.'

'And the holy sisters are really able to control him?' Suzie asked, thinking in the hinterland of her mind of Golly Goldfinch on the loose, coming for her.

'He has difficult times, I gather. But they seem to get less and less. Those nuns are truly wonderful: love him and help him. For most of the time he's with the other patients – and he's not the only one who can be dangerous. What a terrible thing it is, such a birth defect.'

Then again, 'You'd have Max's murderer if Pip was out and about in this country. No doubt about it.'

'Indeed,' Tommy's concentration slipping, showing signs of impatience, wanting to be off, needing Freddy to sign the papers validating the formal identification of the bodies. If you didn't know Tommy well, Suzie thought, you'd think he hadn't taken in what Freddy Ascoli had said.

'Got to see Miss Palmer at some point today, catch her in,' he said. 'Miss Palmer and the delightful Thetis.'

'You won't today,' Freddy looked up. 'Nor for a week or so. Taken the fair young Thetis on a little holiday.'

'Really?' Tommy, well controlled, showed no sign of surprise or confusion, though, standing at his side, Suzie felt it. 'Where've they gone then?'

'No idea,' Freddy smiled as though this was all quite normal for Paula Palmer. 'I rang this morning and the house-keeper – who doesn't live in – told me she was away.'

'Drop round and see the housekeeper then,' as if it couldn't matter less.

Tommy, Suzie thought, could be cool as a cucumber when

push came to shove. She liked that, but then she was in love
with him, wasn't she? The query cycled through her mind:
in love with him, wasn't she? Or was she?

Rick LeClare had Blomwitz, the chief tech of his ground
crew, go over the new airplane with a magnifying glass. It
wasn't brand new, one of the three reserves the squadron
carried. 'Anything mediocre, get a new one, install it, right?
Any other problems, you fix them, Bloomy.'

'Right, Skipper,' said Teddy Blomwitz, whose reason for
living was keeping *Wild Angel* and its crew flying. They got
Anton Echer over to do exactly the same art work on the
nose, mirror image of the first airplane only this time *Wild
Angel II* and the underwear was white not black. White, Ricky
decided, was luckier than black, the colour of mourning.
Juliet Axton wore white satiny things. Liked that.

LeClare got the new boys out and talked to them about
their ship, told them they gotta be proud about serving in
Wild Angel II, and that the men who had already served were
good guys, little Tim Ruby and the waist gunners, Corkendale
and Piakesky – so everyone has to tell a white lie sometime,
keep morale up. The other guys wouldn't let on that the waist
gunners had leaped from the ship the moment they thought
there was trouble, and he made the four new guys come out
to the hospital to visit Peliandros, just as if they had been
part of the crew with him.

The two new waist gunners were Pete Israel and Danny
Spooner. The new tail gunner was a tough-looking bruiser
called 'Red' Moir, because he had ginger hair. Sol Schwartz
was never coming back, his nervous system shot by just the
one operation, and the new upper turret man was a tech-
sergeant by the name of Jim Dodd, calm and taciturn, with
a slow drawl all the way from Texas, the kind of guy you'd
want with you in a saloon brawl. LeClare was determined
to mould these men into a crew that wouldn't panic or react
badly once they were in combat.

Just after lunch, on the afternoon of the day Suzie had gone with Tommy Livermore to have the victims' bodies identified in King's Lynn, Ricky LeClare got the whole of his new crew over to *Wild Angel II*'s frying pan, dispersal hardstanding, prior to going on an orienting, navigational and firing exercise. He had already arranged for Father Christopher, the RC Chaplain, to be driven over, wearing his cassock and a surplice, a white stole around his neck and his attendant, a young sergeant called Brazier, carrying a silver holy water stoop and a missal.

There, Father Christopher said prayers of dedication and blessed *Wild Angel II*, sprinkled it with holy water in the sign of the cross on its nose, then blessed the entire crew.

LeClare was greatly moved by this and was certain they would do well when out on operations, but Pete Israel, speaking on his own behalf and that of his fellow member of the Jewish persuasion, Bob Pentecost, the ball turret gunner, remarked that they should have had a rabbi over to give a blessing.

'I'll get the rabbi over,' LeClare told him. 'Soon as I can I'll get him to come over, long as he doesn't cut off a couple of inches from the ball turret gun.' Which even Pete found amusing.

So they took off and spent four hours working together, going through the in-flight drills, navigating as far as Newcastle-on-Tyne and back, rendezvousing with a tug aircraft, which ducked and dived around the Fortress with a drogue trailing for the gunners to shoot at.

'You're gonna be the best damned crew in the 302nd,' he shouted through the interphone, putting a little extra back-bone into the boys.

Just as *Wild Angel II* was lifting off from the main runway at Long Taddmarten, Tommy was worrying about where Paula Palmer and Thetis had gone. For once he was concerned about his reputation.

Thirteen

They were having the set lunch at the Bull Inn, not bad at three and a kick a head. Tommy read the menu trying to make Suzie laugh, 'Le potage legumes, les omelettes espagnole avec les chips, et le Roly Poly pud avec le custard oiseaux.' Pause, then a change of demeanour, 'Christ, Suzie, I hope I haven't put my big foot in it.'

'Why?' She raised her head and saw his face was clouded with worry: a look she knew but seldom saw: something serious.

They had been to 'River Walk' and seen Mrs Goode, who had absolutely no information regarding Paula Palmer and Thetis. 'I'm sorry,' she said, sounding as if she was blundering round a dark room, 'I've no idea where they've gone off to. Miss Palmer telephoned me again last night, said don't expect them back in a hurry. Said Miss Thetis deserved a bit of a break, I mean she's supposed to be back at school in a week or two. Have to be back for that. Miss Palmer said, deserves a treat, Thetis, poor lamb with her Daddy gone so terribly; 'tis so sad, Mr Livermore.'

'Ever done this before?' Tommy asked. 'I mean has she ever just gone off on a whim?'

'I think they probably went by rail.' Longish pause, working it out. 'Though they left in the car. My feeling is they went on by train.'

'No, I mean on the spur of the moment. Ever gone off and not told you?'

Mrs Goode, who reminded Suzie of a large robin, short,

168

plump with rosy cheeks, seemed lost for words at first. Then, 'As a rule she gives me some kind of address, I must say.'

'Any ideas, perhaps, Mrs Goode?'

'What, where they've gone? None at all, sir. Miss Palmer's a law unto herself as the good book says.'

Does it? he wondered, and studied his shoes. 'This is somewhat important. If she rings again would you ask her to get in touch with me?' Handed her a card, both his Yard number and, pencilled on the back, his number at the Falcon, his special phone, in the bedroom.

She promised she'd be punctilious about it, used that very word, 'But, Miss Palmer's already telephoned. Doubt if she'll do it again.'

Now, drinking the vegetable soup in the Bull Inn, King's Lynn, he wondered out loud if Paula thought telephones to be instruments of the Devil.

'Hardly think that, Tommy. Not the type, is she?'

'Just gone off, leaving no address. Wonder if Freddy would know?'

'What's the real worry, Tom?'

'An old rule, heart. We both know that Palmer's in the frame. Has to be . . .'

'What, you really think . . . ?'

'That she could have orchestrated the killings? Of course I do. It's a possibility, if not a probability,' he admitted gloomily. 'We talked about it.'

As for Paula I think she'd kill, heart. Tough as old boots. Maybe has killed once, could do it again.

'You really think she had a part in this?' Suzie baffled because they had no solid evidence.

'Oh, I'm not like those cops you see at the pictures, heart, you know that, but . . . well, I shouldn't say it but I have a feeling she's not altogether innocent: in my water, so to speak, I sense something wrong.' He gave a one note laugh, 'Ha! But that's how it is. I think she had something to do with it, but there isn't a scrap of evidence. And I couldn't tell you

why I think it: intuition, heart, and that means damn all.'
Another spoonful of soup, and, 'Very good this, eh heart?'

'It is. Excellent. Yes. Tastes just like Mum use to make it.'

'Only Thetis saying she thought the telephone rang in the night, that's the only minute lead.'

'And if there is a connection?' Suzie's eyebrows raised.

'If there is a connection, Thetis'll have forgotten all about that middle of the night call by now. Her mother'd make sure of that.'

'Sometime around three or four,' Suzie remembered, and, 'she went off to sleep again.'

'That's how she recalled it.'

'So what's your terrible worry?'

'It's a first rule. Anyone you haven't really finished with: in the old days you used to tell them not to go abroad, must not leave the country; keep in touch, let us know where they are.'

She had heard as much when they made their farewells to Freddy Ascoli. 'Stay in touch, let me know where you'll be,' Tommy had said to him, repeating it and then once more for the cameras and the insurance.

'I didn't say she wasn't to go away without telling us. Didn't tell her to let us know wherever she was, Paula bloody Palmer.'

'And you think that matters?'

'It does if she has something to hide. Could've done a runner with Thetis, holed up somewhere. Could've dropped out of sight.'

'Oh, Tommy.'

'My fault, heart. Silly damned fault and I've no real grounds for putting out a search – apprehend if seen. Make me a laughing stock.'

'Tommy, I'm sure it's not that serious.'

'I've broken my own golden rule: don't know what I was thinking of. If she's not here I can't ask her any questions, and I've got one or two I should be asking now.'

Throughout the meal Tommy remained distracted, while Suzie tried to keep the conversation going, never had any trouble with talking before, but now she headed him away from the case and it wasn't easy going. They reached a collection of yes and no replies and finally Tommy struck out on his own. 'How's that book going, one you're reading, what is it? *Ruth*? No . . .'

'*Rebecca*,' Suzie supplied.

'That's the one. Knew it was biblical. Ruth, Rebecca, Sarah. Old Testament. How is it?'

'Okay. Interesting actually. The main character's like *I* used to be.'

'How's that then?' lively again. 'How's that, little cracker? Always rushing around? Likes a slice off the joint? Wears enticing undies, eh?' Coming back on form.

'Tommy, no. She's shy, a bit clumsy, awkward, good middle-class girl but not good socially. Just like I was till you taught me the ropes and gave me some confidence. Actually this girl's a bit of a wet egg, as my dad would say.'

'What's her name? Rebecca, is it?'

'No, she hasn't got a name. Well, not till she marries Max.'

'Max? Another Max, eh?'

'Yes. Maxim. Maxim de Winter.'

'The hero, yes?'

'Sort of, I think. Possibly, though he's a bit demanding.'

'Then who the hell's Rebecca?'

'His late wife. She's dead and, to be honest, seems to haunt everything.'

'Dead but she won't lie down?'

'I've just got to the bit where Max takes his new bride back to this wonderful house. Manderley it's called, super-beautiful place on a headland, overlooking the sea. She doesn't say it's in Cornwall but that's where it sounds like.'

'On the road to Mandalay,' he half sang, stopped eating for a moment.

'Rude to sing at the table, Tommy. And, no, Mand*er*ley.

It's called Manderley. Not Mandalay. Beautiful house with a
sinister housekeeper . . .'

'Like Mrs Goode then.'

Tommy was trying too hard. 'No, she's called Mrs
Danvers.'

'It's a creepy sort of book then. Like the place those nuns
have near Thun.'

Suzie thought for a moment. 'Yes, but it's not just a kind
of romance with a dash of Gothic darkness. Somehow there's
more to it than that.'

But Tommy had given up, distracted again, troubled. She
thought, he's searching for answers. She knew Tommy
Livermore when he was really what he called 'into a case':
seen him like it before many times – distracted, buried in
it, his mind crawling around all the possibilities, taking
mental measurements and bearings, pulling people into his
head, examining them, then either dismissing them or putting
them under the microscope of his brain. Most murders, he
taught her, were committed by someone close to the victim.
Often another family member, unless the killing had been
some aberrancy – like this one – the work of a mentally
disturbed person with bizarre, abnormal tastes. Someone
like Golly Goldfinch: and at that her tummy turned over.
For a second she saw the obnoxious Golly with his slanted
grin, so suddenly real that she could have sworn for a wink
of time he was here, with them in the hotel's dining room,
very close.

'You all right, heart?' Tommy, glancing up and catching
her, swaying in her seat, eyes unfocused, touched by terror.

'Yes. Yes. Just for a minute . . .' She was sweating and
didn't even try to put the feeling into words because she
thought it would sound silly.

'You sure, heart? For a minute you looked like you'd seen
a ghost.'

'Perhaps I did.'

'What, on the road to Mandalay again? Too much reading,

heart. Active imagination. Sends you Harpic, right round the bend.'

When they got to King's Lynn Police Station they were taken straight through to Detective Chief Inspector Tait's office, corner of the building just off the main CID room: a correct uniformed WPC showed them in, intoning their names just in case Tait had forgotten them. Tait ran a tight ship.

The Detective Chief Inspector himself stood behind his desk, in front of a large window: light directly behind him, so that Suzie immediately thought of a kind of cartoon crow, larger than life, silhouetted black, his head turning and the beak of his nose prominent, a great aquiline creature, predatory and ready to sink claws into any smaller animal that came into his sights. For a moment or two Suzie felt tiny and vulnerable herself.

'Come in. Sit down, how can I help? The case going all right, eh?'

They seated themselves in the proffered chairs, Suzie noting how Tommy visibly relaxed, spreading himself, stretching out his legs, pointing his well-shod toes and leaning back. She thought to herself, the fur's going to fly, for this was again Tommy at his most dangerous. When his whole body relaxed he was really winding himself up for the spring.

'Case I want to talk about, actually,' he started, a thin smile, not reaching his eyes, which never moved off the Chief Inspector's face.

'Glad to be of help.'

Tommy moved straight in. 'Why, Mr Tait . . . ? Why . . . ?'

'Please, sir. Please call me Eric.'

'. . . Why, Mr Tait, did you think this could be a random series of killings by some vagrant or vagrants seeking revenge?'

'Well, it had the feel of revenge to it, and we'd had a number of problems with vagrants in the area. Unpleasant exchanges on doorsteps, uncouth people doing the rounds, begging, wanting money or food. Both often. Half gypsies, tramps kind of thing. Giving a lot of unpleasant lip to house-holders. We were worried that there could be violence.'

'Nobody told me this.' Soft, almost a whisper. 'You didn't advise me of this, Tait.'

'My officer on the spot was supposed to give you the full picture. Capable man.'

'You mean Titcombe?'

Tait nodded and Tommy gave an irritated cough of contempt. 'Titcombe who spends most of his time giving fatuous and unnecessary advice to my trained and experi-enced officers, but hasn't parted with this information about vagrants? Police Constable 478 Walter Titcombe? That who we're talking about?'

'I'm sorry, sir. I imagined . . . Yes.'

'You imagined wrong then, Mr Tait. Did you imagine that an uncouth vagrant would purposely fire a shotgun into Max Ascoli's face, then reload and prowl the house in search of others to whom he could mete out the same punishment?'

'I've said. It had a taste of vengeance about it, yes.' Tait's voice clipped, bridling, comprehending that the senior officer was out for his blood.

'A taste of vengeance? A *taste*? Ye gods, DCI Tait, it was like an execution in there. Didn't you go in search of Ascoli's links with local people?'

'You mean Paula Palmer and her love child?'

'Her daughter, yes. How many people know about that?'

'She's well known of course. Local celebrity. I suppose there are odd jokes and innuendoes in the Conservative Club bar, and in public bars across the town. You know what men are. They don't do it in front of me because I let them know I won't have that sort of talk. After all, I'm a church warden.'

'I didn't realize that.' Tommy rolled his eyes towards heaven.

'And women such as her – doing well in her chosen

profession – would want to live down a terrible secret of their youth. Paula Palmer is well liked, but I suppose there's always that small percentage of local people who won't forget: won't ever leave it alone.'

'Like me, I suppose?' Tommy went straight on, 'I won't forget, Mr Tait, because I *know* who the father is.'

'Well, many of us do. Or at least think we know. Max Ascoli never made a secret out of it.'

'And now the father's dead. Fourteen miles away with his face blown off and his wife and child killed in the same manner, like some ritual.'

Tait nodded, looking grim.

'And is this just a cosy country secret or can anyone join in, nudge each other in the ribs as Paula Palmer passes by? I for one had to hear it from the Ascoli family, from Max Ascoli's uncle. You didn't even think to fill me in on local gossip, Mr Tait. Negligent in your duties, I'd say.'

Tait did not reply, just kept sitting there with his profile outlined against the window behind him. Finally he murmured something about not really having had a chance to chat with DCS Livermore. 'Busy country area to police. Can't be everywhere, can't remember everything. Thought you'd seek me out when you wanted local colour.'

'That what you call it? Local colour? You weren't by any chance waiting for some opportune moment when you could sweep in out of nowhere and put your colleagues from Scotland Yard in a poor light? Walk in like that stuffy little Belgian of Agatha Christie's, solve the puzzle.'

'I resent that, sir.'

'Resent away, old sport, it won't get you anywhere. Now, have you got any other local gossip you'd care to share with me?'

Suzie was uncomfortable with the fireworks: lightning and the scent of powder in the air between the two men. She sensed a lot of trouble over this: shaping up to be a knock-down drag-out fight. Most unseemly.

Finally it was Tait who spoke. 'In the last year or so there's been talk that she's seeing – been seeing – Mr Ascoli again.' He almost whispered it as if reticent about repeating the rumour aloud.

Suzie thought: Well, he would, being a church warden and all.

Tommy grunted and asked if there was anything else he might not yet have discovered for himself.

'Well, there's the tale about the mad brother.'

Tommy's face stiffened and Suzie moved in her chair.

'What's the tale about the mad brother then, DCI Tait?' They keep him locked up at Knights Cottage, or something?'

Tait rose, towering over them, and to Suzie the silhouette suddenly became familiar. One of Walt Disney's rapacious birds that frightened Snow White in the scary forest.

'I have no evidence,' he began, looming over them. 'No hard facts. The story is that Max Ascoli has a brother. The brother is called Phillip and he is crazily mad, and dangerous with it. There appears to be some truth in this.'

Tommy nodded. Go on, he was saying.

'The other story is that in the summer of 1938, the year before the war started, the year Chamberlain flew to Munich and came back with a little piece of paper with Hitler's signature on it: the peace in our time year—'

'Yes?' Tommy really asking a question.

'It is said that towards the end of August in that year, 1938, Max Ascoli went to wherever his brother is kept – one of the tales is that it is in a sanatorium in Switzerland – and brought his brother back to London and then came up here with him. To Knights Cottage in Long Taddmarten.'

'And?' Tommy asked again.

'There are those who claim to have seen them together. In Taddmarten.'

'And he is still there?'

You'd have Max's murderer if Pip was out and about in this country. No doubt about it. That's what Freddy had said.

'No.' A great shaking of his big head. 'No, the story is that Max Ascoli took him back from whence he'd come. Came back to Taddmarten alone. I can only vouch that it's a tale. It could be idle chatter with no foundation in fact. Something that's grown out of the stories of Ascoli having a mad brother. A dangerously mad brother. You know how people like to gossip if there's a hint of danger. It could be just that. Someone conjuring dark tales to chill the blood and send a shiver up the back of people's necks as they go home, late at night in Taddmarten.'

'How much credence do you give the story?'

Tait frowned, licked his lips, opened his mouth but before he could speak there was a tap on the door and the WPC came half into the room. 'Urgent telephone call for Mr Livermore, sir.'

It was Molly with the news that the shotgun had been found, buried on the grass verge along the main road, beside the chain-link fence that bordered the aerodrome.

'We have to go,' Tommy already on his feet from taking the telephone call. 'But before we do, Detective Chief Inspector, how much credence do you give the story? That the dangerously mad brother was brought to Taddmarten.'

'I don't know, sir, and I've never actually investigated it. I think you'd have to ask in Taddmarten itself. Then make up your own mind.'

Tommy nodded. Then Tait spoke again –

'There is one other thing, sir.'

'Yes?'

'One thing that could be useful. Only just come in. I looked through the reports. Of course you're looking for one woman – the Lavender woman . . .'

'Rosemary Lattimer?'

'That's the one, sir. We think we may have her going under the name of Midge, something or other.' He turned over some papers on his desk to show a drawing of a girl's face.

Tommy nodded. 'Yes, that could just be Lavender. Suzie?'

She nodded. 'Possibly. In the dark with the light behind her. Definitely.'

'Been hanging around with this one.' Another drawing, artist's impression as they liked to call them. 'She's going under the name of Queenie. Would fit together, two of them getting Goldfinch out.'

'I take these?' Tommy asked.

'I have them for you. They've been whoring around the Cambridge and the Newmarket area.'

'Interesting if they helped to extricate Golly.'

'Very, sir.'

Brian got them back in incredibly good time. They stayed on the main road and, well in advance, saw the little knot of people by the roadside some two hundred yards or so before the turn that took you to the aerodrome's main gate: four of the King's Lynn uniformed people keeping a small strangle of village and US personnel at a distance from the spot that had been marked out with saw horses.

Tommy alighted from the car first, greeted by a smiling Molly, pleased with herself. Other people from his team stood around and, on the far side of the fence a pair of snowdrops – US military policemen – stood in a vaguely menacing attitude.

'So you found it?'

'Well, Captain Skeggs's men found it, Chief. And it wasn't really buried.' She led him to the side of the road, pointing down through the grass and weeds that had covered a ditch – three to four feet deep – running parallel to the road, a couple of feet in towards the tall chain-link fence, the boundary to stop people wandering towards the lines of huts and buildings bordering on the aircraft taxiway another three hundred yards distant.

'Whoever did it just dropped the gun down here.' Molly pointed to the overgrown ditch. 'Quite invisible, grass is thick as fleas on a dog down here. Unless someone actually fell into the ditch it might not have been found for months. Ron and Laura have taken photos in situ and of other interesting things.'

'Is it the twin to the other Purdey shotgun we found?'

'No doubt about that, Chief. I've had it taken back to the Falcon and Doc's going to run it straight over to Hendon for all the forensics. Dennis is giving it a good check-up first, okay, sir?'

'Seems you've done everything.'

'Well, there is one more point.' She daintily half-stepped, half-jumped across the ditch, a couple of feet wide, and pointed towards the fence. 'See, Chief. Interesting bit of tampering here.'

The reason for the couple of snowdrops became clear: the chain-link fence had been cut, a slit running from the ground to around five or six feet in height with the outer edges of the slit turned in so that anyone could force themselves on to the aerodrome with no trouble.

'Are we meant to think that whoever dropped the shotgun used a pair of wire cutters to let himself on to the airfield?' Suzie asked.

'So it would seem. The nearest buildings, do we know what they are?'

Molly said they were living quarters, mainly aircrew huts. 'I've been through and had a look,' she said. 'Proper little homes from home some of them.'

'Ron take pictures of this?'

'Done the whole thing, Chief. It'll make quite a family album.'

'And the MPs?'

'Waiting for us to say they can get the thing made good, I think.'

'Well, not just yet, eh. We need a little more time.'

'Ron Worral says that the cut wire has probably been like that for some time. Didn't think it was recent. Week or two old, he says, traces of rust already on the inside of the wire: where it's been cut.'

'He can be sure of that?' Suzie asked.

'You know Ron.' Molly smiled. 'If he tells you it's been there for more than a couple of days then you can bet that's how it is.' Ron was extraordinarily accurate, careful and precise. If he had been uncertain about how long the cut had been there, he would have said. Ron's word was usually good enough for Tommy.

'Have to speak with the head snowdrop I think,' and he called out to the MPs who still waited, patiently but with some menace. 'Where's your senior officer?'

One of the men moved some two paces towards the wire. 'At the Guardroom, sir. Main gate, sir. Major Bragg, sir. He'll either be there or in his other office in the Exec Building, sir.'

Tommy stepped back and guided Molly on to the macadam surface of the road, standing close to her, heads almost touching. 'I want you to secure this site.' He put an arm around her shoulders: fatherly, Suzie told herself. 'Leave one uniform here, Molly. Just for the time being, and for God's sake don't forget about him. I don't want him left out all night on his own. Let's see if we need anyone else, okay?'

She nodded.

'Then you trot along to the main gate and see this Bragg fellow – probably their Provost Marshal, okay? Tell him we're terribly sorry but could he police their side of the wire for a day or two. Be incredibly nice about it. In your hands, right?'

'*You're* not going to talk to him?' Molly Abelard not happy doing her boss's job for a change.

'Not at this stage, heart. No. If I begin nosy-parkering around on the aerodrome they'll have me off fast as fornication. United States territory and all that. I'll do most of my talking to their people either at the Falcon or at the dance tonight.' He gave her a look that signalled duplicity and her part in a conspiracy.

'Right, Chief.' Not altogether convincing.

'Good, I'm taking Suzie back to the Falcon, have a word with Dennis and take a look at the shotgun. See you back there, Moll.'

'I could've done the job with their Provost Marshal,' Suzie griped as she got into the car.

'You forgetting, heart? Forgetting that Golly has a price on your head and that he's out and on the loose?'

She hadn't forgotten, just pushed it out of the way.

A few minutes later, as they left the car and walked up to the Falcon's main door, so a cheeky little blonde came out, hair bouncing against the collar of her thin raincoat.

'I know that girl from somewhere,' Tommy muttered.

'So do I.' Suzie shaking her head, frowning, had a clear picture of the cheeky dimpled face and the spectacles, but couldn't place it. 'Press maybe?' she asked.

'Don't know.'

'That was them,' Lavender said as Queenie slid back into the Austin Seven, patting her blonde wig.

'I know, and I walked right past them without even flashing the buggers.'

Lavender started the car. 'Well?' she queried.

'Yeah, very bleeding well, Lavender. Talked to the daughter of the house, bouncy Beryl. Not over clean, I suspect, but she's not backward in coming forward.'

'They got a spare room?'

'One. One only. Number seventeen and the WDS, the one we want, is in fourteen. I booked seventeen for me and my hubby, Sunday night, name of Mr and Mrs David Powell – that's right, ain't it?'

'Yeah, I've got Identity Cards in that name. You'll probly have to let Golly jump you, Queenie.'

'My pleasure. He's a creepy little beggar, but I like weirdoes.'

181

Fourteen

Tommy talked with Dennis Free for over half-an-hour, having a good look at the double-barrelled Purdey shotgun: twelve-bore with live cartridges in the breech and a lot of mud over the barrels and stock.

'You'll not get any prints off this,' he told Dennis, who nodded in agreement because he'd said the same thing to Molly when they fished it out of the ditch.

'You reckon he loaded it again before he left Knights Cottage?'

'Makes sense,' Livermore nodded. 'In case he met something hostile on his way to the base, or to wherever he was going to be picked up – assuming it's a male.'

'And assuming he was being picked up.'

'Naturally.'

Dennis said he couldn't see a female putting the weapon to anyone else's head and letting them have both barrels.

'You can't?' Tommy coughed. 'Not if it's another woman? Women can be bloody cruel, Dennis. I mean in the right circumstances I could see Molly doing that.'

'Molly's different.'

'Oh, yes. Oh, well,' a kind of chant, amusing and musical if you liked plainsong. 'The Doc's taking this down to Hendon, I gather.'

'Soon as I've done with it, Chief. We any further forward?'

'Straws in the wind, Dennis. I may have to go away for a couple of days. See you later.'

Detective Chief Superintendent the Honourable Thomas

182

Livermore made sure Peter Prime, with a spare revolver hidden under his jacket, round the back, stuck in his waistband out of sight, sat outside Suzie's door, number 14, and accompanied her wherever she wanted to go. Even stood outside the Ladies while she had a comforting pee.

In the meantime, Tommy went back to his room and slaved away over a hot telephone, speaking to old chums, school friends, fellows now at the Home Office and the Foreign Office: one old mate who was in the government and another who was the overlord of travel. It was known as the old boy network and it worked very well for someone like Tommy who had chums in high places because of his education and the fact that he was first son of the Earl and Countess of Kingscote. Didn't approve of it really, but it came in handy at a time like this. Last of all he called Freddy Ascoli, who had got back to Montpelier Square and grumbled about the journey, but finally co-operated with everything Tommy asked him, which, on the surface, was nothing of great moment.

He finally put the telephone down and it rang immediately: the Deputy Assistant Commissioner (Crime) said, 'Tommy, you've been stirring up a mare's nest. The Commissioner's been bending my ear something horrible. You're in hot water.'

'Arthur, nice to hear from you. So what's new?'

'There's been a complaint against you by Detective Chief Inspector Tait. CID King's Lynn.'

'Yes, I know what he is, a right grumble. He's the one in trouble.'

'He admits he made some errors in his part of your current investigation, Tommy. But he's claiming that you tore a strip off him in front of your DS. He seems to think it's worse because your DS is a woman.'

'Silly sod.'

'I should think you're guilty as charged old boy. Tait appears to have rung Harold Brew in Norwich. Brew knows what's what. Told him to ring the Commissioner.'

'Didn't want to clash with me.'

'Probably not, but consider yourself in the old boiling water.'

'With a dash of hot lemon-scented oil. That it? That the end?'

'I spoke on your behalf, Tommy. Think I've kept them off your back for the time being. You know part of the trouble is that all these people're older than you. They see you in an exalted position and say to themselves, Tommy bloody Livermore? How's he got up there, top of the ladder? Must be his pa.'

'Well, you tell them, old sport. Clean living, pure mind and a healthy body.'

'I did.'

'Good of you, Arthur.'

'They're still rolling around with mirth.'

'Glad you called, Arthur, I wanted a word: favour actually.'

'Yes?' Drawn out, a tincture of suspicion. The Deputy Assistant Commissioner was wary of Tommy asking for favours, like Greeks bearing gifts.

'I have to go away for a couple of days.'

'Somewhere nice?'

Tommy told him and he squawked, 'Jesus Christ, Tom?'

'It's okay, I've cleared it all down the line.'

'Except with me.'

'Technicality, old love. Now, you know that bastard Golly Goldfinch is on the run.'

'Uh-huh.'

'While I'm away I need four extra bods.'

'What the hell for, Tom?'

'Keep an eye on my DS. Babysit her in London.'

'Can't she stay up there, Norfolk? You've got almost your whole team with you. Can't they . . . ?'

'No. Up here's dangerous. I'd say Goldfinch is still around up here. In fact . . .' Tommy realized who the blonde could be: the perky little blonde whom they'd spotted coming out of the Falcon. Moment of truth. Maybe it was her, on the wanted list, photo and all. But the hair was different and she wasn't as solid as he remembered her: only seen her the once in an ID parade. Then she was definitely blocky, big shoulders; but people change, maybe she'd won back the trim figure. Possibly? Was it? Uncertain.

'Can do, Arthur?' he asked.

'I suppose. We're hard stretched, but yes, okay.'

'Thanks old boy, I'll be in touch. I'm bringing her up Sunday, so if you can let me know who's going to do it I'll see them at Suzie's flat in Upper St Martin's around ten in the morning. You've got her address.'

'Bags of time then,' said the Deputy Assistant Commissioner, sounding uncertain and quite twitchy.

'Good show.' Tommy signed off.

One more call, this time to the recently promoted Shirley Cox, on the Reserve Squad and at the Yard, old friend of Suzie's from Camford days. Shirley was more than delighted when he told her she'd be staying with Suzie for a few days the following week. 'Have lots of girlish chats, eh?'

Now, he thought, one more interview tonight then he could speak to the girls and boys, tell 'em what was what, so he went in search of Molly, who, by then, had returned from the hedging and ditching operation.

'How'd it go then, Moll? How'd it go with the Provost Marshal?'

'He was a trifle miffed, Chief. Didn't like the idea of his blokes being out twenty-four hours a day looking after the hole in the fence for the foreseeable.'

'Shouldn't have joined, heart.'

'Agreed in the end. No problem.'

'Then you must've used your feminine wiles and convinced him of the necessity of keeping an eye on the spot.'

'I pointed out that we were allies in a great cause for the common good of the world. Quite Churchillian I got, Chief.'

185

She gave a winning smile. 'I also promised him a dance tonight.'

'Ah, thought you'd have asked young Trevor Skeggs to the hop, heart.'

'He was only a one-day stand, Chief. Not for the duration. Have to think about the morale of people like Brian. Trevor's only for practice.'

'Quite the little hussy.'

True praise, she thought, then Tommy said:

'Well done, Moll. Now, I want to see that local PC. What's his name, Titcombe?'

'Call him Wally and he'll be your friend for life.'

'Thought he was causing you little problems, horning in on the cerebral detective work.'

'You have to know how to handle him, Chief.'

'And how's that?'

'With a chair and a whip, sir.'

'Show him who's boss, eh?'

'Don't think you'll have any trouble, Chief. When do you want him?'

'Yesterday. Keep everyone close, Moll, I'll want to talk to the whole team after I've finished with Titcombe.'

Walter Titcombe seemed to fill the whole of Tommy's bedroom: in an enclosed space PC 478 could be intimidating what with his height, the broad shoulders, florid face and bellicose moustache with the spiked waxed ends, take your eye out if you weren't careful.

'Sit down, Wally, nice to see you,' Tommy at his most languid, which made Suzie and Molly, sit up. Languid equalled dangerous: they knew that.

'Thank you, sir. I will, sir.' Gruff voice, part military, part Three Nuns Tobacco.

'Smoke if you like.'

'Well, I do, sir, but I'll wait if I may. Smoke a pipe and it soon builds up.'

'Low cloud base, eh?' Pause to collect his thoughts. 'Wally, old thing, need to pick your brains. If you want local knowledge, you go to the local man, the one they talk to.' A bit loud, playing the silly ass.

'Pick away, sir.' A shade too simple; a little too intimate.

'The late Max Ascoli's brother, Wally?'

Blank. He was very good, Tommy considered, not even a blink deep in the eyes: no shift behind the pupils. 'The brother, sir?'

'That's what I said, Wally. Max Ascoli's brother, Phillip, or Pip as he is known.'

'Right, Mr Livermore, sir.'

'What comes first, Wally, in your book, eh? Your vocation as a police officer, or some promise you made to a local gent now departed this life?' Tommy was flying blind, guessing, pinning the tail on the donkey, as he'd describe it.

'Don't follow you, sir.'

'No?' A further pause, as though he was allowing the sand to resettle on the bottom of a rock pool. 'There's a strong rumour in the village that Max Ascoli had a brother; that the brother was a shade touched. They say that in 1938 Mr Max brought this brother, known as Pip to the family, to Taddmarten. To Knights Cottage. You know about that story?'

'Yes, sir. Right enough. Village were agog. Heard the story many times. Made no comment, sir.'

'And, as guardian of the law, you'd make a point of following up on the story. Yes?'

'Yes, sir. To ease my mind if nothing else.'

'And what did you find? Did you ease your mind?' Like pulling teeth, he thought.

'This would be in the autumn of '38, sir?'

'It would. Early September.'

'Yes. Well, Mr Ascoli had been on holiday, sir. All of August, with Mrs Ascoli and young Paul – little lad he were then. They'd been in France, then Italy, I was told. Mrs Axton, who does for them, said she'd had a card. Always good like that, sir. Always sent cards to them as worked for them.'

John Gardner

'And you got a card. Wally?'

'I did, sir. But it was from Switzerland. Place called Thun.' He pronounced it sounding the 'Th'. Sun. 'I was glad of that; glad they didn't send it from France. Don't like the French, sir.'

'Oh?'

'Nineteen hundred and seventeen, sir. I and a party of men had just captured a German officer. Near Cambrais I think it was. We was standing away from him, he wasn't going to run anywhere. Glad to be captured by the look of him. Then a young French officer rode up, horseback. Saw the Jerry, took out his pistol and shot him. Bang, like that, no hesitation, took the top of his head off. Never liked the French after that.'

Get him back on track before he gives us the complete war memoirs. 'And when they returned from the holiday, the Ascolis?'

'I have to be careful here, Mr Livermore. Why I've been hesitant so far.'

'They had someone with them?' Tommy prompted.

'They did, sir. Stayed some two, maybe three weeks.'

'A guest?'

'A guest, sir. Yes.'

'You meet this guest?'

'I did, sir. And that's a problem because Mr Max introduced me to him, and it was his words that cause the trouble. I met them out for a walk. They were looking round the church, came out into the graveyard and I was wheeling my bicycle down Church Walk. Lovely afternoon. Real early autumn afternoon, trees just turning. That big chestnut at the corner of the churchyard looked a picture. Mr Ascoli hailed me. Introduced me.'

'So?'

'He said, "This is our village bobby. Walter – always called me Walter – this is my friend, Pip."'

'He called him Pip?'

188

'He did, sir. Plain as day. "My *friend*, Pip," he said. Then he said, "Phillip."'

'He refer to him as his brother?'

'No, quite the opposite. He said, conversationally like, "I got a brother the same name: Phillip. And we call *him* Pip as well."'

'So, he was denying that this friend was his brother?'

'I didn't believe he was the brother, sir, no. There was talk that his brother was . . . well not quite right in the head.'

'You ever see this friend again?'

'I did, sir, yes.'

'When was that, Walter?'

'I saw him several times in 1940. Thought he'd come down to stay with the Ascolis. I think he was down again last year. In the summer, and I saw him four or five weeks ago.'

'You spoke to him?'

'Always, sir. Give him a little salute, like I do to all the gentry in the village.'

'He walking out alone?'

'No. No, he always had someone with him. Mrs Ascoli, or Master Paul. Two or three times I saw him again with Mr Max.'

'And how did he look to you, Walter?'

'Meaning what, sir?'

'Meaning how did he look?'

'To be honest, sir, he always seemed a little dazed to me.'

'Dazed?'

'Dazed, sir, yes. I've seen that look in men coming back on leave from the trenches in the last show, sir.'

'Dazed?' Tommy repeated.

'Sort of not quite believing where he was. Like he'd just woken up.'

'And this Pip, you really didn't think it was his brother?'

'No, sir. Not for a minute. Beautiful gentleman, Mr Ascoli. Terrible thing this, terrible.'

'Yes, it is terrible. Walter, Sergeant Abelard here has taken down all that's been said. We'll have it typed up and I'll have to ask you to sign it. We may have to call on you as a witness, if we ever catch the man who did this dreadful thing.'

'I understand, sir. Be glad to be of help.'

'Anyone else see this friend, Pip? Anyone speak to you about him?'

Titcombe gave a ponderous slow nod. 'Numerous people, sir. Many said he must be the brother. Indeed I recall old Bill Treacher asking me, "Is that the Ascoli brother then, Walter? The one they say's a loony?" I give 'em short shrift. Never believed Mr Ascoli could have a brother not quite right. Too nice a gentleman for that to run in the family. Now, Mrs Ascoli could be a bit sharp, a bit acid at times. But there I mustn't speak ill of the dead.'

'Of course not, Walter. Thank you very much.' The hand went out, languorous arm, raised slightly to grip Walter Titcombe's hand. Firm grip as the police constable stood and came to attention in front of his superior.

'Well?' Tommy asked, looking at his two female sergeants once Titcombe had left the room.

'Loyal, faithful,' Suzie said.

'True, salt of the earth,' added Molly.

'But thick as a plank,' Tommy didn't smile. 'Regimented. Only believes what fits, and always believes a senior officer, like Max Ascoli.'

Suzie heard Freddy's words again. *You'd have Max's murderer if Pip was out and about in this country. No doubt about it.* 'You think . . . ?' she began.

'Don't know what to think, heart. But we're going to find out. If it turns out that the guest *was* Max's brother then a great deal's solved, including the reason Paula and Thetis have gone off, lying low.'

'If they have gone off, sir. We don't really know.' Suzie placating.

Tommy was silent, gazing into the middle distance, not looking at Suzie. Not acknowledging what she'd suggested.

'Get the boys and girls together, Molly,' he said finally, stood up and walked over to the window, looked down on the deepening evening shadows. He sighed, and Suzie looked at him with a sudden nervousness.

Then Tommy Livermore quoted Tennyson, learned in fear at his brutal public school:

> 'Or when the moon was overhead,
> Came two young lovers lately wed;
> "I am half sick of shadows," said
> The Lady of Shalott.'

And it was a while before Suzie understood his indigo mood.

With the whole team assembled, Tommy spoke for around half an hour, there, behind locked doors in the privacy of his room.

'Sarn't Mountford and myself have to be away for a couple or three days,' he told them. 'Just tying up loose ends, dotting *i*'s crossing *t*'s. Going through what we've got already. You've just about wrapped up the crime scene, so I'd like you to get on with a door-to-door here in the village. Try to see most people. I want to know what they thought of the Ascoli family here in Taddmarten; I want to know any rumours about them; I want to know how they were perceived here, liked or disliked.

'You should know that there was a rumour, circulating here in the autumn of '38, and also I think in '39 and '40, that Max Ascoli's deranged brother was here, staying at Knights Cottage. I have had one trained police officer's statement to the effect that it wasn't Mr Ascoli's brother but an old friend of the family, coincidentally of the same name as the brother – Phillip or Pip.

'You should realize that Mr Ascoli had a brother by that name, and the brother was certainly dangerously deranged. In fact another member of the Ascoli family has indicated

191

that if Pip Ascoli was around we shouldn't have to search very far for the murderer.'

He filled them in on the question of Paula Palmer and Thetis Ascoli, cleared up several other outstanding matters and answered questions. Finally he came to the form for tonight's dance at the aerodrome:

'I want you all to be there. I want you to keep your ears open, and stay off the booze if there is any. Listen to the chatter, file away any gossip – there'll be locals there, local women possibly, and one or two other civilians. There will be some of our WAAFs around, and some of the Raff personnel as well. Watch your backs, do your jobs and I'll be seeing you back here when I return.

'Sarn't Mountford and I'll be off straight after the dance, Brian. Okay?'

'Means definitely no booze, Chief.' Brian happy that he would be with Molly at the dance.

'Okay. Any more questions?'

When they were alone, Suzie asked him where they were going.

'Didn't I tell you, heart?' All forgetful, innocent and distracted.

'No, you didn't, heart,' with bite and a knowing that came from their long relationship. He stayed silent, absorbed in something else.

'Tommy?' she prompted.

'Heart, listen to me.' He stood before her, both hands on her shoulders, gazing down with his look-at-me expression. 'You're not to breathe this to a living soul, Suzie. Understand?'

'When have I ever broken your rules, Tommy?'

'This is a bit different. So promise.'

'I promise.' Wagging her head from side to side, like a small child.

'You're going back to the flat and you'll stay put, okay?'

'Yes.'

'You'll have company. Shirley Cox.'

She gave a little squeal of delight.

'Shirley Cox and a couple of hired guns from the Yard. Two trained officers – well four actually doing twelve on and twelve off. Don't want any nasty surprises.'

'Tommy, you're not setting me up again?'

'No. No, I'm not setting you up. Not for Golly or anybody else. But I won't be there for three – maybe four – days. Okay?'

'Where'll you be?'

'Flogging peasants,' which was their euphemism for dealing with family business at Kingscote Grange.

'So we can talk on the telephone? Keep in touch?'

'Not this time, heart. No.' The Oracle had spoken and that was that. When Tommy laid down this kind of rule, she knew it was serious.

'Oh, Tommy,' she hugged him tight. 'Whatever it is, be careful.'

'It's nothing dangerous, heart. In fact it's dull and routine, but I'll be extra specially careful. Never fear.'

Suzie felt that they were starting some new phase and that worried her. She couldn't say why, but she felt that something unpleasant lurked out in the shadows that Tommy had alluded to.

Fifteen

Tommy had told Molly to go into Suzie's room, share with her for the evening, get dressed together for the dinner party with the Station Commander, and the dance afterwards. Three years ago he had made a near fatal mistake, taking his eye off Suzie in a place he thought safe, and Golly Goldfinch had got her. He had been so wrong then; didn't intend to make the same error twice.

So he went round the rest of the squad, spoke to every man and woman, told them again to stay sober if there was booze around, keep their eyes open, and 'Earwig everywhere,' he said. 'An arrest may depend on chatter, gossip or conjecture. Go to it.'

He gave his pistol to Dennis Free – 'It'd spoil the cut of my suit, old boy' – told him to watch Suzie so that he didn't have to do that chore alone. Molly, he knew, was carrying a small SIG-Sauer .22 – called it a peashooter – in a little holster hidden in her waistband. Everyone was briefed and knew what the visit to the aerodrome was about – see how the Yanks reacted to the murders, follow any leads, be nice and friendly but be aware that on one night in the past ten days the crew of *Wild Angel* had been to a dinner party with the victims, in the death house of Knights Cottage.

Satisfied, Tommy went back to his room, showered, shaved and dressed – the grey double-breasted made for him by Huntsman's chief cutter, the white shirt from his shirtmakers in Jermyn Street, his Cambridge college tie. The final product facing him in the mirror was indisputably Dandy Tom, Fleet Street's favourite policeman.

Suzie wore her light blue, the neat little number her mother had bought for her at Fenwicks, during the sales last year; while Molly was turned out in a white pleated full skirt, matching white blouse, over that a silk bolero jacket that went down just far enough to cover the bulge where her pistol rested at the back of her right hip. As well as all her other skills, Molly was a mean needlewoman.

Brian drove them to the requisitioned Victorian house that was the Station Commander's married quarters, a mile east of the aerodrome, arriving on the dot of seven thirty, and there was Tommy's old school chum, Raleigh Ridsdale, a group captain at twenty-eight, DFC and Bar, one of 'the Few' now chained to a desk: tall, spare, rangy-looking man with floppy yellow hair and an Errol Flynn moustache.

'Raleigh, old sport, how goes it?' *Rawley, old sport.* Clasped hands, left hand above the elbow, pumping away, both men grinning, as though they knew things about each other nobody else would ever know. Probably did.

'Tommy, nice to see you. Come in, meet the memsahib.' The memsahib being Sally Ridsdale née Sally Noble, high-born lady, father a knight, mother a great partygiver, known for it, and Sally herself still looking the showgirl she had been when Raleigh met her in London, just before the Blitz in the autumn of terror, 1940. Long legs, elegant: walked, turned and spoke like a dream, swept the new arrivals with a smile each would remember as personal.

Once the introductions were made, Raleigh Ridsdale drew Tommy close and murmured, 'You're sitting next to the Skipper of *Wild Angel*: Captain LeClare. Thought you'd like that.'

'Good of you, Raleigh. Look after my little sergeant over there, the one in the blue, okay?'

'Always could pick 'em, Tommy. Come and meet everyone.'

They went through into a long, pleasant room, sky-blue wallpaper, some nice prints and a large London street scene in oils over the marble mantelpiece, circa 1840 with handsome cabs clopping through driving rain and people hurrying along slick pavements. A large bow window spread across the far wall, leaded lights looking out on to an elegant lawn with trees hunched at the far end.

People circulated, glasses in hand, all the fun of the fair and whatever you wanted to drink. There were introductions, Michael and Bunny something, Raleigh's adjutant, Brian Dicks, a WAAF officer, Squadron Officer Long, 'Lottie for short, ha-ha'. There was a civilian called Kevin, who turned out to be a local bigwig, and his wife, Elsie – wouldn't you know it? – and a couple of Yanks. Ricky LeClare, and Will Truebond, who said, 'Hi ya,' shaking Tommy's hand firmly. Until that moment Tommy had never believed that people actually said, 'Hi ya,' outside of on the silver screen.

Then Sally was beside him, saying Raleigh had often talked about him. 'Don't believe a thing,' Tommy smiled. 'Old Raleigh's an inveterate liar.'

'Oh, I know *that*,' she said with a little moue and a wink. 'Great exaggerator,' she added.

Then Lottie – 'Charlotte actually' – asking how were they getting on with the case, so terrible, those poor people, and the little boy. Tommy was suitably vague. 'One day at a time stuff,' he told her, but they'd get whoever did it, never fear.

'My Waafs're a bit scared,' she said as though she owned all the Waafs in East Anglia. ''Fraid there's a maniac about, coming to get them, bogeyman sort of thing, eh? Ropey do.' She struck Tommy as being somewhat horsey.

'They don't need to be afraid. We think there was an element of revenge in this, probably someone close, don't really know yet, haven't got all the ducks in place. But it'll happen. Nothing to worry your girls.'

Across the room, Suzie tinkled with laughter and Tommy thought what a splendid laugh she had, *ding-ding-di-ding-ding* it went, and as far as Tommy was concerned she could go on chuckling out that laugh for ever. He noticed Raleigh filling up LeClare's glass again, softening him up? He wondered what went on in these men's minds. Did they have problems after the battle? Did they have nightmares about fire and death in the skies? Come to that, did old Raleigh get the horrors when he thought back to those summer days of 1940 when it was a daily fight with the Dorniers and Messerschmidts, or was that past reality now packed away for ever in a memory box where it couldn't hurt?

Then, suddenly, Sally was saying that dinner was served and they all trooped through, Tommy taking Sally while Raleigh squired Suzie and the adjutant led Molly through and they ended up in a slightly cramped dining room where Tommy found himself, as promised, next to LeClare on his right and Sally on his left, Sally muttering not to worry about her because she had Mister Moneybags Kevin, the civvie, next to her, indicating she knew he needed to talk to the Yank.

'You're all cops, I hear.' LeClare opening the bidding.

'Yes indeed. Common or garden cops.'

'What about the girls?'

'Yes, they're cops as well.'

'What do they do? Make the coffee, do the secretarial work?'

'No, actually, they're real cops. In fact the one over there,' nodding towards Molly, 'she's a specialist in unarmed combat, as they now call it. She's also a crack shot. Specialist sort of thing.'

'Gee,' said LeClare, not believing a word of it.

'But what about you, Captain?'

'Call me Ricky.'

'What about you, then, Ricky?'

'What about me?' not aggressive. LeClare was a tall, lean, muscular man, tanned, pleasant round open face, salt-and-pepper hair, verging on gold streaks, and a five-mile stare, used to sweeping the air around him.

'You fly those damned great Fortresses, Raleigh Ridsdale tells me.'

'Somebody has to do it.'

'Fly them across Europe, bomb the Nazis?'

'All the time, sir.' Pause. 'No, that's a bit of what your Raff boys call a line shoot. We've actually bombed occupied Europe twice. That's it.'

'Not to be sneezed at. Makes my job look a little humdrum.'

An RAF steward and two Waafs in white jackets served a clear brown soup and LeClare asked if this was a speciality.

'Probably what's called Brown Windsor. Supposed to be a favourite with royalty.'

'Yeah?' Impressed that he was drinking soup that maybe was served regularly to George VI and Queen Elizabeth. 'You're real lucky having a royal family. I hear they were a great help during the Blitz, when it got real bad.'

'Well, they didn't actually take to the skies, or man the guns . . .'

'No, but they helped morale.'

'Not as much as you do with those damned great Fortresses. They difficult to fly?'

'They have their little idiosyncrasies like any airplane, little ways. But they're pretty straightforward. We thought they were impregnable but . . .'

'And they're not?'

'I guess not,' and he was off, told the story of little Tim Ruby getting killed, and coming home again minus two of his crew and a third badly shot up, then wrecking the airplane. Not bragging but getting it all out of his head.

'I'm sorry about that.' Tommy put on his quiet face, relaxed, interested, and as they removed the soup plates he waited as the steward placed the rare beef before him. 'Somehow it looks as though Raleigh has captured one of our British delicacies. Roast beef and Yorkshire pudding. How d'you manage that?' he asked Sally.

'We dig and delve, like the seven dwarfs,' she smiled, then turned back to Kevin the civilian.

To Rick LeClare Tommy said, 'Someone, I forget who, told me you knew the family who were murdered in the village – oh, I remember who it was. Young girl, the late Max Ascoli's illegitimate daughter, Thetis: she told me.'

It felt as though a small charge of electricity passed from LeClare to himself: a kind of instant acknowledgement, a stiffening of muscles, a small shock that told him the American captain was uncomfortable with the facts, knew something about the Ascoli family and didn't want to talk about it.

Queenie MacSweeney's besetting fault was that she would often take action without thinking of the consequences; so it was on the night of the dance at Taddmarten aerodrome. That afternoon she got to know Golly Goldfinch, and, for Queenie, getting to know a man – even one so mentally and physically deformed as Golly – generally meant taking her little drawers down and letting the male have his wicked way with her. No getting away from it, old Queenie MacSweeney liked to be schtupped regularly and often, and it didn't really matter if the man was a sixty-year-old horny letch or a deformed cretin like Golly or any variation in between.

There was danger about Golly Goldfinch, and that added an extra frisson to the pleasure. She didn't stop to think about it, but it was an edge that could possibly be fatal. The only thing against Golly and a bit of the yo-ho-ho was that, because of his distorted mouth he had a tendency to slaver. Apart from that, they had managed a pleasant afternoon and she enjoyed teasing him and hearing his strange breathy laugh when he got excited.

So when the doorbell rang at half-past six she told him to stay where he was. 'Just in case it's one of Lavender's regulars.' Golly understood about Lavender's regulars because he had worked with her when she had clients up to the rooms off Rupert Street in Soho, London. He had taken care of some of those regulars himself, ones she didn't like, and those men never came to see her again.

If it was a regular, Queenie reckoned she would have time for a nice bath. Lavender had a washbasin in her room, so that would be okay.

It turned out to be Ed, the Yank officer from Bury St Edmunds – a major – the one who'd brought the ham, and he was a looker: dark, what they called saturnine – mysterious – which brought a little flip to Queenie's loins.

'You know Queenie?' Lavender asked him, giving him a little kiss, peck on the cheek.

'Gee, no. I've heard a lot about you, Queenie. Real nice to meet you.'

Queenie simpered a bit, but she knew men and could sense that he didn't really mean it.

'Lavender,' he said, turning away from Queenie in a manner she thought quite rude. 'Look, honey, I've got a jeep downstairs all gassed up and ready to go, parked right in front of the house. I got some tickets see, invitations to the dance out at the Long Taddmarten base. Wondered if you'd like to step over there with me.' He leaned towards her, on the balls of his feet. 'And Queenie of course. She's welcome as well.'

Too late, Queenie thought. Wouldn't come if he got down on his knees and begged.

'Nice of you, Ed,' Lavender said. 'I'll have to get ready though. Yes, I'd love to come with you, but you'll have to wait a half-hour or so while I change.' Lavender giving a look at Queenie that said, okay, maybe it'll come in useful.

'You get ready then, honey. And what about Queenie?'

'Oh, I couldn't. Not tonight, Ed. I'm meeting someone, later.' Very firm.

'Well, in case you change your mind you can bring him along, if you get transport.' And he handed her two invitation tickets to the dance.

Immediately, Queenie, being Queenie, began to have the stirrings of an idea.

Lavender said did he mind if she dressed up and changed how she looked and Ed seemed bemused and asked what she meant, changed how she looked?

'I've a friend in the theatre in London. Get's me these proper professional wigs. Changes your appearance.'

'Bet it still makes you look sexy.'

And it did. When she came out in her little grey dress, with the long pleats that made the skirt rise and fall as she twirled – gave onlookers a peek at the bridge – she looked quite different to the Lavender who'd gone into the room. Neater figure, much shorter girl without heels, myopic, with the spectacles and ravishing deep dark-red hair, almost aubergine colour, sweeping back, making waves against her shoulders.

'Gee,' Ed said. Then again, 'Hey, Lavender, you look a million dollars.'

'Not Lavender, Ed. Not tonight. Tonight I'm Daphne, right?'

'Daphne? Okay, so you're Daphne.'

'Good. Don't forget it, sweetheart.'

When they had gone, Queenie went through to Golly, woke him up. 'Come on sleepy head, how d'you fancy a ride in the car, go on out to that 'drome at Long Taddmarten, go to the dance?' It was a typical Queenie cock-up, really believed it was a good idea. Idiot.

'I can't go to no dance, Queenie. Get recognized straight off. They'd have me quicker'n a fart in a box.'

'I didn't mean you to come into the dance, Golly. I mean you could hide in the car, get into the base and we might have a wander round. Everyone'll be at the dance. There'll be a lot of empty rooms. People leave stuff lying around in empty rooms. Might make ourselves a bob or two, have a root round the aerodrome. How about it?'

Golly started to chuckle, the breathless laugh. 'Yeah,' he

201

said. 'Yeah, Queenie, better'n a kick in the arse wi' a frozen foot.' And he began to laugh and laugh, getting out of control, so Queenie did what Lavender had told her, gave him a little slap and shouted at him.

Golly stopped laughing, stood crouched in the middle of the room, breathing heavily, eyes going from side to side, this way and that as if looking for someone out to get him, creep in the room and kill him.

'Come on, Golly,' Queenie smiled at him. 'Let me get ready, change, and you put on those plimsolls Lavender got for you and we can go out.'

'I watch you get changed, Queenie?'

'Course you can, you little devil. But you mustn't touch.'

'Yeah. Right.' Golly began to laugh again.

'Was it you, Ricky, who knew the late Ascoli family?' Tommy tackled his beef, which was not as tender as he would've liked, though the Yorkshire pudding was a treat: great drowned in gravy and covered in mustard.

'Yes.' Ricky LeClare didn't meet his eye, kept his head down, refused the horseradish, which was probably wise of him. 'Sure, yes. I met them. Had the whole of my crew in to dinner. Great party. Nice people.' Somehow didn't ring true coming from him.

'The Ascolis simply invited you, just out of the blue, eh?'

'No, well, no. I knew Jenny Ascoli before. When she was still Virginia Anstead.'

'Really?' Surprised, as though he had no idea until Ricky told him. And how did you know she was here, married to a famous legal eagle?'

'Well, we kinda kept in touch over the years. Leastways *she* kept in touch. Little letters followed me round and around wherever I went. See, I went with her for a while, when we were both at the University of Virginia. U.Va. Charlottesville. Her daddy approved of me.'

'Really? And you went to see her for old time's sake?'

Ricky laughed, a deep satisfying laugh. 'No, I went to see if she'd changed at all. You see, when I knew her, Virginia Anstead was just about the most unpleasant woman I've ever known.'

In spite of himself, Tommy repeated the 'Really?' response yet again. 'And had she changed?' he added.

'Hardly. If anything, I guess Jenny Ascoli was even more unpleasant than the girl I knew as Virginia Anstead, which is saying quite something.'

'What was so nasty about her? I'm asking because I've only heard good things. The rest of the Ascoli family seem to think she was the thing Max needed most in his life.'

'Sure.' *Shore.* 'That was the impression she liked to give, the façade if you will. The whole picture that the sun shined out of where the sun don't shine, if you know what I mean. I'd imagine the family thought she was God's gift. But underneath she was a conniving, manipulative, two-faced bitch of a woman who must have been running poor Max Ascoli ragged.' He paused for a moment, then shook his head. 'Shouldn't really talk like that, should I? Shouldn't speak ill of the dead, and she's not yet buried. I'm sorry.'

Tommy just stopped himself from adding yet another 'Really?' 'Oh, one can't . . . and you saw this from the minute you met her again?'

'When I met her again . . .' Rick had cut up all his meat, the vegetables and the Yorkshire pudding. Now he was quickly forking the food into his mouth, as if he'd been brought up in a family who only allowed you the minimum amount of time to consume a meal. 'When I met her again she was alone – Max was in London during the week and young Paul was staying with some school friend. I called on her and she could hardly wait for me to get into the house before telling me how she'd landed a real chump of a guy, only thought about his work, brilliant at that. Said he always put his position in society first, which in a way suited her because she couldn't really bear him.

'She wanted to take Max for most of what he had in the way of money: why she'd married him in the first place, she said. Quite open about it to me. Told me she had been on the verge of taking him and getting out when the war came. Said she'd never wanted children, certainly never wanted to be married to a stuffed shirt like Max. Her words. On the other hand he'd given her some standing in London, and now, locally. She liked being a queen bee who could despise the man who brought her a pleasant lifestyle.'

'How about when you met her with his whole family?' He remembered Willoughby Sands – *Happy as a sandgirl. Loved it, couldn't get enough – of being a legal wife that is. Brilliant, great organizer, splendid hostess, the whole magic thing. Looked like a permanent honeymoon from where I was sitting.*

'Embarrassing.' LeClare nodded to himself as though remembering certain incidents. 'Very embarrassing. She'd make snide remarks, put him down in public – well, round the dinner table she did. My crew commented on it after we'd had the dinner party. She said things like, "My husband's too busy keeping criminals out of prison to be bothered with things down here."'

'It doesn't sound much, I know, but it was constant – "Any fool can stand up in court with a silly wig on his head and argue some stupid case for five minutes at a time. Not as if it's arduous." Lots of remarks like that. It was constant. She never let up and I know about being on the receiving end of that kind of thing, because I've been there.'

'She ever get violent?' Tommy knew well enough how a barrage of snide, hurtful remarks could wear down even the most placid man. He'd seen it before. Knew it could drive people to kill.

'The violence was in the way she went about talking at him. And she could switch the moods off if she felt she should impress others.'

'I meant physical violence.'

'She was much too clever for that, sir. Listen, when I first met her I thought she was the most lovely creature in the world. She had that knack of making you feel you were at the centre of her life, the one person who could give her everything she most needed: and she was able to convince everyone around you that your relationship was unique. It was only after a short time, when you were kinda suckered into this situation that you realized she had another set of values. She was like a spider, pulled you in, gave you everything then strangled you. It was weird, but it was also . . . gee, how can I best describe it . . . frightening, I guess. She had the ability to emasculate you, drain away your confidence. Did to me anyhow.'

'And you reckoned she did it to Max Ascoli?'

'That's what I saw when we had that dinner. Sounds glib now, but I tell ya, she was some unpleasant lady when she got going.'

LeClare told him of the kind of remarks she would use to wrong-foot Max. 'He asked a question and she'd counter with another. Like, if he asked, "Are we having cream with this?" She'd say, "What do we usually have with it, Max?" And she'd go on and on, getting him to make some response: "Come on, Max, tell me what we usually have with this trifle." Or, "What did you see in the kitchen this afternoon?" It was mean remark after mean remark, as though she was exposing a childish side of her husband, or showing her husband as an elderly man starting to become an idiot. He'd say, "I saw cream this afternoon," and she'd make a big thing out of him saying it. You know, "That's right Max. So what d'you think we're going to have with the trifle? What do you really think? Can you make the connection, Max?"'

'I suppose some people'd get a laugh out of that kind of thing.'

'Yeah? They'd think it was cute? It wasn't cute, sir. This was downright unpleasant.'

The stewards were now bringing the pudding, a kind of blancmange, made from jelly, milk and tinned mandarin oranges, 'God bless the 8th USAAF,' Raleigh said loudly. 'They provided the tinned oranges.'

LeClare seemed to have got his second wind now, starting to give Tommy more illustrations of the way in which Jenny Ascoli crushed Max. 'To be honest, sir, when I heard there had been murder done I thought to myself: He's killed her at last. Something's snapped and he's killed her. Unhappily it wasn't so.'

The man's still obsessed with her, Tommy thought. She had given him the business and sucked out some measure of his courage, leaving him haunted by her former self. What he was hearing added up to one man's preoccupied memories. Aloud he asked how long he had been paired off with the woman at university.

''Bout three months, I guess. One pleasant month, then a couple of months of having my confidence taken apart every day by her.'

'It's a wonder that Max was able to function,' Tommy said. 'They were married for over ten years.'

'Jesus, yes. Life sentence.' LeClare screwed up his face, trying to beat a path into his past.

They were served coffee back in the pleasant drawing room and Tommy sidled over to Suzie, muttering out of the corner of his mouth, like an old lag in the prison exercise yard. 'It would seem that Mrs Ascoli was a prime grade-A bitch.'

'I thought she was the light of Max's world.'

'To some of the outside world, but not deep in the heart of the marriage. Destined for murder, I'm told.'

'Crikey,' Suzie whispered under her breath.

Eventually people began to drift away, making excuses that they should put in an appearance at the dance, and Raleigh eased over, suggested they went over together. 'It'll do no harm for you to be seen with the likes of me, Tommy.'

'Has it come to that?' Tommy said. 'How will they take it, all these civilians with one brass hat?'

* * *

206

The hangar was vast, a great cavern cleared of all but one of its usual inhabitants: at the far end, one B-17 Flying Fortress – *Able Mabel* – stood, its nose pointing towards the dance floor, laid especially for the evening, a large raised dais for the band, who were throbbing their way through 'Chattanooga Cho Cho' to the delight of the dancers. Cigarette smoke hung up in the metal rafters and the couples on the floor gyrated, twisted and stomped their way through the number, spinning, truckin' and jiving, faces serious, concentrated or grinning as they forgot the daily grind, burying themselves in the music that took them away from the hard realities of the war.

Close to where the Station CO's party had entered to shivering salutes from the snowdrops on door duty, a lanky sergeant in shirtsleeves – silver aircrew wings pinned to his left breast – danced with a short, dumpy but very tidy Waaf, who spun away from her partner and back again with a precision that delighted the onlookers. Suzie thought to herself that the girl was like a very neatly wrapped package, her figure folded into her blue uniform to make waist, hips, breasts and legs conform to a definite, and erotic, pattern that was even exaggerated by the music and the way in which she spun backwards and forwards in time to her partner as the brass exploded its brazen chords across the temporary dance hall.

Dennis Free was by her side, reaching out to dance with her and she found herself joining in, not really knowing how to jitterbug or jive but just getting into the rhythm and leaping around, catching Tommy's eye for a second and seeing his eyebrow raise as she strutted by, then twirled and the band shifted the tune, sliding into 'String of Pearls' then 'Kalamazoo'. She was getting it now, being consumed by the music, following her partner as their hands became damp and she was filled with the exhilaration of the moment. I shall remember this until the day I die, she thought: not for Dennis and dancing with him but for everyone, for Tommy's

hoicked eyebrow and amused expression, for the faces of the
GIs, US officers, Waafs and village girls she saw in the
dancing crowd as they whirled past.

Then, out of the smoke, noise and sweat she saw someone
she recognized: someone who she immediately knew did not
want to be recognized. She was twisting towards Dennis and
twirled close to his right-hand side. 'Get me towards the
Chief, Dennis,' she said right into his ear as she went past,
and he nodded, not missing a beat or a step as she kept an
eye on the girl she'd seen coming out of the Falcon the other
night. The girl called Queenie MacSweeney who they knew,
because they'd discussed it, was a friend of the much wanted
Lavender.

Dressed in her best, the pink skirt with all the buttons up
the front that the men adored, even had bets on how high
they could get, Queenie MacSweeney had trotted down to
Newmarket railway station and got the Austin Seven out of
their lock-up. Then she drove back to the house and went up
to the flat, where Golly was trying to choose what to wear
from his small wardrobe. Before the escape, Lavender had
scrounged clothes for him mainly from jumble sales, which
was a game and a half. Shopping at jumble sales was an art,
somewhat like rugby football, because the same types of
women appeared at jumble sales, made an attack on the stalls,
a scrum and dash. Lavender had fought with the best of them
and got a couple of jackets, some trousers and shirts that
would fit him. She'd bought mostly dark clothes, like the
dark-brown plimsolls. 'Black as night,' she'd say to Queenie.
'That's what he'll like so he can blend in with the dark, hide
away out of the moonlight That's what Golly does best.'

So, Queenie got up to the flat and there he was, Golly,
arguing with himself like a small child, which was, of course,
what he really was – a small strong, ruthless child. 'I thought
at first I'd wear this shirt, then I wondered if I should wear
this one, maybe go better with the navy sports coat. Oh,

Queenie. I wish I had my duffel coat here, 'cos the duffel coat kept me nice and warm in the winter.'

'But it's still summer, Golly.'

'I know but I'd be on the safe side if I had my duffel here and now, like I wish I had that pair of boots that Micky Mangle got for me. They was good boots, them.'

'Come on, Golly, make up your mind then we can get going.'

'In the car, Queenie. We going to have a ride in the car?'

'Yes, Golly, and you'll have to keep nice and quiet in the back.'

'Under a rug, Queenie, yes, I know.' His half-daft smile. 'Will I have my wire that Lavender made for me?'

Queenie didn't know the ins and outs of that; didn't know what Golly was capable of with the piano wire with the ends bound up with insulating tape so he'd get a good purchase on it.

She got him dressed in the dark slacks, black shirt and the dark-brown sports coat. 'Now, have you been?' she asked him.

'I don't need to go.'

'I think you do, Golly. You go, just to be on the safe side.' And off he trotted, singing and humming away to himself, leaving out lines, changing words –

> *'I know where I'm going,*
> *And I know who I'll marry.*
> *Some say he's black, but*
> *I say he's horny.*
> *Fairest of them all,*
> *My handsome, winsome Jornny.'*

And the tunelessness of it with those words beat upon her whorled ear and clattered into her brain, making her frightened, not knowing what she feared.

She got him into the back of the car, got him settled down

with the tartan rug that Lavender had got for them – another jumble sale – then he wanted a drink, worse than a two-year-old. She brought down a flagon of Bulmer's and he sucked at it, there in the back of the Austin Seven, under the blanket. So they set off on the longish drive to Taddmarten where she'd have to show one of the tickets she'd got from Ed the Major.

Of course they had to stop on the way, because Golly wanted to get out and have a pee behind a bush by the roadside but they finally made it.

As they came into the village of Long Taddmarten, Queenie slowed down and turned left, off the main road. 'Stay down, Goll,' she said. 'I want to take a look at something.'

She drove very slowly along the narrow road, then went down to a crawl as she approached the house, saw there were no coppers standing on guard outside.

'Quickly, Golly. Take a look at that.' Still dusky light outside, Double British Summertime.

'What?' he raised his head, peeping the wrong way to begin with, then swivelled round. 'What m'y lookin' at then?'

'That's the house, Golly. See, Knights Cottage.'

'What is?'

'The house, there. That's the house where those three people were murdered. The ones being investigated by that lady policeman you're always talking about.'

'She there then?' He raised the upper part of his body and reached towards the door.

'No, there's nobody there now, not at the moment but I expect that's where they come to do their detecting.'

'Ah, right. Yes. Knights Cottage. Ah.'

He stayed looking out while Queenie drove back to the main road, where she made him duck down again under the blanket. 'And lie still, Golly.'

'I am lying still.'

'Just you, ma'am?' the guard at the gate asked her when she stopped.

'Just me, yes. Little me.'

'You won't be alone long, ma'am. Wish I was over to the dance tonight instead of pulling this duty.' And a snowdrop came up behind him and asked if everything was okay, smart in his white helmet and webbing with a big Colt .45 on his hip, showed her which way to go and where to park, on the hardstanding park. 'Not many people've come in cars,' he said, mistrustful.

'I got it, 'cos I work for the US Forces,' glib and word perfect, aware of movement behind her in the car, Golly under the blanket. 'Go around the bases filling in for girls off sick or on a rest period.' Got the lingo off pat. 'Working in the PX and Officers' 'nd NCOs' Clubs.'

'Okay, ma'am. Move right along.'

It was like being in a foreign country, the rows of Quonset huts and the prefab buildings, over in the distance the shape of the big aeroplanes against the moonlight. My, Lavender will be surprised, really surprised to see her. And pleased an' all.

'Golly, keep still.'

'Laughing my head off, Queenie. It's so funny under the blanket,' and behind her the blanket heaved with mirth.

'Now,' she parked between a jeep and a big lorry, put the lights off, killed the engine so that the sound of the band came throbbing out into the night from the hangar. 'I'll go and find Lavender, Golly. You have a look around then come back here in about an hour, eh?' Gave him the spare key so he could get back down under the blanket. 'You be careful, eh Golly.'

'Yeah. Yeah, Queenie, I'll be really careful,' another burst of laughter as he slid out into the night and she was amazed how quickly he managed to disappear into the shadows but remembered that Lavender had told her he was good on his own, had moved around London and not got caught for several days: knew how to hide and, in spite of his deformities, how to get from place to place. 'Has incredible eyesight in the blackout, Queenie.'

All smiles from the snowdrops on the door. 'Evening, ma'am, come to have a bit of fun? Leave your coat with the sergeant over there in the cloakroom.'

She exchanged her coat for a ticket, went in to the little cloakroom and tidied her hair: gave her bodice a little squirt of *4711* she had in her handbag. Thought they had a lot of military police on the door, but a friend had told her how strict the Yanks were about counting girls on and off their bases.

Then, all pretty in her pink dress with the buttons down the front, she walked into the wall of music and the heaving movement of the crowd and, just inside the door, spotted Lavender almost at once, waved to her and began to walk in her direction. Why was Lavender looking so glum? Thought she'd be pleased to see her.

Tommy had just been introduced to the Commander of US Forces, Long Taddmarten, General Pritton, clasping him by the hand when Suzie almost bumped into him, almost sending him flying. 'Over there, Chief. Across the room. The girls, *that* Queenie and probably Lavender as well,' and she was away with Dennis, bobbing and bucking to the sound of 'Tuxedo Junction'.

Tommy followed her gaze and it was as though his eyes had the power of a zoom lens, binoculars. He seemed to see the girls' faces in close-up, like at the cinema, Queenie with the blonde hair falling to her shoulders and the other girl, the one they had searched for, for so long, changed, shorter now with the deep and lustrous red hair. Tommy's brain stripped away the hair and the lipstick, the glasses and the shape, the height and carriage and there was Lavender looking angry and mouthing off at the other girl, Queenie, he thought, Queenie MacSweeney.

'How do I arrest a couple of civilians in your hangar, General?' he asked, calmly, no flap, hardly raising his voice but knowing that time was possibly limited because he had the feeling that Lavender had connected with him, knew what was going on.'

'You don't arrest anyone in my hangar.' The General was a bluff, hearty man who, one thought, would have been happier on a horse, somewhere out west, riding the range. 'What we do is, *we* arrest them, then we have a parlay about if you can take 'em off the base, 'cos this is United States territory, sir. What you want 'em for anyway?'

'Murder.' Tommy still didn't raise his voice. 'They killed a nurse/warder from an institution for the criminally insane.'

'You betchum.' The General raised his voice. 'Major Bragg?'

'Sir?' The Provost Marshal, controlled, but only just.

'Do what this gentleman requires. He's a police officer.'

'Sir.'

And that's when it stopped being low-key because the band finished playing and the dancers began to applaud just as Dennis and Suzie arrived in front of Queenie and Lavender, Suzie stepping close to Lavender and starting to say that she was arresting her: '. . . Rosemary Lattimer . . . I arrest you in the name . . .' and Major Bragg's whistle screamed out across the building, summoning four big snowdrops just as Lavender was screeching that her name was '. . . Daphne Strange . . . and I won't . . .' while Dennis was closing in on Queenie and Suzie grabbed at Lavender's hair and it all came away in her hand and everything began to get dead dramatic as the snow-drops took over and Tommy was shouting at Suzie and Dennis to stand back.

'Better than the pictures,' Raleigh Ridsdale murmured.

'Now,' Tommy said with a huge smile, more of a grin actu-ally, 'what's Lavender getting so worked up about?'

Sixteen

They took the two girls to the Guard Room, where they were shackled – the whole thing, wrists, ankles and the chain around the waist – and suffered other indignities, put in the cells, refused legal representatives and told they would be formally charged with murder.

It was in the Guard Room that Tommy had the parley with General Pritton and the Provost Marshal, Major Bragg. The parley took longer than anyone expected because Major Bragg was, to put it mildly, a shade hidebound and appeared to resent any proposition that did not follow the strict process laid down by US military law.

These two girls, women, had been arrested on what was technically United States territory; Major Bragg had no charges he would, or could, bring, and it was his view that they should be immediately set free. Tommy gave Molly and Dennis the nod and they slipped out. Tommy then said, 'Okay, let the girls go.'

So they did, escorted them off the premises.

Molly and Dennis arrested them as soon as they stepped through the main gate where everyone had to hang around waiting for Brian and the Doc to bring the cars up while Tommy rang King's Lynn nick to arrange cells and interrogation rooms.

So now, round midnight, with a host of telephone calls made to numbers all over the country, Tommy and Molly sat down opposite Lavender, who still maintained that her name was Daphne Strange and had a blue National Registration

Identity Card – the one all civilians carried – in that name, but registered at a fictitious address in Newmarket.

'I don't know nobody by the name of Adam Arthur Goldfinch, never ever heard of him,' she stated with a coarse brashness, surprising even Tommy who thought she was a more sensible type of criminal who'd see they'd got her bang to rights. 'Should've known,' he said later, 'after all she was the one who programmed Golly to kill. Ruthless little bitch.' He thought to himself. Why had she been the cause of Golly's escape? Must have had a reason. Lavender wasn't the kind of woman who did things just for the hell of it.

'But, Lavender, I know who you are,' Molly Abelard told her. 'We've spoken before, when you were a tom working near Rupert Street, down the Dilly, back in 1940. We also knew you had a house in Camford, Dyers Road, where you lived under the name of Rosemary Lattimer.'

'You're mixing me up with someone else.' Lavender putting up the shutters and flatly denying everything.

'You're saying that you're not Rosemary Lattimer, also known on the street as Lavender, Daphne Strange, Midge Morrison and Old Uncle Tom Cobleigh and all?'

'Corse I am. And who's Tom Cobleigh when he's at home?'

'Man in a song, like Little Sir Echo.' Tommy speaking without a trace of humour.

'So you didn't go tomming out of those rooms we finally raided off Rupert Street.'

'Never.'

'And you didn't keep Golly Goldfinch as your minder?'

'Never. Who's Golly Goldfinch?'

'You're a silly girl, Lavender,' Molly said, looking exceptionally stern.

'Tomorrow, then.' Tommy sighed. 'Tomorrow, we'll have the two other Nurse/Warders from Saxon Hall over to identify you and Queenie as the people who took Golly off in an ambulance, then promptly disappeared into the night. We'll do a couple of line-ups, identity parades . . .'

'They're never going to . . .'

'Recognize you?' Tommy laughed.

'Different wig, a bit of this and that?' Molly still didn't smile. 'Lavender, it's not going to be a problem for us, we've got you trussed up like a Christmas turkey as it is. All we need to know now is which of you stiffed Nurse/Warder Edgehill, because if we don't get the truth about that you'll be going for that nine o'clock walk with Mr Pierrepoint, both of you up the dancers wearing the hemp necktie.'

Almost certainly they'd both be hanged for the murder anyway, but Molly was all for fostering a tiny ray of hope if it helped the case along. Once they'd got Lavender's identity sorted they'd have a pile of serious charges they could bring: charges going back to the days when Lavender was setting Golly Goldfinch loose to kill her selected targets.

In the meantime, in another room in the King's Lynn nick, Suzie Mountford and Dennis Free were questioning Queenie, using shrouded threats and claiming this was a matter of routine, that Lavender had already coughed the lot and it was simply a matter of time before they'd be brought in front of the beak, and the tumbril of justice could start rolling.

But Queenie was as obdurate as Lavender, denying everything, and remaining silent for much of the time, punctuating the questions with surly demands to see her brief, wanted her lawyer.

Then, just after quarter past midnight, DCI Tait went into the interview room being used by Tommy and indicated that he'd like a word in private.

'We've had a bit of a breakthrough from Newmarket, sir.' Very correct with Tommy, not rocking the boat, out here in the corridor.

'What kind of breakthrough?'

'A DI in Newmarket knows the girls, knows where they were living under the assumed names, though he didn't know they were assumed: Midge Morrison and Queenie MacSweeney. They hauled a magistrate out of bed, got a search warrant and just tossed the place. Ashes of Goldfinch all over it. Clothes, some notes, the full moment.'

'Then I can be on my way while the rest of the team go about the investigation.' He explained he had to be away on business concerning the Ascoli murders. 'Off for a few days, I fear, DCI Tait.' Pause. 'Eric.' He turned away with his tongue in his cheek, called him Eric. Then he looked back and caught the sneaky expression of triumph on Tait's face.

'I hear you didn't like the way I spoke to you in front of WDS Mountford.'

'I've put my concerns in writing, sir.'

'Yes, and I've talked with the Assistant Deputy Commissioner, Eric. It's all been dealt with, but I can reopen it again if you like, bring your shortcomings into the daylight.'

'Your decision, sir.'

Right berk, Tommy thought.

'Yes, well we've got to get along for the time being. Need your cooperation, Eric.' He gave his horrible smile. 'Faynites?' he asked, the old grammar-school word for truce.

Tait nodded grudgingly, 'Faynites.'

Tommy flashed his horrible smile. 'Okay, let me put you in the picture. I have to be away for a couple or three days. I'm leaving WDS Abelard in charge – very responsible woman, knows what's what. I'd be grateful if you could uncle her along. She'll need to have a couple of identity parades, establish the two little totties in your cells are in fact the women who got Golly Goldfinch out of Saxon Hall – and killed a Nurse/Warder to boot. At the same time she'll be looking for Goldfinch, and dealing with the murder investigation in Long Taddmarten. Lot on her plate while I'm off attending to other matters.'

There was a longish pause while Eric Tait appeared to be making up his mind whether to cooperate or not. Finally he acquiesced. 'I'll do all I can to assist, sir.' Knew which side his bread was buttered, though still couldn't meet Tommy Livermore's eye.

'Good man. Thank you.' Magnanimous in victory, just like he'd been taught on the playing fields. 'Keep an eye out for Goldfinch as well. He's a scary type. Very scary. You don't want to bump into him alone on a dark night. I know. I've done it.'

Having settled the current problems, Tommy now sought out Molly, who was all for going on and interrogating Lavender yet again, yearning for what she regarded as the good old days, waking Lavender just as she'd got off to sleep, get her disoriented then put her on the rack, thumbscrews, or pieces of rubber hose to inflict pain.

'No can do, Molly,' Tommy told her, then went through what he wanted her to deal with while he was away – a daunting amount on her shoulders.

'Nothing else I can do for you, Chief? Would you like me to go out on a bombing raid with the Yanks perhaps, or mount some kind of commando operation along the French coast? I could always do it in the evening when we've finished inter-rogating the girls, doing the house-to-house in the village and looking for the Ascoli killer, and Golly Goldfinch of course. I mean, you know us, Chief. No problem. Work round the clock.'

'Glad to hear it. Just share the load with the rest of the team, and keep Billy Mulligan informed at the Yard.'

'You'll be calling in though, won't you, Chief?'

''Fraid not, Molly. I'm going to be out of touch. Essential. Good idea if you telephoned Suzie from time to time . . .'

'She's not going with you?'

'No.' Clipped and final.

'Can't you give me a hint . . . ?'

'No. Out of the question. In the fullness of time, Molly. And for heaven's sake keep an eye out for Goldfinch. Good idea to alert the aerodrome, Yanks and the Raff.' A flash of concern flicked over his face. 'The girls are here, so maybe Goldfinch's here as well.'

* * *

Golly's nerves jangled, fizzed and trembled through him as he lurked in the shadow of one of the Quonset huts across from the hangar where the music had come from, and where Queenie had gone.

He had been away, skulking and scouting in the dark, came back in around twenty minutes to a spot close to where they'd parked the car: lots of ideas for devilment, some for theft, a lot concerning illegal entry. Then came the commotion and he was like a man suddenly rolled over by an attack on the nervous system, confidence and amusement sucked from his soul, control removed from his body.

He could feel the strings under his skin, deep in his flesh, strands being stretched to breaking point, pains in his head and the sense that he was going to explode. He was being wrenched apart and the madness seethed in his bones, through his arteries and veins, his whole body hostage to howls of agony. He hadn't taken his medicine for almost three whole days now, so the calmness had left him: waiting for the voices to return telling him what to do, who to attack.

He had heard the hubbub from inside the hangar, wondered if it was real, the loud music stopping, petering out, ragged, the shouting and the doors opening and, in the sudden shaft of light from inside, he'd heard and seen Lavender and Queenie, heard the yelling, and for a brief second, saw the lady policeman caught with them in the quick streak of light. More screaming and the shuffling sound of feet as they were all marched off. He began to be concerned and anxious because all this puzzled him, not being certain sure whether this was fantasy inside his head, or reality taking place, here and now.

They'd been hustled off by the police and the soldiers, Lavender and Queenie: his friends, his saviours. What to do? Oh, what to do now? He wanted to weep. It was like his mother dying all over again.

It had been wonderful for a few minutes, hearing the music and jigging away on the grass, in the black shadows: jumping around to the blare of the music: dancing. Then the clamour, the cries and yelps, the girls being led away. Didn't like that, no.

'Shit,' Golly said softly. Then again, 'Shit.'

Slowly, the calm started to flow over him and he knew what to do. He smiled in the darkness, chuckled, took a deep breath and remembered other times when he had been alone and survived: in the dark.

His back against the outer wall of the hut, Golly began to edge towards the rear, glancing up at the windows to make certain this was the one. Inside there was no blackout, no beds or signs of life like there were in the other huts. Across the hardstanding being used as a car park the music started again from within the hangar: 'St James' Infirmary Blues'. Golly knew that, knew the words, whispered them as he moved –

'Went down to St James' Infirmary,
To see my baby there,
Stretched out on a long white table,
So cold, so stark and so bare.'

Giggle, hold back, move. Someone's baby would be laid out on a long white table before he was done with them. Lavender had told him she wanted the lady policeman and the honourable copper, the Thomas Livermore, out of it, 'dropped down a well and left,' she'd said. That was okay. He'd do that, do it for Lavender and he'd begin by having a little sleep in the empty hut.

He tried the door and it opened, creaking a bit. Creaked and opened wide. Golly went in. No light, no blackout and nothing but bare boards on the floor, bit of newspaper spread over it. Didn't mind the smell of damp wood and the scent of emptiness.

He was in a small room that led through another door into the long room that was the larger interior of the hut. He'd stay here, in the little room, curl up in a corner and think about what he would do. He'd be okay because he'd always been okay, 'cept when they'd caught him, but he'd pay them back for that.

Golly curled up in the corner: used to sleeping rough. Before, when they hunted him they'd followed him with soldiers and police, the freezing earth hard as iron, water like a stone, Christmas time and they'd even followed him with aeroplanes. He recalled sleeping in a bitter ditch, and then, when the aeroplanes came, in a hunter's hide. He'd still escaped, walked out, got to London and holed up. He'd do it again, but not so far. He'd get off the aerodrome, find the murder house that Queenie had shown him. He'd get in there somehow and wait. The lady policeman was bound to end up coming there because that's where they were doing their detecting. That's what Queenie had said, so that had to be right.

He didn't remember all of before when he had so cheekily survived, dodging, ducking, diving out of sight. For instance he didn't think about all the people who'd helped him, driven him to London, lodged him safely in an unknown flat, fed him, looked after him. In memory he'd done it all by himself.

He rolled up his jacket, used it as a pillow, slid off into sleep and to the good dreams of when he'd had the power, when he'd crushed the necks, killed with the wire.

It was almost four in the morning when Brian pulled up in front of the Edwardian apartment block in Upper St Martin's Lane and Suzie and Tommy were able to climb out, stretch their legs.

They even invited Brian up to Suzie's flat, have a cup of coffee. Brian was silent as the proverbial, could be trusted but didn't like going too far, never took advantage of knowing things that were secret. 'I'll kip down here, Chief. If it's all the same to you.' Chose to sleep in the car.

'I'll bring coffee down for you, Brian,' Suzie said, voice brighter than she felt.

'No,' Tommy said as he walked her to the door. 'No, Suzie. Once inside you're not moving out again unless it's with me when I'm back. Remember that walking disaster, bloody Goldfinch, and heaven knows what else there is out there. When you get in your flat, you aren't moving until I return, not even for Hitler, right?'

'Right, Chief.' Imitating Molly who she always thought was his biggest fan, nearest to her of course; but then she wasn't really sure about herself any more – where she stood; what she wanted.

In the flat, Tommy, tired and weary, checked every room, looked under the beds and behind curtains, flushing out bogeymen, making sure the windows were still locked, especially the one leading out to the fire escape at the back of the building, their undoing at another time.

Suzie had boiled the kettle by the time he'd finished his sweep, boiled the kettle and found they were almost out of milk. Eventually he carried a cup of cocoa, not coffee, down to Brian, going through all their old safety routines, locking the front door behind him, pausing at each landing, checking out the dark corners in the main lobby.

'What time's Shirley coming?' Suzie asked him. 'In the morning, what time's she coming?'

He said she should be with them around nine and he had to be away by ten. 'There are a couple of other people dropping in as well,' he told her. 'Guys going to be baby minding you.'

'Then come to bed now, Tommy, so that we can at least get four hours' sleep. You don't need to pack me in cotton wool, you know, I'm not *that* fragile.'

'Neither is Goldfinch, heart.'

Golly woke with a start, to a creak and whispering.

'Ricky, you sure, love? We won't get caught, will we?' A girl speaking. Golly didn't move.

'Nobody's gonna come near here, honey, this is okay. We

can't go into my quarters, so come on, through here. I want to be your Romeo again, Juliet.'

Loving couple, Golly thought, saw their shapes in the doorway, getting light outside. So he lay there, not moving as they felt their way through into the main body of the Quonset hut. Don't stir, Golly, he thought. Lie still: and he did, saw them creep, full of giggles, going out of sight now.

They're going to be at it, he thought. They're going to be at it like stoats. Lord, the very idea of it's giving me a touch of the beat.

'Come on, Juliet, baby, this is quite comfortable here. Yeah, that's it, honey.'

'Oooww, Rick, what've you got there? You could poke the fire with that. Ooow.'

'It's your fire I want to stir up, darlin', only your fire. Jesus, Julie, that's good.'

And so on and so forth until they got on with it and were saying, 'Yes . . . Yes . . . Yes!' or 'Oh-Oh-Oh!' down to the short strokes and Golly was getting more excited and thought he could feel the floor swaying, but that was his imagination, because of the bumping noises coming from the other room, and the panting and the great howls of jubilation when they rang the bell at the end. He'd like a bit of that, Golly would.

They were kissing now, lickspittling. He had to hold his mouth closed with his hand, stop himself from laughing out loud.

Then they started to talk.

'I still haven't figured out this money, Julie. You were teaching me, huh?' Little smack of a kiss on her cheek or her lips. Maybe it was the other cheek, lying there with a bare bum, Golly wondered.

''S easy, Ricky. Nothing to it.'

'There ain't no logic to it, your Limey money, hon.'

'One pound, how many shillings?'

'I got that. Twenty of your shillings to the pound.'

'Right, then there's another note.'

'Yeah, five pound note, big white sucker.'

'No, Ricky. Smaller than a pound.'

'Oh, sure, the ten shilling note.'

'That's the one, what else we call it?'

'Ten bob?'

'That's the one. The ten bob note.'

'Other names for a pound, Rick.'

'Sure. A quid?'

'That's it. A quid. A quid or a nicker. How many shillings?'

'To the pound? Twenty. Ten for the ten bob and twenty to the quid.'

'There you are, Rick. Easy. Now, half crowns?'

'Yeah. Half-crown. Two shillings and a half.'

'Two shillings and six pence, Ricky. Two and six, two and a kick, okay?'

'I got that. And two half crowns is five shillings, five bob.'

'Got it. Twenty shillings to the pound and twelve pence to the shilling. Easy, Rick. Ow no, not again, darlin', no, not . . . Oooww, Rick.'

Then they were bumping and humping all over again and Golly was feeling more and more like playing bury the bone, have to find some way. He thought of Queenie and what they'd been up to only a few hours ago. Have to find a way of getting Queenie out from the cops.

They were moving now, the guy, Ricky and his Juliet. Standing up and scraping around.

'Okay, hon?'

'Let me just fasten these fiddly little buttons. I'll be glad when we can get elastic again.'

'Just stick 'em in your pocket.'

'How'm I going to get out, Rick? Everyone else'll be gone by now.'

'Easy, sweetheart. There's a break in the fence, in the wire, the chain-link, about fifty yards behind these huts. Old Allan Bragg the PM . . .'

'What's a PM? Prime Minister?'

224

'Provost Marshal. He's supposed to have a guard on this break. Twenty-four hours, but he doesn't bother. We can slip through there, then I can walk you home and slip back in again.'

'No need for that, darlin'. That takes me out on to the main road, yes?'

'Sure.'

'Only a spit and a stride to Knights Close. I only got to walk through Knights Close, then up to Church Lane and Pheasant's Row and I'm home.'

'No, I'd have to see you home.'

'Don't be bloody silly, Ricky. There'll be nobody about this time in the morning. What is the time, anyway?'

'Quarter after one.'

'Just see me through the gap in the fence, then you go and get some sleep.'

'Well, if you're certain. I'll see you again tomorrow, then on Tuesday unless they suddenly decide to change things and we have to fly. We can go up to London with the whole crew, that's the plan. Have a night in your capital city.'

'That'll be lovely, Ricky, really lovely.'

Then they started up with the mushy talk as they came out into the smaller room where Golly was lying. Keep still now. Hold your breath.

'You do love me, Ricky? Really love me?'

Yuck, Golly thought he'd be sick. Yuck.

'Course I love ya, baby. Course I do. Wanna marry you when this's all over. Take ya back home to the States. What d'ya say.' Yuck-Yuck.

'Ow, Rick.'

Oh shit, thought Golly. Can't be doing with all that kind of gloop.

They were in the doorway again now. In the doorway and canoodling, wrapped up in each other, do it again, probly, Golly thought. Do it standing up in the doorway. Ow heck.

'See, there's just enough light to see the fence. There, see.

There's the gap. Cut it myself. Well, with help from the boys. After that night we had dinner with the Ascolis, when I first saw you, waiting at the table, and couldn't keep my eyes off'uv you. You want me to walk you to the wire?' all the loving sincerity gone now he'd had his fill of her.

'No, I can see it. Duck straight through that. Be home in ten minutes.'

'You sure you don't want me to come with ya?'

'You're flying tomorrow, aren't you, Ricky? You get off to bed now and don't worry 'bout me.'

'Well, if you're sure. Watch out for the Ascoli ghosts, then, Juliet.'

'Ow what you want to say that for, Rick? Ow that's 'orrible.'

'Only kiddin', honey. See ya tomorrow night over the Falcon.'

'Yes, then we can make plans for Tuesday.'

'Sure can. See you then. Take care of the ditch other side of the fence.'

Couldn't get out quick enough. Golly heard him walking away on the little path that ran down past the other huts, crew's quarters he'd reckoned when he was having his root around them, earlier. Last night, he thought, when they were playing the music over in the hangar, when they'd taken Lavender and Queenie away.

He climbed up and took a pace towards the door. They'd left it open, the loving couple. He could see out to the fence and the girl, Juliet, was just climbing through the slit that ran from top to bottom of the chain-link.

Take care of the ditch other side of the fence.

Golly put his hand in his pocket, laid hold of the piece of wire with the taped handles so he could grasp it properly.

I'll have some of that, he thought. Have some of it, then find that house. Began to move fast towards the fence: fast and silent. One thing Golly knew, how to move quickly at night. Specially when there was a nice woman at the other end, tasty.

Seventeen

Suzie and Tommy were hurled out into the new day by the clamour of the telephone, bog-eyed, unsteady and dry-mouthed as they came suddenly up from sleep.

'Ugh?' Suzie said into the instrument, asking who was at the other end.

'It's me. Shirley,' Shirley Cox said into her ear. 'Been ringing your doorbell for the past ten minutes. I'm in the phone box round the corner.'

'Ugh. Oh. Ah?' Holding up her wrist, closing one eye to focus, tell the time. 'Christ!' She'd go to hell for blaspheming like that, Sister Lucy May at the convent had told her many times. 'Christ, Tommy,' putting one hand over the receiver, shaking his shoulder, 'we slept in, Tommy. It's almost half past nine.'

Tommy exploded from the bedclothes, shaking his head and looking bewildered.

'Hello,' Shirley Cox said into Suzie's ear, through the telephone.

Palm over the receiver again she shushed Tommy, mouthing at him, telling him to get in and out of the bathroom bloody fast because Shirley Cox was here.

'She got anyone with her?' he mouthed back.

'Shirley?' too loud and bright, take it down a shade. 'Woops, Shirl, sorry, we – I – slept in. You got anyone with you?'

'Not yet, but they'll be here shortly. Big Larry and Mickey the Fin are on the way, said they'd meet the Chief at your place.' Big Larry was Laurence Manderson who's strength wasn't in his brain, while Mickey the Fin was Michael Farnham, good with the fists and the muscle but not the brightest set of handcuffs. Both were good at obeying orders, thumping and intimidating people.

Suzie could tell that her friend was laughing: Shirley had known every move between Suzie and Tommy, but had to pretend she hadn't a clue because Suzie didn't want Tommy to know the secret was out.

'Yes, the Chief,' Suzie burbled, 'he's only just arrived.' A lot of splashing noises coming from the bathroom. 'I'll be down to let you in quick as I can, Shirl.'

They had been close friends from the day Suzie was posted to the Camford nick in 1940, done a great deal together, been out on the town, got their first glimpse of Dandy Tom Livermore at the same moment and shared the secrets of their lives. In a way, Suzie was responsible for Shirley being invited to join Tommy's famous Reserve Squad, but until now they hadn't worked on a case together since the dangerous days that were the prelude to Golly Goldfinch's arrest.

Suzie put on her thick woolly dressing gown, the one she had used when still at school, blue with darker blue collar and cuffs, frogging on the sleeves, and a thick tasselled cord for a belt. She went through to the kitchen, lit the gas, filled the kettle and put it on, then went down to the front door, forgetting about the security routines.

Shirley stood outside, leaning against one of the stone pillars that were part of the entrance. She wore her grey trench coat, was bare headed and carried a medium-sized suitcase plus a copy of the *News of the World*.

'All human life is here,' she announced with a cheeky grin when Suzie opened the door, then inclined her head back towards the two plainclothes men – Larry and Mickey – who were just getting out of a car drawn up in front of the building.

The Wolseley was still there from the early hours, Brian lifting a hand, turning in his seat, obviously been away for a shave and whatever, acknowledging Suzie who was putting on a welcoming smile for the cops coming to stand guard over her and tell them the Chief had arrived. 'Come on. He's using my bathroom at the moment and he's in one hell of a hurry.'

'Good job we're not,' Big Larry muttered, and Mickey the Fin repeated it. Neither looked ecstatic about their present duties. Baby-minding a WDS wasn't the most stimulating work for them, happier when they were menacing suspects, getting confessions the hard way, just like her former boss at Camford, now in the clink, doing time.

They began the toil up the wide stairs to her flat on the fifth floor. Shirley started to whistle the main *pumpty-pumpty* theme from *The Sorcerer's Apprentice*, '*Dum-dum-dum, dudilly-dum-ti-dum-ti-diddly-dum-ti-dum-ti-diddly*,' and Suzie thought of Mickey Mouse and all the brooms and buckets of water in *Fantasia*. You had to be there but the rhythm took them up the stairs, and there was Tommy making tea in the kitchen.

'Right,' he nodded his greeting, pouring out an earthenware mug of tea for himself, emptying half a week's sugar ration into it. 'I have to go in a minute. Already late. Car waiting?' raising his eyebrows, questioning Suzie with a look.

'Yes,' she nodded back.

'Right, you all know what's going on. Goldfinch is on the loose. I hardly think he's got to London yet, but you never know and it's a safe bet that he wants to finish what he started a couple of years ago. Sergeant Mountford was his target last time and her safety is your concern. You two,' looking at the men. 'You two. One at the back and one at the front. Nobody goes in or out without your say-so. There's food in the kitchen for the ladies.' Tommy had worked some magic with his parents and the cornucopia that was the home farm. Last night Suzie had discovered the cold cupboard stocked with a ham, chops and a small joint of beef, while there were vegetables, eggs and milk in the larder.

'. . . so there's no need for you to leave the flat. Understood?'

They nodded.

'Good. But if anyone *does* have to go out it'll be you, Shirley.'

'Chief,' she acknowledged.

'And if that happens, one of you boys comes and sits with Suzie. Got it? No matter how short a time. I do not want Suzie to be left in this flat by herself.'

'How long you going to be away?' Big Larry asked in his particular brand of verbal shorthand.

'Couple of days. Three at the most. You've got people coming to relieve you?'

'Two of the heavy mob're coming up later. We'll do eight hours on and eight off. Round the clock.'

'Good lads. Sarn't Mountford, with me for a second.'

Suzie followed him into the hall, where there was a small suitcase ready for him – explained what he'd been fiddling about with in the early hours, doing his packing. Tommy picked up the case and took hold of Suzie's arm, leading her outside the door, out of sight. 'Behave yourself,' he said, spun her round and kissed her, muttering, 'Stay safe, heart. Hope to be able to make an intelligent guess about the Ascolis' killer when I get back.' Another quick kiss, little pat on the bum and he was gone, down the stairs, out on to the street and away to Lord knew where.

Suzie was amazed, felt bereft and couldn't go back into the flat straight away: didn't know where he was going or what he was up to, but thought he was probably putting himself at some kind of risk. There were uncalled-for tears in her eyes and her bottom lip trembled. Silly bitch, she said to herself, silently. Come on, Suzie, pull yourself together. Now! And she marched back inside, shut herself in the bathroom for ten minutes, until the lads had gone. Then she went out and talked too loud, laughed a shade shrilly, and that went on for most of the day.

They sat around, caught up on their news, talked about the things that mattered most, like the clothes they couldn't buy because of rationing, the food shortages, and the general drabness of life in wartime London, how bloody tired they were.

'How's your fearless fireman? What's his name, Bernie?' Suzie asked as they prepared lunch. Shirley had been going out with a member of the Auxiliary Fire Service in Camford.

'The way of all flesh,' she shrugged. 'Double-crossed me. Married a barmaid in Maida Vale. Been having a canter round the park with her the whole time he was taking advantage of me.'

'Rotten bugger.' Suzie was quite shocked. 'But you didn't exactly discourage him, Shirl.'

'Not actively, no.'

'What about his friend, Ernie?'

'Oh the one we went out with, you went out with. What happened with him? You played rolling in the hay with Ernie, didn't you?'

'Just a bit of tongue.'

'And the rest.'

'Let him have a little fumble.' Suzie blushed.

'Before Tommy made a woman of you?'

'Something like that.' Suzie thought to herself that Shirley had kept her figure and still looked a bit like Hedy Lamarr.

Molly rang in the afternoon, just after four. 'You okay, Suzie?'

She could tell by Molly's voice that something was wrong. 'I'm fine,' she said. 'Shirley's here and we've nothing to do but wait.'

'Good.'

'What's up, Molly?'

'You remember that girl, Juliet Axton, daughter of Mrs Axton who worked for the Ascolis.'

'Yes,' hesitant, sensing something bad was coming, Molly's voice over the telephone wires like paint stripper: like it was caught in her throat.

'She's dead.'

'Dead?' Shock, immediately knowing who'd killed her.

'Found in Knights Close. Wally Titcombe found her this morning, tucked away among the bushes near the main road.'

'What happened?'

'You sitting down, Suzie?'

'No, but it's . . .'

'She was choked with a piece of wire.'

'Oh, God . . .'

'Yes, it was Golly. No doubt about it. His MO. Everything.'

'Golly's himself again then.'

''Fraid so.'

She had a flashback, a vision quite clear and focused in her head: Molly in her bathroom with a gun, extending it towards a cringing Golly Goldfinch. That was real. Had happened, here in this flat.

PC Walter Titcombe had telephoned Molly from Knights Prospect, corner of Knights Close and the main road, big house set back among trees, bit damp some said because of the tree roots; big buggers those roots, Buster Gregory, local gardener said. Dr and Mrs Habland never complained though – Dr of Philosophy, him, retired now, Doctor of Drink, some said.

Wally Titcombe had gone there straight off – well, the body was half on their property, small glade just in from the road, beautiful this time of year, mossy bank and what Titcombe thought of as greensward – could walk through the trees straight to it off the road. Good place for a bit of how's-yer-father on a soft summer night. Titcombe'd seen the body plainly just lying there as he cycled past on his morning ride round the village. Recognized Juliet straight off, went and roused the Hablands, asked to use their telephone. First rang Mr Tait in King's Lynn, who told him to inform Mr Livermore. Rang the Falcon and found Mr Livermore away, so asked to speak to the senior officer, turned out to be WDS

Abelard, not his favourite woman, didn't really approve of women coppers: against nature, he reckoned.

The first thing Molly Abelard asked was had he touched anything, as if he would. 'I am a trained policeman, Sarn't. Not likely to tamper with a crime scene.'

Molly looked at the body, horrible, head thrown back revealing the deep scar round the neck where wire had bitten in, blood oozing down on to her collar, eyes open; teeth bared, the dreadful grimace. Her fists were clenched and she had obviously fought back. Molly had seen others like this and knew immediately what it meant and who had done it.

Most of the team had also seen Golly's handiwork and this subdued them as they carefully went about their work, looking for clues, combing the grass and putting up a screen so nobody could see the cadaver from the road – local press already there, champing at the bit.

There were no footprints, the ground already too hard for that, and when the doctor arrived he said the victim had almost certainly been killed there, in situ, in the little glade. She'd also almost certainly been sexually molested, but he'd have to take a look when the body came to King's Lynn for the post-mortem. Could have been gang-raped, the doc thought.

Ron Worral was moving round taking the pictures, looking as serious as a judge.

'They can take her as soon as you've got enough snaps,' the quack told Molly as though this was an everyday occurrence.

They finished a little after midday and Molly went off, taking Dennis with her, to break the news to the mother, one of the most unpleasant jobs she'd ever known. Never got used to it.

Elderly Mrs Axton rocked back and forth in her chair, keening, little wails of distress. 'She were only twenty: just. Twenty in July, whole life before her.' Heart breaking, crying again. 'I en't ever going to have grand-babies now, never.'

Molly asked the routine questions. Had she been to the
dance at the aerodrome? Yes. Was she going with anybody?
Yes, Violet Sparrow from lower down Pheasant's Row. Two
doors down. Were they meeting anyone, did she talk about
a boy friend? Oh, yes. Our Juliet were meeting an officer.
Very proud she had an officer boy friend. Had she got his
name? Yes, it was a captain something, Eclare or something.
Ricky, and he was a captain. Pilot. Flew one of those Fortress
things that make all the noise. Mrs Axton sometimes thought
the roof would come in, the planes made so much noise,
rattled the whole cottage.

Molly got a neighbour in to sit with Juliet's mother, said
the doctor'd be round shortly. Went back to the Falcon and
telephoned the doc in the village, asked him to trot up and
see Mrs A.

Then she telephoned the Provost Marshal. Tommy had said
she must go through the Provost Marshal regarding anything
connected with the men of the 8th USAAF and she'd already
been going to phone him, ask him if they could look around.
She'd spoken to the telephone people at the GPO and found
that Midge Morrison had a blue Austin Seven, so wanted to
see if it was anywhere on the aerodrome. Neither Lavender
nor Queenie had owned to having any transport, but Molly
would have laid a large bet that they'd driven in, or at least
one of them had. Probably with Golly aboard.

She met the Provost Marshal just after two in the afternoon, taking Dennis with her – the others were now back
doing the house-to-house enquiries in the village.

Seeing the Provost Marshal wasn't something Molly had
looked forward to – after all she had been with Tommy during
the arrest of Lavender and Queenie the previous night, so
knew what a difficult man Major Bragg could be. In the
event, as soon as she told him about the murder he lost his
aggression, petered out, was even quite pleasant, and
certainly calmer than he had been after the dance.

'Sure. Sure, I saw that girl with one of our people at the

dance. Real peach of a girl.' Molly had shown him a photograph they'd borrowed from Juliet's mother. 'Now who the
heck was it?' scratching his head.

'Her mother said she was meeting a Ricky Eclare, a pilot?'

'LeClare,' the major actually smiled. 'Ricky LeClare.
That's it, who I saw her with. Gee, they were having a dandy
old time and all. I'm sorry, very sorry about this.' He picked
up the telephone – they were in his Guard Room office,
which he seemed to prefer when talking to civilians; probably easier to get them off the aerodrome straight from the
Guard Room.

'Captain LeClare is flying, up on an air test, but should
be back any time now,' he told her after holding a brief
conversation. 'Tell you what, why don't you both come along
to the Officers' Club, have a bite to eat. We'll catch Ricky
LeClare when he comes in after he's done flying.'

'That'll be very nice, but I don't think Dennis can make
it. You've other things to do, Dennis? Right?'

'No, I'm with you all day, Sarg.' Big smile and a narrow-
eyed look from Molly, who wanted to eyeball the Yank facil-
ities on her own.

The major's jeep was summoned and they were driven
across to the Officers' Club, a fairly lavish building and not
as formal as the Officers' Messes of the British Forces that
Molly had seen – among them she had been to the Raff Mess
at Middle Wallop, following up work that Suzie had done in
1940. That was a fairly formal place with erk waiters and
Waaf waitresses trolling around in white jackets. Well, there
were white jackets inside the Officers' Club but it was a
much brighter and easier atmosphere. She thought of Trevor
Skeggs, wondering what his mess was like: hadn't heard from
him since they'd found the shotgun.

'Care for some chow?' the major asked when they had
ordered drinks in the bar, and they accepted immediately, not
showing any polite reluctance, because they wanted to see
how the Yanks did for themselves.

'Best meal I've had in months,' Molly said later. They had to line up for the served buffet, canteen-style arrangement, but the food was hot and plentiful – hamburgers, solid meat in tomato sauce, chips – which the Yanks called fries – beans and peas, plenty of freshly baked bread, and three or four kinds of salad. Molly grinned at Dennis as they returned, plates loaded, to the table the major had taken for them.

'Yeah, I guess we do ourselves proud here. We fly stuff in from home. It's pretty regular but we don't eat as well as our troops still stationed back in the US of A.'

They finished off the meal with apple pie with ice cream, 'A la mode,' Bragg explained. Then, shortly after they moved out into the bar and main club area, he saw Ricky LeClare come in with some of his crew.

'Like a gun dog,' Dennis said, watching the major walk quickly over to LeClare and quietly pull him aside, talking to him as he eased him away from his fellow crew members.

'LeClare, yes. He was at that dinner party last night. Sat next to the Chief. Chief wanted to talk with him. He knew the Ascolis, well, knew Mrs Ascoli. Knew her a long time ago. In the States.'

As she spoke, Molly saw the young officer falter, his face going white, and she swore under her breath. 'Bloody Bragg, he's just told LeClare about Juliet Axton. We should've done that, Dennis.'

'Yes, indeed we should.' Dennis looked up at the advancing men as Bragg brought the pilot across to the table.

The Provost Marshal introduced Captain LeClare, who was clearly shaken, ashen-faced and uncomfortable.

'I get you a drink, Ricky?' Bragg asked. 'A brandy, perhaps?'

'That'd be good, Major. Thank you.'

'Steady your nerves, I guess.'

'Yes, he's just told me,' tipping his head back towards Bragg. 'You're the police, yes?'

Molly introduced herself and Dennis, explaining, telling

him they had to ask him some questions. He was shaky but understood, and told them he'd been with Juliet all evening, 'I picked her up at the Falcon. After the dinner party. The RAF Station Commander had a dinner party . . . Oh, you were there, ma'am. I saw you there. I spoke to Mr Livermore – that right? That his name?' Very polite, no messing around.

Molly acknowledged that was his name. 'Detective Chief Superintendent Livermore. Yes, I remember seeing you there.' She then asked why he hadn't seen Juliet home from the aerodrome, and he told a long involved story about her not wanting to bother him, knew he was flying today, said she'd go straight home.

'Would that've involved her going into Knights Close? You know Knights Close? That's it's name. Knights in the plural, no apostrophe.'

'Yeah, that would be her way back. She said she was going that way. She told me, Knights Close, then up Church Lane and into Pheasant's Row. She said she'd be home in ten minutes. Jeez, I can't believe it. She seemed so happy. Now I feel . . . Well, I feel dreadful. It's my fault . . .'

'You weren't to know, Captain LeClare. You went straight back to your room?'

'Sure.' *Shore.* 'I went straight back. Sat on my bed, smoked a cigarette, had a shower, then went to bed. It was around 01.25 hours, I took my watch off,' he lifted his left wrist. 'Took my watch off, laid it on the night table, and that was that. Jesus, she was coming to London with me and the rest of the crew. Tuesday. We had it all planned.'

Bragg returned with the brandy and LeClare took a gulp, winced at its burn going down. 'Murdered?' he said again. Then, 'Murdered? You think it had anything to do with the Ascoli business? I mean Mr and Mrs Ascoli had the whole crew in to dinner couple weeks ago.' He shook his head. 'Where I first saw Juliet Axton. Her mom used to help out at the Ascolis' and Juliet came in to assist that night; serving all five courses. She helped me with all the knives and forks

237

I'd never seen before. Pointed to the right ones as she served, said later that she only knew them 'cos Mrs Ascoli taught her. Where I come from we hardly bother with that kind of thing. Took a fancy to her straight away, Juliet. Christ, murdered?' Then almost to himself, 'I told your Mr Livermore about the dinner party last night, the dinner party with the Ascolis and my having known Mrs Ascoli in, what would you call it? Another life I guess. This have anything to do with the Ascoli murders?'

'We're pretty sure it had nothing to do directly with the Ascolis,' Molly said, and went on to tell him they knew the identity of a dangerous man. 'This guy's around here somewhere, Captain LeClare. We're not making a big fuss about him but he escaped from a mental institution: pretty dangerous sort of guy. I think you should know that he's killed before. Just for the hell of it, I suppose.'

She asked if Juliet Axton said anything else about Mrs Ascoli.

'Said she could be a bit sharp, then admitted that was an understatement, seeing as how I'm the world expert on Mrs Ascoli.' Then suddenly switching as if he'd only just taken in her reference to the 'dangerous sort of guy'. 'Not Pip?' he asked.

'What did you say?' her head whipping up, eyes a shade wider.

'I . . . er . . . I said it's not Pip, is it? Mr Ascoli's brother, Pip?'

'What d'you know about Pip, Captain?'

The silence was too long, trailing out across the room, she thought. Something not quite right. 'Not much, I don't know much about Pip. But I know he's supposed to be dangerous.'

'Really, how do you know that?'

'From Mrs Ascoli. From Jenny. It worried her.'

'You tell that to Mr Livermore?'

'We didn't get that far into it, no.'

'You want to tell me?'

He shook his head, eyes on the brandy, then slewing towards Major Bragg, who was starting to get restless.

'Well?' Molly asked. 'Do you tell me, or do you wait until Mr Livermore gets back?'

'It's nothing,' shifting in his chair. 'Really, it's nothing.'

'All right.' Molly made as though to stand. 'We have to take a walk round the car park,' she said to Bragg.

'Yes indeed.' He rose.

'If you want to talk further, Captain, just ring me at the Falcon.'

'I'll do that. Yes.' Seemed like he meant it.

'Good.' She still had a great deal to talk about with Ricky LeClare; felt uneasy leaving it all unsaid, but he wasn't going to talk in front of the Provost Marshal.

In the car park, outside the hangar where they'd all danced the night before, they found the solitary Austin Seven. Blue.

Molly immediately sent Dennis back to the main gate. 'Get Doc to drive you around the village, find Ron and Laura. I want them to go over this car with a toothcomb, see if Golly had been in it, brought on to the aerodrome. I'll wait here, make sure nobody touches it. That okay, Major Bragg?'

'Sure, I'll send one of my guys over to keep things regular, 'cos I gotta go and sort out some stuff with the old man. You don't mind?'

'It's good of you, Major. We don't want to be any bother.'

'No, you're okay. We've had a memo saying that we have had to accord you every possible help and assistance. Seems your boss, Mr Livermore that is, well he seems to have friends in high places.'

'Tell you something, Major Bragg. Tommy Livermore is really the Honourable Tommy Livermore. That usually means he has a little extra pull when he wants to use it.'

'Honourable, huh? That's something special, huh? Sounds chink to me – Honourable Number One Son. Uh?'

'Just a lot,' Molly said. Disgusting, she thought, that by an accident of birth someone could have an open door to heaven knew how many powerful places. Still, the way of the world.

Alone on the hardstanding they had used for the car park she was surprised to see Captain LeClare striding towards her from the direction of the line of Quonset huts she knew made up the aircrew quarters.

'Just wanted to pass on something, Sergeant.' He saluted as he approached, wearing an officer's raincoat over his uniform, his 'crusher' cap at an angle, the stiffening removed so he could wear it with headphones on in the B-17 flight deck.

'You had second thoughts, Captain?'

'Some. I just didn't want Major Bragg to hear what I had to say.'

'So?'

'So, Juliet Axton didn't leave by the main gate last night – well, this morning actually.'

'No.'

'No, Sarge. That hut at the end there,' pointing. 'It's not occupied yet, not finished really, inside that is.'

'Go on.'

'She and I – Juliet and I, well we went in there for a spell. Kinda . . . well, I guess you'd call it canoodling.'

'Yes.' Molly knew what she'd have called it.

'So she didn't leave much before around one fifteen. Went out through a split they got in the wire, the chain-link, 'bout twenty, maybe thirty, yards down from where the main road turns into Knights Close.'

'I know it. Thought they were keeping a guard on that hole in the wire.'

'Kinda rolling sentry. They go take a look about once every hour.'

'And you saw her go out that way?'

He nodded and said, yes he did.

'Anything else?'

'About poor Juliet Axton? No, except I cared for her. I feel dreadful about it.'

'Don't, Captain LeClare. There was no way you could've known. Anything else?'

'About Jenny Ascoli? I've told Mr Livermore about that.'

'All of it. You've told him about Pip?'

The silence stretched out for several seconds. 'I told him that she was not the nicest woman around.'

'And you knew about that? Personally.'

'I did.'

'And Pip? Mad, bad Pip.'

Again a wait while time went by.

'Max Ascoli brought him to Long Taddmarten in 1938.'

'Really?'

'Yes, really. Mrs Ascoli, bitch that she was, she was terrified of Pip. Truly frightened. It was as though he had – this sounds stupid – as though he had impregnated the whole house with his madness. She thought Pip would kill her.'

'You'd better go over all this with Mr Livermore when he gets back.'

'Sure. Yes, sure I will.'

Back in his quarters, as the sun came out from behind the clouds, Ricky LeClare lay on his bed, eyes closed, and wondered what he should do. Should he go to the Livermore guy and tell him everything? That could be a problem. They wouldn't be happy with him. They wouldn't be happy with the truth. Two lots of murders, unconnected except by him. They'd take him off flying that was for sure: once that particular cat was out of the bag.

What if something happened to him? What if they got hit bad and had to get out of the ship? If he was taken prisoner, or worse? Nobody would ever know, who or why.

Ricky LeClare got off the bed, went over to the metal wardrobe and opened it, got writing paper and his pen, started writing everything, writing a long letter which he finally folded and put in an envelope marked 'For Detective

241

Livermore. In the event of my death'. Felt someone walk over his grave as he sealed it, tossed it into the drawer next to the other one. The one to his wife back in the States. The one that started, 'Dear Angel, If you get this you'll know I've gone. Now don't be sad, 'cos it happens to a lot of guys here, that's the nature of war . . .'

It went on like that for over six pages. Basically he thought Angela would be relieved, theirs was not one of the great marriages, wasn't that conventional.

Molly rang Suzie that night, told her the latest and said she really had to speak with the Chief the minute he got back. It was very important. She said that they had found traces of Golly all over the Austin Seven they'd picked up in the car park.

'Couldn't he have ridden in it during the escape?' Suzie asked brightly. Too brightly.

'Looks like he was brought in to the aerodrome. Under a blanket in the back. Both Queenie's and Lavender's prints're all over the front and Golly's traces're much more recent. If that's the case he possibly watched Juliet Axton go through the wire fence, probably followed her. Then killed her.'

'You know Golly,' Suzie said brightly, and Molly thought that a little odd. 'I'll phone you again tomorrow,' told her. 'You okay?'

'Never better,' Suzie slurred. 'Me and my old friend Shirley Cox, here and happy.'

They had found two bottles of Gordon's Gin and a bottle of brandy, some tonic waters and a soda syphon. Neither Suzie nor Shirley could feel any pain. It was the first time that Suzie had ever got really paralytically drunk and later she admitted that it was because she missed Tommy. He had only been away since that morning but she missed him as if he'd been away for weeks.

It was the same all through Monday. She kept saying things like, 'I wonder what Tommy's doing?' Not out loud to Shirley, who was quite funny about their state on the previous night, and on Monday night they didn't drink anything, went to bed still feeling very fragile, as Shirley put it.

Golly was comfortable. He had a nice cosy bed right at the top of the house: bed by the window, a dormer window poking out from the roof. Spare room in what had once been an attic.

After he'd had his fun with the girl, Golly had walked down the road, quietly, softly, smiling to himself, had a good time with the girl, she didn't argue and try to stop him, not anything.

He gave a little hop and a skip in the darkness, up the road.

With Golly, killing a girl with the wire was no more than a means to an end – most times anyway, no more'n killing a beetle or a pretty butterfly, that was it, what the girl was, pretty butterfly.

He got to the house that Queenie had shown him. The house where there'd been this murder, these murders. Nobody about, not overlooked by anyone. Got over the gate, white gate with a name on it, K . . . something . . . K-N-I-G . . . Kernights, and Cottage, he knew cottage. Kernites Cottage. Vaulted over the gate and stayed on the grass to the side, the verge to the flowerbed on the right. His eyes had adjusted to the darkness a long time ago. He was good in the dark, like an owl, eh? Owl on the wing, catching mice. Voles. Came up to behind the house, back of the house, started trying the doors and windows. No luck, then a little window at the back, led into a passage by the looks of it, half-open at the top with the catch off, slid down nice, no problem and he hoisted himself up, squirmed around and was in: inside this big old house, could smell it around him, house welcoming him with the smells of tile polish and beeswax: knew those smells of old, those big round tins with the red polish in them, and the beeswax in a smaller tin.

He had to stay awake on that first night, let his eyes adjust to the deeper darkness inside.

Golly began to sing under his breath, happy because he knew that this was a murder house and it meant that the bloody lady policewoman, who'd been the cause of them shutting him away, would be bound to come back doing her investigating and that. The copper as well, the honourable one, he'd come in here also and they wouldn't know what they were walking into.

He sang softly –

> *'I had the craziest dream last night*
> *Yes I did.*
> *I never dreamt it could be*
> *But there you were, humping me*
> *I found your lips close to mine and I kissed them,*
> *And you didn't mind it at all.'*

He giggled, his low shaking giggle, because the nice girl didn't mind him kissing her and touching her. He'd had the craziest dream. Yeh-eh-eh-eh. Yeah-eh-eh.

Eventually they'd come to him. When he could see as it started to get light, he explored all over the house, saw the blood stains, picked out where he could sleep, nosed about, poking into cupboards and drawers everywhere: in the bedrooms, down in the dining room, ever such pretty pictures they had, liked the paintings, liked all of it, the whole house. When it got night again he knew they wouldn't be coming, so he went up to the room he now called his bedroom and got into bed. Had a good kip. Slept like a baby. Maybe they'd come tomorrow. They'd come though, 'cos this house'd be like a magnet to them. And when they come, he'd give them what for.

'Do we count today as the second or the third day?' Suzie asked, talking to Shirley, thinking about Tommy coming home: looked forward to it and dreaded it at the same time. Knew that eventually Tommy would start talking about a wedding again and she was split in two about the wedding.

Molly telephoned in the afternoon, said they'd almost completed everything Tommy had told them to do. 'But I had some really interesting conversations with one of the guys on the aerodrome. Must speak to the Chief about that as soon as he gets back. Just telephone me at the Falcon, Suzie.'

Suzie said of course. Yes of course she'd do that.

Molly was still there at the other end, saying nothing until, 'You any idea, Suzie? Any idea where he's gone?'

'Not a clue. Not even a clue to a clue, but he did say he might know. Might know who'd killed the Ascolis when he got back.'

'Oh. Oh, really?'

And he came back.

About half past eight that evening, when they'd had supper and given up any hope of him getting back that night.

Suzie, sitting in the kitchen eating a bit of bread and cheese – they'd had some fried rashers and chips that Shirley had made – 'You make the best really rinky-dink chips, Shirl.' Heard the key in the door, heard it open, got up, walked to the kitchen door, and –

'Dad's back,' said Tommy looking bigger than ever.

She threw herself at him, and knew that, whatever it was, the news wasn't brilliant.

Eighteen

Tommy wanted coffee but Suzie wanted to know what was going on. 'Where've you been?' she demanded, her voice slightly on the hoydenish side, grating, unladylike, her mum would have called it. In return she got one of his infuriating smiles.

'Coffee,' he said, opening his case and handing her a packet of the real thing so she got out the percolator and dusted it down. 'Where have you been?' she asked again but Shirley kept quiet, wasn't supposed to know that her friend Suzie had this thing going with the Chief: very obvious now.

At last he said, 'I've been visiting, been to see Pip Ascoli. Fillipo, Max's loony brother.'

'But he's—'

'Yes. He's supposed to be in Switzerland. Hospital called Alpenruhe, ten miles south of Thun: like the bloody castle in Thun, resonance of Dracula there. You ever been, heart? You stand in front of the Rathaus – Town Hall – and look up and you could be in Dracula country, castle looming over everything. Could be Frankenstein even.'

'And you've been there? Couldn't you have rung them, what're they called?'

'Not quite the same as being there, heart. Sisters of Compassion. Spend their time working with nutters. Needed to look them all in the eye, Pip included.'

'How? How've you been there?' As though she couldn't comprehend the logistics.

He told them the story, sipping freshly brewed coffee and

saying the Swiss still did the food wonderfully, absolute knockout. 'Don't realize how much we're missing.' He had pulled strings, at the War Office, at the Yard, at the Home Office and Foreign Office. An aircraft went out to Lisbon about three times a week – sometimes twice, sometimes four a week, depended. He had got himself a seat on Sunday's flight. 'Not exactly an easy thing to do.' Connected with other flights including a Swiss aircraft to Zurich – 'Damn great Ford Trimotor, full of shady-looking customers, spivs, spies and such.'

It was Tommy's first time in an aircraft with more than one engine. 'A Lockheed Hudson out of Northolt and then the Swiss plane from Lisbon. Those films have got it wrong by the way. In the cinema you see everyone sitting and chatting, talking to each other. Rubbish, can't hear yourself think. The waitresses have to scream at you. Oh, and the wings flap: move. Snap off if they didn't I suppose. Flew over part of Italy to get into Switzerland. Then took one of the Swiss toytown trains to Bern, then on to Thun, they're bloody good the Swiss railways. I'd forgotten how good, eat your lunch off the station platforms. Meticulous the Swiss.' He laughed. 'Stayed at a nice little place, the Falken, down by the river, lovely. Interesting, eh? Same as where we're staying in Taddmarten, but chalk and cheese. Fed me damn great veal steaks on spaghetti – four-course meal and splendid. Much as you wanted. Then I rang the Alpenruhe, Peace of the Mountains – though you're miles away from any mountains, they glower at you from a distance. The nun who answered the telephone said I'd needed to see Mother Brigitta, Chief Nun, sort of Commissioner of Compassion. Got a car to take me next day, Monday. Yesterday.'

The convent turned out to be as creepy as Willoughby Sands had described it – 'Lot of gargoyles, cloisters. Inside, it was a hospital with bars and damn great steel shutters and doors, smell of polish and that stink you get in hospitals: embalming fluid. They called it a Clinic, but what's in a name?'

Mother Brigitta welcomed him. He couldn't even guess at her age, smooth face, wrapped up in black habit with a white gown over it. 'Catching the blood, I suppose. Had clear grey eyes, looked into your soul. Didn't feel comfortable with her but I don't know why. Spoke faultless English. Supremely confident. God's got his hands full with that one.'

'You're a policeman,' she began. 'From England. I suppose it's something to do with the Ascoli family. We've been praying for their souls.' Which surprised Tommy. 'Oh, we get news here, and we know a lot about the world – the physical world. We've a sister house in Paris and there's another just outside Salisbury in England. I often think of us as God's secret agents, the Almighty's spies. Now what do you wish to know?'

Tommy asked if it would be possible to speak to Pip Ascoli, and she said this wouldn't be practicable as he wasn't there, in the clinic, and Tommy blew his top. 'Think I shouted at her, but she just sat and looked at me as if she was reading off a list of my sins. Make a damned good inquisitor.'

It turned out that Pip had been taken from the good sisters' care in the late summer of 1938, then brought back in mid-September. 'Max Ascoli didn't want his brother far away from the family in time of war, and we all thought war was inevitable in '38.'

It had been Willoughby Sands who had come out and taken him back to England. They sent a Sister Rachel back with him. 'She was bound for our English house, so it was convenient for her to go with them.'

'And Willoughby Sands brought him back?'

'No. Sir Willoughby had visited at least once a year for a long time. We had a standing joke about his weight. But it was Max Ascoli who brought him back, and Max Ascoli who took him to England again the following year. Late August, 1939.'

'Was this safe, taking Pip out of your care?'

'Personally I didn't think it was safe. Neither did Dr

Gaspard, who had worked with Pip for many years. The doctor did everything possible, though. He sent very full notes so that doctors in the UK would know the severity of Pip's illness. He also made absolutely certain that Max could get the drugs necessary to control him. There was little danger if Pip was kept on the soporifics and tranquillizers. He was able to function, walk, think and talk – after all, he was highly intelligent. But as for it being safe. Well . . .' She flapped her arms in a controlled gesture that said, What can you do? 'Max Ascoli promised that Pip would be taken back to our Salisbury house if there was any problem. I didn't like to remind him that if there was a problem it would probably be too late. If you're looking for him, perhaps you should start there.'

'Even gave me the phone number,' Tommy said in the present, here in Suzie's flat. 'Looked in at the Yard on my way here, phoned them. No dice.'

Naturally, Tommy asked Mother Brigitta about how Pip had been doing. 'Was there any change? He getting better?'

It depended what was meant by better. 'Sounded like that egghead on the wireless, Professor Joad.' Joad appeared on a BBC programme called *The Brain's Trust* – named after Roosevelt's description of his advisers. Joad often began his answers to difficult questions by saying – 'It depends what you mean by . . . ?' Tommy called him a 'pedantic little bugger'.

Mother Brigitta had then launched into a long explanation of 'Pip Ascoli's problems'. As she called them.

'Bit of an understatement if you ask me.' Tommy pulled a face.

'I was a novice when he was first brought here,' she told him. 'So, one way or another I've been with him for a very long time. In the beginning it really was a matter of restraints, keeping him locked up, arms and legs manacled for a lot of the time, in a most secure environment. He was dosed with different kinds of tranquillizer as well.'

Shades of Golly Goldfinch, Tommy thought.

'He was that dangerous?'

'Undoubtedly, and the biblical "soft answer turneth away wrath" didn't work either. But we made progress. Dr Gaspard is advanced, uses radical methods: he's farsighted and has tried many things. He sat with Pip for hours, trying to analyse him. By the mid-thirties we didn't need the restraints all the time. Only when he became upset, and we learned the warning signs.'

The warning signs were that Pip 'took against people', as Mother Brigitta put it. 'You knew instantly if he didn't like someone when he first met them, and if that person went on seeing him an incident would follow, as night follows day.' By 'incident' she meant violence. 'Also, he got sullen and moody about twenty-four hours before throwing one of his fits,' she said, and continued, 'I always felt that his whole life was lived through violence. It was his only answer to problems, and it came as naturally to him as breathing. If someone crossed him, if he disliked a person, if he was thwarted in any way, or just got into a mood, violence would follow: real violence, I'm not talking about the temper tantrums we get from some of our patients. With Pip it was always the hard edge, real life-and-death physical attacks. I always thought he had inherited a particularly bad gene from his family. They were not noted for being peaceful people you know.'

'Sat up at that,' Tommy told his two sergeants. 'Sat up and took notice, probed a bit and found the story was that the Ascolis had been known as people who took a short cut now and again. That's what Mother Brigitta said – "a short cut", euphemism for being bloody gangsters. Those nuns had a tendency to look for the good side in everything, and the good in everybody. Told me Pip was a poor lost boy. Right, lost boy who stabbed a nun in the eye with a pen, which he did in Alpenruhe, made a knife out of a piece of wood, went for another nun with a cord he'd hidden away. Damned near

killed the doc, Gaspard, on two occasions, went for him with
a table lamp the last time. Gaspard spent a week in hospital.
Came out, went to see Pip straight away and said to him,
"That wasn't very nice, Pip. If you go on like that I cannot
continue as your friend."'

According to Mother Brigitta Pip wept. 'Like a baby,' she
said, 'sobbed for a day because the doc threatened to pull
his friendship.'

Later, during the afternoon, Mother Brigitta talked about
the family as a whole. 'I met them all,' she said, rather
proudly, as if she collected autographs. 'All of them, even
the boy's grandfather, old Antonio, famous man had to leave
Italy because enemies threatened to kill him if he didn't.
They told him he had broken some deep and secret law. Took
it seriously and left.'

So Tommy asked how she found them, the Ascolis, and
she said, 'They were charming, always brought silly gifts
for us as well as the boy – as he was then. They were all
charming, their women were charming, except for Max's
wife: it's a sin to say it but Pip always acted like a rabid
dog for the first few hours after she came. He was getting
over that when he came back to us after the visit to England
in '38. But they all had charm, the men in particular.
Immaculate, glossy. Yet . . .' She paused, looked away and
then said, 'In the midst of all that smooth and polished
charm I felt only a step away from steel, the old steel hand
in the velvet glove. What is it Shakespeare says in another
context, "Gentlemen of the shade, minions of the moon"?
That's what I always felt they were, but nearer darkness
than moonlight. They were criminals, Mr Livermore, they
ran criminal organizations – even when they lived in your
country. They had great power, power over life and death,
but God can forgive at the last. Gentlemen of the shade,
minions of the moon.'

Then, Tommy said, she turned it around again, gave them
a way out by quoting Keats –

251

'Aye on the shores of darkness there is light,
And precipices show untrodden green,
There is a budding morrow in midnight,
There is a triple sight in blindness keen.'

Always the hope, always salvation behind the darkest act. She said the Ascolis always made excuses for poor Pip, Sammy's boy, as they called him. They're a family and counted him as one of them – that was why Max wanted his brother back in wartime England. 'They closed round one of their own like a Praetorian Guard around an emperor,' she said. 'Would hear no evil spoken of him. They would deny him any complicity in crime. But that's how they were, a law unto themselves.'

'Very keen mind, that Mother Brigitta. Gave me a photograph of Pip, with his brother before he left for the last time. They look like two men who love one another – in a fraternal sense, of course. Brigitta said, "Siamese twins, yes?" and I knew what she meant. Bound together by ruthlessness in a way; joined at the soul.'

'And where's Pip now?' Suzie asked.

'Heaven alone knows, but I reckon we've got our murderer. All we've to do now is find him, and I'd like to do that without shouting it from the rooftops.'

'So where do we start looking?'

'Only certain places *to* look, heart,' raising his head and catching Shirley's eye, saying, 'No good you smirking, young woman,' which made her blush.

'What certain places, Tommy?' throwing caution to the wind, using clichés in her head.

'Homes of the brave of course. Ascoli homes. Montpelier Street, the gaffe up in Scotland where Freda spends most of her time. Even the Palmer drum in King's Lynn. Point is that even though Pip shot down a brother, an Ascoli bride and a child, the others would probably form a square round him, hide him from the world.'

'What about Sir Willoughby?' Suzie frowned.

'No point, not yet. Willoughby's a lawyer. He'd stop us at his door, make life uncomfortable for all of us, warn the others, so we'll keep well out of old Willoughby's way. Interesting about the Ascolis and their connection with organized criminal activity in Italy, eh?'

He made his excuses, asked Suzie to knock him up some of that ham – 'Sandwiches, heart, smidgen of mustard if you would, Coleman's' – and went through into the bedroom where he had this second telephone line which answered to his number in what he called his sordid hovel in Earl's Court. First he dialled Billy Mulligan's private number.

Mulligan had been his senior NCO, general overseer and major-domo since Tommy had been in charge of the Reserve; there were tales that – like Brian, his driver – Billy had worked for Tommy's father. Now they discussed which magistrate they could get to sign search warrants for Montpelier Square and Scotland, told Billy the whole situation, talked about when they should pounce. 'Get the warrants tonight, Bill, and I'll come in and we do it around eight in the morning, catch Freddy and Helena, plus Benny's widow all in one place, not exactly the dawn patrol, eh? Who've you got handy? Bert and his people, they'll be good and I'll do the charm offensive on the righteously angry senior Ascolis. Now, Scotland . . . Yes between Strachan and Birse . . . Marecht Hall . . . Yes, Billy, very good address. Not quite spitting distance of Balmoral but near enough to be select. You have reliables up there? . . . Good . . . probably only a housekeeper but tell them to be careful. Yes send it by a dispatch rider tonight if you can, then they can execute first thing in the morning, or the morn's morn or whatever they bloody say up there . . . No, I'm aware they won't be best pleased . . . Then, of course we should really deal with Paula Palmer and Thetis . . . Yes, that's what I thought you said . . . You get those search warrants plus the Palmer one – "River Walk", King's Lynn. Yes, get it here, I don't want any loose talk going on, you never know who's listening in King's Lynn nick and we won't be using it until Thursday . . . Yes, I'll talk to Molly tonight. See you at the Yard around seven so we can go in at eight . . . No, I'll bring Suzie and Shirley with me . . . Yes, I'll talk to her now.'

He rang off, went through and ate his ham sandwiches, telling them the good news, 'Going to turn over that smart house of Freddy Ascoli's in Montpelier Square.'

'When?'

'Got to be at the Yard around seven.'

'Better get my hair washed tonight, then,' Suzie grinned. 'Shirley coming?'

'Course, and she can come up to Taddmarten with us, extra pair of hands dealing with everything there.'

Suzie ran off to tell her old friend. Excited, told herself they'd close the case in a matter of days now. Tommy had said if they didn't find Pip's spoor in Montpelier Place, Scotland or in King's Lynn he'd use the photograph and go on the offensive across the country.

Tommy smiled, ate his sandwiches and closed his eyes, drank his coffee and dreamed of cracking this one. Get bloody Pip Ascoli, put him away for good.

Suzie came back, 'Means we've got two mad killers floating round, then.'

'There's a difference.' Tommy put on his serious look. 'Pip Ascoli's utterly cracked, kills people because it's a compulsion, likes doing it. Old Golly's been programmed. Different. May not even know he's doing wrong. Maybe thinks God's telling him to do it.' Remarkably enlightened view from Tommy.

As Tommy was chasing up Billy Mulligan, so the crew of *Wild Angel II* were having dinner at the Ritz. Well, some of the crew, the officers – Ricky LeClare, the Bombadier, Will Truebond; Navigator, Jimmy Cobalt; Willie Wilders the Radio Op; and Bob Crawfoot, LeClare's second pilot.

They had spent the day together, one-day pass and had to be back by 23.59 hours, could just do it by taking the last local train out of London – flying tomorrow, an operation.

The meal, they agreed, had been good, beautifully presented, served with style and élan. Now LeClare was making a little speech, sitting down, naturally, didn't want to draw attention to themselves.

He couldn't know it of course but Ricky LeClare was echoing sentiments expressed in a letter written by Paula Palmer to Max Ascoli in October 1939.

'Gentlemen,' he began, his eyes stealing around the table, fastening on each man in turn, holding for a second and then moving on. 'Gentlemen, we have spent a pleasant day in this great city and seen many things, Westminster Abbey, Tower of Big Ben, The Houses of Parliament, Buckingham Palace, St James's Palace, Hyde Park and Regent's Park. Now, it is fitting that we should be dining here in the Ritz Hotel. We spend a large part of our time fighting this war close to the angels in the heavens, and we all know about that damned nightingale singing in Berkeley Square. We've all sung, "There were angels dining at the Ritz . . ." Well. Here we are boys, the crew of *Wild Angel II*, angels dining here, at the Ritz.'

The young men around the table tapped on it softly, their applause, then they lifted the glasses in a toast. 'To the angels dining at the Ritz,' they chorused.

Back in the flat in Upper St Martin's Lane, Tommy had managed to get in touch with Molly Abelard: left a message with Mrs Staleways at the Falcon asking if Sergeant Abelard would telephone him from the line in his room. 'Let her have the key, Mrs S,' he said. 'I've got a nice piece of ham here to bring over for you. Little thank you,' and Hettie Staleways simpered away like a young woman being told that the French perfume was forthcoming from the man of her dreams.

Molly telephoned ten minutes later and sounded flustered. 'Having a drink with the lads,' she told him, 'then old mother

Staleways came bustling in, full of importance, said to me
very loudly, "The Honourable Thomas Livermore says you're
to telephone him at his private number. Come with me."
Thinks you're God, Chief.'

'Don't disillusion her then, Molly.' Then he briefly filled
her in on his travels around Europe, and went on, 'There's
only one person in the frame now, Moll. It's got to be Pip
Ascoli, Max's brother, so we're going after him, no holds
barred.'

He explained how he was taking a team into Freddy's house
in the morning and another team in Scotland would be going
through Marecht Hall, the Scottish house that had belonged
to Benny and his wife, before that to Antonio himself. 'Any
traces of Pip I want followed up, and I *don't* want Mr Tait
or the Norwich blokes tipped off, so don't let the lads talk
freely.'

With luck he would be in Long Taddmarten by the
following night, bringing Suzie and Shirley Cox with him.
In the meantime he wanted the team in Long Taddmarten to
take a quick look at the situation in King's Lynn. 'Nothing
too heavy. Just take a surreptitious peep, see if Paula and
Thetis have come back from their jaunt.'

Molly, conscientious as ever, repeated the instructions back
to him, said she looked forward to seeing him sometime
tomorrow and closed the line. Never wasted time chatting
on the phone about extraneous matters if there was work to
get on with. In fact, Molly had a nice gin and tonic waiting
at the bar downstairs and it was almost closing time. Brian
was still in London and Trevor Skeggs had come over for
the evening, to see Molly.

Fancied his chances.

Golly was in the house, up in his bedroom inside Knights
Cottage. They had not come today, the police, but they would
be here tomorrow, or the next day. Tonight he had gone out
into the dark, hiding away in the shadows.

He had broken into a little shop, 'Chamberlain' it read above the door, only it was too dark for him to see that. Cheap rubbishy lock on the door and it was a black dark night. He stole some food, not much, just biscuits, two packets, a little jar of jam and some cheese, all waiting there to be stolen, and he went back keeping clear of the men laughing and joking as they went home to the aerodrome, one of them with a girl in another doorway getting his hand up her skirt.

Golly was like a ghost – he thought – noiseless and unseen, flitting from corner to corner. He got back and ate biscuits and cheese, drank water, sat in the dark and went to bed again.

They would come when they were ready. In the meantime he thought he was like a big fat spider waiting at the centre of his web, laughed at the picture in his mind of him having eight legs and the ability to spin a web. He'd wrap them all up and bite them to death when they came. He thought that was funny and he laughed to himself.

They would come.

Sure of it.

Nineteen

At just after eight o'clock the following morning three cars turned into Montpelier Square, Brian driving Tommy, Billy Mulligan, and Suzie in the Wolseley, Shirley with Bert and his team in the other two cars.

Tommy Livermore had been explicit in his instructions, taking his time, talking to them in the big conference room of the Reserve Squad's offices on the fourth floor of Scotland Yard. Just after seven that morning, he'd prepared them for what was to take place, saying they were lucky he could actually speak to them at this time in the morning.

Polite laughter.

'The members of the Ascoli family who we're walking in on this morning are not going to be as happy as nuns weeding the asparagus,' he began. 'They won't want us there and they'll be exhibiting signs of outrage. Be polite but firm. They'll be shouting for briefs and they'll be expecting injunctions against the search warrants, keeping us out. Don't let that worry you, these people may seem to be straight-up honest British ladies and gentlemen of the middle classes, but they're not. You'll meet one man, Freddy Ascoli, the last Ascoli in the male line. The last but for Pip Ascoli, the man we now know killed his brother, Max, Jenny and young Paul Ascoli, in their home at Long Taddmarten. Pip has spent most of his life in a clinic for the mentally unstable in Switzerland. Now we're looking for him. That's what this is all about, and when we catch him we're going to put him away for the rest of his natural life.

'Sadly, no court'll sentence him to death, which is what he deserves, would save a lot of money.

'Right, first we're going into Freddy Ascoli's house on Montpelier Square. At the same time, colleagues in Scotland will be turning over a house belonging to the late Benny Ascoli and his wife. We're going into those properties to see if we can find any traces of Pip Ascoli. Look for anything that seems not quite in keeping with the house or the people in it, look for possible hiding places, or signs of disturbance, and remember that, and I've only just been made aware of this, these people will gather round their own and protect them. Although Pip has killed his brother and his brother's family, Freddy won't want him to fall into our hands. He'll have the overwhelming desire to take care of this business himself.

'You see, I'm sure that when this war is over and we get a peep into the files in Freddy's native Italy, we're going to find that the Ascolis ran a large segment of crime in Rome, Milan and many major cities on the Italian mainland. Possibly in Sicily as well.

'So, I want you to take Freddie Ascoli's nice home to pieces; when you empty cupboards really empty them, then examine the interior walls; measure up the thickness of partitions and walls, see if there are any hidey holes built into the place; if you see a picture hanging skew-whiff take it down and examine the wall beneath; if a carpet is rucked, take it up and examine it. You're to go through the place like a hurricane.

'Don't heed the ladies either, they'll make a fuss, they'll complain, take no notice of them; and if we do flush out Pip Ascoli, watch out for him because he's truly dangerous.'

Tommy leaned on the electric bell at the front door, Suzie a couple of paces behind him, the rest of the squad taking positions to her rear so the whole phalanx of policemen, some in uniform, were intimidatingly arranged in front of the house when Freddy himself opened the door.

259

'Can't get the help these days, can you, Freddy? Have to do it all yourself.' Tommy smiled at the tall, greying immaculate man, whose eyes were lifting, taking in the police outside his own front door.

'Awfully sorry to bother you, Freddy, but I'm afraid I've got a search warrant, to have a little look through your house.'

'What the hell . . . ?' Freddy began, his eyes losing their usual twinkle, becoming cold, possibly angry, Tommy thought.

'I'm sorry, really, but it has to be done.'

'On what grounds?'

'Not required to answer that, sir.' Tommy could feel a menacing anger coming off the man, it seemed to spray over him in waves, an invisible tide carrying with it unpleasant, and frightening vibrations. Tommy was still armed, a pistol holstered snug behind his right hip.

Later he was to say he had never missed Molly so much: Molly would have been the right backup for him, always gave as good as she got, always ready. For a few seconds Fredo Ascoli appeared to be stripped bare of pretence, the bonhomie gone, only power and aggression left in its wake. 'I believe you know why we're here, sir,' Tommy remembering Freddy's own words – *You'd have Max's murderer if Pip was out and about in this country. No doubt.*

'And I believe that I can speak to my lawyer before you enter the house.'

'Not necessarily, sir,' Tommy formal now as Helena and Freda suddenly appeared with a clatter of heels on the hall's marble flags. 'But, as we know who you are, and are aware of the strain you're under, I'll wait for you to make your telephone call.' There was muttering and sharp looks as the two women closed on Freddy. 'What? . . . Why? . . . How? . . . They can't . . . I'll talk to Willoughby.'

A long table stood against the far wall of the hall, on it a telephone and an electric lamp made from an antique oil lamp. Freddy crossed to the telephone, picked up and when the operator came on asked for a number. When there was an answer he spoke rapidly, his back towards Tommy, his speech low.

Eventually he turned and imperiously beckoned Tommy. 'Sir Willoughby Sands wishes to speak with you.'

So, Tommy was in. He walked to the 'phone and held the warrant in front of Freddy. 'Willoughby?' he said pleasantly into the telephone.

'What the bloody hell's going on, Tommy? Some kind of harassment, is it?'

''Fraid not Will old chum. This is a serious matter.'

'Not connected with Max, I hope?'

'Very much connected with Max.'

'But you can't think . . . ?'

'We're looking for someone, Willoughby. You know, old love. I know you know. You have left undone those things which you ought to have done. Book of Common Prayer. The General Confession, Wills, remember that?'

'I know you aren't obliged to say anything to Freddy. Can you tell *me*?'

'I've told you. We're looking for someone, and you should know who that someone is. You should've told me about him. Erred, old love, erred and strayed from thy ways like lost sheep. Book of Common Prayer again. Want to hear any more?'

Willoughby made a noise like a kind of bleating. 'Tommy, if any damage is done to Freddy's house I shall hold you responsible.'

'Of course old horse. Sorry about all of this.'

'Tommy, you have to understand that my life and my practice are integrally bound to the Ascoli family and their various businesses. Put Freddy back on, would you.'

'I probably understand more than you know,' and Tommy handed the phone back, flicking his hand in the direction of his waiting officers, who began to enter the house.

Helena and Freda began to make more noise, loudly demanding to know what the police thought they were doing.

A uniformed officer stood guard outside and a small crowd was starting to collect.

Freddy finally put the telephone down and turned to Tommy. 'It appears that you win, but—'

'I know about the but, Freddy. Let us get on with it and we'll be out of your hair.'

It took them until after five o'clock that afternoon: searching every room, going through the attics, the cellars and the small outbuildings. They found no traces of anyone either hiding or having hidden and, as the day wore on, so Freddy and the Ascoli women became more annoyed. They damaged nothing, but there could be no doubt that the lovely house was clean.

Around three in the afternoon Tommy allowed Shirley Cox to go back to her digs and collect clothes. 'I need you up with me in Taddmarten tomorrow,' he told her, 'so I suppose you should have at least a change of clothes so that the eyes of the locals won't get bored.'

He also received a message from Scotland, late in the afternoon, dispatch rider from the Yard on his BSA motorcycle. Nothing of any significance had been found at Marecht Hall. He was pleased to be able to tell Freda that his people were now out of her house because she had raised seven bells of hell when her housekeeper had telephoned to ask what she should do.

Tommy remained polite to the Ascolis throughout the search, and particularly courteous when he thanked the still seething Freddy for his cooperation.

They went back to the Yard, and after an hour's deliberation Tommy instructed Brian to take them up to Taddmarten, calling in at the Upper Grosvenor Street flat to collect cases and what was left of the ham he'd promised to Mrs Staleways.

They also took one of the other cars with them, Shirley at the wheel, a most competent driver, having worked through the verbal assaults of her old DCI at Camford who believed all women drivers had two left arms and three left feet.

As they made their way out of London, Tommy said, 'Let's hope we have more luck in Taddmarten, or rather at "River Walk" in King's Lynn. He's got to be hiding out somewhere and I'd rather like to stop him before he goes berserk and kills someone else.'

Wild Angel II had taken off from Long Taddmarten aerodrome at a little before ten. Six aircraft – six ships as the American jargon had it – initially heading to a point above Felixstowe, where they climbed to their bombing height of 23,000 feet, orbiting for almost ten minutes, together with two squadrons of Spitfires – including the recently equipped 308th from the 31st Group 8th USAAF – climbing, turning and waiting for the six other B-17s out of Earl's Colne. The target was the same one they had attacked on the very first operational mission on 17th August, the railroad marshalling yards at Rouen-Sotteville. In all, the Spitfires were orbiting for almost eighteen minutes before the airplanes out of Earl's Colne got themselves into position and the whole formation could head out down the east coast of the UK, then off across the Channel. As they got into that final formation, one of the American Spitfire pilots broke radio silence: 'We're gonna have to leave the big brothers before we reach the target,' he said, but the pilots of the Fortresses paid no attention, thinking the guy was having a joke at their expense. 'We were on time,' Ricky LeClare said over the interphone as though this was all that mattered, we were on time, therefore all was bang-on.

The whole crew of *Wild Angel II* was excited, their first proper operation since the original crew had been split up by death, injury and the twitch, as in the case of Solly Schwartz, who had frozen over the guns in the upper turret during the St-Nazaire trip. Now, Jim Dodd was in the upper turret, swinging the guns round, always alert, his eyes tracing through the clear cold blue sky, watching for the dots which would grow and were out to get you. Pete Israel and Danny

Spooner in the waist positions were also alert, everyone looking for a good scrap.

With Will Truebond in the nose, hunched over the Norden bombsight, and in control of the airplane on their final run, everyone was relaxed, even when Navigator Jimmy Cobalt said, 'Uh-oh, our little friends're leaving.' The Spitfires peeling away, unable to remain with the formation, running out of fuel because of the long wait they'd had over Felixstowe.

Then the flack started, the nasty little smudges of grey-black against the sky and the occasional rocking of the airplane when one came a little too close.

'Bombs away,' Truebond spoke calmly, and *Wild Angel II* lifted, relinquishing the weight of the bomb load, then tipped to one side, the nose slewing, jerking to starboard as they felt another thump, invisible hand grabbing at them, the outer port engine suddenly belching smoke, a flicker of flame deep in there, for a couple of seconds, and there was a swift crackling noise.

'Feather port outer,' Ricky said using the interphone, and Bob Crawfoot repeated the instruction as LeClare steadied the ship, working as a team to shut down the damaged engine, pressing the button that fired the extinguisher through the nacelle to quench the fire.

Immediately the ship began to slow and lose a little height. 'Keep your eyes peeled everybody, we're going out of formation.' Ricky was doing what he had practised many times, his voice calm, controlled to dampen any anxiety among the crew.

Then Bob Pentecost in the ball turret yelling, distorted in LeClare's ears, 'Two coming in, five o'clock low!' Followed by the tuck-tuck sound of bullets and cannon shells hitting the metal fuselage.

LeClare looked left and saw an Me 109 turn away, close enough to see the pilot's head move as he worked the stick, pulling against the force pressing him down against his seat. 'Yellow noses,' LeClare said, again calmly, seeing the bright-yellow spinner on a second aircraft so close that he felt the wash of its slipstream. Yellow spinners meant Gruppe II/Jagdgeschwadern 26, the Abbeville boys from Drucat aerodrome outside Abbeville, veterans of the Battle of Britain.

As he was thinking, so Pete Israel in the port waist position shouted, 'Port, three o'clock high!' Then louder, 'Four of the bastards coming in!'

Almost at the same moment, LeClare felt something cross the cabin in front of him as a 22mm cannon shell took off half of Bob Crawfoot's head, spraying the entire cabin with a film of blood.

Danny Spooner was hit, standing in the starboard waist position, feet slipping on the shell casings from his guns. Danny felt a fist bang into his chest, saw what looked like a film of blood, filling up his eyes, heard his mother calling for him, 'Danny . . . Danny . . . You fighting again, Danny . . .'

In the tail, working his guns from the stand-off position at the bottom of the tall tailplane with the linked sight that operated the guns facing backwards out of the tail, 'Red' Moir gave another warning, 'Two, coming in on the tail, six o'clock high,' and he saw the flicker from the cannon in the spinner of one of the Me 109s, then the other one, the teeth-shattering blows somewhere just behind him followed by a dizzying lurch downwards as the entire tail section was blown from the ship. 'Red' screamed all the way down.

Pete Israel sat among the shell casings laughing. He had felt this terrible burning pain, sat down knowing he had been hit, ripped at his electrically heated suit to render some first aid to himself. Torn the suit open with his knife and saw what had happened, laughed, throwing back his head. He had wet himself in the excitement and shorted out the wiring. The terrible burning pain was electricity from the shorting wires snapping at his leg. He was still laughing when they blew up.

Up in the nose both Truebond and Cobalt lay dead, rolling

around the nose cone, imprinting the plexiglas with their blood. In the cabin, covered with Bob Crawfoot's blood, and some of his own, Ricky LeClare felt the seat under him wallow and tip. He felt detached as he looked out on to the port wing and saw a flicker of fire somewhere between the two engines, the outer one still gushing smoke and, he guessed, some gasoline in there, starting to take hold. Aloud he sang some of the old song from U.Va. –

'From Vinegar Hill to Ivy Road,
We're gonna get drunk tonight.'

He saw the blood in his head and thought it was a good job he'd written to Mr Livermore otherwise they might never have known what happened, how he'd gone for a walk in the middle of the night, and seen the lights – Hey, that's real pretty, he thought as the fire struck out of the wing, blossomed and formed a huge roaring fire sliding up to the wing root.

'Wow, Bob,' he said to the headless corpse jiggling about next to him. 'Hey, Bob, look at her go,' and the flame reached out to consume the entire wing and fuselage of *Wild Angel II* with a huge whumping sound that leaped up and licked Ricky's ear, felt it singe him.

'Son-of-a-bitch!' he muttered.

Twenty

They didn't get back to the Falcon Inn, Long Taddmarten, until almost midnight, stopping off for an execrable meal near Chelmsford – soggy chips, overcooked beans and a grilled steak that Tommy swore had come off the sole of some boot attached to a corpse at Dunkirk.

Molly was waiting up for them and Mrs Staleways came rumbling out. Tommy gave her the ham and she asked him if he would like some sandwiches. 'Ra-ther,' two words, Tommy grinned at her and Suzie added, 'Little mustard, Coleman's please.' Cheeky little grin, extracting the urine from Tommy.

'Right away, right away,' Hettie Staleways almost bobbed a curtsy and trundled off to do Tommy's bidding.

'Think you're in with a chance there, Chief,' Molly said, and he glared at her, said, 'Could've done with you today, Moll. Sore pressed we were.' He led the way to his room, and they sat around the table, Tommy, Molly and Suzie. Brian had sloped off, knew he wasn't required.

'She's back, Chief,' Molly said, sitting across from him.

'Who's back?'

'The fair Paula and her daughter, Thetis.'

'How d'you find out?'

'You asked me to take a peep, so I sent Laura over to keep a weather eye on "River Walk". She phoned to say they got back around five this afternoon.' Glancing at her watch, 'I mean yesterday afternoon.'

'Alone, just the two of them?'

'Alone, that's the good news. The bad news could well be

267

this letter.' She handed him a cream-coloured envelope addressed to 'Detective Livermore. In the event of my death', written in blue ink.

'It's from?'

'Captain Ricky LeClare. Major Bragg brought it over. It was with LeClare's effects and marked to be given to you in the event . . . Bragg said he bought it, him and all his crew, got the chop over Rouen this afternoon.

'Oh! Oh, I'm sorry.' Tommy looked just a tiny bit stricken, for several seconds, not long.

As he was tearing the envelope open, Mrs Staleways tapped at the door and brought in a tray with the sandwiches and a pot of coffee.

'Lord knows where she got the coffee from,' Tommy said when she had departed, took the letter out of the envelope, longish letter, several pages.

He started to read, eating a sandwich at the same time, got on to the second page and said, 'No, Molly, this isn't bad news. It's quite good actually, not for poor old Ricky of course, but quite good for us. Listen to this.' He started to read.

Dear Detective Livermore,

I guess I should have bit the bullet and told you all this when we last spoke. I nearly told your nice sergeant when we met, but didn't have the guts. See I wanted to go on flying, doing operations against the Nazis. Once I came clean over this I was pretty sure they'd take me off flying and operations. I don't know what they'd charge me with, but I guess it would be something to do with tampering with evidence, so you'll get this if I'm taken prisoner, or if the bastards get me, which will mean I'm dead.

Okay. First, I know you're aware of the wire being cut behind the aircrew quarters. Well, the crew of Wild Angel did that. Stupid, foolish and against regs, but we're all pretty stupid. We did it to save ourselves the trek up to the main gate, and it plays a part in what I got to tell you.

On the night of 16th/17th August 1942, I couldn't sleep. I guess it was nerves and excitement. See we knew we were going on our first bombing mission in the morning. Didn't know the target but we did know it was some Nazi base in France. I tossed and turned, just couldn't sleep, so I thought I'd get up and take a walk round the block. I'd done this before, through the metal fence, across the road and down Knights Close, back on to St Mary's Drive that takes you to the main road again.

I put on a shirt and trousers, a pair of soft shoes and set off, going through the opening in the metal fence, turning left, crossing the road and heading towards Knights Close.

As soon as I got into Knights Close I could see something was wrong, Knights Cottage – where the Ascolis lived – was a blaze of light. I thought this couldn't be right, it was like a signal to any bombers that could be overhead, a huge beacon shining in the darkness.

I remember walking fast, then running and I got to the white five-bar gate at the bottom of the little drive in front of the house when the lights suddenly went out. The blackouts weren't in place I'd realized when I first saw the lights. Now, first the upstairs lights went, then downstairs. I stopped by the white gate and suddenly the front door burst open and somebody came running towards the gate. I stepped aside, almost into those bushes on the left, and the guy pushed the gate open and went haring up Knights Close, toward the main road. I guess I should have followed him then, but the front door was wide open so I ran down and went into the house. Foolishly, I reckon, I switched the hall lights on again and saw the horrible state of the hallway. Max Ascoli was flat on his back with his face shot away and there was a shotgun lying by his feet.

I didn't know if he'd shot himself or what, and of course I didn't know anything about Jenny and young Paul. And I didn't want to know. I only heard when we came back from the operation in the afternoon and I reasoned that probably the man I'd seen running from the house had something to do with his death and I recall thinking that I should follow him. See if I could identify him. To follow him meant that I would be putting myself in some kind of danger, so I grabbed the shotgun. There was blood everywhere, right across the marble floor and around Max's body. But I grabbed at the gun, got some blood on me doing it as well. I thought about the blood constantly. I kept getting this picture of blood all around me. In my head the blood followed me everywhere. I even thought of it while we were flying, on the raid.

Whoever used the gun had been a cool guy, reloaded it: there were spent red cartridge cases on the floor and new ones in the breeches. I broke it open and looked.

I switched the light off again, took my handkerchief and wiped the switch because I didn't want to leave fingerprints around. Then I left the house. I remember slamming the door and running like hell up Knights Close, heading for the main road. As I reached it I was aware of a car engine and saw whoever it was just getting into the car, the engine gunning and the car being driven away at speed. I was just left standing there, like a dummy. I can't tell you what kind of car it was, nor the license plates, but I did get a sense that it was a woman driving and that she had opened a door for the guy to get in. I got a feeling, no way I could prove it, that this had been somehow arranged. That the car had been waiting nearby, had dropped off the guy and was now picking him up.

So, there I was, standing in the middle of the road with a shotgun in my right hand. I went straight over to the fence, walked along to where we had cut it, wiped off the gun with my handkerchief, and dropped it into the ditch beside the fence, climbed through and walked back to my quarters. I saw nobody else. I noticed my watch said exactly four fifty-five. Sorry, I should have told you all this before.

It was signed Richard C. LeClare.

'Well,' Tommy sighed, 'what I'd give to ask Captain LeClare a few questions, his sense of the fleeing guy's height, how he moved.'

'Thetis thought she heard the telephone ring between three or four,' Suzie said.

I had some silly idea it was sometime around three or four. What Thetis had said at the interview in 'River Walk'.

'Mmmm,' Tommy grunted. 'Yes, that would fit. But why would Paula respond to a call from Pip?'

'If she'd set it up. If she'd finally gone cold on Max. If Max had refused, one last time, to leave Jenny. Could happen.' Molly convincing.

'It's an idea,' Tommy frowned. 'But I'd have to be persuaded. Those letters are so . . .' He struggled for the word.

'Passionate?' Suzie tried: after all she'd read the letters as well.

'It's more than passionate. There's a kind of profound love, attachment. They split up because of the danger, when Max discovered there was someone nobody else had found, what was his name? Edgar Turnivall?'

'Edgar Turnivall,' Molly agreed.

It had to be an incredibly strong bond between them: all that stuff in the letters Max hung on to, and kept in his little safe, right under Jenny's nose.

'I suppose we could give her a bit of really hard interrogation tomorrow – Paula. Her and Thetis.'

'You think she'd have told Thetis? Max's daughter after all,' Suzie asked.

'Wouldn't have thought so.' Tommy shook his head

violently as though to rid it of some vile thought, like LeClare
trying to get the blood out of his head. 'Sleep on it, eh? I'll
tell you in the morning. Wake me early, Molly dear, for I'm
going to use a bit of guile on Paula, I think.'

Molly said goodnight and left while Suzie lingered.

'What's bothering you, sweet?' she asked.

'A million things, heart. Sometimes I see the whole thing
clearly then another puzzle pops up. There are moments when
I even think Tait's right, that this was some passing ruffian.
Now, I just wish I could talk to LeClare, what kind of car
was it? Old banger? What? Why did you think it was a
woman? You see her? Or . . . ? Hell, heart, I just don't know.'

'But I thought you were certain it was Pip, the mad, bad
and very dangerous brother.'

'I do,' Tommy said slowly, raised his head and looked
terribly tired. 'Yes, in my heart of hearts I know it was Pip.
Most things fit. Just don't like the loose ends.' He smiled
ruefully and wrapped her up in his arms, holding her tightly,
and she felt she loved him more than anything, then found
herself questioning it: had she had enough experience?
Tommy for the rest of her natural? For ever's a very long
time, she thought and gently drew away from him.

'Don't stay tonight, heart. Might be a bit restless, eh?'

Suzie nodded, kissed him on the chin. 'Early doors?'

'Early doors it'll be, heart, yes.'

In the attic at Knights Cottage, Golly still waited. When? he
asked himself. When will they come, the lady policeman and
the honourable cop? He wondered what was happening to
Lavender and Queenie, shivered 'cos he thought he may never
see them again, knowing they were locked up. Wondered if
Lavender would be able to stand it, being locked up. Good
sport Lavender was, but she didn't like to be in the same
room all the time.

He remembered when he was her guard in the little rooms
off Rupert Street, up the Smoke. She'd once said, 'As bad as

being in prison, being in this room six days a week, Goll.'
Then she'd laughed. Had a lovely laugh, Lavender had. Real
gutsy laugh. He'd see her right once he'd put the lady
policeman and the honourable copper away.

Yes, he'd see Lavender and Queenie right.

Just you wait and see. Eh?

The morning brought another fine, clear day. It also brought
a dispatch rider from Billy Mulligan at the Yard: the report
from the team which had been to Marecht Hall, doing over
Benny's drum, as Tommy said. He also said, 'Bloody interesting. The housekeeper was uneasy, telephoned Mrs Ascoli,
Freda, but we know that. We were at Freda's end. However,'
he said with great emphasis. 'How-Ever, the guys up there
at the house said there were signs that someone had stayed
there recently, two beds stripped down, one single and one
double. Interesting. Both had been slept in, they reckoned.
Housekeeper said she was doing all the beds while Mrs Ascoli
– the widow Ascoli – was away feeding the ducks in London.
That's what she said, and she explained herself. "That's what
I always say. When she's away I say she's off in London
feeding the ducks. That's because she once told me it was
one of the things she liked doing best, going to the park,
Regent's Park, and feeding the ducks and the squirrels. She
canna say squirrels by the way. Canna say it properly, gets
stuck on the 'squi' bit." What you think of that, eh?'

'Bloody interesting,' Suzie said, sotto voce, and Tommy
gave her a sharp look.

'Going to see Paula today,' he continued. 'Just drop in
unannounced. Laura, what's the situation over there? Can we
keep obbo on the place, understand you were out there 'til
all hours?'

Laura Cotter was quite a wizard at a number of jobs, one
of them being surveillance. She was a short dark-haired girl
with little dress sense and, according to Billy Mulligan, she
could fade into the background with almost chameleon ease.

'Put her in a crowded room and she becomes the wallpaper. Put her outside a house and she blends into the brickwork across the road,' Billy had said when giving his pitch to get her into the Reserve Squad.

'It's not easy, on the other hand it can be done, back and front.' Even her voice was quiet and she spoke with minimum movement of the lips. 'You know that "River Walk" stands on its own and the front of the place has a stand of trees shielding the façade. Well, the address is "River Walk", River Road. Diagonally across from the house is the corner of a children's playground that's gone almost to ruin. Dodgy swings and those chain things on a pole, like a maypole, they're rusted to blazes. Kids do go up there, but you can get yourself nicely tucked in among the bushes on that corner and the view is straight through the trees, spot on to the drive she uses for her car. Takes in the front door and you can also see if anyone goes round to the side door. I was up there with a pair of night glasses yesterday and it's great. There's also a telephone box less than a minute's walk, through the side gate of the playground.'

'Good,' Tommy grinning. 'Where'd you get night glasses from, Laura?'

'Did a favour for a naval lieutenant, sir.'

'Must've been a big favour.'

'It was, sir. Favour of the month.'

Laura Cotter, top of the bill comedienne.

'Really, and what about the back, Laura?'

'Oh, it's fine now, sir. Just twisted it a bit doing the favour.'

Laughter, rolling in the aisles.

'I mean the back of "River Walk".'

'Oh, easier still, Chief. Little coppice about fifty feet from the far boundary of the garden. It's on higher ground, looks down on the whole place. You can see everything.'

'And communication?'

'Not as quick sir, but you can do it and back within seven minutes. Timed it last evening.'

'Another telephone box?'

'Yes, sir. Armby Road. Spit and a stride, sir.'

'Right, Laura, I want you to take Peter and Dennis – Peter Prime and Dennis Free – show them these two obbo spots, lend Dennis your night glasses, will you?'

'For a small favour, sir. Yes.'

Another little ripple of laughter.

'Okay. We're going over with the search warrant for "River Walk". Just a gentle stroll, all the cars and all of you. Suzie and I'll go in and have a little chat with Paula and Thetis. Tell her it's for her own good, having the place searched: Pip on the loose, prowling round, could be thinking of pouncing on her and/or Thetis. Put the wind up her and the girl, find out how much she really knows. Also find out where she's been.'

There was a murmur and nodding of comprehension from the team.

'I want you all to stay in the cars. Outside. In plain view. Everyone except Dennis and Peter. Laura'll show you two around, put you in place so that you can keep the house under surveillance. Got it? Good, do that quietly, don't make a fuss. Just stay put. We'll call the rest of you in when we're ready to do the search. In the unlikely event of me finding some reason to bring Paula and Thetis in to the nick, give 'em a verbal going over, we'll signal you. That's unlikely though. Questions?'

There were none.

'Good. We'll go in about four this afternoon. Teatime. Hope she's got a few custard creams in. I'm partial to a nice custard cream. Cool your heels and have lunch and we'll leave here around three fifteen.'

Suzie suddenly felt cold. Like the shiver you get when they say somebody's walking over your grave. She felt unhappy about the whole thing but couldn't tell why. Silly, superstitious rubbish, she told herself.

Twenty-One

'You going to tell Mr Tait over at King's Lynn nick, Chief?' Molly asked as they went out to the cars, three fifteen in the afternoon, sun shining, birds flying around, as someone once said, just for the hell of it.

'Not likely. Not prior to going over to King's Lynn, Molly. Maybe when we get there I'll get on the blower, just to be courteous.'

'Bet he'll know though, Chief. His little dicky bird's just passing by,' pointing out Wally Titcombe, cycling through the Market Square and looking their way.

'Bugger it,' Tommy said, showing off his university education.

The DCS went in the Wolseley with Suzie, Brian at the wheel. Molly drove Laura, Peter Prime and Dennis Free in the spare car while Doc took Shirley Cox and Ron Worral in the claret-coloured Railton.

They arrived just before four o'clock, Suzie and Tommy getting out of the car, walking up the flagstone path, everyone else staying inside, the cars drawn up so that they blocked the road, not allowing anyone else to get near.

Laura waited until the Chief and Suzie were inside the house, keeping the ladies happy before taking Dennis Free and Peter Prime to the surveillance points. Tommy had already told them they could be in for a long wait.

Paula Palmer opened the door, looking beautifully groomed in a camel skirt and a white blouse with a complicated gold design on it, her hair styled in gleaming waves and rolls circling her head, the hair itself with a sheen to it, smooth, silky. To Suzie she looked like a woman that all men would desire, the kind of woman who men could die for. 'You've brought a lot of your friends, Chief Superintendent,' she said. 'Are they coming in, or will they be happy waiting in the cars?'

'They've come to do you a favour, Miss Palmer. But I'd like a word or two first.'

She nodded pleasantly, and pulled the door wide open, with what looked like a benign smile and a twinkle of amusement in her eyes.

Thetis came out of their drawing room, into the hall. She also looked untroubled, not in the least concerned that the police had called again, greeting them as though they were old friends, ushering them into the room. Tommy thought they looked like people who had got away with something unspeakable, and knew it.

Tommy sat down next to Suzie on a long settee, the material covering it decorated with clusters of tea roses.

'Care for a cup of tea at all?' Paula asked, very gracious, lady of the manor.

'That would be delightful,' Tommy smiled back and Suzie said she would love some custard creams if there were any. There were no custard creams but Paula had made a cake that morning. 'We've been away for a few days so the larder was fairly bare. But I managed to get some good strawberry jam in Scotland. Brought it back and made a jam sponge.'

'Mummy makes super jam sponges,' Thetis said, and Suzie looked around to see if Thetis kept a jolly hockey stick around anywhere. She thought if she found one she could belt the girl round the head with it. Oh, Mummy makes super things for tea. La-di-bloody-da. She raised her head and through the window caught a glimpse of Laura skulking off with Dennis and Peter: taking them to the obbo points.

Finally they were settled, bone china on a silver tray with solid handles at each side and a larger plate on which rested the magnificent jam sponge. They had smaller plates and cake forks: all these things appeared to be very important to Miss Palmer, who now asked the most obvious question, in an even more obvious way, 'So, to what do we owe this honour, Chief Superintendent?'

He switched a smile on and off. 'Several reasons.' Tommy had changed down in his approach, serious now, no smiles, face grave. 'I'll explain in a moment. You say you've been away? Scotland was it?'

'Yes, Dundee. I have friends there.'

Dundee, where the cake comes from, Suzie thought, nearly said it but stopped herself in time and wondered why she was being so frivolous, came to the conclusion that she was nervous. Possibly frightened as well. Probably amazed by the two women's controlled demeanour. Underneath the calm exterior, getting away with murder, but both mother and daughter occasionally displayed concern, the worm in the eye, the wariness of manner.

'Nice, Dundee,' said Tommy, unhurried, taking his time. 'Miss Palmer, I must ask you how much you know about Pip Ascoli, Fillipo Ascoli. Max Ascoli's brother?'

Now he saw the worm deep in her eyes, the worm that moved and gave away her secret. Suzie saw it also and felt her heart skip and her stomach turn over. Paula Palmer was about to lie, she thought, about to tie them up in knots.

'As a matter of fact I know rather a lot about him, Mr Livermore. After all, he was my daughter's father's brother and dear Max used to talk about him a great deal. He was constantly trying to get advice about Pip. For Pip. He didn't think that his brother should be locked up year after year in that Swiss asylum.'

'He tell you that? That it was an asylum?'

'It was nuns, I know that, just as I know they called it a clinic.'

'Ever meet him, Paula? Ever meet Pip?'

'As a matter of fact, I did. Once. In the autumn of '38.'

'And how did you find him? Was he raving, crazy, or was he just a very nervous young man; nervous and misunderstood?'

'Don't like you calling him names, Mr Livermore. I found him charming, like all the Ascolis. Charming and cultured.'

'Cultured people don't usually go around shooting the faces off their brother and his family.'

'Charming and cultured and terribly frightening. What d'you mean by that? About shooting off his brother's face?'

'So, you were frightened of him?'

'Terrified.' She spoke calmly, at odds with what she was saying. 'What do you mean?'

'What made you so frightened of him?'

'His manner, his obvious delight in intimidating people. He was a very creepy man. What do you mean about shooting off his brother's face?'

'Did you know that Max brought him back to England again?'

'I knew he brought him in '38. I just told you.'

'He didn't tell you he brought him back again in '39.'

'In 1939? Just before the war? You say he brought him back?'

'He did. Even people in Long Taddmarten have vouched for that, saw him walking around the village.'

'Mr Livermore, what do you mean about him shooting off Max's face? Mr Tait told me it was some itinerant, some troublemaker.'

'I mean what I said, Miss Palmer.'

'Really?' Trying to sound wary, maybe concerned, her face showing the fear that she'd confessed to. Thetis, sitting in a large easy chair cringing back as if trying to force her body through the stuffed chair back. They had changed, suddenly after he had spoken about Pip Ascoli.

'Yes, really, Miss Palmer. In fact we've come to the conclusion that it is probably Pip who killed Max and his family. We have a witness who saw him, or someone very like him, getting into a car driven by a woman at the junction of the main road and Knights Close in the early hours of 17th August. And that person had just been inside Knights Cottage; had just seen Max's body.'

Thetis gave a little intake of breath, a noise of shock possibly. Either that or she was a good little actress.

'The point is,' Tommy continued, 'we are most concerned for your safety. Pip Ascoli is on the loose; we think he killed Max and we're concerned that he might wish to harm you or Thetis.'

Again the tiny jerk of shock from Thetis, like the sound of a small animal in pain, just for the fraction of a second.

'I'm sorry, am I frightening your daughter? I don't mean to, Thetis. But we must face facts. I think you are both in danger—'

'Nonsense,' from Paula, a touch strident, but she was looking around, as if searching for someone hiding in the room, or just outside the door.

Suzie thought the two women must be marvellous actresses because both of them were ashen in colour, Paula's cheeks like parchment. You can't just do that at will, Suzie thought. There was something wrong here; this was not acting, this was real, you could almost touch the fear.

Tommy had seen it as well. He spoke softly, 'My people want to come in and give your lovely house a good going over.'

'What d'you mean by a good going over?' Sharp.

'I mean they'd like to search the place, from top to bottom. They'd also like to search your garage and your car and anywhere else that you own.'

'You sound as though you're about to accuse me of something. Collaborating with Max's murderer, or something.'

'Nothing was further from my mind,' he lied. 'However, I'm exceptionally concerned for your safety. The safety of you both.' Suzie could see he was disconcerted by the fear transparent in the two women. Again he spoke softly, 'I'm afraid you have no say in the matter,' reaching inside his jacket to remove the search warrant, explaining what it was, and giving the nod to Suzie, who went outside and gestured to Molly.

'Are you sure there's no other . . . ?' Paula perplexed, grasping for words.

'Please,' Thetis said, and it was difficult to work out what she was pleading for.

Then the rest of the team were in the house, starting their search, methodically moving from room to room, opening cupboards, tapping walls, their footsteps moving upstairs, their muted conversation in the hall.

'They can go into the garage but they can't see the car.' Paula's voice catching in her throat. 'It's off the road, in Hunter's, the local garage. Left it in the car park at the station while we were away. Wouldn't start when we got back last night. They came down and towed it away. I'd hoped to have it back today . . .' trailing off.

'Don't worry, just stay quietly here, we'll see to everything.'

'Christ,' Paula said, to nobody in particular. End of her tether, Suzie thought.

Tommy went out and brought Shirley in, told her to stay in the drawing room with Paula and Thetis, then took Suzie into the hall.

'More confused than ever,' he whispered, cocking his head, listening to the sounds coming from upstairs.

'They really don't seem to know about Pip, certainly the girl doesn't. That's real fear,' Susie said.

'Yes. Something very strange going on. Full of confidence when we arrived. Going to pieces at the first mention of Pip.'

Together they took a quick look around downstairs, calculating the number of rooms above them: a large house with six and a half bedrooms, two attics; and in the garden, the studio, built for Paula Palmer in the twenties.

Ron Worral had done the studio. 'Not a thing,' he said.

'The house is clean, ordered, nothing out of place. Mother and daughter living here with people coming in every day. No sign of a third party either living here or hiding.'

'You want to come upstairs for a moment, Chief.' Molly whispering, leaning over the banisters.

Suzie went up with him, to the first landing, a wide carpeted area, doors leading off to little passages, left and right, and a large bookcase facing the stairs, heavy with old leather-bound books.

'Must've had this built in at some point,' Molly grinning like someone who's found gold. 'Look.' She crossed to the bookcase. 'Thought it was odd, a lot of the books are fakes,' reaching up and pulling at the spine of a leather volume on the far left of the centre shelf. As she pulled so the entire bookcase swung out like an unusually thick door, revealing a long narrow room behind. 'Nobody home at the moment,' she said, making a gesture, showing off her find. 'Measurements didn't fit.'

The room was fitted with a thick white carpet, there were pictures on the walls, a single bed pushed against the left-hand side, and a small table at the far end: no windows and no sign that the room had been recently occupied.

'I wonder,' Tommy said, as though the room had led him to the answer of a particularly knotty crossword clue, turning to Suzie. 'Can you remember the name of that agent fellow who was doing that big deal for her?'

Suzie nodded. 'Johnny Goodman. The Goodman Gallery, Bruton Street.'

'Good girl. Think we should give him a bell?'

'See if he's at home?' Suzie asked.

'Close that up.' He indicated the bookcase. 'We never saw that room, right? We're satisfied and we're going home. Don't know why they're so frightened, but I think we should really go, just leave Dennis and Pete in place. I mean what's it take us to get back? Fifteen, twenty minutes? I really think we should do it. Play it absolutely straight. If I ring old Goodman

'Will you please take WDS Mountford back to Long Taddmarten in the spare car.'

'Of course, Chief.'

'And come straight to my room when you're back. Brian . . . ?'

'Yes, Chief.'

'Home Brian, and don't spare the horses.' In his funny Music Hall turn accent.

The Wolseley took off like a rocket, followed by the Railton.

Molly leisurely started the spare car, put it in gear, and drew away with Suzie sitting beside her.

Twenty-Two

Golly was bored, had the attention span of a gnat. They still hadn't come – the lady policeman and her boss – and he'd spent most of the day poking around, waiting: took some books off the shelves in the little study round the back of the house, leafed through them but they had no pictures so he left them on the floor.

When it got to dusk he went back up to the attic room, lay on his bed and dozed, thought about going out again in the darkness, nicking a bit more food because he was hungry: hungry in every way.

Then he heard it.

Someone in the house. Came in through the back door. Footsteps in the hall, then into the body of the building.

The lady policeman? No. Steps were heavy. A man? The honourable copper? Maybe.

He reached into his pocket, running his fingers round the wire, pulling it out, testing the tightly fitted insulating tape wound on to each end, the wire turned over in a hook right at the ends to keep it tight, stuck into the thick coils of tape. He had washed off and cleaned the wire when he first came into the house, cleaned it and dried it on a towel found in the bathroom, blood and bits coming off on the towel from that nice big girl he'd used it on up the road: the one who'd been doing it with the Yank in the hut.

He slid off the bed, glad of his plimsolls: he'd practised creeping about the house, able to do it without a sound now. Went to the door and realized something was funny, odd.

286

Whoever had come in hadn't turned the lights on. He didn't understand that because the lights were working – he'd tried them and they'd worked but he couldn't leave them on. Couldn't put them on again either. He knew that if anyone saw the lights on in the house they might investigate and where would he be then?

He came out of his room, peered down, over the banister rail running along the landing, saw right down past the second floor and into the dark that was the hall. There was a flicker of light somewhere. A torch. That was it. The other person in the house was using a torch. Golly, standing on the landing, tried to work out what that meant and finally decided that whoever it was didn't want to be seen either.

He heard a cough, knew it was a man in the house now and took another pace towards the foot of the stairs, craning his neck forward, trying to get a glimpse of the intruder, one end of the wire tight in his hand.

Then the other noise, the car drawing up outside, doors slamming, footsteps, people running.

Golly shrank back towards the door to the attic room, his room.

Molly drove most carefully, wasn't really worried about how long it took. If anything she dawdled, talking away the journey between King's Lynn and Taddmarten.

'You know what he's up to?' she asked Suzie.

'Being the bumbling detective, heart.' Suzie had Tommy's intonation off to a *t*, the pauses and everything.

Molly said she was wicked and Suzie said, 'I don't know what all that was about. I think it was really for the benefit of Paula and her scrumptious daughter. She's going to have problems with that girl before she gets much older.'

Molly laughed, '*If* she gets much older. There's something very strange there, something irrational. I mean their reaction to Pip Ascoli.'

'Pip must be a scary kind of man. But what Tommy was

doing's a different matter. He *was* playing the bumbling detective. Tommy has that clarity of mind which he cloaks by doing his imitations, and he does the bumbling detective by a choice of words, and his delivery. What he says is usually the complete antithesis of what's going on in his head.'

'The real question to ask,' Molly said, impressed by Suzie's comprehension, and then thinking that of course she knew Tommy's ways: they were lovers and it would be strange if she didn't have an insight. 'The real question to ask is why he was doing all that double talk? There's a reason for everything the Chief does, and what do you make of this sudden latching on to the agent – John Goodman is it?'

Suzie nodded in the darkness, and Molly continued. 'Apart from one mention a few days ago, we've heard nothing about Goodman. Don't even know what he looks like.'

'There'll be a reason.'

As they were coming into the outskirts of Taddmarten, Molly said she was going round past Knights Cottage. 'Just take a quick butcher's.'

'Yes, make sure it's still standing, Molly.'

They turned left, up Knights Close, and as they drove towards the cottage, Molly stiffened in the driving seat. 'See that?'

'What?'

'Look. There again. Someone's in the bloody house.'

And Suzie caught a fast flash of light downstairs.

'That's someone with a torch.' Molly brought the car to an almost screaming standstill abreast of the five-bar white gate and was out of the car, her hand going back to draw the Smith & Wesson .38 from behind her hip. 'You take the back, Sue. I'll go in the front,' her other hand reaching for her keys – Molly had charge of one entire set but kept the front door key permanently on her chain.

Suzie wondered how she was expected to get in, thought maybe she wasn't; perhaps Molly would flush the interloper out through the back, making it her job to trap him. But when she got to the rear door it was open: wide and fully ajar. She pushed on in and heard Molly shout from the hall, 'I am an armed police officer, come out or I'll shoot!'

Suzie didn't even see the person who charged her as she was feeling her way into the kitchen, heard only the sudden rattle of feet, heard the rasp of breathing and was knocked to one side by someone running full tilt, heading for the back door.

He had shoulder-barged her, sending her spinning against the wall, bumping against it hard, knocking the wind out of her as she rolled along, then fell, recovered, took a deep breath and began to run after him, shouting as she went.

In the darkness outside she could just make out the running figure, hurtling up the garden, going through the gate in the wall like magic, and on towards the meadow on the other side of the trees and fencing. She heard a loud grunt as her quarry hit the door in the wall, cracking it open, heard the thud of his footsteps going up the rising ground. She would never catch him now, and she knew it as the query came into her head, asking herself what had happened to Molly? She should have been out here by now.

Suzie turned and began to walk back, hurrying and aware of a car engine she could hear up past the far trees, in the distance, starting up on the other side of Bob Raines's field.

The lights were on deep within the house, in the hall she reckoned as she hurried through, coming into the glare and being dazzled by it going from dark to the light so suddenly.

And not believing what she now saw, in the middle of the hall, on the flagstones where Max Ascoli's body had been.

She felt a terrible surge of nausea, tasted the bile in her mouth. Molly was standing in the centre of the hall, her feet dragging on the ground and behind her, Suzie's nightmare tugged at her: Golly Goldfinch with his wire around Molly's neck, his dreadful skewed face and the mouth slanting in a panting grin, making a deep grunting noise as he dragged Molly towards death.

She had her head back, the wire pulling at her neck, eyes bulging and her mouth an unnatural oval, tongue beginning to loll out over her bottom lip, the crushed face pleading for help, and as Suzie stopped, then recoiled from the sight, Molly dropped her pistol, fingers going slack and the gun hitting the stone, skittering towards Suzie.

In a blink of time questions slid through Suzie Mountford's head: this couldn't be real; couldn't be happening, not to Molly because Molly knew all the moves, Molly was the expert, knew exactly how to duck and dive and give the lethal punch and knock out a six-foot man with the flick of her wrist. It couldn't be happening to Molly, not to Molly.

But it was, and Molly was starting to sag on the wire cutting deeply into her neck, Golly giving her the *coup de grâce.*

And as Suzie was thinking these things, streaming through her mind, she made a dive for the revolver, still moving on the flagstones.

She scooped it up, turned, spread her feet just as Golly laughed and dropped Molly's body free of the wire.

'Lady policeman,' Golly said in his slow, breathy speech. 'Lady policeman.' Joy in the words.

Suzie, arms extended, squeezed the trigger twice, heard in her head Tommy say, 'No, heart, keep the bloody thing still, you're waving it about like it's got balls attached! Not like that, heart!'

She was deafened by the report as she fired, then again, the double boom of the two shots and, looking over the muzzle with her eyes wide open she watched, disbelieving as Golly Goldfinch's face exploded in blood, bone, flesh and gristle.

He made no noise from what was left of his mouth, but she watched as he was lifted from his feet, body levitating for a second, arching backwards towards the front door, hitting it sideways on and dropping in an uncoordinated jumble of arms, legs and the rest of him, thudding down on to the stone.

Once she had done it, actually shot the beast dead, Suzie heaved twice, then shook her head and leaped towards Molly, who lay rasping, breath coming in laboured moments of exertion and her head cricked unnaturally on the floor.

Later, Suzie couldn't remember using the telephone, summoning an ambulance and getting Tommy, who brought almost the whole team with him. Eventually she recalled desperately trying to telephone the number of the instrument in Tommy's room, but he was constantly engaged. She had already rung for an ambulance, identified herself, but was still trying Tommy when the medics arrived.

She closed the line again and again asking for the number and finally had to get the operator to break in on the conversation: Tommy yelling at her, 'Where the hell have you got to?' She must have told him because he arrived, cradled her in his arms, in spite of the others being there. She saw Laura almost in tears, and Ron looking exceptionally grim.

Then Laura was left with her while the others piled into the cars and drove away, using the signal bells to move any other traffic.

One of the medics had come over and suggested to Laura that Suzie was in shock, 'Should get her into the warm, if I were you, miss.'

She walked, with Laura hanging on to her, staggered really, right to the Falcon and up to her room, with young Laura fending off both of the Stalewayses, getting Suzie on to her bed, everything a bit of a blur.

'How's Molly?' she finally asked, and Laura looked away, bit her lip, and said they didn't know yet. 'Touch and go.'

She pulled herself together after a while, couldn't stop shaking, then began to cry for quite a long time, asked Laura to get her a brandy, 'A double.' Laura fluttered off, bringing her a glass of what looked more like a quadruple, her hand shaking so much she could hardly hold it.

All the time she kept seeing Golly's face exploding in front of her, feeling the jerk of the revolver in her hands and the deafening roar punching at her ears. She knew it was the shock that made her so unsteady but after an hour or so she felt ashamed of her reaction. Bloody softy, she called herself, and cursed that she wasn't there for what she was certain must be the end of the Ascoli business.

It wasn't until very late that night that she learned what had happened. Tommy banished everyone else from her room and talked to her gently, sitting beside the bed while she kept apologizing and telling him it was the shock.

'I know, sweet. Take it all back,' he told her. 'You can shoot properly and you did. Wonderful, heart. Absobloody-lutely wonderful.'

Before anything else she asked about Molly, and Tommy gave her a long, sad look. 'I'm sorry, heart. Molly died. They could do nothing for her. She was dead before she hit the ground. You saw her die, couldn't have done anything for her.'

Suzie let out a long, shuddering wail, trying to stifle it with a hand over her mouth, sure that Molly had still been breathing when she got to her, on the flagstones. 'How?' she asked again.

'How, Tommy? How? Molly knew it all. All the moves.'

'Taken by surprise, Suzie. Only answer, taken by surprise. Can happen to any of us.' He put his arms around her, to hold and comfort her. 'Molly always carried a weapon, in spite of everything she was vulnerable because of the weapon and her skills, so she always knew the risks, and she accepted them.'

'But, Tommy, it's so unfair.' She thought that if Molly hadn't decided to take a look at Knights Cottage, she'd still be alive now, and thought of her, the confidence, single-mindedness, everything about her. When they had first met, she remembered that she hadn't really liked Molly. It was only with the passing of time that she came to understand and respect her. Molly had taught her so much.

'I'm going to miss her, Tommy.'

'We're all going to miss her,' he said. 'I never had to worry about my personal safety when Molly was around. Going to miss her a hundred times over. Can't really believe she's gone.'

He was silent for a good minute, then said if she wanted to blame anybody she should blame Max Ascoli. 'Oh, yes, heart he's still alive.'

It was Max who had come into the house, driven over in Paula's car, came back to get those letters Molly had already found in his little safe. They'd found the safe open tonight after he'd gone.

As the evening wore on, he told her what else had happened after he'd received her telephone call.

Dennis Free and Peter Prime were left in position at the observation points looking out, and down, on the house called 'River Walk'. About nine o'clock Dennis tried to get in touch with Tommy who had left Shirley manning his telephone at the Falcon. Dennis, who had been watching from the corner of the playground, had seen a car drive in, thought it was the garage returning Paula's car at first.

A man got out, went to the door of 'River Walk'. Dennis, watching through Laura's night glasses, saw him take a key from a pocket and let himself into the house. That caused alarm. Before going any further he rang from the telephone box, tried to get Tommy but spoke to Shirley who said he should proceed with caution – good old police terminology – take Peter with him, go in and check on the stranger who had just walked into the house.

He signalled for Peter to join him and the two of them went up the flagstone walk to the front door, where they heard raised voices. They rang and knocked loudly and were eventually let in by Thetis, whom they described as being in a highly emotional state. She was shouting and crying, 'Stop them! Please stop them!'

Later Dennis said, the words looked a bit simple when

293

written down, but in reality the girl had been in a dramatic and excited, highly charged condition.

Loud, melodramatic shouting was coming from the drawing room. Afterwards both men said they were unprepared for what they found, couldn't believe their eyes seeing a dead man in the middle of an outrageous slanging match, Paula screaming at Max Ascoli, accusing him of manipulating her and of being a cold-hearted murderer, guilty of fratricide, while their daughter sobbed in the doorway.

Within a couple of minutes Dennis and Peter had heard enough, they separated the pair and arrested both of them, at which point each went silent, refusing to answer questions.

When Tommy arrived he sorted out what he could and charged them jointly with the murders of Jenny and Paul Ascoli and Fillipo Ascoli.

'That's what happened? Max killed his brother *and* his wife and child?'

'Not certain yet,' Tommy said. 'Suspect it was neatly set up and I have doubts about Max killing his own child. We won't know everything for some time, if ever, but my guess, heart, is that Max had Pip in the house against the day when he could set him loose to prowl around without taking any medication. Like so many patients, Pip was controlled by a balancing act of drugs. Don't forget that people in the village saw him regularly for a while, going about seemingly quite normally.

'That didn't seem to last for long though. After the end of 1940 there are no reports of people seeing Pip in the village. I suspect he was kept to the house and the garden at Knights Cottage. You must have noticed the way the whole of that garden is protected – the wall at the end and the trees and fences around the rest of the property. The story about Piglet romping in Mr Raines's field, that was only when the door in the brick wall had been "accidentally left open".'

'No, I believe he purposely allowed Pip to deal with Jenny and Paul; even let him dress in Max's old clothes, and finally shot him in the hall, they were not unalike, Pip and Max. I didn't begin to suspect it until quite late on, and I still can't work out how Max programmed him to blast their faces off – a most necessary part of the whole thing.'

'And Paula? Did she not know . . . ?'

'About Pip? Obviously not. Those two couldn't really live without each other and I suspect they found it difficult to live with each other, if ever there were star-crossed lovers, drawn back to each other again and again. Unable to resist the magnetic pull. I suspect they emotionally plundered each other. Drank each other dry. He probably gave her some cock and bull story about who the man was – dead in his hall.'

It was going to be an interesting investigation over the next few weeks. In the end Paula became a prosecution witness and then backed out at the last moment, and there were many questions never answered. In the years to come, Tommy thought much would be unearthed about the Ascoli family in Italy; and that Max's final Machiavellian plan, to free himself from one family and continue with the other, had all the cunning of a great Italian plot.

'The only thing I can't understand, heart, is how Max kept up the façade for so long and was able to put up with Jenny, who turned out to be a real harpy.'

'You brought up John Goodman's name when we were all in "River Walk" . . .'

'Smoke and mirrors, heart. Smoke and mirrors.' His terrible smile once more.

Molly had left explicit instructions for the disposal of her body: wanted it buried with Christian rites near to where she was at the time of her death.

They buried her in the graveyard of the Church of St Mary Magdalene, Long Taddmarten, on a rainy Thursday in September. Suzie remarked at the time that there seemed to be a sea of umbrellas around the grave, stretching to the edges of the churchyard and even out through the lychgate.

Early in January 1943, Tommy and Suzie returned to see the gravestone they had ordered. It was a simple marble stone with the inscription:

WOMAN POLICE SERGEANT
MOLLY ABELARD
WHO DIED IN THIS VILLAGE ON ACTIVE DUTY
AUGUST 1942
REQUIESCAT IN PACE

Golly Goldfinch is buried nearby in an unmarked grave.

On that visit, Tommy and Suzie did not stay at the Falcon Inn, but at a nearby hotel on the recommendation of Eric Tait with whom Tommy had made his peace.

As Suzie was sitting at the dressing table in their room, preparing to go down to dinner on the Saturday night, Tommy came up behind her, put his hands on her shoulders and asked when she was going to make an honest man out of him. They hadn't mentioned the subject since the end of the Ascoli case.

'When're you going to marry me, heart?' Tommy said, and Suzie looked at him in the mirror, standing behind her.

She had a moment of inspiration. 'Tommy, about the Ascolis: why did King Edward VII arrange for them to become British citizens without any fuss? Why would he do that?'

'One of the great mysteries, heart. Haven't a clue.' Count of six. 'Heart, when're you going to marry me?'

She felt the old sinking feeling. 'Well Tommy . . .' she began, desperately searching for excuses.